The Last Fandango

To Darling Jenny
with much love

Lenché
x
2017

The Last Fandango

Robin Hellaby

First published in 2017 by
    Robin Hellaby
    Website: www.thelastfandango.com

ISBN: 978178808946

Edited by Joseph Wood
Cover design by Wishful Thinking
Layout by Janice Cheong

Printed by Vinlin Press Sdn Bhd
2 Jalan Meranti Permai 1
Meranti Permai Industrial Park
Batu 15, Jalan Puchong
47100 Puchong, Selangor, Malaysia

To those who are seeking the courage to love.

"Be happy for this moment.
This moment is your life."

The Rubaiyát of Omar Khayyám

Prologue

A SOLITARY RED CARNATION

T he dream woke me again last night.

The same dream. The one that has wrenched me from my sleep, trembling and perspiring, for the last ten years.

I dreamed that Marco could dance again.

It's not a nightmare – it's sheer joy, not terror, that overwhelms me when I see Marco strutting out onto that starlit stage in Granada.

Here he comes, his eyes fixed on mine – thumping and stamping his way across the boards, making straight for me! The nails in his boot-soles smash against the wood with a din that ricochets like gunfire across the vast auditorium. The guitars and box-drums have fallen silent. He leaves the audience of thousands gasping in wonder at his utter mastery of the dance. His heels move at the speed of light – he reaches his arm out to me, his hand miming the clacking of a castanet. I extend my fingers to touch his –

But, of course, there's nothing to touch.

Marco has vanished, like mist at daybreak. The stage is empty except for one solitary, blood-red carnation.

The scene shifts. A thunderous roar engulfs me, sucking all the breath out of my lungs like a tornado. It's the moment the helicopter hauls itself into the sky from the Village churchyard, with Marco and his father both strapped down inside – the last time they were ever together.

I see my old friend Trelawney, but no longer is he the unfailing tower of strength that saw us through the worst years of our lives.

In my dream, he's a helpless old man, trembling in confusion on the doorstep of his house in the Village, blood streaming from a gash on his face.

There's always blood in the dream – blood on my hands, blood drenching the bed where we spent our first night together.

And tears – of sadness, yes, but of joy and laughter too: as if from a vantage-point in the sky, I see us careering from Africa across to Spain, up to Scotland and all the way back again, our friends cheering us on as we crazily pursued our own dream and made it come true.

For a while. For that brief, golden era of our lives.

But that was then, and this is now, I remembered.

I could hear Beth snoring gently in her bedroom at the back of the house as I wandered through. I had no fear of waking her as I set about mixing a stiff drink to see me through the night. She'd shared all our experiences over the last ten years, but they hadn't scarred her as they had me.

As I took my glass through to the lounge, I glanced across at the life-sized portrait of Marco at the height of his powers, and Beth's intricate drawing of a honeycombed ceiling in the Alhambra Palace hanging next to it. When Beth sketched that drawing, she was no more to me than a friend Marco had known since his childhood. Now, she was closer than any blood relative I'd ever had. Over the years, she'd become the cornerstone of our odd little family.

I lowered myself onto one of the long chairs on the veranda. I picked up my book, but soon found it held no interest. Gazing in the direction of the unseen Mediterranean below, I let my mind wander. I recalled, with a shudder, what my life in this house had been like before … well, before Marco.

I pictured myself embarking on the journey to Africa that led me to him, as the familiar bulk of the Rock of Gibraltar loomed into view on the horizon.

Part One

Invitation to
The Dance
1999

Chapter One

Even from thirty thousand feet, the Rock of Gibraltar exudes majesty and authority. It is the unmistakable, monolithic harbinger of your departure from a world where life proceeds, more or less, as you expect it to.

As the plane edged past the Rock on that bright September day, I felt the first tingle of anticipation, the thrill of adventure. This evening I'd be joining the autumn gathering of friends at Trelawney's home, an event I'd attended for more years than I cared to remember. Now I could forget my ordinary life and immerse myself in the fantasy world that Trelawney had constructed for himself in his beloved Village, perched on a clifftop high above the African coast.

I caught one last, heartwarming glimpse of the Mediterranean before its turquoise waters vanished forever into the grey Atlantic. As our progress became steadier, I dozed off and by the time I awoke, we were already tacking and weaving our way down to land.

A solid wall of heat slammed into my face as the plane door swung open, followed by the familiar assault on my nostrils from the commingled fragrances of spice, sweat and sewage. One glance at the airport roof was enough to assure me that Trelawney had arrived. No-one else would dare be seen in the huge black fedora he always wore for airport trips "just in case anybody should miss me."

When he met me at the exit barrier, I saw the rest of his attire hadn't changed, either: a flowing white shirt of the finest linen; khaki shorts of a length that surely disqualified them from being called shorts; and boy-scout socks, replete with green ribbons peeking over the turned-down tops. But something was amiss. Instead of his usual aura of contented self-confidence, there was a sense of anxiety. His brow was wrinkled into a frown that did not bode well.

Nevertheless, he wrapped his arms around me in a long bear-hug as soon as I walked past the barrier.

"My dear Peter! It is always wonderful to welcome you to my adopted homeland, and never more so than today. You must be parched. Let's make our way to the vehicle immediately. Tamir is there preparing the usual refreshments as we speak."

Trelawney insisted on treating his visitors in style, right from the moment they arrived at the airport. Thick, steaming hot coffee or ice-cold beer would be waiting for us when we reached his ancient Land Rover, to be savoured as we watched the sun dip over the darkening sea.

We headed for the furthest corner of the car park where the battered green Land Rover stood. On the bonnet, a welcoming tray was set with bone-china coffee cups on saucers, silver spoons, and a plate of assorted English biscuits.

Tamir, Trelawney's companion for the last seven years, strode towards us. Despite the indulgent life he had with Trelawney, he remained as svelte as he was when I'd first met him.

"Lovely to see you Mr. Peter, nice flight?"

I returned his kisses.

"Yes, thank you Tamir, nice flight, lovely to be back. You well?"

"Top form thank you, Mr. Peter!"

Tamir's English had become expressive, if antiquated, during those seven years. You sometimes had the impression that he was a ventriloquist's dummy operated by Trelawney. "And I got important news!" he said.

"One thing at a time," Trelawney intervened. The waspish tone of his voice was unfamiliar. Something was definitely up.

While Tamir loaded the luggage into the car, Trelawney and I sipped from our slightly chipped Spode coffee-cups.

"What's this news of Tamir's, then?"

"Nothing much. It won't change things, I don't suppose."

Trelawney stared at the ground. It seemed unwise to interrupt him. "He's getting married."

"What? You're not being dumped again? But..."

"We'll discuss it later. No surprise — I've told you thousands of times how things work here. But there's other news as well."

"There always is in that blasted Village," I said. "It's like a primitive organism, ingesting and excreting nothing but gossip."

"That may well be so. But this is somewhat more serious than usual."

Trelawney's face clouded over completely; the bonhomie of his welcome had evaporated.

"There's trouble with the government."

This was unheard of. For decades, the Village had been a privileged enclave, untouched by anything that happened in the rest of the country.

"You remember that South African journalist who came to Mulberry Villa with the rather nice companion..."

"Vaguely. I never met them."

"And he wanted to buy the villa. Well, suddenly the government has stepped in to stop him. They won't say why. But now they're saying that houses in the Village can only be sold to families with at least two children, if you please."

"So, what's the problem? You don't want to buy another one, surely?"

"No, of course not. Trelawney Towers is my name, and Trelawney Towers is my residence. But you know what it's like here. You always get a warning when trouble is on the way." He paused to mop his brow with a large handkerchief. "And you ignore that warning at your peril.

I don't want any trouble when our residence permits come up for renewal, so I'm having to mobilise forces down at the Consulate. I'm having Sir Brian from the British Residents' Association up to dinner on Wednesday."

"That old screamer."

"Quite. He has as much to lose as we do."

"We? I'm just a visitor!"

"You know you're part of the establishment here, Peter. You belong to the Village as much as we all do. Show some commitment for once!"

Trelawney was clearly rattled by these developments. If half of what he said was accurate, it could even evolve into a situation that would force him to abandon his home. And the idea of Trelawney living anywhere but the Village was simply inconceivable.

On the other hand, with the detachment of a newcomer, I was tempted to dismiss it as just another of the petty happenstances of Village life that its residents liked to blow up into existence-threatening melodramas.

Trelawney took the wheel for our journey to his home. He produced a massive pair of tortoiseshell-rimmed spectacles held together with sellotape and perched them on the end of his nose. I went to get in the front, but Tamir opened the back door for me.

"I have to sit in front with Mr. T. in case the glasses drop off, you see!"

I didn't particularly relish the prospect of spending the longish drive hunched up next to the luggage in the back, with occasional bouts of mirth as Tamir rescued Trelawney's plunging spectacles. But by now I was quite tired, so at least I could rest silently.

"Oh, I knew there was something else I had to tell you before you drop off, Peter. Had a couple of visits from a young Frog. Half French, anyway. Unusual specimen. Very dark, quite a charmer, but damned if I can remember his name now. Melvin, Marcus, something like that. Remind me to tell you about it when we get home."

I was hoping for a speedy trip up to the Village, but I was to be disappointed. A strapping blond backpacker was standing by the airport exit road, thumbing a lift.

"It is of course an act of charity to give a lift to an *ugly* hitch-hiker," Trelawney said as he clanked down through the gears. "Pity this one doesn't qualify. I'll have to find some other way of being charitable today. Hutch up, Tamir, and make the fellow welcome. He'll only want to go into town, I imagine."

It turned out he was German. He introduced himself as Florian, a name I'd always found rather romantic. Although I could have spoken to him in his own language, I knew that Trelawney revelled in any opportunity to recount the peculiar history of the Village to newcomers. As I began to doze off, I heard him bawling out the familiar tale for Florian's benefit.

"So, you see after the forest fire, there was nothing left of the Village but charred foundations and rubble, with burnt olive and fig groves all around – paradise on toast, they called it. The locals couldn't be bothered to rebuild it and it lay there like an eyesore through the fifties and sixties. Used to be the most beautiful spot on the whole coast. You'd think you were on one of the Greek islands. Then the government came up with the idea of getting foreigners to buy the ruins dirt cheap, provided they would repair them, you know, make them liveable. So, that's what we've done."

Trelawney's narrative was punctuated by violent gear-changes as we swerved to avoid the worst of the pot-holes in the "Airport Expressway".

"And we are, I'll have you know, the only one hundred per cent foreign community within the whole country. The Head of State himself gave the project his blessing. Even sent one of his daughters to open our Village Hall when it was completed. A kingdom within a kingdom, he called us. Mostly English of course – you should see the Women's Institute fête at the end of summer. The Ambassador comes up from the capital to award the prizes, but a few Frogs and Krauts and what not – er, I mean, well, we welcome other Europeans, all part of the Community vision you know..."

Florian was now attempting to contain some fairly violent squawking, although I couldn't tell whether this was prompted by the prospect of the European vision being realised by the lady jam-makers of a fire-struck African village, or by the slow but inexorable progress of Tamir's left hand, which had carefully massaged each of his vertebrae and was now well on its way down towards the top of his underpants.

I dropped gently asleep, glad to be back in this wicked wonderland.

Chapter Two

We set our passenger down at a dilapidated hostel near the city's bus station. Judging from his finely preened appearance, I gave him about two days here before the absence of functional plumbing would become insufferable. Trelawney watched in satisfied silence as the concierge used Florian's passport to squash a particularly well-nourished cockroach, casually batting its squelched remains from the document before pocketing it.

Then Trelawney clasped Florian's hands in his, fixed him with an earnest stare, and said in his most avuncular tone: "Now you will call us if you have the slightest problem, and come up to see our lovely Village as soon as you get bored with the delights of the city, won't you?"

He produced one of the embossed visiting cards which, I knew from long experience, read:

Trelawney Towers, Esq.
Trelawney Towers
The Village
Telephone El-Velaj 3

Florian clutched the card as a meagre substitute for his impounded passport. "Most certainly, yes. I look forward to seeing us as soon we can!"

He directed this remark mainly at Tamir, who shot a wink and a winning smile back at him. I guessed what was coming next.

Trelawney turned to Tamir.

"Isn't it about time you paid a visit to that aunt of yours in town, dear Tamir? Why not stay down here tonight and take the bus up to the Village tomorrow? You could pick up that suit I had altered at Mustafa's while you're at it."

"My aunt'll like that, Mr. T. It's very kind of you. I just help new friend with luggage first."

Trelawney hugged Tamir and watched him disappear into the hostel behind Florian.

We piled back into the car, this time with me in front. Trelawney seemed disinclined to talk about anything until we'd threaded our way through the city's maze of alleys. To me, it was incomprehensible that he could allow his lover to go off and spend the night in bed with a complete stranger, especially given the history of their relationship.

They'd originally met one night at a café in the *souk* and had ended up in the Village. Discovering that Tamir was homeless, Trelawney allowed him to stay on. When a drunken father eventually made irate contact, Trelawney invited him up to the house, charmed him completely, and obtained his written permission for Tamir to stay on in the capacity of houseman. The police soon tracked Tamir down on a charge of minor theft but Trelawney paid the bribes required to keep him out of prison. When a second charge materialised, and Tamir actually went to jail, Trelawney visited him every day, bringing food parcels and clothing. He paid no heed to the glares and spitting he had to endure as he waited with the relatives of the other prisoners. Once Tamir finally emerged from prison, Trelawney set about having him educated, and there was even hope that he might train as a chef at the government college in the capital.

"So, Peter, here we are again. All well at home?"

"Can't complain. Doña Elena is using my absence to try and rearrange the entire house, as usual, and Pepe is out shooting rabbits dawn and dusk."

These were my gypsy housekeeper and her taciturn brother, who tried valiantly to instil some order into the acres of wilderness that surrounded my tumbledown farmhouse in southern Spain.

"No change, then. I must say, in your case, it is still the lack of a partner which strikes one most."

Trelawney was almost the only person to whom I opened up about my emotional life, or rather, the lack of it. But it was too soon in my holiday for that discussion, so I remained silent.

"What's this about Tamir getting married, anyway?" I eventually asked.

"Yes. Next spring. I'm delighted."

He couldn't have been more curt.

"How can you possibly be? He's lived with you for seven years and now he's abandoning you for some..."

"No, no, no." Trelawney thumped the steering wheel with both hands, causing the vehicle to lunge into the middle of the road where we nearly had a catastrophic encounter with an oncoming truck. "You still don't understand the first thing about relationships in this part of the world. Appearances have to be kept up at all costs. The outside world must see what it *expects* to see. What goes on once the shutters are closed is an entirely different story. As I'm sure Tamir will confirm, he has a very happy life with me. The only way he can hope to continue that is by getting married. Otherwise how would he ever have any standing in society? Or even with his own family?"

"But won't it break your heart?"

"He won't be leaving. Of course, they'll have to have a house, and as you know, the Village Council doesn't encourage natives, so I'm buying them a little one in Beetlebridge."

This was the settlement at the bottom of the road leading up to the Village; its real name was Beit al-Burj but as most of the Villagers couldn't cope with this, it had been known for years as Beetlebridge.

The Village itself was never called by its original name; even the locals referred to it as El-Velaj.

"So Tamir will still be with you?"

"As long as he wants. That's another thing you don't understand – Tamir and I have been through many phases: he has been my lover, my assistant and even my nurse. But most of all, he is my friend. And friends let one another do what they want to do. He will still be my friend if he decides to go off and become a model family man. Based on the effusive welcome he is doubtless giving our German friend as we speak, I think that's unlikely, but stranger things do happen. What do you expect me to do – lock him up in the cellar, forbid him to marry and blackmail him into being mine forever?"

"But you've done so much for him, and now off he goes..."

Trelawney expelled a stream of air through pursed lips. "Surely you see that it is *I* who have benefited most from the giving? You sit there on that terrace of yours with those yapping hounds and that dragoness of a housekeeper snorting around the place, and you fail to engage in life. As soon as there's the least hint of a risk, you flee. You're waiting for a cast-iron guarantee that someone will remain loyal to you, present with you and attendant upon you until your dying day."

Trelawney had dashed my hopes of avoiding this sort of conversation, which usually took place late at night as the whisky bottle emptied. I put his sharpness of tongue down to the stress he was under. Perhaps it was easier for him to analyse my life instead of focusing on his own.

"You stand on the sidelines of life, and others are deprived of all you have to give."

"That's not true. I saw Alex just before I came here."

Other than Trelawney, Alex was the only other person I could truly call a friend. I'd met him through my work: a Scot by birth, he'd made good as a translator for the Swiss banks. Like me, he was in his mid-forties, so it came as a horrific shock when he was diagnosed with lung cancer a year ago. Since then, he'd been undergoing a series of harrowing therapies. I'd flown to Zurich to accompany him on a visit to yet another specialist who bombarded us with a vast quantity of technical information. It all boiled down to the stark fact that nothing more could be done.

I stayed with him that night.

We sat up into the early hours, coolly considering the courses of action. Grim options, indeed. Emotionally detached though I may be, people tell me I've always been a good listener. Faced with this ghastly situation, all I could do was to nod and make occasional gentle suggestions or comments. Nevertheless, it was one of the most draining nights I've ever spent.

"And how is he?"

"No better. He refuses to give up hope, but he's realistic about his chances. The main thing he wants is not to lose control of his mind."

"That can't have been easy for either of you. And I'm sorry, it was quite unjustified of me to say that you don't engage in life. I know there are many people around who have benefited from your kindness. Perhaps I'm a little more ruffled about this residence permit business than I care to admit. Forgive me, Peter."

By now we'd moved out of the harsh orange glare of the city and were making good progress along the coast. Here and there, a twinkling cluster of lights high up in the mountains to our right marked the presence of a hamlet. To our left, the rollers crashed shoreward behind the dilapidated beach hotels and casinos that had sprung up and quickly fallen into disrepair at intervals along the highway.

"So who else is around?" I asked.

"Nobody yet. As the first to arrive, you're in Heliotrope."

The various guest-rooms at Trelawney Towers were colour-coded, though the system carefully avoided anything so vulgar as a primary tone: Magenta, Amethyst, Cornflower and Anthracite (for last-minute arrivals) were among the other shades on offer.

"Purvis arrives shortly."

Purvis was an old friend of Trelawney's who kept himself in considerable style by a variety of less than transparent financial dealings. "And those people who run the delicatessen in the Cotswolds are due about the same time." (It was actually a corner shop in Swindon, but I saw no point in correcting Trelawney's description.)

"What about the younger generation?"

"Well, I rather fancy we'll be seeing our German friend again. The goatherds are down from the mountains already so that alleviates the situation, and Tamir has a few soldier friends seeking respite from their duties. Then there's his brother, you know, the butcher. But there is a certain − er − odour problem involved there."

"What was that you were saying about a French chap?"

"Ah yes."

We were now pulling into Beetlebridge at the bottom of the hill leading to the Village. Even at this time of night a couple of shops were still open, and in one of them I spied a massive round tray loaded with honeyed baklava, topped with bright green pistachio shavings.

"No, Peter, hands off. No good will come of it."

"The French chap?"

"No, the baklava. Well, the same might apply to the Frog. Ah yes − *Marco* − that's his name. Not Melvin or whatever. He's actually the son of that odd couple who have the next-to-top house in the Village. He pitched up at the house the other day asking if I was a friend of Doocie from next door. Said he wanted to find Doocie to help him with some research he was doing on gases in greenhouses or something, wherever it is he studies. Some university or other in Scotland, I suppose, that's where his father's from. His mother is that

Frenchwoman who does the accounts for the Village Council. Or she might be from one of the French colonies, by the looks of her. I don't think I've ever spoken to either of them. Money to burn, and the three of them cooped up in that ivory tower looking down on the rest of us with total disdain."

"So he came in?"

"Of course he came in. You know my rules of hospitality. We are in a land where the stranger must always be made welcome. Naturally I smelt a rat. I know Doocie's a university lecturer, but I don't think he knows any more about greenhouses than I do. Not the sort of chap you'd forget in a hurry, young Marco – shockingly outspoken but very bright, asks far too many questions but listens to the answers. The sort who decides what he wants and stops at nothing to get it. Cut out to be a real heartbreaker one of these days, I'd say."

I should perhaps have paid more attention to his choice of words.

We now began the climb up to the Village through a series of terrifying hairpin bends, made still more hazardous by the potholes that seemed to multiply as the years went on. Trelawney made an initial effort to avoid them but then gave up, with spine-jolting consequences.

"So, what did he ask?"

"He asked whether Mr. Doocie and I were lovers. Pah! The very thought of it!"

Trelawney produced a sweaty handkerchief to wipe away the spittle he'd propelled onto the windscreen at the memory of this outrageous suggestion. Doocie and Trelawney were always quarrelling about one neighbourly issue or another. Last year Doocie had turned off the water supply to Trelawney's hosepipe because Trelawney had built a "Juliet balcony" overlooking Doocie's flat roof, where he liked to sunbathe with his exotic girlfriends. Though they would never admit it, he and Trelawney were actually the best of friends.

"I told him in no uncertain terms that we were not. And furthermore, that the nature of my relationship with Mr. Doocie was none of his business.'"

"He must have been terrified at that!'"

"Actually, he took it quite well. 'That is very frank of you, sir', he said, or something of the sort. I offered him a drink, but he said he'd better be getting back as his mother was waiting with his tea. I was rather touched when he asked my 'permission' to visit me again. I mean, he's a well-developed lad – six foot I'd say – and he comes across as very adult. He shook my hand, slight lingering of thumb in palm, and then off he went for his tea."

Trelawney now crashed through the gears again to haul us up the last gradient into the Village itself. "I expect he'll be back. Curiosity aroused, appetite whetted and so on. Give them an inch ..."

As we swung over the brow of the final hill, the whole Village was suddenly revealed: a neat and well-lit collection of gleaming white houses clambering down the side of a ravine that plunged into a deep inlet of the sea, invisible in blackness at this hour. The church with its belfry presided over the community. Subtle illumination and well-trimmed cedar trees enhanced the contrast between simple, homely architecture and breathtaking natural grandeur.

"Good God!" Trelawney exclaimed.

This was not a spontaneous response to the beauty of his adopted home, however. His house was a star-shaped white stone complex built around a central spot lit pool with a fountain that was almost as prominent a feature as the church. But outside it, the road was blocked by a large, battleship-grey Hillman Minx. This uncompromising vehicle was half-backed into the entrance to Trelawney's shed at a jaunty angle, suggesting that its owner had every right to leave it there. We both knew exactly who that owner was, but mentioning her name at this precise moment would spoil the magic of my return to his home.

The obstruction forced us to negotiate a narrow alley and park behind the house. My friend stepped out of the Land Rover and released the secret trap mechanism on the oaken back door. Once we passed through, I knew we'd leave all semblance of reality behind and enter a world of our own, where any dream, but thankfully few nightmares, could come true. My friend preceded me over the threshold, turned to take both my hands, and pulled me in as if I were boarding a boat.

"Welcome home again, dear boy. I hope your stay will leave you with something to remember."

As it turned out, his hopes were fulfilled in ways neither of us could ever have expected.

Chapter Three

Trelawney's house was just as familiar to me as my own home, and a good deal more welcoming. Over the years, he'd transformed his burnt-out ruin into something between a run-down English country house and a Bedouin caravanserai. Among massive bronze lamps, sumptuous brocades and luscious Persian carpets stood dumpy over-stuffed leather armchairs with mahogany feet and baize-covered card tables. The Heliotrope Room, with its own little balcony looking down the ravine towards the sea, even contained an old church harmonium as well as a high four-poster bed with a wooden canopy, painted pale blue inside with gold and silver cherubs floating along on little white clouds.

I unpacked a few essentials and rejoined my friend for a nightcap in the main room.

Trelawney poured us each a generous Scotch. After he'd downed most of his in one gulp, I judged it safe to raise the subject of the Hillman Minx.

"So," I began gingerly, "why has Greta dumped her car outside your front door?"

"Quite simple. She's stating her price for sorting out the fuss Doocie has created over my new balcony. She wants my shed to keep that wreck of hers in over the winter."

Greta Lindberg, a loping Norwegian giantess now in her early nineties, was the driving force behind the whole Village project. Forty years before, she'd used her diplomatic contacts to obtain the approval of the Head of State, and was rumoured still to have his ear should it be required. Every commune in the country has its elected or appointed *mukhtar* or Headman. The Village was no different in this respect, and Greta was duly installed in the office. But as no feminine form of the word *mukhtar* existed, she became the nation's only female Headman. Nobody had dared question her right to the post since then.

She'd established a veneer of democratic freedom by setting up a Village Council, but not a single member would dare stand in the way of her numerous projects aimed at embellishment and improvement. It was her idea to have the old school converted into a little chapel with a belfry, although national law only allowed the bells to be rung on very special occasions. Cases such as that of the balcony and the water tank kept her mind in sharp focus, and she usually found a way of turning them to her advantage.

"As usual, Greta will get what she wants," Trelawney sighed. "I'll have to kowtow to her tomorrow morning – it's Tuesday, Elevenses day, so we'll find her at the Olive Branch."

I logged the 'we'.

"Smart attire, remember. Long trousers, please."

He drained the last of his whisky and rose. "It's marvellous to have you back, Peter. I wish you a peaceful night – ah – if that's what you want. Help yourself if you're hungry. I'll see you at breakfast."

With that, he ambled off his bedroom, a magnificent domed chamber, tented in scarlet and gold, leaving me to raid the pantry for a simple supper.

I carried my tray of sandwiches through the inner courtyard of the house, pausing to listen to the only sounds that broke the thick black silence of the night – the inevitable chirrup of the cicadas, the occasional modest monotone of a nightingale, the splashing of the fountain. Above me, the stars were painfully clear in a moonless sky, framed by luxuriant fig trees and lofty Canary palms soaring from the oleander bushes that edged the yard.

I set the tray down by my bedside and stretched out on the huge mattress. It could easily accommodate four and I chuckled as I remembered more than one night when it had. As so often in this house, but so rarely elsewhere, I wanted to let my mind rove freely and imagine what my life could have been, and what it might still become. If only I could be as fearless as Trelawney in achieving my own version of contentment, no matter what the rest of the world might think.

I recalled some words that Alex had spoken to me during that long night in Zurich.

"So it seems that I'm to die without knowing what it is to have a lover."

I was unable to come up with a response.

"Make sure you don't do the same," he added. "I've only lived half a life. Make sure you get the full deal."

Alex's advice had returned to me time and again since then. I was beginning to see my life as many outsiders must have done: a vaguely impressive outer shell encasing vast inner emptiness.

At least I'd avoided the hell my parents created at home. While my classmates rode the roller-coaster of first love, I was learning how to detach and suppress every feeling that surfaced. I would stay silent as my parents devised ever more effective ways of torturing one another. My poor mother would plunge abruptly from the heights of demented elation into suicidal depression; my father was a smouldering volcano of rage – fuelled perhaps by the marriage he found himself trapped in, or perhaps he would have been like that anyway.

After fifteen years of enduring this, I'd concluded that intimate relationships were nothing but a recipe for heartache, suffering and festering hatred. I dropped the few friends I made at school as soon as they tried to move in too close. When swimming lessons were introduced, I realised that girls held no physical attraction for me –

but boys most certainly did, and that made the whole business more complex. Or, rather, terrifying.

By carefully constructing a self-contained, solitary life, I thought I'd reached some sort of equilibrium. But Alex's comments had begun to disturb it, and now Trelawney's carping on about 'the lack of a partner' had continued the process. I didn't like the edge of discomfort I could sense sharpening all the time. Smoking cigarette after cigarette in the easy familiarity of that room, I realised it wouldn't go away. At least here I might be able to confront it.

As I lay on that magnificent bed, I was overcome with weariness and regret for all the years I'd wasted being absent from life. With a childlike prayer, I called on the special magic of this place to transform my life – overnight, if possible. Then I fell into a deep and dreamless sleep.

⎯⎯⎯⎯ ⋗⋖⋗⋖ ⎯⎯⎯⎯

But not, as it turned out, for very long. I awoke with a sense that something or someone was moving in the room. I held my breath in instinctive fear, then realised that a scrabbling noise was coming from outside the French windows. I sprang from the bed and searched for some kind of weapon. The best I could find was a rolled-up golf umbrella in a rack behind the door. Seizing it, I tiptoed to the window.

To my horror, someone was now standing on the balcony and tapping quietly but firmly on the wooden shutters. I knew you could climb up from the lane below because I'd done it myself one unusually drunken night when I'd forgotten my room key. For the same reason, I knew the shutters could be forced open from outside. I stood by the window, umbrella raised, ready to strike. Sure enough, whoever was out there started to prise the shutters apart.

"Who's there? *C'est qui?*" I growled as sternly as possible.

There was a soft titter from the other side of the shutters.

"Mr. Peter, don't frighten, I come say you hello!"

I nearly passed out with relief when I realised the voice belonged to Zeki, one of the goatherds from the hills behind the Village, who'd spent a few tender and memorable nights with me the year before. I'd forgotten everyone here knew everything about everyone. My arrival would have been widely expected and monitored by unseen eyes.

I unhooked the hasp and opened the shutters. Zeki was always cheerful, with a broad, toothy smile; now he burst into a fit of uncontrollable laughter.

"What's the matter?"

"You think it gonna rain, Mr. Peter?"

I must have cut a rather bizarre figure, standing in candy-striped boxers, grasping a huge and equally garish umbrella in one hand. Before I could come up with an explanation to salvage my dignity, Zeki threw both arms around me and planted a long, wet kiss on my mouth.

He drew back and passed the side of his index finger gently over my cheek.

"I wait for you, Mr. Peter. Welcome back. I stay?"

"You stay, Zeki. You stay."

He carefully closed the shutters, took my hand, and led me back to the bed. He was reassuringly strong and muscular; as our embrace grew tighter and more passionate, I felt my mind empty itself of all the thoughts that had been whirling through it. Warm, tender flesh – the most powerful drug for me – sponged away my pains, regrets and anxieties, and I let myself float away into fantasy, imagining how it would be if I could always feel like this. If only.

Chapter Four

I was awoken next morning by the soothing coolness of a flannel passed over my forehead. It was barely seven o'clock, but brilliant shafts of sunlight were shooting through the gaps in the shutters.

Zeki was already dressed. I felt a jarring mixture of sadness that the gentle (and not so gentle) pleasures of the night were over, and relief that there was no need to find some way of passing the time once we were out of bed. I took Zeki's hand and began to speak, but he silenced me by placing his index over my lips. He took a cigarette from the pack on the bedside table, lit it, and transferred it from his mouth to mine.

"I go now," he whispered. "I go work."

I motioned him to wait and got out of bed. I always hated this part.

"Would you like cigarettes, Zeki, or … money?" I tried to make it sound like a casual enquiry.

"You got American cigarette?"

I fished a carton of duty-free Marlboros from my bag and handed it over. For me, this custom – " the gratuity," as Trelawney called it – nearly always spoiled the memory of the night. What had seemed so genuine was, after all, just another version of the transactions I performed in the bath-houses of Zurich or Madrid. Still, a carton of cigarettes felt less brutal than a twenty-dollar note.

"I see you again, Mr. Peter? Tomorrow?"

I nodded as I pulled on a dressing gown, and then we padded barefoot over the courtyard and down the steps to the back door. Its unspoken purpose was to enable local visitors to emerge into the lane where nobody could possibly see them. Zeki hugged me again and kissed me softly on the lips.

"Why you sad? I come back tomorrow!"

"I'm not sad, it's just...never mind, Zeki. You take care." As if he could understand what I was mumbling about.

"*Ma salama*, Mr. Peter."

"*Ma salama*, Zeki. See you."

With that, he was gone into the already dazzling daylight. I swung the wooden bar back over the door and returned to my room, where a mixture of human and animal odours lingered – not totally unpleasant, but not altogether agreeable either. I turned the fan up and rolled into bed for another couple of hours' sleep.

When I eventually emerged, Trelawney was already installed at the head of the long refectory table, swathed in a billowing cream kaftan. A bright orange bath-towel wound around his head made him look even more like a minor oriental potentate from a Gilbert and Sullivan opera. Trelawney always lavished enormous care on every part of his body, but his hair received particular attention. Crates containing modestly-labelled but highly pungent lotions were regularly shipped to the Village from a venerable address in Jermyn Street, and the results were clear to see. At sixty-two, he still had a full head of thick, silvery-blonde hair that cascaded down the back of his neck in rows of carefully crimped curls.

"Good morning my friend. A satisfactory first night?"

"Oh, you heard..."

"Heard, be buggered! Zeki's asked me when you're coming back every time I've seen him. He would have walked from the other end of the country to see you if he needed to. He really is quite fond of you, you know."

"Well, he's a nice lad. Straightforward, simple, sort of. But he still needed paying."

Trelawney snorted. "You really don't understand how it works here, do you? The gratuity is *not* a payment. This house is *not* a brothel, and

Zeki and the rest of them are *not* prostitutes. But when you hand over the gratuity, you make the whole thing acceptable. It allows the man to feel no guilt about the act he has just so clearly enjoyed. Someone like Zeki couldn't cope with thinking that he really was a homosexual, even a part-time one. Don't forget most of them are married – I think Zeki has two children already. The gratuity lets him think that it was a favour, beyond the normal call of duty. You both enjoy the sex, he feels good about it, and you feel good because you are assisting the poor of the Third World. It's a perfect system – all participants are satisfied."

"Well, I still have mixed feelings about it, I mean..."

"Oh for heaven's sake, stop analysing and start enjoying. You'd do well to remember what dear Miss Stein said – a fuck is a fuck is a fuck, I seem to recall it was. Have some toast, or are you going to start looking at the ethical aspects of the combustion of bread as well?"

Last night's waspishness clearly hadn't worn off.

"Now, I've been giving some thought to today's agenda. We shall have to put in an appearance at Elevenses."

Every Tuesday and Saturday lunchtime, anyone who was anyone in the community was expected to call in at the café-cum-pub that was the hub of the Village's social life. This establishment, The Olive Branch, was run by June, a busty, red-headed Liverpudlian who'd eloped with an Egyptian policeman decades ago. The policeman disappeared without trace but ever since, various reasons had prevented her from returning to the Mersey. These included a succession of impressively built lovers from south of the Sahara.

Greta and June had waged open warfare for many years. Greta unsuccessfully tried to have June ejected from the Village on moral grounds, while June had made equally vain attempts to oust Greta from her position as Headman, alleging incompetence and corruption. Like spectators at a cock-fight, aficionados would go along to Elevenses in the hope they might see sparks fly, since this was the only occasion they appeared in each other's vicinity.

"But Elevenses is merely the start of it," Trelawney went on. "Then we'll need to go into town. Dear Tamir has telephoned and I've arranged to meet him to help us with the shopping. There's next to nothing to eat in this house, as far as I can see. Also, there's the matter of Sir Brian, who is dining here tomorrow night, and that has to be a rather grand occasion. My continued presence in the Village is at stake, don't forget."

The agenda was beginning to fill up, I thought, with the promise of Zeki's return late on Wednesday night as well.

"There will be numerous guests and vast quantities of provender will be needed. Purvis may arrive by then, making matters even worse, and God knows who else. A swim on the way back up, and then Tamir will cook us a quiet supper here. Will that suit you?"

"Fine by me," I replied. It never ceased to amaze me that life in this remote outpost was so packed. Although my home in Spain was close to some of Europe's most popular holiday resorts, I lived the life of a hermit by comparison with the hectic routine of the Village.

"I remind you again to dress appropriately for Elevenses, please. I shall be ready to leave at twelve."

It would have been unthinkable for a Village event named Elevenses to start at anything like eleven o'clock. Though I objected to wearing long trousers and a jacket in the midday heat, the sacrifice was worth it to load up on the latest morsels of scandal. Trelawney rose from the breakfast table and made a stately exit. In this garb, it occurred to me, not for the first time, that he could easily have had a distinguished career as a female impersonator.

And perhaps he had, for all I knew.

Chapter Five

I appeared as requested at twelve to find Trelawney now changed into an obviously hand-made suit of the finest white linen, a silk handkerchief spilling out from the breast pocket, a Panama hat with a broad band of fabric that matched the handkerchief, and an ebony shooting-stick. I felt rather overshadowed in the lightweight sports jacket I usually wore to see my bank manager.

We paused to check our appearances in a huge gilt-framed mirror, Trelawney standing behind me as I straightened my tie. He placed both hands firmly on my shoulders and made me turn around to face him.

"My dear friend," he said. "I say this with love: I am concerned about you. In the past, I have been amused, frustrated and enraged by you. I have been bored by you and interested in you. But I have never been concerned. Now I am, because I see you are unhappy. Deeply. You know this is true, Peter. I don't know what I can do to help, other than open my home and heart. You don't need to answer. Just remember that I know, and that it changes nothing in our friendship."

This was not what I'd been expecting. I was so glad to be back in the Village, to be reunited with my friend. After my night with Zeki, I thought I was feeling rather chipper. In any case, as a guest, I always tried to keep such emotions well hidden. But of course, Trelawney was right. I knew what he said was true, and I had another pang of that sharp, discomforting sensation I'd been feeling on and off since I was with Alex in Zurich.

"Please don't worry about me. There's nothing to..."

"No point asking that, my dear. Enough said for now. Let us sally forth into the fray."

He rotated a sort of ornate spanner that released a cascade of locks, allowing him to swing the huge door open. It took five minutes to walk to the café, but it was nearly at the top of the hill and the alleyways became steeper as we went. In the searing heat, I was so out of breath by the time we arrived that I was incapable of thinking any more about what Trelawney had just said.

The Olive Branch consisted mostly of a garden, with just one splendidly aged olive tree in the middle. Graceful palms lined the perimeter and much of the area was heavily shaded by vines entwined around an overhead canopy. Through the open window, I spotted June behind the counter, cigarette wedged between pouting puce lips, torrents of red hair tumbling out of a polka-dot bandanna. A totally shapeless floral print dress covered everything from her neck to her espadrilles. She stomped over to the door and flung it open, waving us inside with a regal sweep of her chubby hand.

"My, my, my, what a well-pruned pair of poofters!" I looked round quickly and was relieved to see that the room was empty. "Peter my darling, lovely to see you back. My boys always come back to me."

She kissed me full on the lips, then made a show of scrunching her nose up.

"Hmm, I do believe I can smell goat already. Early start, was it?"

Trelawney broke in. "June, you are outlandish, outrageous, and out of keeping with the exclusive and sober tone of this Village. I fail to see why we put up with you!" He leant over and kissed her first on the right cheek, then the left, then the right again. "But then, who else would put up with *us*?"

"Too right, love. Such a shower I never seen in my life. They're all through there, the sipping spinsters, waiting until something happens to stop rigor mortis from setting in. And now with you two here, their prayers have been answered in style!"

"Is the Headman with us?"

"Need you ask? On her usual perch, just behind the Colonel and his missus. Plenty of room at her table if you want to join her."

"I think we'd better do that. Matters of state to discuss, as you may have heard."

June rolled her eyes heavenwards, eloquently signalling her utter contempt for the Villagers' pettifogging squabbles. "Usual for you, Mr. T? Peter?"

"Heart-starter coffee please, June."

"I'll be over in a minute. Don't be offended if I don't join you at the table, I've only got a few marbles left and I can't afford to lose any."

Trelawney strode into the garden and I followed. There were twenty or so assorted Villagers, and a few nodded or raised a hand in Trelawney's direction as we passed. We headed for a table in the far corner where Greta was sitting in solitary splendour, her back ramrod-straight.

Trelawney bowed slightly as he approached. "Good afternoon, Greta. All well with you? May we join?"

"With the very greatest of pleasure. Peter! How lovely to have you back among us. So nice to see Trelawney with such pleasant company of his own generation. I'm always glad to welcome intellectuals to my Village." The *my* was uttered with all the cool authority of a monarch speaking of her kingdom.

Greta's appearance was imposing enough – she had the rugged, deeply tanned features of a mountaineer, with brawny, masculine arms and vast square shoulders, but her voice was what struck you most. There could be no arguing with those precisely enunciated vowels, delivered in a powerful baritone. You couldn't help being awed by her perfect command of English, even though it was not her native tongue. She and Trelawney went into a huddle about the matter of the Juliet balcony while I scanned the garden.

I'd encountered most of the inmates during my stays in the Village over the years: dreary Colonel Twelvetrees and his dimly smiling wife; a family of Swedes with blond-cropped children arranged around their table in order of height; an elegantly coiffed Belgian lady sitting in total silence opposite her pasty husband as he pored over his newspaper with a magnifying glass. In a far corner was Dr. Steingass, slouched over the table, his head perilously close to an almost empty bottle of cheap red wine. He'd apparently been an eminent physician in Heidelberg, but was struck off many years ago for reasons that were now all too obvious.

My attention was caught by a middle-aged couple I'd not seen before, pipe and cigarette-holder, fingers jabbing at a map spread on their table. The wife had one of the most striking faces I'd ever seen – a complexion the colour of rich Arabica coffee with a dash of cream, and a nose sharp enough to puncture gunmetal. Her husband and son sat side by side with their backs to me. I could tell from the way the son slouched in his chair that he was bored stiff by the entire proceedings.

However, the general air of subdued calm in the garden was disrupted by the ruckus emanating from another family in the opposite corner from Greta. The bleary-eyed, beetroot-faced father was lashing into his teenage son as the mother tried in vain to calm them down. The daughter had her head and arms slumped on the table in a pose that suggested she'd been through this ordeal far too many times. Her thick black hair was gelled into a crown of aggressive spikes, and what I thought was some sort of injury on her temple turned out to be a silver piercing through the fold of skin next to her left eye.

Looking at her more closely, I remembered that this was Beth Horrabin, a child who came to Trelawney's house almost every day one summer several years ago. She'd begged permission to pick figs from one of the trees in the courtyard, and I'd gladly allowed her to when nobody was around.

Empty beer-bottles littered the table. The argument was reaching such proportions that other conversations were suspended as the Villagers turned their attention to this latest drama.

With a surprising turn of speed, June swooped across the garden and planted herself squarely in front of the caterwauling family.

"Mr. Horrabin, it's time for your party to be leaving my premises if you don't mind. Sort it out at home, will you?"

"You tryin' to eject me?"

"No question of an attempt, dearie. I *am* ejecting you."

"And where's your bouncer, might I ask?"

Now on his feet, Mr. Horrabin was by no means a midget, but June had to lower her face by several inches to bring it level with his.

"You're looking at the fuckin' bouncer. Now OUT!"

They knew better than to put up any resistance. Horrabin senior slapped his son across the cheek, telling him it was all his fault while his wife started ferreting around for money in a huge, over-stuffed handbag. June snapped it shut, gesturing that their departure would be ample payment.

Beth, roused from her torpor, seemed to recognise me as she turned around and shot me a glance of helpless, weary embarrassment. She'd grown tall and broad, her father's fleshy lips adding a sensual note to a face that was handsome rather than pretty. The four of them clattered off, and relative peace was restored.

"Dreadful, dreadful people," Greta said. "Sometimes I weep when I think that the future of my Village is in the hands of people such as they. What on earth are we going to do, my friends?"

Trelawney seized on this opening.

"The first thing we can do, Greta, is to stop wasting our time on silly little squabbles about hosepipes and windows. That way, people like me would have more time to help you in your noble work of development, so the Village would attract a better class of person in the future."

"You are so right, Trelawney. As you well know, I can resolve a minor matter like that by signing a couple of documents and having them delivered to you and Mr. Doocie. He simply has to abide by the rules. Of course he must restore your water supply, and of course he must accept that your elegant balcony does not project onto his property and is therefore none of his business."

I didn't have long to wonder whether Trelawney had been forced to pay the full price for victory.

"I'll have the documents typed up and drop the copies off when I pop my car into your garage tonight. So nice to think it'll last me another few years now it can spend the winters under cover. More tea, gentlemen?"

Though Trelawney's demeanour remained impeccable, I could tell from the twitching of his left eyebrow that he was close to implosion.

"Very nice of you, Greta," I said, "but I think we'd better be getting down into town now. I'll call in and see you in a few days."

"I shall await your visit with particular pleasure. Do enjoy your holiday with us, Peter."

We made our way out of the garden, through the main room where I congratulated June on her performance. We plodded in silence through the bright white alleyways into the coolness of Trelawney's courtyard.

I started to ask what he thought of the deal that had just been struck, but he cut me off sharply.

"Just don't say a word until I have had a prolonged siesta. Please wake me at four if I'm not in motion by then."

He tramped off into the inner reaches of the house, and I decided that I would follow suit, exhausted by all the excitement of Elevenses.

Chapter Six

Back in the Heliotrope Room, I threw off my clothes and stretched out on the bed. I couldn't even be bothered to unpack the rest of my bags. I was looking forward to a well-earned siesta when I suddenly heard footsteps in the courtyard.

I dressed, cautiously swung the door open, and looked around.

At first there was no one to be seen. Then I heard a slight cough and a rustle from the oleander bushes. An intruder? I decided to be authoritative.

"Yes? Who's there? What do you want?"

An unusually tall, slender young man emerged from the bushes and stood looking at me sideways. He was as dark as any Arab, but his features were distinctly European.

"I'm sorry, I didn't mean to – I mean, I came to, I thought Mr. Towers was … are you … ah?"

This intruder was obviously harmless, but I thought I should uphold my firm line.

"This is a private house, you know. Now who are you and what do you want?"

The young man switched suddenly from confused shyness to confident, even aggressive, assertion.

"I know it's a private house because I've been here before and Mr. Towers knows me *personally*. I am a resident of this Village and I have come to consult Mr. Towers on … on a matter. My name is Marco. Marco Blaine. May I ask who you are – sir?"

As he was speaking, I stepped forward and he turned to face me squarely. It was the mole on his cheek, just half-way between his left eye and his nose, that first caught my attention. Also, a little bump on the bridge of his nose that somehow made his face less perfect, but more interesting. His black eyelashes, long and gracefully curved, were magnificent. Perhaps I noticed them because he was blinking so much now he was on the defensive. They were hazel – deep brown one minute, almost amber the next.

He wore a T-shirt emblazoned with the motto "Madonna For Pope" – which made no sense to me at all – and khaki shorts. I took in his deeply tanned, powerful legs. They were covered in downy, reddish-brown hair and, looking back to his face, I noticed a faint tint of the same auburn in his hair, which I'd first registered as black.

It's hard to remember exactly how you felt when you first saw the person who was to turn your life upside-down.

A tremor rose through me, starting in my chest, moving up to my head, twitching my lips and freezing my tongue. It seemed I'd already known his face and body all my life. At the same time, a delicious but troubling pang of lust shot through me, for he was undoubtedly stunning. I was sure he'd see my excitement through my boxers.

Maybe hindsight has coloured the memory of my first reactions to Marco, but whatever was happening, I was now breathless and unable to speak.

"Are you all right?" he asked. "Now I've told you who I am, are you going to tell me who you are?"

"Of course. I am Peter and I am..."

"Peter what? I like to know people's full names."

"Peter Carter. Why?"

"It gives you more of an impression of their character. I've read it gives you more power over them as well, but I'm not sure I believe that. Actually, I have four names: Marco Thomas Duncan Blaine." He extended a finger to go with each name, then spread both palms out as if he'd performed a conjuring trick and was waiting for a round of applause.

"Well," I said, "I only have the two. My parents weren't so imaginative."

"Do you wish you had more? Don't you feel inadequate with just two?"

"I hadn't thought of it that way. I suppose they might be useful. For bank accounts or passports, or that sort of thing." I was amazed but equally charmed by the way Marco launched into such personal comments on the basis of a chance encounter.

"Well, if you say so. I've got two passports, one French and one British, but they both have the same four names in them. And I wasn't even born in either of those countries." His English bore not the slightest trace of a French accent, but he put a Scots roll on his r's at the end of words like "passport". Somehow this struck me as highly sensual.

"So where were you born?" I remember thinking: I have no idea where any of my other friends were born.

"Madagascar. Formerly known as the Malagasy Republic. It used to be a French colony and that's where my mother happened to be when I arrived. That's where she's originally from, you see, and her people have some sort of firm there. Fruit, in fact. I was born in the capital, which used to be called Tananarive. Now it's called Antananarivo. Too many syllables whichever one you use. So I just say Madagascar, which most people can at least place on the map. However, you look quite intelligent so you may know some of this."

This was rapidly turning into one of the most ridiculous conversations I'd ever had, but I had no wish to cut it short.

"I am slightly familiar with that part of the world, but I've never been there." My work as a translator made me 'slightly familiar' with an endless variety of obscure subjects. "What's it like?"

"Well, I can't be expected to remember anything much. Hot and wet, basically. Masses of disgusting animals. I left when I was three, you see, my parents moved on, and I've hardly ever been back."

"Ah. And, erm, you're looking for ... Trelawney? I mean, Mr. Towers?"

"Yes."

"Well I'm afraid he's resting. Perhaps..."

"In that case, I'd quite like to go on talking with you. Actually, I've already seen you once today. At the Olive Branch."

Now I realised: this was the young man I'd seen earlier from behind in the Village café, so obviously bored by his parents' discussion over a map. This morning, though, I had no chance to sense his overpowering magnetism.

"Yes, everyone in the Village has to show up there, I suppose."

"Ghastly. Monstrous." Marco made a stage gesture, as if he were flicking flies away from himself. Then, as casually as if he were checking the time, he asked: "Are you a homosexual?"

"Look, I really..."

"Oh, come on, we're all in this together. I don't mind telling you I'm one. But I've only become absolutely sure of it just recently. Are you and Mr. Towers lovers?"

"Well, seeing as you ask so nicely, yes, I am a homosexual, but no, I am not Trelawney's – ah, Mr. Towers's lover."

"You've never even had sex with him? I mean, that's one of the reasons I'm so pleased to be gay. You can have all sorts of combinations that straight people would never even think of."

"No, they probably wouldn't, Marco." This was the first time I called him by his name. Why on earth should that have given me such a thrill?

"But you'll also find that gay men, we gay men, can form fabulously strong friendships, and sex needn't ever enter into it. Shouldn't, in fact. Sex would be more likely to destroy a friendship like Mr. Towers' and mine, not that either of us have ever wanted it."

Where on earth was I dredging this garbage up from?

"I know what sex can do. Would you like to hear how I lost my virginity? Actually, you've already seen the person I gave it away to."

"I suppose I'll have to tell you how I lost mine in return."

"If you can remember that far back." He tittered. "Sorry, you shouldn't take that as an insult – you don't look *much* over forty. Anyway, you remember the girl who was with her family in the Olive Branch before they got chucked out?"

"Beth Horrabin. She's quite a woman now. I remember her as a little girl only a few years ago."

"Not such a little girl as you'd think, actually. We were best friends ever since I can remember, because we were the only two kids in the Village for all those years. Apart from Mickey, of course, that's her brother. You saw old man Horrabin walloping him earlier, as usual. I'm actually more of a brother to her than Mickey is, but that's another story. I fell in love with her. My first time. Then she let me fuck her. Also my first time. After which things went all cold and prickly between us. I know that was because of the sex. Now we're sort of friends again on the surface, but I still love her, and I've turned out to be gay. As a matter of fact, I think she probably is as well."

"You're sure this isn't..." He joined in and we said the words in unison, "… *a phase I'm going through?*" At which we both burst out laughing.

"I have to tell you, I've never had a conversation like this with anybody I've just met. Would you … like to continue it in my room? We'll be waking Trelawney up if we're not careful."

He smiled rather wearily, like a parent letting a child have its own way to keep the peace. "Okay. I can't blame you for asking. Over here?"

He set out for the Heliotrope Room and I followed. He sat down on the edge of the huge bed, crossing his legs in a way that forced his genitals up and out rather than down and in. My heart began to pound.

"Do you like the room?"

"Get on with it! Is that all you're going to ask me?"

I couldn't believe this was happening. The man of my dreams had just stormed into my life, and seemed to be offering himself on a plate.

"Well, would you like to, ah, lie down?"

For the first time in the conversation, there was a short silence.

Marco looked at the floor, as if he were making a calculation, and then, quietly, deliberately, but without the least anger or malice, said, "No thank you, I wouldn't, actually."

Damn, damn, damn! What a feeble line. Why did I ask in the first place? Given the way he'd seized total control of our encounter so far, if he'd wanted to have sex, he would have dropped his shorts or pulled me on top of him. In fact, it was he who had more or less forced me to make my clumsy advance. Maybe he wanted to see me squirm. Now I was the one who felt like an embarrassed child, about to be upbraided for talking badly out of line.

Marco raised his eyes to meet mine. A broad smile crinkled his face.

"I've decided that hanky-panky with you is not on my agenda. But I just *love* the way you put it – I must remember that!"

He started tittering again and then burst into shrieks of laughter. "*Would you like to lie down?* I've never heard anything so cheesy in all my life! Has that ever worked?" He thumped the bed with both fists in mirth.

"I don't think I've ever used that line before, actually," I replied, deadpan. "Would you like a cigarette, without any obligations?"

"You really are quite an oddity, aren't you? Yes thanks, I thought you'd never ask."

I lit it, glad to see my hands were no longer trembling, and passed it over. He drew deeply, blowing smoke out in a long cone that glinted gold and grey in the sunbeams.

"Now, where were we? You think I'm going through a phase. Well, since Beth, I've had sex with thirty-seven men. I keep count, and I record the details in a diary – in code, of course. With a score on a scale of one to ten. I never had to use any "lines", as you call them, at all – but then with my looks and age, you wouldn't have to. Each time it's got better, not worse, and each time I want more. Apart from the locals, that is, but they only want one thing, and seeing as I want the same thing as they do, it doesn't really work out."

"Your back door is firmly bolted, as they say."

"What? Where in God's name does that come from? I think I'll have to stick around with you just to pick up the lingo. I've never heard anything like it – *in all my born days*!" He turned the last words into a lampoon of my own public-school-and-Oxbridge accent.

"I'm glad to be of interest. If what you say is true, and I've no reason to believe it isn't, I reckon your gay phase is set to last about half a century. I wish I'd known at your age – it would have saved me a lot of heartache."

"Do you know how old I am, then?"

I studied his face. He could have been twenty, he could have been thirty. He was in the peak of physical fitness, glowing with the exuberant energy of youth. But now I detected something about the cast of his features – a maturity that had escaped me at first, a hint of sadness, a certain hardening – perhaps the imprint of bitter experience.

"Well, I believe you're doing research at university, aren't you? So, mid-twenties, I'd guess."

He looked at me ruefully. "Peter, I haven't even got a *place* at university yet. I go back to Scotland in a week to a ghastly institution for lazy rich kids who fucked up at school. I'm nineteen years old. *Nearly* twenty, though."

Now my heart took another plunge as it dawned on me I was

having one of the most intimate conversations of my life with someone less than half my age. Trelawney *had* told me he was a research student, hadn't he?

Marco could obviously read my thoughts.

"Nobody would ever think I was that young, so don't torture yourself. I'm the oldest in the whole place, of course. I missed a year at school thanks to my parents' inability to keep their arses parked in the same place for more than five minutes. As usual, they do what they want and I pay the price. Anyway, only two terms to go at the crammer and I'm out of there, whether I get a place at uni or not."

I didn't want us to stop talking, but now he was looking at his watch, a rather elaborate diver's model. "Christ, it's nearly four o'clock. I have to get home to go on some stupid drive – one of Mama's archaeological field trips. And you have to wake Trelawney up, I think."

"So I do. Well, Marco, I've thoroughly enjoyed talking to you. Can we do it again?"

For some reason I couldn't quite grasp, this provoked a new fit of laughter. "God, you're so pompous! In a nice sort of way, I mean. Quite quaint, as my mother would say. Which reminds me, just don't ever think of trying to contact me at home. But I've decided I like you. Although you've hardly told me anything about yourself. Do you like dancing?"

"I don't mind it. I mean, I'm not very good at it."

"Can't do this sort of thing, then?"

He leapt suddenly to his feet and broke into a dramatic frenzy of foot-stamping, clapping and arm-flailing that climaxed with him snapping the fingers of both hands just below my eyes, his lips pouted in mock passion.

Of course I knew what it was. "Flamenco. *Venga!*"

"So, you know about it, do you?"

"I've lived in Spain for the past ten years. I didn't get a chance to tell you that."

"*Have* you now?" This was the first thing I'd said that seemed to give him genuine pause for thought. "Well in that case, you'll know exactly what sort of flamenco I just showed you."

I didn't. Even in the small town near my house, it was performed regularly, but I'd never taken much interest in it. "Sorry to disappoint you."

"That was the *bulerías*. The only one where the man is allowed to leap, that's why I like it. Dancing is my *absolute* passion. I know I'm good enough to be a professional. So far I've just taught myself from videos, though. And I speak Spanish – that's what I want to study at uni, if I ever get there. Which is doubtful, as I have other plans. Now – what's this?"

He arched his entire body backwards and slowly raised his arms in graceful, spiralling motions until his hands met, far above his head. He remained at that impossible angle for several seconds, a delirious expression on his face.

It was the most seductive movement I'd ever seen a man make.

"No? Surely you know that one? It's a *fandango*. Danced by a courting couple, usually."

"I didn't even know there were different types of flamenco, to be honest."

"Hmmm. You've got a lot to learn. In various respects, by the sounds of it. I've got to go. We shall meet again. *Hasta luego*!"

He sailed out of the room and I heard him letting himself through the secret door – he'd obviously memorised the geography of the Towers from his previous visit. Or perhaps there'd been more than one. I was left exhilarated, buoyed up by our talk, bursting with curiosity about this extraordinary young man.

Looking back, I see that all the seeds of my obsession – and my desire for ultimate possession – were sown in that very first encounter. Nothing about Marco was predictable, nothing fitted into any mould I knew.

But it had already gone four o'clock, and as he'd reminded me, I had to go and rouse Trelawney.

Come to think of it, how did he know that? He must have been waiting and listening outside the house when Trelawney and I returned from the Olive Branch. For the first time – and not the last – the truth of the situation only dawned on me after Marco swept from the scene. There was no element of chance – he'd planned the whole thing.

But that just made me feel even more fascinated, and flattered.

Trelawney's wake-up call could wait. Anyway, I was still quaking from excitement, and it wouldn't do to appear in his bedchamber in such a state of disarray. Chuckling, I stretched out again and savoured the hour I'd just spent with Marco, wondering whether it was the first and last – but hoping, already, that it was the first of many to come.

Chapter Seven

When I finally decided to head to the main part of the house, I found Trelawney already ensconced on the terrace in a cane chair with a huge peacock's-tail back. He was scrutinising the marriages column in the copy of The Times I'd given him when I arrived.

"D'you remember Jonathan who was here three or four years ago? Father was Ambassador in the Gulf somewhere? Well, it appears he's getting married to one Lady Lavinia ffrench-Smith. I didn't realise people still had names that started with two small f's. I fancy Lady Lavinia has quite a surprise in store if and when they make it to the nuptial chamber. Big boy, that one. I wouldn't predict a lengthy marriage unless he's radically changed his ways."

I poured some coffee and took a seat. As I stirred in the sugar, I realised I hadn't taken in a word Trelawney said.

"Sorry? What? Who?" I mumbled.

"Jonathan. Lovely cook. Don't you remember those hampers he used to pack up for the beach trips that autumn?"

"Oh yes, of course. Getting married, you said?"

"Peter, what's wrong with you? If I didn't know you better I'd think you'd been on the bottle. I hope you're not starting with a bug."

"No, no. I … I had a visitor while you were asleep."

"So you're shagged out, to use that charming expression of the younger generation. Not very wise in view of our packed programme, but I suppose as a guest…"

"No. It wasn't like that. It was Marco – the fellow you told me about. We just talked. Actually, he talked most of the time."

"I heard nothing. Greta drove me to medication and I slept the sleep of the relatively innocent. Well?"

"Well what?"

"Oh dear, Peter." He snorted in a deep and noisy breath through his nostrils. "I don't like the sound of this. Getting defensive already?"

"What do you mean, defensive? I..."

"*That's* what I mean. Have you become *fond*?"

"I'd hardly put it like that, after one brief conversation. It's just – I rather like him, he rather likes me, in fact he told me so, and I would – no, *we* would – like to see one another again. To talk, you know."

"You really didn't fuck? It's not against the house rules."

"We did not."

"Well remember this, then. You never, ever will."

"How can you possibly know that?"

"Peter, I've met Marco, I know the type. It won't happen. Accept that and you'll be fine. But knowing you, I rather fear..."

The telephone rang and Trelawney sprang up to answer it, leaving me to ponder his latest intrusion into my emotional life. He'd managed to spoil the warm, chirpy mood I was in, but now it bubbled up within me again. Maybe he was jealous that I'd found a nice young man, with a friendship in view that wasn't based on the exchange of bodily fluids or money. Pleasant though they were, the Tamirs of this world were barely up to discussing the weather forecast. How on earth did Trelawney pass the time with them once they were out of bed? And he'd already told me he was worried about me – well, here I was, launching a new initiative to change the situation.

From inside, I heard Trelawney bringing the telephone conversation to an end. He came through the French windows onto the terrace, smiling broadly. "That was our German friend. Change of plans: we're meeting him after our shopping trip and he's coming to stay for a few days."

I still sensed some tension between us as we bumped along in the Land Rover, but Trelawney's conversation turned to less touchy matters. A wind was beginning to blow in from the north, making the sea look like a wrinkled bedspread, but it did nothing to diminish the relentless heat. By the time we reached the outskirts of town, sandy gusts were buffeting the car like miniature hail showers and shreds of litter were sailing along the streets.

"We're meeting Tamir at Abdul's restaurant in the Copper Bazaar. He's already been busy this morning, organising the *meze* and the meat, bless him."

Any dinner in the Village was judged by the selection of starters – *meze* – endless combinations of stuffed vegetables, various bits of seafood cloaked in batter, mixtures of yoghurt, goat's cheese and herbs, cracked wheat and creamy thick chickpea paste with pools of olive oil floating on the top. You had to provide enough to make sure that the table was still quite full when all your guests had finished, and then you lived on the remains for the next week.

We parked the car by the crumbling archway leading into the bazaar and threaded our way through the labyrinth to the restaurant. Old Abdul and Tamir were seated on classroom-style chairs, drinking tea at one of the simple steel-and-plastic tables. Abdul was gaunter than I remembered him, and his skin had the same yellow tinge that I had seen on Alex's face only last week in the hospital in Zurich.

We all exchanged pecks on the cheek and took our seats. Abdul clapped his hands for more steaming tea with fresh mint leaves plunged into the glasses. This was the only form of tea I ever drank: I was so fond of it that I'd planted mint bushes outside the kitchen door of my house in Spain. Yes…Africa, Switzerland, Spain – not a bad routine. Most young men would be happy to share such a varied international lifestyle.

You really are quite an oddity, aren't you! Where on earth did that line come from? I could hear Marco speaking as clearly as if he were beside me, rolling the *r* in the word 'earth'.

Trelawney's voice brought me back to the present. "Are you still with us, Peter? Feeling the heat?"

"Sorry, yes, I haven't had time to acclimatise yet, I think."

Tamir smiled. "I get you some cold water, Mr. Peter. Perhaps not sleeping so good, first night." He winked at me as he headed off into Abdul's kitchen.

Abdul spoke to us in French. I knew he really had a better command of Spanish, and he had family up near Seville, but the Spanish were still disliked here; we only ever spoke that language if nobody else was around.

"Tamir has told me his good news. I am sure you will be giving a *dîner augmenté* to mark the occasion, Monsieur Towers."

"Indeed I will, Abdul. And of course I shall want you to put on a first-rate banquet. A whole roast sheep, and much more besides. I think it will be early next summer."

"I shall be delighted, if God so wills."

"Indeed, Abdul," Trelawney responded, "who knows where any of us will be by then?"

Abdul's *insha'allah* set me thinking about what might, what could happen in my life over the next year or so. For the first time since I could remember, I was actually looking forward to the future ... to a future that might just include Marco ...

"Peter!" I heard Trelawney bellowing, as if from some distance away. "I'm quite worried about you – you keep drifting off as if you're sickening for something!"

Tamir appeared with a glass of water which Trelawney forced me to drink. The restaurant waiters began to pile sheaves of foil-wrapped kebabs onto the table, and the *meze* was packed into a collection of plastic ice-boxes. Trelawney handed a thick wad of grimy notes over to Abdul as we left, a procession of waiters following us to the car with various boxes balanced perfectly on top of their heads.

"We've to be at the Phoenicia for Florian by seven, don't forget," he said pointing to his watch, "and it's nearly that now. Tamir had better drive."

I heaved an inward sigh of relief. Trelawney on the open road was terrifying enough, but Trelawney in the chaos of rush-hour was a guaranteed recipe for screeching brakes, near or actual collisions and endless screaming-matches.

We arrived just on time at the Phoenicia, a decaying but stately hotel set back from the coast road leading to the Village. It was built in the nineteenth century by a Belgian brewer who had a fascination for the city "in the days when the city was still fascinating," as Trelawney put it. Florian was sitting patiently on a gilt-and-plush chesterfield in the lobby, headphones over his ears, bulging backpack by his side. He leapt to his feet as we entered, enthusiastically offering his hand all round.

"It's so kind of you to invite me, Mr. Towers. I look forward to numerous adventures up in your marvellous Village. I already saw some photographs in the tourist office and I know its history in full. It is a most unusual enclave, I think. Mr. Carter, how nice to see you again too. *Marhaba, Tamir, keif halak?* Who would like a drink?"

An impressive performance, I thought – a little dose of attention carefully meted out to each member of the company. I admire the Germans' thoroughness – indeed, I've borrowed it myself and my professional success as a translator is founded on it – but I wondered how long we'd have to put up with this sort of thing. On holiday, with a few drinks or joints inside them, some of his compatriots descended to the same level as the rest of us. Hopefully Florian would turn out to be like that, otherwise I could see my work receiving more of my time than I thought.

Trelawney marshalled us out of the hotel and fitted us into the car. This time it was Florian's hand which slid confidently up the back of Tamir's shirt.

"You don't have to mind us, you know," Trelawney said, not looking away from the road but perfectly aware of what was going on beside him. "You're among friends here. Peter, could you put that into German so that our guest feels more at ease, please?"

I did as Trelawney asked but somehow it seemed as if I was the only passenger in the car who had to establish his credentials. The two young men settled into one another's arms in a display of intimacy that already looked well-rehearsed.

"Peter, I'm whacked and the youngsters are busy. I think under the circumstances we might just go straight back and make supper out of what we have on board. Don't you?"

"Absolutely. Why don't I get the food ready while you shower and Tamir settles Florian in? A video evening, maybe?"

It had been a bit of a bumpy start this time, but here we were, the old trooper and his faithful sidekick, hauling our latest catch back up the hill for the time-honoured ritual of supper on the terrace, a bottle of Johnny Walker and maybe a joint or two, the pretence of watching a movie from the cushions on the drawing-room floor, limbs slowly becoming interlaced ...

The evening went very much as I expected. Florian, of course, was in awe of the Village astride its ravine, and as enchanted by the house as every visitor always was. We barely made any inroads into the huge amount of food that had been assembled for the next night's feast.

Florian was more affected by the alcohol and hashish than the rest of us, probably letting himself relax for the first time since he'd arrived in the country. He disappeared to the Anthracite Room after about half an hour of the film. Then Tamir snuggled up on Trelawney's chest, giving my bare feet an occasional prod with his own. Out of common decency, I'd always kept my hands off Trelawney's partners, tempting though they might be. We were pleasantly dopey by the end of the video, in that lovely state where you just don't need to say any words at all. As we rose blearily from the floor, Tamir gestured with his hands to ask Trelawney whether he should sleep in his bedroom or with Florian. Trelawney pointed him graciously in the direction of the Anthracite Room. The three of us kissed one another gently on the lips, and retired contentedly to our various beds. Yet again, the Village was casting its spell.

Chapter Eight

As I resurfaced from a deep sleep, three words were banging around in my head as if a crowd were chanting them: "Madonna for Pope!"

I could clearly recall the slight concavity in the fabric of Marco's T-shirt under the word "for", where his breastbone tapered to its apex. I was still none the wiser as to what the words meant. I couldn't imagine Marco taking a great interest in the affairs of the Catholic church, although his origins might have made him a nominal member. Of course, I knew that a singer called Madonna existed, but I had no idea what her religious beliefs might or might not be. I added this question to a long list of others that were queuing up in my mind for our next meeting.

But when? I would certainly heed Marco's request not to phone his house. The fact that the Blaines had a telephone line was an indication of their high standing in the Village – they must be in Greta's good books. This was one of the many favours that lay within her gift. Mobile coverage had not yet reached the Village, and conversations over the few landlines in the village were usually drowned out by crackling and hissing.

I spotted Florian taking breakfast on the terrace as I emerged, so I went up to join him. Crisp white tennis shorts and shirt had been carefully chosen to show off his tan. He rose courteously to greet me.

"Good morning, Peter! You seem very happy today, we think!"

I took it that the "we" included Tamir, though nobody else was present. "Good morning to you. And why do you say that?"

"We heard how you were whistling and then singing in your bathroom just now. It was like a free public concert!"

I had no recollection of this. I wasn't noted for my good humour in the mornings – in fact, unless I was on holiday or with friends, I avoided the forenoon altogether.

"Glad you enjoyed it." I hoped Florian wasn't going to be commenting on my every gesture and movement. "Where are the others?"

"Trelawney sleeps still, and Tamir is already working in the kitchen, he has so many jobs to do for the big party tonight."

The quality of life at the Towers took a radical turn for the better as soon as Tamir returned to his duties. I helped myself to fresh croissants and poured some coffee for us both. Somehow I seemed to lack the energy to keep this conversation going. Apparently, Florian expected me to say something.

"So, you're having a nice time with Tamir?"

"He's so sweet. And he teaches me such a lot in bed. It's just a holiday romance, what do you call it in English – a sling?"

"Nearly. A fling."

I decided to switch to German, to avoid the conversation turning into a vocabulary lesson. "You know a bit about Tamir?"

"Of course I know he's Trelawney's lover – that was almost the first thing he told me when he came to the pension the other night. I'm surprised Trelawney isn't jealous."

"No, Trelawney's not like that. You won't have a problem there unless you try to steal Tamir away completely. Which you won't be able to do anyway." Just in case he was stupid or infatuated enough to try.

"I realise all that. But I've got another problem. You see, I have my girlfriend at home in Frankfurt, she's a lovely girl, and..."

I groaned inwardly. I had nothing against bisexuals as long as they didn't belabour me with their ramblings about the agonies of being spoilt for choice, which is precisely what Florian now began to do.

I found my attention drifting again as he unburdened himself.

"... first time I started to feel something deep...don't want to hurt anybody..."

He was quite attractive, I had to admit, in a very off-the-shelf Germanic sort of way. As Alex used to say, "If it was in bed already, I wouldn't throw it out." But in any contest with Marco, well…

And all this clap-trap about mixed loyalties – I registered that a photograph of Magda or Maria, or whatever she was called, had been proudly produced from his wallet. None of that nonsense with Marco! What was it he'd said, right at the start of our conversation? 'I don't mind telling you I'm a homosexual'…That must have taken some courage.

"... an older man. How about you?"

My views on older men were pretty clear: I didn't fancy them in general, and I certainly had no lustful interest in the specimens who tended to gather each autumn in the Village.

"Ah – no, not really, Florian. Not my sort of thing, actually. Perhaps when I was younger..."

He seemed somewhat dissatisfied with my answer.

"Oh well," he mumbled, "I hope you didn't mind me asking."

I thought I'd better say something encouraging. "Actually, Florian, if I were you, I'd just carry on experimenting, have as much fun as you can in the process, and one day you'll wake up knowing just what you like and what you don't like, and feeling perfectly comfortable with your life."

"Thank you Peter, that's very good advice. I need to reach my conclusion." Yes, how very German, I thought. "Then maybe I'll get to be as happy as you are. It shines out of you!"

I was astounded but rather flattered to hear this, and acknowledged the compliment with a gracious smile.

"Now, why don't you take Trelawney a cup of tea? The old boy has a hell of a day before him and he needs to be moving."

At this point, the French doors leading into Trelawney's bedroom were flung open and our host emerged in his kaftan.

"The old boy *is* moving, thank you very much. Good morning, young ones. I'm glad to see you two getting to know each other."

In other words, he had lain there trying to listen in to our conversation. I should have remembered that keeping a secret was always an enterprise doomed to failure anywhere in the Village.

Trelawney strode over to us and poured himself a cup of tea. Three sugars; a sure danger signal.

"Developments have already taken place. I was awoken by the telephone at six. Purvis will be touching down at the airport as we speak. He will, of course, have to join us for dinner, which is unfortunate as I hardly think he and Sir Brian are a match made in heaven. Can't be helped now. I have arranged a vehicle for him – nobody can be spared to fetch him; all hands are required on deck here."

Trelawney was clearly going to extract every ounce of drama from the preparations for tonight's gala dinner, and judging from past experience, we would all be frazzled wrecks by the time the first morsels passed our lips. I decided to make a getaway while I still could.

"I'm just off to the shop for a couple of things. Anything you need?"

"Rather an unusual move, Peter, since we spent most of yesterday shopping. But we'll let you go. Could you ask June to lend me a proper carving knife while you're up there, please? You could ride bare-arsed to Benghazi on the one in the kitchen. Assuming you're going to drop in to pick her brains about things, that is?"

Instead of replying to this, I just made a noise like a cat hissing and got on my way, much to Florian's amusement.

June allowed visitors to use her telephone for cash payment, so I decided to call Alex in Zurich. Trelawney was rather fussy about guests running up his phone bill and in any case, there was never any chance of privacy. June at least made a pretence of not listening in.

She spotted me panting up the last few yards to the archway that led into the Olive Branch.

"Anyone would think you wasn't getting enough exercise, though that's not what we hear on the grapevine, dear. Come on in and rest your weary bum, hardly anybody in yet. Caffeine required?"

"Yes thanks, June, and plenty of water, please. Can I use the phone first?"

"Course you can dear. Help yourself, you know how the meter works."

I got through to Alex's home number in Zurich, but his answering machine was switched on. I heard that he'd changed the message; his once sonorous voice now had a rasping, husky edge to it.

"Sorry I can't speak, I may be out, or maybe I just can't cope with phone calls just now. I'll do my best to reply to your message. Depending on..."

I waited for his recorded voice to finish the sentence, but that was it.

If Alex's intention was to make his callers stop and count their blessings, he certainly succeeded with me. Anyone who knew him would understand that he wasn't fishing for sympathy. I couldn't think how to follow his words, so I mumbled something inane about blue skies and endless fun, left him Trelawney's number, and said I would ring again in a couple of days.

I cast an eye around the garden. In the farthest corner, intently copying something from an open book onto a drawing pad, sat Beth Horrabin.

"Hello, Beth. Do you remember me?"

"Course I do, Mr. Carter. I hope you didn't get it in the neck from Mr. Towers for giving me all those figs that summer!"

Trelawney had actually exploded in rage when he found out. "I've nothing against the child, but I absolutely refuse to give sustenance to that vile father of hers and the so-called principles he stands for. The very worst type of Charlie Brit!"

But I wasn't going to tell her that. "Nothing to worry about, Beth. What are you up to?"

"Calligraphy. They taught us how to do it in school last year. I found I had quite a knack for it, but it needs a lot of practice. Most of it's the Koran, but this one is a poem in a book I nicked from the school library."

"I didn't know you went to a local school. That must have been a challenge."

"Yeah, the Village school in Beetlebridge." But she pronounced it in the Arabic way. "It was quite tough at first, me being the only foreigner, and a girl as well. But once I got the hang of Arabic I started to do better than the locals, and then they were really pissed off because I got top marks in the grammar exam. Half of them can't even speak their own language!"

"When do you start back?"

"I don't. That's it now – my education's finished." She shrugged her shoulders. "The local school can't keep me any longer. My folks talk about sending me to school in England, but I know there's no money to do it."

She kept inking in the characters on her piece of paper as she spoke. Her work was strikingly graceful.

"How unfair."

"Life isn't always fair, is it? Take my Dad, for example. You know what he's like, you saw him in here yesterday, but do you know he's a war hero? You must have heard the story in the Village."

I'd heard a variety of rumours about her father's past, but nothing as flattering as this, so I just nodded silently.

"He saved three men's lives in some country in Central America, and he should have got a medal, but his commanding officer made up a pack of lies and got the medal himself.

And now the army won't even pay him a penny of pension money. He's written a book about it, but it's still waiting to be published."

I knew better than to probe her any further. I had an awful picture of her father scribbling away in red-faced fury over his beer bottles and could imagine the publishers' expressions as they reviewed the first couple of pages of his diatribe.

Conveniently, June chose this moment to bring my coffee and a stone flagon of chilled water. I asked her for the knife Trelawney wanted and used the interruption to change the subject.

"I met your friend Marco the other day, Beth."

She lay down her pen and heaved an exaggerated sigh. "Marco the Magnificent?"

"Is that his nickname?"

"No, that's the title he invented for himself. You're looking at the world's greatest living expert on Master Marco Thomas Duncan Blaine."

"Really? You know more about him than his parents, even?"

"Them? Pah!" She took a swig from the Coke she was drinking. "Half the time, I think they forget they ever had a son. They packed him off to some fancy boarding school in Scotland as soon as they possibly could. Still, he comes in handy at *Madame* Blaine's dinner parties." She produced a chilling imitation of the type of Parisian landlady that would strike terror into the most robust of tenants. *'Now then, Greta dear, everybody, Marco will just give us a little Schubert on the piano to help us digest our dinners.'*

I couldn't help bursting into laughter.

"So, he didn't go to school with you?"

"Oh, no way! He was at the French school in town before they shunted him off to Scotland. Now of course he's being groomed for university." Her hands imitated a hairdresser teasing curls. "*Papa* wants him to go to a Scottish university, but *Mama* wants him at that one in Paris."

"The Sorbonne."

"Whatever. But what Madame Blaine wants, Madame Blaine usually gets. Then again, she's hardly got the son she would have picked from the catalogue, has she?"

Now she coloured slightly, thinking she might have gone too far. Just lately I seemed to have found a talent for loosening young people's tongues.

"Oh, I'm sorry Mr. Carter, you're not…you and Marco aren't…"

"No, no, Beth, I understand what you mean, it's nothing like that. And please call me Peter. We just had a friendly chat, that's all. But he's certainly a character in a million."

"I'd very much hope so. Actually, it would do him good to…to be with someone sensible like you. Maybe you could teach him about some of the things his parents haven't managed to."

"Like?"

"Like love, and pain, for example. About giving and receiving both." She laid her drawing aside. "What's this?"

She reached over and prodded me in the ribs with her index finger. It hurt quite badly.

"That's Marco Blaine trying to tell you he loves you."

She inclined her head and smiled broadly as she said this.

"Sounds to me as if you've got quite a soft spot for him in spite of what you say."

"Oh, of course I do. Except for my brother, we were the only two kids in the Village for years, so we had to get on. We did everything together."

I tried not to catch her eye, but she shot me a saucy wink. She obviously knew just how much Marco was likely have to revealed to a complete stranger.

"Yep, I do mean everything. And growing up in this place is bound to make you unique. We shall always have that bond, as long as we live. I suppose I *am* quite fond of him really, for all his faults. Are you seeing him again?"

"I'd like to. I thought he was very – ah – original. We have quite a few things in common."

"Well, I'm not the one who should be teaching you anything, so all I'll say is: just be careful. Flies like a vulture and stings like a scorpion, that's Marco. Talking of Master Blaine, I'd better be off up the hill to get him out of bed."

"What?"

"Oh, yes, he needs to be woken up with a nice cup of tea, bowl of breakfast cereal, bath run, that sort of thing…" She was packing her books and papers carefully into a tattered brown leather satchel as she spoke.

"You mean, you go into his parents' house and…?"

"No way! Marco has his own little suite built onto the side of the big house. He made it quite clear he wasn't prepared to carry on living in the same space as his parents. He's like his mother in that respect. What he wants, he will get." She slapped the satchel to emphasise each syllable. "And if he doesn't, everybody suffers."

"Well, it's very loyal of you to do that, Beth."

She scrunched her nose and pouted her lips in an expression of resignation. "I've nothing better to do – there's no chance of a job for me round here – and at least it keeps me away from home a couple of hours longer." Now she reddened. "How long are you here for, anyway?"

"Three weeks or so. Why?"

"I just wondered. It's – nice having you here, that's all!"

I didn't know whether to feel sad for Beth as I wandered out of the café – she'd had the benefit of a childhood in that extraordinary place but unlike Marco, she had none of the advantages – or disadvantages – that wealth could bring.

June chased after me with the carving knife, which I'd completely forgotten. "Won't even offer a penny for your thoughts, dear. You'd forget your head if it weren't screwed on!"

She was right. I was wandering along in a trance, barely aware of my surroundings. *Bound to make you unique*, I repeated to myself as I made my way back to Trelawney's house. You could say that again. Or maybe it was just that I'd never really taken the time to talk and listen to the new generation of teenagers. Surely they couldn't all be as outspoken, as experienced in the ways of the world, as these two?

I wasn't looking forward to the evening as much as before – back to the tired old gossip of assorted elderly queens, trying to cap each other's saucy innuendos, lewdly reminiscing over wasted years and decades. But then I thought back to Alex, not even able to muster the energy to cope with a telephone call, and decided to make the most of whatever opportunities the rest of the day had in store.

Chapter Nine

When I reached the corner of Trelawney's street, I saw that an antique and mud-encrusted red Citroën 2CV was blocking access to the front door, its engine coughing and groaning. Two figures were engaged in a heated argument from either side of the bonnet. One, an extremely fat, perspiring middle-aged Arab in an ill-fitting, grease-stained grey suit, was shouting and swearing in his own language and then English, while the other remained silent and aloof.

"You will regret this! You are a dishonour to your countrymen," the Arab bellowed. "The terms of the contract are quite clear and you are in breach of them. No customer has ever treated me in this way. You are a thief. A cheat. A thug!"

His remarks were phrased in impeccable English and he punctuated them by thumping the bonnet of the car so hard that its flimsy bodywork was set quivering.

His adversary showed no sign of being bothered by the heat or the verbal onslaught. He was a short, stocky fellow with a stance that suggested you'd be unwise to engage him in physical combat. A toothbrush moustache and combed-over slivers of mousy hair did little to make his fleshy, pink face more attractive. A faded beige garment of the type marketed in England as a "safari jacket" was slung across his shoulders. He seemed totally absorbed in a scrap of paper bearing a few lines of handwriting which his pudgy fingers were pinning to the bonnet of the car.

This was Purvis.

I held back behind the wall at the corner of the street, not wanting to get embroiled.

By now, the Arab was pacing up and down in rage. "There is nothing else for it. The police must be called." That prompted Purvis to stifle a yawn and speak for the first time.

"Yes, I suppose you could do that. Mr. Towers would let you use his phone, or maybe you could try up at Greta's, I'm sure you know her, most accommodating lady. Bit cut off up here otherwise, though, innit?"

Purvis had a rasping, nasal voice and an accent that wouldn't have been out of place in the Petticoat Lane market. "I'm looking at the contract we signed here, Mr. Mahboob, and it doesn't quite match what you say. Just have a squint at this, or maybe it's easier if I read it for you? 'Sole valid contract for the transport of Purvis, plus two items luggage from airport to Village, 120 kilometres, all other terms and conditions excluded, all other agreements to lapse herewith. Price: twenty pounds sterling, payable in cash on delivery of the above destination.' Now there you are, today's date — and we know that's your signature because you only signed it two hours ago in front of me. Remember that, do you?"

He withdrew an immense bundle of twenty-pound notes from the pocket of his grey flannels and peeled one off. "And there's the payment, as per contract. Witnessed agreement, service performed and payment in cash as per contractual conditions. What more could an honest trader wish for? I'm a trader myself, and I'd be delighted if all my clients were as businesslike as I am."

The other man started ranting again. He fished out his phone and frantically began pressing keys to no effect except to deepen his distress.

"If you were a touch more reasonable, of course, there might be another job or two in it. As luck would have it, I'm in town next week to meet somebody from the – what is it now, Ministry of State Affairs – hold on, I've got his card here somewhere. Now, a reasonable trader would have spotted a good punter and possibly got another run out of it. Ah yes, here we are, maybe you'll recognise this."

Purvis pushed a large gilt-edged card over to his adversary who snatched and examined it. The Arab's face glazed over in dismay.

"This is a joke. You cannot possibly know this man. He would not spare one minute of his day for the likes of you."

"I *don't* think he'd like to hear you say that, my friend. I'm told he's got a terrible temper if he's upset. Or, indeed, if someone upsets a friend of his."

For the first time in the encounter, Purvis actually looked at the poor man who had hired him the car, and quietly bowled him a couple of sentences in the fluent Arabic he'd acquired during his Gulf days, when Trelawney had apparently first met him. Mahboob's defeat was complete.

"Now, if you'll just give me a hand with the cases – just the two, you'll note, as per contract – you can be off back to town for the next lucky customer. Don't forget your twenty quid. Honest day's pay for an honest day's work, that's what I always say. The watermark's fine, you needn't check."

Totally crestfallen, the Arab slowly raised the tailgate of the Citroën and lifted out two battered suitcases. I judged it was safe to make my presence known. Purvis acknowledged me without particular emotion, as if I'd only left him five minutes before.

"Afternoon Pete, just giving this chap an elementary lesson in contract law. It might help him on his way to fortune and prosperity. Heavy night, was it? You still look a bit rat-arsed. No need for the knife." I was still carrying it blade-up like a dagger. "I sorted things out with no recourse to physical violence. Chummy here thought he'd hired me the car for two weeks but I don't think it would even last that long, do you?"

"You amaze me, Purvis. Normally they won't come up here for love nor money because of that blasted road, but you get here for twenty quid. It costs that to get from the airport to the Phoenicia!"

"The professional approach, Pete." Purvis tapped a finger against the side of his bulbous nose. "Put it down to pure professionalism. Normally, I find one professional recognises another and treats him as such. Sad to say, our Mr. Mahboob doesn't make the grade."

He tapped on the driver's window of the car as its owner was about to leave. "Here, sunshine – a tip for you." The poor man was actually taken in by the mention of a tip, and seemed to think his luck might have changed. "Always read the small print. It'll save you a lot of bother."

The rusty wreck shuddered off in a cloud of dust and putrid exhaust fumes.

"Let me help you in with the luggage," I offered.

"No need Pete, thanks all the same." Purvis must have been ten years older than me, but he seized the cases and marched up the hill with the vigour of a man half his age.

"Trel around, is he?"

Nobody else ever called me 'Pete'; that was bad enough, but I was even more irritated by the abbreviation of Trelawney's name that Purvis always used. And nobody, not even Trelawney, ever addressed Purvis by anything but his surname.

"Trelawney was up when I left half an hour or so ago. Big night, tonight, you know. Sir Brian Bishop from the Residents' Association is along for dinner."

"So I hear. Never fear, old Purvis is here."

He let me work the trap mechanism on the oaken door, and then he lumbered up the steps in front of me. Trelawney's face appeared from the balcony as we negotiated our way around the furniture.

"Dump the cases in Purvis's room, Peter, and come for a drink. I'm opening a bottle of imitation champagne in his honour, to try and persuade him to give Sir Brian an easy ride tonight."

Purvis was the only guest at the Towers who occupied a room without a colour code. His quarters, at the far end of the courtyard, were simply known as "Purvis's Room".

He was the opposite of Trelawney in almost every respect, but there was a close bond between these two men that I'd never been able to understand. Trelawney always treated him with respect, if not deference. Knowing Trelawney's tastes, their relationship could not possibly have been sexual. I'd heard rumours that Purvis had extricated Trelawney from a financial mess years ago, when they were in the Middle East together. Purvis had built a career on his ability and willingness to manage other people's money and keep them just on the right side of the law. Several residents of the Village apparently had him to thank for protecting their assets from the prying eyes of the tax authorities in their own countries. But you never found out exactly what he did, or who the beneficiaries were.

By the time I'd performed the bell-hop's duties and returned to the terrace, Trelawney was already recounting the events that had necessitated tonight's gathering.

"... so you see, some party or parties have decided they want the Village to be a model of Victorian family life. The Ministry has refused permission for that South African and his gentleman friend to buy Mulberry Villa."

Trelawney shot me a disdainful glance and cleared his throat pointedly. "And while Peter was out running his errands just now, Doocie came charging in from next door. No mention of the balcony but all in a panic because the Ministry have called him in for an interview about renewing *his* residence permit. Normally it's just a matter of posting them the old one and you get the new one automatically."

Officially, the Village came under the wing of the Ministry of Tourism, but Greta's careful work over the years meant there was little need for liaison with the authorities.

Purvis nodded as he contemplated this information before responding.

"I can see why you're getting a bit antsy, Trel, but you know how it is round here. Give 'em a bit of time and they'll find something else to occupy their tiny brainboxes. You lot probably pay as much in rates and taxes as half the population of the country put together. They're not going to kiss goodbye to that."

The telephone rang and Trelawney rose from his seat to answer it, clamping a handkerchief to his brow in a stage gesture of fatigue.

"If the trouble comes from the Ministry itself, you're probably right, it'll blow over. My concern is that the shit's being stirred on my own doorstep, here in the Village. Excuse me a second." He stomped off into the far recesses of the drawing room.

Purvis and I sat in silence for a while; he was making some notes on a little pad that he always carried with him in the breast pocket of the safari jacket. I thought back over the many autumns I'd spent in Purvis's company here, but couldn't recall once having a real conversation with him. The confrontation I'd witnessed between him and poor old Mahboob was typical of his style. He would let you talk yourself out, give you a little lecture and then leave the room, underscoring the finality of his words. He shocked and offended other guests with his blunt and usually gloomy views on virtually everything. I recalled an evening when the discussion turned to AIDS in the days when it still meant a death sentence with no remission. He for one had his plan clear in his mind, he told us smugly; he'd laid in a stock of Nembutal

to "finish the job" were he ever to find that he was infected. He
also had an annoying habit of storing away and then exploiting any
item of information you might mention in his presence. Before Alex
became too ill to work, for instance, he told me Purvis sent him some
documents to translate, quite out of the blue, citing me as the point of
contact. I couldn't recall mentioning Alex to him, let alone passing on
his address, but put it down to a lapse of memory. After all, we seldom
retired to our beds sober at the Towers.

"Rather rum, this business." I was so absorbed in silently
cataloguing what I saw as Purvis's shortcomings, I'd almost forgotten
he was there. "Just like old Trel to get rattled over a bit of tittle-tattle.
Should have been nipped in the bud before it got this far. You lot are
going to have to watch your step for a while."

"Well," I replied brusquely, "you spend more time here than I do,
Purvis, so you're in the firing line as well."

He sniffed. "Don't worry about me Pete. I know exactly who's
behind this and believe me, they'll rue the day they decided to stir up
trouble in my back yard." The aggression he put into this remark was
quite unsettling. "I've a hunch things will get messy before it's sorted
out."

I waited for him to continue, but he clearly had no intention of
disclosing his privileged information to me. The strained silence
between us resumed until it was broken by the unusual sound of
Trelawney swearing at the top of his voice. He burst onto the balcony,
his face several shades redder than when he had left.

"Damn the lot of them. In fact, *fuck* the lot of them. That was June.
Her friend in town rang her to ask – *so* kind – if she knew all about the
latest scandal in the Village. Apparently there's an article in this week's
Telegraph."

This flimsy publication, aimed at the scattered English-speaking
community on the North African coast, managed to pack even more

right-wing vitriol into its few pages than its British namesake.

"Ministry to promote family values in Village," Trelawney went on, "closer vetting of candidates for residence. Social dropouts, bachelors and others of loose morals to be excluded. A response to the decadence in the countries to the north of us. And more of the same *horse-shite*. June couldn't get the whole story out of her friend, but I've already heard enough."

"Can't believe everything you read in the newspapers, Trel. You should know that at your age."

"Pah!" Trelawney was pacing up and down in agitation. "How nice of June, how typical of her, to warn her chums right away. I've asked her to join us tonight, for drinks at least. She's really one of us, anyway. I'll have to get Sir Brian to bring a copy of the Telegraph with him, he's bound to have seen it. Damnation, dam-fucking-nation!"

Purvis remained utterly calm as Trelawney continued his ranting. He reached over to top up Trelawney's glass with the last of the 'imitation champagne'.

"Where will you go if they boot you out?" he asked.

Trelawney exploded. "It won't come to that. It can't possibly come to that. Greta will not allow it to come to that."

"You can always come to me in Spain, you know," I offered, wanting to be helpful.

"I – am – not – going – *anywhere*!" he yelled. "Will you kindly get that into your heads? Where's Tamir? I need something stronger than this gnat's piss."

"Calm down, Trel. We've got out of worse fixes than this, you and me. Go and get Tamir, get a proper drink and we'll deal with it. You've got the best brains in the country coming here in a few hours, and if we can't work it out together, nobody can."

As instructed, Trelawney went back indoors and Tamir emerged a few minutes later to tell us that the master of the house was now busy supervising the preparations for dinner, and would expect us at seven, ready for the evening's entertainment. Purvis asked for a stiff brandy sour – the Village's favourite cocktail. I decided that enough was enough, and retired to my room to gather my strength for the challenges of the evening ahead.

Chapter Ten

It was already half past six when I was awoken by knocking at my door.

"Mr. Peter! You all right?" Tamir enquired. I shouted through the door that I'd be upstairs in ten minutes. But I hadn't locked the door and before I knew it, Tamir was in the room, dressed in a *djellaba*, the loose cotton robe that he would be wearing to serve dinner.

He paused at the door, drew a deep breath, smiled broadly and turned, swiftly shoving the bolt home. He strode over to the bed, flung his arms around me and lowered his lips to mine. The robe fell gracefully to the floor, freed by some unseen button – revealing that it was the one and only garment he'd been wearing.

The silent encounter only lasted five minutes, but judging by its climax, both of us must have been bursting for release. Whoever had taught Tamir the arts of love – and it must have been Trelawney – had taught him very well indeed.

Then, with a stab of panic, I realised I'd just broken my own unwritten rule and let myself be seduced by my best friend's partner. I must have shown my anguish, for Tamir raised his index finger to his lips, wagged it to and fro and pointed upstairs to signal that nobody else would know (including Florian, I hoped). Tamir went and turned the shower on, grazed my lips with another kiss, and made the gesture of wiping it away with his fingers.

When I finally emerged onto the terrace, I saw that the entire area had been transformed while I was asleep. The floor was covered in deep-hued carpets, with bulging bolsters and gilt-threaded cushions lined up against the walls for the guests to recline upon. A long, very low table swathed in white ran down the centre of the terrace, already set with sparkling copper and brassware, multicoloured bowls and dishes containing the cold *meze*. The sun was on its way down, the sea glinted orange in the distance; torches stood ready to light in the corners of the balcony and the parapet walls were lined with tiny glass bowls, each containing a flat circular candle floating in water.

Trelawney had emerged from the house and was standing behind me. "Will it do?"

"Trelawney, it looks fabulous, and you know it does." I was half expecting reproaches for being absent so long, but Trelawney had now reached the stage where all his attention was focused on creating the best impression for his guests. No extravagance and no trouble were too much when the doors of his home were opened to welcome visitors from afar. But consummate professional though he was, Trelawney was always nervous and needed reassurance on these occasions.

"Did Tamir fix your shower? He told me the pipe had come loose again."

Not only a superb lover, but quick-witted as well.

"It's fine now, and so am I. Even if it's only for this evening, please stop worrying about me."

"Actually, Peter, I owe you an apology. I've been harsh about your interest in Marco Blaine. Catty, even. What you make of it is up to you, and no-one else. Of course I want to protect you, because I love you. But all the strain I've had with Doocie and Greta, and now this blasted article in the paper – I've been taking it out on you. That's *also* because I love you. Please forgive me, my friend."

Then to my surprise, he kissed me on the lips, very lightly, but long enough to look me straight in the eye. There was nothing sexual about it – but from that slight contact, I felt a surge of warmth, closeness and strength. Then I panicked again: could he taste Tamir's saliva on my lips, I wondered, or smell the odour of him lingering on my skin? If he could, it didn't seem as if he was going to make an issue of it. He broke the mood by clapping his hands and fishing a bottle of wine out of one of the ice-buckets.

"Red on ice? The champagne is no doubt open and warming up nicely in the drawing room. You'd think I'd never taught that boy anything, wouldn't you?"

He laughed a laugh of such deep affection that I now deeply rued what I'd allowed to happen. "Tamir? *TAMIR!*" Trelawney bawled, and they started fussing about with the bottles and buckets like a pair of old spinsters. I left them to it and went into the drawing room where I found several of the dinner-guests already assembled.

In one corner stood June, her hair piled high and pinned with a huge jet brooch, an undeniably elegant figure in a kaftan of mauve and silver. She was chatting to Doocie from next door and a petite girl who, I presumed, was his latest travelling companion.

Opposite them, Purvis and Florian were seated on either side of a carved hexagonal table, playing Chinese Checkers. Purvis was a genius at this game, and he'd introduced first Trelawney and then all the rest of us to it. He would often spend the whole evening playing it with one or other of the younger visitors to the Towers as the rest of us lolled around on the floor cushions, gradually sinking into a comfortable stupor.

But when it actually came to the crunch and we were pairing off for the night, he would already have disappeared without us noticing. It was known that he liked to take long walks around the Village late at night, and sometimes I'd hear him stomping back across the courtyard at three or four in the morning. Most unusually in this circle, nobody seemed to know anything about his sex life. Florian and Purvis...well, nothing was impossible in the Village.

Standing to attention by the drinks table were two young Arabs, wearing identical cotton robes to the one Tamir had recently removed. I recognised one of them as Tamir's younger (and rather tubby) brother Abdullah, who went to Libya a couple of years before to try and open a butcher's shop. The project foundered after six months, but Abdullah had forever become the "butcher of Benghazi".

Abdullah clasped my hand in both of his. He hardly spoke any words in any language except his own, but managed to introduce his companion.

"Is Brahim. My friend. Good people." If you didn't know, you'd have thought Brahim was Tamir's brother, not Abdullah, for they were equally tall and slim. I had no doubt that Brahim had been hand-picked to minister to Sir Brian's needs during the evening's festivities, and probably afterwards as well.

Tamir and Abdullah circulated respectfully with huge gleaming trays of drinks and delicacies. Trelawney, now changed into an immaculate white dinner suit, flitted among the guests. Brahim sat cross-legged in a corner playing the plaintive North African lute known as the *oud*. As the sun vanished, the torches and flickering candles on the balcony bathed the drawing room in a magical light. The atmosphere of warmth and good companionship, so much a part of this house, seemed to swell by the minute. Soon, Tamir signalled to Trelawney that the guests of honour had arrived and they moved to the top of the balcony steps to welcome them.

Sir Brian looked, and indeed was, the quintessential British diplomat of the old school. Now in his seventies, he dressed and moved with the grace of a man half his age; his darting blue eyes betrayed an intelligence that was undimmed by the years. By his side was his partner of thirty years' standing, Jean-Louis, a retired Parisian actor, still debonair and elegant. Such was Sir Brian's sway in the diplomatic corps that they'd been able to live openly together on their last few postings. They were followed in by a driver trailing two tiny tan Dachshunds –

Cantaloupe and Honeydew, I remembered – who were unleashed to nose their way around.

Once their owners had been introduced to the guests they didn't already know, they immediately and skilfully set about defusing the slight tension that sometimes follows the arrival of minor celebrities. Jean-Louis was flinging his arms around June and they performed a mock can-can, apparently in memory of some other raucous occasion. Sir Brian crouched down by Brahim and quizzed him in fluent Arabic on the details of the *oud* he'd been playing. Despite my earlier reluctance to face the evening, the company was so varied and congenial, and the setting was so utterly delightful, that I was now eagerly looking forward to it.

At this point, although the noise level was rising, I heard the telephone ring in the background.

I paid no attention because Jean-Louis and I were already deep in conversation about our mutual dislike of the new euro currency. As we spoke, I noticed that Tamir was hovering by us, waiting politely for a chance to speak.

"Somebody wants you on the telephone, Mr. Peter. He says it's urgent."

It could only be one person: Alex calling from Zurich, with more bad news. Hardly anyone else had the number here; even the total destruction of my house in Spain wouldn't bring Elena or Pepe to overcome their fear of telephones. I excused myself and hurried with foreboding to the alcove behind the drawing room. I tried to put as much warmth and confidence into my "Hello" as possible, but the voice that answered was completely unknown to me.

"Hello? Peter Carter? Now listen. This is a dire emergency. You've got to help. I can't think of anybody else who can."

"Sorry, who is this?"

"It's Marco, of course. Surely you can't have forgotten already?"

I hadn't, but his voice sounded amazingly adult over the telephone.

"What's happened? What's wrong? Are you all right? What can I do?"

"You can rescue me from a ghastly crisis." A calculated dramatic pause followed. Then: "Have you got any condoms with you?"

I couldn't believe my ears and made him repeat the question.

"What a thing to ask! Not *on* me, no. I'm at a dinner party, Marco. I told you about tonight, remember?"

"Yes, yes, I know, Sir Brian and all the other old farts. What I mean is, have you got any condoms in your luggage? There's enough of it, I noticed."

"I do have some in my room, but – "

I had no time to decide whether to be delighted or outraged.

"Good. Can you lend me a couple? I'll be waiting by the gate to the church in ten minutes. Don't worry, I'll make sure nobody sees me. I'll be your friend for life. But get a shift on, please, it's absolutely vital. Bye-ee!"

And he put the phone down before I had a chance to say anything else.

I could hardly have been more dazed even if it had been Alex on the line asking me to rush back to Zurich. I lit a cigarette. Of course, there was no question of leaving the party. What bare-faced cheek!

But equally, there was no question of missing this chance to deepen my ties with Marco. After all, my absence wouldn't be noticed for a few minutes, and I could always say that the call was bad news, and I needed a little time to gather my thoughts.

I hurried along the corridor, through the kitchen and down the back steps to my room. Luckily, none of the guests had moved out onto the terrace, so I dashed into my bathroom, grabbed a handful of condoms from my wash-bag, tiptoed back across the courtyard and let myself out of the 'guest door' as quietly as I could. No noise I made could be heard above the hubbub from the party, mingled with the strains of *oud* music and Dachshund yelps. Not wanting to arrive in a breathless sweat, I paced myself as I began the steep climb up to the church.

I realised I was thoroughly enjoying this. In fact, I hadn't had so much fun since – well, since I was a schoolboy!

Chapter Eleven

I made my way to the arched entrance of the church. The walls enclosed quite a large expanse of land – almost the only flat terrain in the Village. There was no sign of Marco, so I lit a cigarette and consulted my watch. I was taking the last draw on the cigarette when a sudden poke in the ribs nearly made me jump out of my skin.

That was twice in two days I'd been prodded in the same place, and it hurt.

"Follow me," Marco hissed. "Head down!"

Although the Village was deserted, I went along with the game; he took my hand, shooting a sensual thrill through my body.

He led me through the small cluster of tombstones to a clump of trees. I knew I had every right to demand a full explanation from him, but as soon as we came to a halt I found I was shaking with uncontrollable laughter. I felt unbelievably light and free, as if I were floating on some narcotic cloud. I couldn't actually manage to get any words out, so I took the condoms from my pocket and counted them into his hand like banknotes.

"You're an absolute darling, Peter. And to prove it..." He thrust his face towards mine, and I parted my lips in delirious expectation, but the kiss landed on my right cheek, followed by another on the left.

I found my voice. "Marco, just precisely what is going on?"

"I'd have thought it was fairly obvious. I've got a shag lined up, but I've run out of supplies and you're more likely to find an elephant than a condom in my parents' bathroom. Talking of whom – can you light me a fag, by the way – there's another problem."

I lit a cigarette, drew on it and passed it to him, and lit another for myself.

"You butt-suck your fags. Vile. Anyway, I've got to ask you something else. My parents were supposed to be out tonight but the bloody, buggering idiots –"

"That's no way to talk!"

"Shut up and listen. They've just come back, and even I can't risk shafting someone in my room while they're on the premises." He blew a cloud of warm wet smoke straight into my face. "Do you think, possibly, at all, *dear* Peter, *sweetie*, that we could use your room at Trelawney's place, only for an hour, or so – I mean to say, that huge party's on down there…"

"Full of old farts?"

"Well, be honest. That doesn't apply to you or June or Trelawney, but look at the rest of them! Anyway, they'll be gassing on all night, you can hear the noise from here, so nobody would notice, would they?" Now he grabbed my hand and squeezed it tight, mocking a baby girl imploring her mother for sweets. "Pl-eee-ase, *pl-eee-ase!*"

The situation had careered completely out of my control within a couple of minutes. Trelawney would be less than pleased if he found out, but he was far too preoccupied with the party. Nevertheless, I thought I'd better show some token resistance.

"Couldn't you do it here? Churchyards are quite romantic, and it's lovely and warm!"

"You must be mad. What if Greta came along on one of her night prowls? Anyway, it's holy ground and a Moslem would probably object."

"And who is the Moslem, might I enquire?"

Marco inhaled the last of his cigarette, tossed it onto the ground, and stubbed it out forcefully with the toe of his sandal. "I've an idea you might know him," he said, charily. "He's called Zeki. But as he's not a stranger, that means there's no security risk. So, is it all right then?"

More bits of the jigsaw fell into place. They probably had no need of the condoms at all, but the ruse had lured me down here, and now I was fairly well cornered.

"You are the limit! I suppose, being as you're so well informed, you also know that Zeki had – ah – an arrangement with me for later on this evening?"

"So he'll be there on the spot already for you. Couldn't be better! I won't wear him out, I promise you."

"Marco, why I should take such a risk for you?"

"Not for me to say. But somehow I think you'll do it."

I paused to let him sweat, though I doubt whether he did. "Yes, you're right, I will. But you need to appreciate..."

"Yes, yes, fine, lovely, course I do. All that crap can wait. Now how do we arrange this? It's a quarter past eight. Why don't we meet you at Trelawney's back gate at half past, exactly?"

He grabbed my hand, deftly undid the strap of my watch and peered at the dial. "I'll synchronise your watch with mine."

He fastened it back on my wrist, but with the dial on the underside, the way he wore his.

"What you mean is, you've already told Zeki to meet you there at half past."

"What on earth gave you that idea? Now, you'd better run on ahead and we'll see you down there."

He prodded me again and like a dutiful child, I trotted off down the hill and back to the Towers.

<hr />

On the way back, I tried to plan a strategy. People were bound to have noticed I was missing from the party by now, but Tamir would have said the phone call was an urgent one. If necessary, I would have to use

Alex as an excuse. How did I want the evening to end up? With Zeki in my bed and Marco safe at home? Or …

The party had taken off by the time I climbed up the balcony steps and sidled into the drawing room. I'd forgotten that Sir Brian was a gifted musician. He'd now taken over on the lute while Brahim accompanied him on an ornate Berber drum. The South Africans of Mulberry Villa fame were there and Jean-Louis had clearly struck up a rapport with them while June, already the worse for wear, was holding court to a group of new arrivals. Florian came up to me and asked me kindly if I was all right, saying I looked rather distressed. So much the better!

It looked as if there was still some time before the food would appear, so I went down to the kitchen in search of Trelawney, who was supervising the final touches to the trays of *meze*. He clamped his hand on my shoulder.

"Peter, what's the matter? Was the telephone call what I think it was? Tamir said your friend sounded awfully upset." This was perfect. I didn't have to lie, technically.

"Well, the situation's changed, all of a sudden. It's rather knocked me for six, actually."

"I quite understand. You probably don't want to be around all these people. Just do what you need to. I'm sorry I can't offer you much support, but you see how I'm fixed. If you like, someone will take some food down to your room when it's ready and you can just stay there."

No, room service would be gilding the lily – though I wouldn't put it past Marco to ask for a snack while he was 'on the job'.

"Of course not, Trelawney, I'll be perfectly OK. I just need a while to think. Any progress with the main business of the evening?"

"No, I shall tackle the subject when food and wine have done their job. But Sir Brian did bring the Telegraph – it's on top of the fridge. I'm afraid it doesn't make very pleasant reading. Actually, there's something on the Letters page you should have a look at. You don't think you'll have to go back to Switzerland for Alex, do you?"

"I really can't say. You just forget about me and get on with being the perfect host. I'll be fine."

I picked up the newspaper and looked at my watch, but of course the dial wasn't where it should have been, and I awkwardly turned my wrist round to check the time. Trelawney noticed this odd manoeuvre, but made no comment.

I left the kitchen and crossed the courtyard. Looking up, I saw Florian and Purvis standing on the terrace, deep in earnest discussion. With any luck, they wouldn't notice the slight creak of the back gate. But people were beginning to drift outside, so I couldn't risk bringing my guests this way; they would have to reach my room by scaling the wall up to the balcony, as Zeki did on my first night.

They were waiting in the shadows when I opened the gate. Zeki started to speak, but I put my finger to his lips, returning his gesture of a couple of days ago. With exaggerated sign language, I made him understand how they had to get in. Like a stooge in a silent film, he repeated each movement after me, finally miming the throwing-open of the shutters followed by a burst of ecstatic pleasure.

Marco impatiently broke the conspiratorial silence. "What the fuck are you two playing at?" he hissed.

"Shut up and follow him, otherwise the deal's off!" I hissed back.

I left them to make their way around the side of the house and went back to the Heliotrope Room.

I opened the shutters. Zeki was already slithering up the wall up to my French windows. He leapt gracefully onto the balcony, cheekily pinched my nose and then kissed it better.

Marco, however, was having far more trouble making the ascent. Half-way up, he missed his footing and fell all the way back down. At first, Zeki and I tittered, but then we saw blood pouring from a cut on his arm. His face was like thunder, but at least he managed to keep quiet. In the end, Zeki had to climb back down and lift Marco onto his shoulders; I grabbed his hands from above so that he could haul himself onto the balcony.

"Doctor. Ambulance. Emergency. I could die and it's all your fault. How am I supposed to perform under these conditions?" He threw himself face-down onto my bed.

"I'm sure you'll manage. I don't think you'll bleed to death from that scratch…"

"It's a deep wound. A gash on a major artery. My condition is critical."

"… but we'd better get it washed and bandaged up."

We frog-marched Marco to the bathroom, and Zeki supervised the washing while I cast around for something to use as a tourniquet. I couldn't risk going back into the house in search of first aid materials. Eventually, I decided to sacrifice a pair of my boxers which I took into the bathroom and ripped apart.

"I can't possibly be seen in those things, even as a bandage. People would think I'd lost all my fashion sense."

As I tore up the boxers, the craziness of the situation seemed to dawn on all three of us and we were overwhelmed by shrieks of helpless laughter. Once the bandage was secured in place, we returned Marco to the bed, propping his arm up on a pile of pillows and towels.

"Right," I said. "I'll keep to my word. You have one hour, starting from now."

Marco looked at where his watch should have been, but it was no longer there. "Oh, Christ. It must have been ripped off when I fell. That was my father's diving watch. How the fuck am I going to explain this to them?"

"Passion has a price, Marco. I'll go for a walk and if I find your watch I'll keep it safe. I'll be back at ten o'clock, by this alarm clock.

In fact, I'll set it to ring at ten to ten in case you get too absorbed. Cigarettes in the carton, don't smoke in bed. Anything else?"

"Well, you could bring us a little something to eat back with you. Oh, and, Peter, sweetie —"

"Yes?"

"Do you have any lube?"

I decided not to answer this. They would find it in the bathroom, if they got that far. By now, I genuinely needed a few minutes on my own to quell the juvenile silliness that had engulfed all of us before I could return to the adult world upstairs. Picking up the copy of the Telegraph from the table by the door, I left them to their fun and headed out into the night.

Chapter Twelve

inner was in noisy progress on the terrace but as the guests were sprawled on the floor, nobody could look over the wall into the courtyard below. I let myself out into the lane by Trelawney's compound and strolled up and down, smoking and thinking.

I was in a bubbly, euphoric sort of mood – a welcome contrast to the grey resignation I'd been feeling lately. But somewhere beneath the lightness there was a sharp, unpleasant edge of discomfort I couldn't properly identify. I wanted to go on enjoying the childish fun, but this needling sensation was starting to spoil it.

I wandered back towards the house in the shadows and followed the wall around to the window of my room. Sure enough, Marco's watch was there, glinting on the dusty ground in the light cast from above.

The strap had been wrenched off and the glass on the dial was cracked. I cupped the pieces in my hand, clasping them more and more firmly, then took a few paces back and looked up at the window.

They'd left the shutters open but the mosquito nets hid the inside of the room from view. All I could glimpse was the outline of two standing figures locked, motionless, in a warm embrace.

I was repelled, yet mesmerised, quite unable to look away until a searing pain shot through my hand. I'd been clenching the broken watch glass so tightly it had cut through my flesh.

Then, as I raised my hand to my eyes, I saw teardrops starting to splash on top of the rivulets of blood that were trickling down my palm.

Blood and tears.

I truly didn't recognise the awful, black churning sensation within me for what it was as I stood there, sobbing uncontrollably, excluded from my own quarters by my own decisions. I had no idea whether I wanted to stop them, join in with them, take Zeki's place, or even take Marco's place. I just knew that I hurt so badly, so acutely, that I had to get away – and fast.

It was actually poor Alex who, one day soon, would give me the words to describe what I was feeling. Alex, who understood better than anyone how, and why, I'd reached my forties with my emotions bottled up to bursting point.

I have those words of his written down. "Wanting something more than you've ever wanted anything," Alex told me, "and not being able to get it, is bad enough. But watching somebody else take what you want, as easily as a bee sucking pollen – that's the pits. That's when you feel jealousy, pure and simple. People say it's born of love, but it kills love, and everything else, if you let it."

So far, my life had simply excluded emotional anguish on this scale. Yes, there had been disappointment when young men I invited to stay with me in Spain had to be sent back for one reason or another. But there would always be another one, and my regrets were forgotten as soon as I was in the next dark-room or the next clump of bushes. As each of my parents were laid to rest, I drummed my fingers with boredom while feigning an acceptable level of grief. Of course, I was terribly sad to see Alex himself suffering and declining, but saw no point in dwelling on it. Or rather, I refused to dwell on it, as I refused to dwell on anything unpleasant. I liked my life to be a nice, even and preferably uneventful progression, not the sort of roller-coaster that tonight had turned into.

I had to do something to suppress the pain within me, not to mention the sharpening ache in my wounded hand. I found just what

I needed on the drinks tray in the deserted kitchen: a few quick nips of Scotch, and I began to get a grip on myself. Like a floundering swimmer whose feet touch the sea bed again, I felt relief as life began to regain its customary good order. Perhaps it would be a good idea to distract my mind for a couple of minutes. I remembered I still had the local newspaper stuffed into my pocket, so I began leafing through it.

The front page was full of the latest manoeuvrings over Gibraltar, on which I had strong views as a loyal resident of Spain. Then I came to the famous article about the Village, but it really said nothing we didn't already know. June's friend had obviously exaggerated its contents, because there was no mention of "dropouts" or "decadence". It merely stated that, in line with the founding principles of the Village community, more efforts were to be made to attract families with children. Some slight changes to the approval procedure for new residents would be introduced to encourage this.

Hardly grounds for the panic that had been drummed up by Trelawney, Doocie and the rest of them.

I was about to fold the paper up and rejoin the party when the Letters page caught my eye. There was only one letter on it, in fact, and I still have that page of the newspaper today. There is no need to reproduce it in full: a few sentences are quite enough to give an accurate idea of its tone.

"*Sir,*

As responsible and respectable parents of children whom we endeavour to bring up in the Village, we feel that the time has come to take a stand. It was a proud moment in the annals of the nation's history when the founding charter of the Village was drawn up, embodying a remarkable combination of Christian and Moslem principles which would serve any young person as a guideline for an upright and useful life. The Village came to be a bastion, secure against the plagues of decadence which have beset the countries to the north of us – drug and alcohol addiction, the decline of the work ethic, wanton sexual excess and, perhaps the vilest act of all, homosexuality, striking at the very roots of the family unit and bringing with it the dreadful spectres of AIDS and an existence beyond the pale of civilised society. How sad we are to see that little by little, undesirable elements have been allowed to creep into our Village, bringing with them the putrid germs which…"

The sermon continued in this vein. It was so overlarded with the classic jargon of prejudice that I actually began to chuckle at it. One passage in particular made me burst out laughing, in view of what was happening only a stone's throw away at this very moment.

"When a youngster walks the lovely lanes of our Village, we of the responsible generation must fear the little one's virginal innocence may suddenly and forever be corrupted by the base and loathsome creatures who are now at large. We say loud and clear: these perverts and drop-outs MUST GO, they must PAY THE PRICE OF THEIR UNNATURAL ACTS and our defensive walls must be fortified against this tidal wave of FILTH."

Thinking of Trelawney's outbursts against Beth Horrabin's father and the "so-called principles" he stood for, I was certain that this was his work. The call to arms was so long that it spilled onto the next page , so I had to turn over to confirm my suspicion. And this, I found, was how the letter ended:

"Yours in disgust,
The Hon. DUNCAN BLAINE, O.B.E., M.C., Commander, R.N.,

WM. J. HORRABIN, sometime Lance Corporal, Her Majesty's Lancaster Fusiliers,
JANICE HORRABIN (Mrs.)
OLIVER TWELVETREES, D.S.O., Colonel, King's Own Suffolk Infantry.
Residents of the Village and Members of its Council."

I couldn't really grasp the full implications of seeing the name, honours and rank of Marco's father at the bottom of this ridiculous and venomous tirade, but I knew full well that they were both numerous and serious.

I took my glass out into the courtyard for some fresh air before braving the crowd upstairs, and sat down cross-legged behind the oleander bushes.

It was abundantly clear to me that the author, indeed, the senior-ranking signatory, of such a document would not deal lightly with one of the "base and loathsome creatures" who had aided and abetted his son to engage in "the vilest act of all". Of course, I'd performed no "unnatural acts" with Marco Blaine... but at this very moment, he was in the embrace of a goatherd on *my* bed, wearing one of *my* condoms ... the Commander and I were probably within shouting – or shooting – distance of one another, and the remains of the Commander's watch were in my pocket, caked in my own blood ...

I simply couldn't pursue this train of thought any further. But I had little doubt that the Honourable Commander Blaine would have no scruples whatsoever about pursuing it, and he sounded like the sort of man who had the power, money and contacts to pursue it right to the bitter end.

Phrases I'd heard about Marco began ringing in my ears – *flies like a vulture and stings like a scorpion...what he wants, he will get, and if he doesn't, everybody suffers...be careful, be careful, be careful ...*

The next thing I knew was June's reassuring bulk towering over me as she slapped my cheeks to bring me round.

"Christ, luv, we thought we'd lost you there. What on earth have you been up to, darlin' – blood all over your jacket, and you stink like a distillery – you're lucky I was invited down here for a little intimate moment with a gentleman admirer I met upstairs, otherwise you could've laid here till dawn. Them queens are all too pissed to care, anyway."

A middle-aged man in a tuxedo pushed through the bushes with a jug of water and a stone cup, which June filled and pressed to my lips.

"Now, drink this. Upset about your friend, was you, dear? Trelawney told us he was having a very rough ride."

"Yes, June, I'm upset about my friend," I slurred. "Rough ride, that's for sure, but much rougher to come … for all of us." I heard my voice degenerate into a humiliating drunken whimper.

She gave her friend one of those humouring-the-insane looks. "Yes, yes, Peter, you keep drinking the water. You'll feel better when you've slept it off. Now we'll just get you to your room."

"NO!" I screamed. This brought me straight to my senses. "I'll be perfectly all right. Just give me a couple of minutes." I tottered inelegantly to my feet. My view of Trelawney's courtyard tilted violently up and down, as if I were in a plane that was banking before it landed. Things stabilised after a couple of moments and I was able to take a few reasonably steady steps.

"June, you're an angel. I'll come and see you tomorrow."

June's friend had disappeared again, so I hugged her and set course for the Heliotrope Room. "Thank your friend for me – and enjoy him, won't you?"

She clucked and tutted in response as if I were a disobedient child, and blew me a kiss.

I dreaded to think what lay behind the door of my room. In fact, everything seemed in fair order as I tiptoed in.

However, my bed was not empty.

Whoever was in it was entirely hidden under the quilt, snoring very gently, on the opposite side from where I'd chosen to sleep. I went over to the bed and was about to lift the cover when I saw a note written on a torn-open cigarette carton.

"You can get in bed. I know I can trust you. Thanks 4 everything. Love, Marco."

I still have that piece of cardboard, too. His writing then was huge, and some of the words — 'know', 'trust', 'everything' and 'love' — were entirely in capitals. His own name occupied as much space as the rest of the text, with an elaborate curlicue below it ending in an 'x'.

He was lying in the embryo position, facing away from where I would sleep, clutching a pillow to his breast. He was naked except for a pair of skimpy white underpants and the remains of my boxer shorts wrapped around one tanned forearm.

I went to the bathroom and cleaned myself up. My hand had stopped bleeding, but it hurt like hell when I tried to wash the clotted mess away. I took the pieces of Marco's watch out of my pocket and arranged them carefully on the bedside table. Then I undressed, keeping my boxer shorts on, turned out the lights, and climbed into bed beside him.

I lay on my back for a while, my head resting on the wrist of my injured hand, hoping that the weight would help to freeze the pain away. I thought I was far too tense to sleep as the wildly contrasting episodes and moods of the evening played through my mind, but I was just dozing off when I felt another burst of pain from my hand.

Marco had reached over in his sleep and taken my hand in his.

Wide awake again, I let his fingers mesh with mine. At first, the pain was worse than ever, but I desperately wanted to keep my hand locked in his. Little by little, the acute physical discomfort and the turmoil in my mind ebbed away as a warm, deep serenity washed through me. I must have fallen fast asleep in that awkward position, because I remember nothing more until I woke up, alone, with the sunlight streaming in through the open shutters.

And that was how Marco and I spent our first night together.

Chapter Thirteen

The first hint of autumn was in the air next morning. Below my French windows, strands of grey mist lurked eerily among the shadows of the ravine. The heat had lost its searing edge, but my head felt like a bag of marbles clattering against one another every time I tried to move. I forbade myself to think about the consequences of what had happened and focused as best I could on showering, tidying up my lacerated hand and making myself presentable enough to get upstairs for some coffee.

I gulped down a double dose of painkillers, crunching them up to accelerate the effect. Some time passed before I felt well enough to risk the first cigarette of the day. Hangovers simply didn't feature at home, and the last time I passed out on the floor must have been during my student days a quarter of a century before. Even so, I chuckled when I recalled June's horror-struck expression as she tried to shake me into consciousness last night.

I spotted the remains of Marco's watch lying on the bedside table next to the note. I folded the watch fragments up in the cardboard and put the package into my pocket. Eventually, I judged that I was just about robust enough to brave the outside world, so I headed out and up to the terrace.

Tamir and Abdullah, stripped to the waist and aided by a couple of heavily-veiled local girls, were busy clearing last night's debris away. They froze to attention when they saw me, brooms held upright like halberds. In this country, the foreign guest always received the marks of polite respect in public, no matter what intimacy or debauchery might go on in private. With everything else that had happened, I'd completely forgotten the five sweaty minutes Tamir and I had passed the day before – but the wry look in his eyes quickly reminded me.

"Morning Mr. Peter, well done, you're the first one! Everybody sleeping with everybody." Tamir couldn't possibly have described the situation any better.

"Except Mr. T, of course," he added. My heart sank a little. I still needed some time to compose myself. "He's in the study now, coming for breakfast in a minute. You need coffee, I think. All ready."

"Tamir, you're a marvel."

"I put chairs and table down there, by the bushes, too much work up here for quiet breakfast."

He pointed, unfortunately, to the precise place by the oleanders where I'd spent an unspecified part of the previous evening. I walked back down to the spot rather timidly, but a quick survey revealed no trace of my earlier presence.

I shakily poured myself a cup of coffee and sat back. Looking around at Trelawney's beautiful home, I saw Casa Morena – my own house back in Spain – for what it actually was: the physical symbol of my attempts to isolate myself from the real world.

Trelawney's arrival broke my train of thought.

"My warmest congratulations, Peter! You have survived! Reports from the front had you close to death from various causes, but I see you have come through your ordeals unscathed."

Instinctively I moved my hands out of sight under the tablecloth. I had no idea of what he knew and what he didn't.

"Yes, I seem to have done. It wasn't quite the evening I'd been expecting." That seemed to cover all eventualities.

"I don't blame you in the slightest. A good skinful does no harm when you're feeling rotten and there's nothing constructive you can do about it. Now, tell me, what is the news from Switzerland?"

"Actually, I can't tell you. Poor Alex was so incoherent I couldn't make much sense out of it. That's what really upset me."

Here I was, lying to my oldest friend for the first time. Thank you, Marco.

"I'll have to try and find out more today," I went on. "I'd prefer not to dwell on it, if you don't mind, Trelawney. There's nothing to be done."

"Except go back early," he suggested. I had a hunch that it was wise to leave this option open.

"Let's wait and see. Now, tell me, what did I miss?"

"What you missed, Peter, may well turn out to be the last party of the golden era of Trelawney Towers. The house, I mean, not its owner. To some extent, the debauchery is still continuing."

I was relieved when he steered the conversation back onto the usual party post-mortem lines.

"So who's where, and with whom?"

"The configuration is complex. I think I should install one of those baize map tables with markers and croupiers' rakes, of the sort dear Winston had in the basement of Downing Street during the last war. Sir Brian and Jean-Louis are in Amethyst. They are not alone there, and I am not referring to those two cylindrical creatures they trail around with them. You may have spotted that one of the cleaning squad is missing."

Trelawney helped himself to coffee as he continued his situation report. "To everyone's amazement, Purvis and Florian spent most of the night hunkered over the longest game of Chinese Checkers I have ever witnessed. I cannot believe that any closer form of intimacy occurred, but stranger things have happened within these walls. I can vouch for Tamir's whereabouts during the night myself, so he was certainly not pleasuring our German guest."

He swivelled around to point at the rooms on the other side of the courtyard.

"In any case, Cornflower and Anthracite are both silent. What is more, Magenta had to be pressed into service to accommodate dear June and a gentleman who came in on the coat-tails of our South African friends. They have now vacated, ready for the fumigation of the room following what, in this house, passes for an *unnatural act*. So, for once, yours may have been the only bed that remained free of wanton sexual excess, of the *tidal wave of filth* – do those phrases mean anything to you?"

Although he was now becoming agitated, Trelawney was clearly delighted that everyone had been suitably fixed up. I certainly wasn't going to dispel his illusions about the virginal state of the Heliotrope Room.

"Yes, I read the letter in the Telegraph. That didn't help my mood, either."

"I didn't think it would. As you know, Peter, what you do with young Blaine is your own business, but that letter has one immediate consequence which I ask you to note. No member of the Blaine or Horrabin families, of any generation, may step over this threshold again while I am the master of this house. That is not negotiable."

I hadn't expected this. Not so long ago, Trelawney was giving Marco "permission" to visit him again for the next lesson in how to be a happy homosexual.

"Isn't that a bit harsh on Marco? How do you think he'll feel when he reads the letter? Who can he turn to?"

"Yes, it is harsh. How he feels about the letter is not my concern. He must turn to someone whose home will not be put at risk by having him in it. I do not really care whether that person is you, although I can think of no one better. But no such meeting will ever take place on these premises. Is that quite clear, Peter?"

"Of course." His tone was so severe that I trembled inwardly. "So, it's battle stations, is it?"

"Regrettably so. Sir Brian is going to try and pull a few strings in the Ministry, but Blaine – Commander Blaine, I should say – is a force to be reckoned with. It turns out the Foreign Office are thinking of making him the next Honorary Consul here. Then there'll be no stopping him. Of course, we could probably unearth some skeleton in the cupboard from his younger days in the navy – high jinks in the hammocks, perversion on the poop deck, and so on. But I gather that a simple principle tends to apply here: what Commander Blaine wants, Commander Blaine usually gets."

From what I was hearing lately, these Blaines were a remarkably well-matched lot. "Sir Brian wasn't able to wave a magic wand?"

"No, and he views the situation as extremely grave. He came up with a plan that could ensure my continued presence in this house, but it would mean going against the traditions of the Village."

Trelawney seemed a little less obsessed about the crisis, judging from the leisurely way he was tucking into the croissants Abdullah had brought down during our conversation.

"Well?"

"It's very simple. As soon as Tamir is married, he and his wife move in here. A little construction work will be necessary to give them the privacy they, and I, require. One of the lesser rooms may have to go, I'm afraid. Once this house is the home of a married native couple, not even the Head of State himself will be able to touch it. Especially if there are children. Utterly sacrosanct."

Try as I might, I simply couldn't imagine the patter of tiny feet across this particular courtyard.

"But it'll still be your house, won't it?"

"Not necessarily. If I have to give it up to Tamir in order to stay here, that's what I'll do."

"You trust him that much?"

"Absolutely. And more. Have you not yet learned that love and trust go hand in hand? By coming to this house all those years ago, Tamir entrusted his future, his freedom, his very life to me. Why should I not do likewise?"

There was no faulting Trelawney's logic, but would I ever dream of doing the same? Or, for that matter, would anyone ever be prepared to trust me that far? I needed a cigarette, and as I reached into my pocket for the pack, my hand encountered something unfamiliar.

Slowly, I realised it was the torn piece of cardboard; I rubbed my fingers over the surface where Marco had scrawled those selfsame words – love, and trust.

"I think I might be learning that lesson at last. Seems I've got a lot of catching up to do."

"You can learn the most surprising things in this Village," he replied. "As, it seems, you are discovering." He raised his coffee cup and clinked it against mine. "To your happiness, dear boy."

I started to gulp violently and felt perilously close to throwing up again. I couldn't take much more of this, so I excused myself politely, saying that I really had to find June and thank her for saving my life last night.

Chapter Fourteen

At the top of the hill, I paused for breath and turned to gaze down on the view. Far below, the sea had gouged out countless inlets and secluded coves where the bathing was superb if you were prepared to stagger all the way down and scramble back up again.

All of a sudden, I longed to plunge into the cool waves, to lie by the waterline and feel the sea lapping the nape of my neck. Perhaps that way I would achieve some relief from the chaos that had invaded my life since Marco had entered it. I decided to hire a car and take myself down to the coast alone that afternoon.

Someone coughed just behind me, startling me out of my skin. I turned my head abruptly, giving myself a vivid reminder that I still had a considerable hangover.

Florian had followed me up the hill. The night hadn't taken such a toll on him, judging from the sparkle in his eyes.

"It makes you feel like a king up here, doesn't it, Peter? All the world is at our feet, waiting to be conquered."

This wasn't quite how I was feeling about the world this morning, but I let it pass.

"We didn't see much of you at the party last night," he went on.

"No, I had to deal with a few things. I gather you've learned how to play Chinese Checkers."

"Yes, *and* I heard all about the amazing life of Mr. Purvis. What a talker! He was telling me about all the countries he's lived in, the wars and revolutions he's seen, the famous people he's met…"

"Really?" I said, with an undisguised lack of curiosity.

"Yes, I was fascinated by every word he said."

I was in no mood to hear a second-hand version of Purvis's life story after all these years on the receiving end of his aloofness, but I did wonder why he'd chosen to take Florian into his confidence. As far as I could see, Purvis never did anything without a motive, and only one came to mind. Given what I presumed were Florian's preferences, I could hardly envision him spending the night in the perspiring embrace of a plump, pink Englishman making graceless headway through his fifties. But as Trelawney said, stranger things did happen.

"In these days I am learning such a lot about the world of…ah… men who like men. I was sad when you…rejected me yesterday, Peter…"

With a shudder, I realised what Florian must actually have asked me while I wasn't listening at breakfast the previous day. Well, that was a compliment, I supposed. Or perhaps he was planning, with typically German thoroughness, to fuck his way through the entire population of Trelawney Towers during his visit. Anyway, he deserved a little more courtesy than I'd shown yesterday.

"I'm so sorry, I didn't mean to be so blunt, Florian. I had a lot on my mind."

Florian raised those steely blue eyes. "So I was double-pleased when I found I liked Mr. Purvis — so much that I invited him to my bed. And he too refused. Very politely, like you, but he refused. So we carried on talking and playing the game. I'm quite sharp at it now – you and I should play sometime. We only finished our conversation in his room at dawn, so I am taking some fresh air before I sleep."

Of all the possibilities on offer at the party, I could think of none less enticing than a night-long recital of Purvis's autobiography. Even with the blood and the tears, my night seemed like paradise by comparison.

"Oh, and Peter, as I was coming out, I met your friend."

"My friend?"

"Yes. Letting himself out of your room in quite a rush. Marco Blaine, he introduced himself."

I tried desperately to think of an explanation that might have even half a chance of sounding convincing.

"That's right. Marco had just...there was a bit of a crisis, he was..."

"Peter, I don't need to know. You are very lucky! Mr. Purvis taught me exactly the right English expression to describe your friend."

"Which was?"

He smiled dreamily, fluttered his eyelashes, and pronounced the three words with long pauses between them.

"Drop. Dead. Gorgeous."

"I don't think I'd disagree with that."

For the first time, I felt pride welling up within me that Marco was seen as my "friend". Let Florian think what he wanted. I wasn't going to confirm or deny anything. In fact, it was high time to leave before my concentration waned again and I stored up more embarrassment for myself.

"Now, you have to sleep, and I have to get on and make a phone call. I'll see you back at the house."

I watched him stride down the hill. Perhaps I'd have taken up his "invitation" back in the days when life was simpler – two days ago, in other words. But it would most likely have been a somewhat mechanical coupling, and the pillow talk would doubtless have been conducted with rigid formality. Compared with my sparkling, headstrong, hectic Marco, he was a stolid, stomping chap. I thought of Marco: the faint hint of auburn in his hair that you could only see when the sunlight picked it out; that long, gently tapering back with the scar from some childhood injection, just below the left shoulder blade; the whorls of thick hair on the backs of his broad brown thighs, spilling out from his underpants...

When had I taken all these details in? If I'd let my eyes linger so long, had I allowed myself to do anything else? Was that why Marco was in such a rush to get out?

Suddenly I could see it all – he'd awoken, horrified at the position I'd manoeuvred us into, and had run out of the room shrieking – God knows what he *really* told Florian. At this very moment, he could be pouring out the most incriminating tale to his parents – and how else could he explain his wounds and bruises to them?

Panic seized me. Somehow or other, I had to find out what really happened in bed last night. Or at the very least, I had to share my fears with someone, otherwise I would implode.

June. Dear, blowsy, frowsy June. I half-ran up to the door of the Olive Branch.

It was open, but June was nowhere to be seen. Old Larbi, who helped her out in the kitchen, was doing his best to cope with an onrush of customers. I might as well go ahead with my plan to get down to the coast – the Village was starting to suffocate me. I signalled to Larbi that I wanted to use the telephone, and rummaged through a box of grubby business cards on the counter until I found the one with the number of the garage in Beetlebridge: "Motor Mahboob. Latest Luxury Limousines."

When I got through, a disinterested representative of the Mahboob enterprise quoted a price in French – five times what Purvis had paid, but I didn't even bargain. Yes, somebody could bring the car up the hill in the next hour if I would drive back down with them again.

"*Vous êtes anglais? Un instant, Monsieur, s'il vous plaît.*"

There was a long pause and in the background, I heard some kind of heated slanging match. Eventually the voice returned.

"*Ce n'est pas la maison Trelawney, par hasard?*" Not Trelawney's house? Instinct prompted me to say no, it wasn't – I wanted the car delivered to the Olive Branch, unless it was more convenient to bring it to Trelawney Towers.

"*Non, au contraire, monsieur,*" came the answer.

In a sinister tone, the speaker told me the garage was "no longer authorised" to hire cars to that house. Purvis's brow-beating tactics had obviously had their effect, and I really couldn't blame Mahboob for his reaction after the way he'd been put down. Unfortunate for Trelawney. I must remember to tell him that he was blacklisted.

Meanwhile, Larbi had made me a cup of coffee, so I took it through and scanned the garden of the Olive Branch. Beth was installed in her usual position at the back, books and sketch-pad arrayed on the table. She waved me over to join her, but to do so I had to pass by a table occupied by old Colonel Twelvetrees and his wife who were sedately sipping mint tea with Greta towering between them.

"Good morning Peter, what a delightful surprise to see you mingling," she boomed. "As it happens, I would like to have a quick word in your ear. Would you mind if I just finished my conversation with the Colonel, and then perhaps you could give me five minutes of your time?"

"Certainly, Greta. I shall be with *that* young lady in the corner." She looked over to see who this was. When she spotted Beth, the expression on her face suggested that some particularly disagreeable component of her breakfast had just found its way back up her windpipe.

"I see. Very well, then," she said, resuming a posture of rapt attention as she listened to Mrs. Twelvetrees' mumblings. The Colonel stared straight through me without a word.

I set my cup of coffee down on Beth's table.

"Hello, Peter. I can see it was quite an evening!" She laughed, though not with the least malice.

"That bad?"

"I could lend you some makeup if you like!"

For a moment, I was tempted to accept, just to see what Greta's reaction would be.

"Look, Beth. I need you to do something for me. Are you going up to the Blaines' to get Marco out of bed?"

"My life wouldn't be worth living if I failed in my duties," she replied, lowering her head in a mock bow of obedience.

"Can you give him a message for me? Please? It's vital. Well, I mean it's quite important."

"I can see that. You've started sweating, Peter."

"Yes, well, that's what happens if you have too much whisky and you're not used to it. Can you ask him to meet me at twelve?"

If he failed to show up, I'd know that I'd gone too far. I could forget Marco and carry on as normal. If I could remember what that meant.

"OK," Beth answered. "Where, though?" I hadn't thought this out.

"Oh, just say – in the usual place, in the churchyard. He'll know where I mean."

"So you guys have got a *usual place* now, have you?" I didn't realise it would come out like that. "Sounds to me as if the pair of you *are* getting close. But actually, I think that's a good thing for Master Blaine. He needs someone to look up to. So, yes, I shall play my part in the intrigue."

She seemed quite gleeful about the whole thing. I was going to start probing to see how much she knew about the newspaper article, but she raised a finger to her lips and signalled with her eyes that I should look behind me.

"Looks like you're wanted by the Headman."

Greta had been striding purposefully towards our table, but she halted and stood to attention a couple of yards away as if there were some kind of invisible sanitary exclusion barrier around it. Fortunately, this position left her out of earshot.

"Twelve o'clock, usual place." With a mock salute, Beth raised her hand to the piercing in her brow, which I now realised was a silver scorpion.

I drained my coffee and rose to join Greta. She waggled her hand at me as if she were addressing an unruly puppy, indicating that we should move out of the contaminated area.

"Greta, what can I do for you?"

She steered me firmly over to a deserted area of the garden.

"It is more a question of what I can do for you, Peter. And that, I am afraid, is limited to issuing a well-meant, but firm, warning." Her steely tone was enough to set me trembling. "The situation in the Village for gentlemen of your ilk, if I may use that expression, has suddenly become rather...*ticklish*, let us say. Have you seen this week's local newspaper?"

"I managed to catch a glimpse of the Telegraph last night. It was quite a busy evening, so..."

"Of course it was. I know that Sir Brian was – is – here, along with dear Trelawney's usual houseful of exotic guests. It may surprise you to know that I would love to be a member of the house-party myself, but circumstances do not permit. Have never permitted. I have devoted my life to public duties, to the exclusion of other pursuits. Now I see events taking a turn which may force me, in my official capacity, to take decisions and actions that could be personally *harrowing*. We ladies conduct our affairs in a somewhat less flamboyant manner than you gentlemen, if I may say so. That places us a little further from the firing line."

Her face as she spoke was totally impassive, the hawk's eyes focused firmly on a point between her feet and mine. I was thunderstruck. Was I hearing the first ever public disclosure of Greta's private inclinations? Or had Trelawney just kept me in the dark all these years – and if he had, what else had he concealed from me?

"I have spoken in this exceptional and, of course, totally confidential manner in order to underscore the gravity of what I have to say. I would strongly advise you to leave this Village and this country as soon as you can. Until your departure, I would beg you to exercise the utmost caution in your dealings with everyone. That applies particularly to the younger generation, be they natives or not."

For the first time in her monologue, she stared me in the face. She couldn't know *everything* that had happened last night, surely? A trickle of cold sweat made its presence felt half-way down my spine.

"Please feel at liberty to pass my warning on to the other temporary residents of the Towers. I shall, of course, take the earliest possible opportunity to talk with Trelawney myself. His position is naturally rather different and, I have to say, even more perilous."

At this point, her face began to betray some emotion. Her lip trembled ever so slightly, and her aged, pale eyes exuded a profound sadness. She reached out and touched the back of my hand with her gristly fingers.

"I truly wish I could do something more to help. You are, so to speak, my brothers. So listen, and heed. Now I must continue my rounds as if all were well. Goodbye, and *bon voyage* if I don't see you again."

All I could do was to return her farewell and make for the door in a stupor. I cannot imagine the effort it must have cost her to lift even this tiniest corner of the veil that always shrouded her personal life. Rumour and ribald speculation over the years had conjured up some wildly improbable scenarios – a secret marriage to a tribal chieftain in the wilds of Mauritania, a string of terrified goatherds forced by whiplash to satisfy her every whim. But even in our unrestrained circle, it had never been mooted that the Headman herself might be part of the "tidal wave of filth" that was pounding against the defensive walls of her own Village.

I didn't have long to wait for the car. The same 2CV that had transported Purvis from the airport lumbered around the corner and juddered to a lop-sided halt outside June's doorway.

Sure enough, the tilt was caused by Purvis's corpulent adversary of the previous day. He unloaded himself from the driver's seat, gingerly planting one foot after another on the ground as if he were stepping off a ketch in which he'd circumnavigated the globe.

"You, sir. Here, sir." He beckoned. For the second time in an hour, I had the impression that I'd been mistaken for a dog. "Here, as you see, is your limousine, and here is your contract of hire." He slapped a substantial wad of documents down on the bonnet. "But we have a problem, sir."

"We do?"

"To be accurate, sir, you do. You have not been truthful. I know that you are staying at Trelawney Towers. Along with that criminal, that cheat, that crook from yesterday. You are maybe a better man than him. It would not be difficult. But that is not where the problem lies."

His English was almost as impressively correct as Greta's.

"So, where *does* the problem lie?"

"You belong to that house. We cannot do business with that house. Orders from the capital."

"Look here, Mr. Mahboob, I have nothing at all to do with Mr. Purvis." I decided to try and establish an alliance against the common foe. "In fact, just between you and me, I probably dislike him just as much as you do!"

"Nothing to do with that. The problem is much bigger. Authority has instructed us not to do business with that household."

The menace he put into the word "authority" suggested that my head could be lopped off there and then if I were unwise enough to ask for further details. My stomach heaved as I realised what was happening. A boycott was being launched against Trelawney Towers and anyone at whom that revolting letter was targeted. The silent, patient tactics of the East ruled supreme here, but if he could play by the rules of the bazaar, so could I.

Without a word, I removed my wallet from my pocket and extracted the opulent Swiss banknotes that were still in its back compartment after my trip to Zurich. I counted them to myself (over eight hundred francs), folded them up in a different order, tucked them back in the wallet and returned it to my pocket.

He watched with a show of nonchalance; I could all but hear the mental arithmetic going on in his head.

"I'm sure there's a way round this," I ventured.

"Eight hundred."

"Six."

"Seven, and my lips will be sealed."

"Done. We shall return together to Beetlebridge now, and I shall hand the limousine over to you there."

I passed over the banknotes and scribbled on the forms. We climbed into the car and he drove me down the hill.

Mahboob rolled the car to a halt on a stretch of wasteland just outside of Beetlebridge, and we stepped out.

"Just one thing," I said as he offered me his hand, "I may need to leave it in town. Perhaps I have to go home suddenly."

"You call this number."

He extricated a dog-eared business card from the top pocket of the suit jacket, which had gained a few more creases and blotches since its last appearance.

"At your service. Twenty-four seven." He squinted at the document he was holding so as to decipher my name, and then he addressed me without hostility. "Mr. Carter, if I were you, I *would* go home suddenly. Very definitely. The best days are over. It could get very unpleasant now." He winked almost imperceptibly. "Ah – the weather, I mean, of course. *Ma salama*, Mr. Carter."

He plodded off into the midday heat and I set off back up to the Village. In between negotiating the potholes and trying to judge when it was safe to move out of second gear, I remembered Trelawney once telling me that in the East, you were always given a warning from an unexpected quarter when your time was up. Well, I thought, I'd now received two in the course of the last hour or so.

If the brewing storm forced Trelawney himself to leave in spite of his master-plan, I could be of far more use to him in Spain than here. At least he would have a place of refuge relatively close by. But whatever it might cost me, I was not going to leave without seeing Marco for just one more time. Whether or not it was to be our final meeting, I knew in my heart that it would change the course of my life for ever. And how right I was.

Chapter Fifteen

ll this haring up and down the hill had used up most of the
morning. Noon was only a few minutes away when I parked
the 2CV outside the Olive Branch. I made straight for the
churchyard, ready for a long wait and steeling myself for a bitter
disappointment.

I pretended to be making a study of the little cluster of Villagers'
graves in case anyone came along. I discovered that a James Anthony
Horrabin (d. 1979) was at rest here, beneath a considerable accumulation
of lichen in the shade of the cedar trees. I was wondering if there were
any Blaines scattered around when Marco came panting up, bright red in
the face, his arm in an elaborately tied sling.

"It's not as bad as that, surely?" I asked.

"Of course it's not, it's only a graze, but Mummy enjoyed playing
nurse. Fag!"

He deftly removed his injured arm from the sling and held two
fingers out twitching, ready to receive the cigarette. I lit one for each
of us and he took several deep drags before speaking again.

"So? Why have I been summoned, not to mention frog-marched
here by Miss Horrabin? She's on guard outside the gate, by the way, in
case you were thinking of a graveyard passion scene."

"I hope you know there's no risk of that sort of thing after last
night. You slept perfectly well, didn't you?"

"And you're easily fooled, aren't you? I was watching every move
until I saw you were dead to the world. Come on – what's this all
about?"

"Several things. Mainly, Marco, I may be leaving very soon, so I wanted to give you my address. What are you doing this afternoon?"

"Piano lesson at seven. Mrs. Twelvetrees. The Village's answer to Dame Myra Hess. Nothing much till then, but I'm not hanging about here for much longer. Far too risky."

"Well, I have a car now. So we could go down to the beach for a swim, if you like."

This seemed to appeal, but Marco elaborately finished and extinguished his cigarette before answering.

"All right then, provided Beth can come. It'll do her good to get out of the Village. They even had to sell the car to pay her father's booze bills, so she never gets anywhere."

"You mean, you'd feel safer with your bodyguard."

"If you like to put it that way."

Of course I'd have preferred Marco to myself, but if that was his condition for coming, so be it. "All right. Should we go now?"

"Fuck no! Get real. We can't be seen getting into a car with the likes of you. Drive down the hill and meet us near that patch of waste ground about a mile down. In about half an hour."

Hastily re-inserting his arm in the sling, he ran back out of the churchyard. I waited until he was well out of sight and headed back to Trelawney Towers.

Half an hour later, having raided the kitchen to pack a picnic basket, I set off down the hill once more. Marco and Beth jumped out from behind a row of overgrown oleanders, leapt into the back of the car and crouched on the floor for the first part of the journey. Then Marco allowed Beth to sit up on strict condition that she kept her eyes skinned for any Villagers who might be about.

"Is all this pantomime really necessary?" I asked.

"It's in your interest more than ours, sweetie. After all, you're one of the *base and loathsome creatures* staying at Trelawney Towers, which we all know is the breeding ground of the *putrid germs*. Don't think we haven't heard about the letter in the Telegraph. You could be corrupting us at this very minute!"

"Ah, so you know. That was the first thing I wanted to ask. I brought a copy of the paper in case you hadn't seen it. If you reach down into the boot, you'll find it in the picnic basket."

"Marvellous!" Marco yelled, launching into a manoeuvre which ended up with his substantial backside in the air and his bare feet on the dashboard. My hand was forced to rub the inside of his thigh when I changed gear but this passed without comment. He extricated the newspaper and began reading it aloud in an exaggerated Old Etonian voice. When he came to the "lovely lanes" and "virginal innocence" paragraph, he dissolved into shrieks of mirth. Beth seemed rather less amused.

"Marco," she said sternly. "You don't appreciate how serious this is. If I were a gay person – "

"Which you are, sweetie, you are but you won't admit it to yourself! *Get real*!"

She bridled at this. "Marco, you manage your life, and I'll manage mine."

"Nonsense, you've no idea of what you want and you need me to bring out the best in you. And we need to stock up the gay population in the Village."

"That brings me to the next item of news," I broke in. "You realise all this fuss is probably going to drive all of us out? I've already been advised to leave, Trelawney's seriously worried about his residence permit, and the character who hired me this shackle told me the garage has blacklisted the Towers. And by the way, neither of you two must come to the house at the moment. It's too risky."

These snippets of information provoked a lengthy silence. When

I looked round again, I saw that Beth and Marco were having a whispered but virulent argument.

"Peter, I want to apologise on behalf of my parents," Beth said in a solemn tone. "You've been very kind to both of us and this is the treatment you get. What have you got to say, Marco?"

"I can't apologise for my parents. What they do is their business and they have every right to do it. I have no control over them, but what they don't seem to realise is that they have no control over *me*. I choose my friends." He reached over and prodded me in the ribcage. "And I'm choosing *you*, Peter Carter."

My heart missed a beat. Several, probably.

"Don't let that go to your head, though. Do you *really* have to go?"

"Put it this way. If Greta said you ought to leave the Village, for your own safety, would you go?"

They both let out a shocked "Oh!" in unison.

"This may even be my last afternoon."

Beth let out a spontaneous cry of disappointment. "Right! Let's make the most of it. Shall we take you to our private beach?"

"I'd love that. Point the way!"

Just before the road climbed up into the craggy section of the shoreline, we turned off and bumped over parched yellow fields, scattering the grazing goats on either side of us. Swerving around boulders and miniature crevasses, we followed a dried-up river bed that eventually opened out into the shimmering sea. A sharp breeze took the sting out of the afternoon heat and lofty rocks provided ideal shade for our picnic. If this was to be my last afternoon in this country, whether for now or for ever, there could be no more perfect setting for it.

The age-old tranquillity of the cove was shattered as Marco and Beth chased one another screaming and giggling down to the shore. He cornered her in the rocks so that she was forced to retreat into the water, still wearing her T-shirt and shorts. He splashed in after her and made out that he was rescuing her, though she was clearly an excellent swimmer.

"There, you see, now I've saved your life," I heard him yell. They swam to shore together and ran out of the water holding hands, clothes soaked and clinging to the contours of their bodies, vibrant with the sheer fun of the moment. Marco raced back to where I was laying out the picnic.

"Hand out! Eyes shut! I've brought a contribution to lunch. Something really delicious!"

I held my left hand out and he pressed a small spiny object into it. I started as the thing began to move. Opening my eyes, I saw that it was a perfectly formed miniature crab. I dropped it immediately – one injured hand was quite enough.

"Careful! They're delicious, but you need hundreds of them and they have to be boiled. I'll kill this one and you can keep it as a souvenir."

Selecting a couple of pebbles, he skilfully sandwiched the creature between them and applied pressure until there was a slight cracking noise. He laid the crab out on the ground: it was clearly dead, but not damaged in the least. I knelt down and watched the operation, fascinated.

"Now, you see, its innards will drain out and you can take the shell home to Spain with you. We used to do all this stuff when we were kids here: diving for sunken treasure; trekking through the mountains; living off honeycombs and berries for days; sleeping in snake-infested caves."

"I'm sure you're exaggerating."

"Occasionally I do. But you can imagine, it was a fantastic childhood – what a place to grow up. Until..." His bright face clouded over again, as it had done earlier in the car. "Until sex, I suppose. Sex arrived and things started to change. Fuck sex, it ruins so much."

"What an extraordinary thing to say!"

"It started very early for me, you know. What I told you about, with Beth – we were just kids when that happened. But it was the end of childhood, for both of us. Bang, bang. Now then, when did *you* pop your cherry?"

Another question I'd never been asked before, certainly not in those words.

"I was eighteen. At university."

"Who was he? I *so* know it was a he, you're *such* a poofter. I'd bet a fortune you've never done it with a woman. You're just not hip enough."

As he said this, he reached into my shorts pocket to extract the packet of cigarettes and the lighter. I let him go ahead, as if it was his right. He took two out of the box, lit them, and passed one to me.

"Well, Marco, you're right on both scores. He was a policeman, actually."

"A policeman! A bobby on the beat! Well slap my thighs and tickle my tits!"

He let out a shrill giggle and then burst into the chorus of 'A Policeman's Lot Is Not A Happy One', in a surprisingly rich baritone. "I've had a very broad musical education. Mrs. Twelvetrees adores Gilbert and Sullivan, as you might expect."

"He wasn't on the beat...but he worked on the telephone switchboard at county police headquarters. He did have to wear a uniform to do that."

Now Marco was reduced to total, body-shaking hysterics. "Beth has to know this. Come on – she's got to hear it from your own lips!"

He grabbed my hand and made me run with him down to the rock pool where Beth was sitting half in, half out of the water, engrossed in a study of the various forms of life to be found there. He made me repeat the information, clearly taking pride in my performance as if I were a well-trained circus animal. Beth tittered politely, but the news didn't seem to have the dramatic effect on her that it produced in Marco.

"Well, what do you think of that?" he asked her. A mischievous glance flashed between them.

"I think," she replied very deliberately, "I think – Peter deserves a prize. Which will be in the form of a swimming lesson!"

They each grabbed one of my hands and dragged me into the foaming waves between them. I'm quite a strong swimmer and I was almost able to stay level with them as they sped away from the shore. I soon turned and attempted to head towards land, but before I knew it, Marco had swum up to me and grasped my feet, while Beth blocked my progress by diving in and out of the water in front of me, splashing water in my face every time I tried to protest.

The salt water sent acid spasms of pain shooting through my cut palm, but I couldn't have cared less. The sense of utter release from the tedious, repetitive gloom of the life I had been leading was overwhelming. A clean, jubilant thrill swept through me, more liberating than any orgasm I'd ever experienced. Even that first one with the policeman, of whom I was now reminded again as their voices echoed over the water in strident counterpoint.

Eventually, they let me return to the beach while they swam off back into the rocky creek on the eastern side.

I staggered over the pebbles, elated but totally drained, and stretched out on a towel. I half-dozed in the luxurious warmth, floating on that comfortable borderline between reality and dreamland.

The heat roused me but when I looked around, neither Marco nor Beth were anywhere to be seen. The sun was already plunging down towards the horizon and the shadows from the cliffs were lengthening by the minute. I shielded my eyes with my hand to scan the rocks. High up there, standing out sharply against the orange glow of early evening, was the taut, erect outline of a body that I now recognised well, facing out to sea and poised as if ready to dive.

Except this time, that body was completely naked.

This was what I was dreading. Things were moving far too quickly. I'd organised an innocent beach picnic, and I'd done very well to resist temptation last night, but now I was terrified of losing control over – I might as well admit it – my urgent need to caress every inch of that body with my hands, to run my cheek gently down that smooth, tapering back, to moisten it with my saliva, and then –

"That's quite some arse, isn't it?"

The words stunned me as if I'd been dealt a physical blow.

Not only because I thought I was alone, and not only because my mind had been read. But above all because those words were spoken by Marco, who'd crept up silently behind me and was now crouching at my side.

Which meant the subject of my lurid fantasy was not him, but Beth. Of course, it was just a simple mistake, caused by the failing light – even so, the fantasy had been vivid enough to produce a bulge in my bathing trunks.

Marco had no doubt seen it, but didn't seem bothered.

"You can see why I was tempted, can't you?" he said quietly.

I could indeed. She was still waiting for the right moment to dive, or maybe just enjoying the warmth of the evening sun on her skin. Had Marco not been here beside me to prove otherwise, I would have sworn that it was him on that rock, not her. And though I was no psychiatrist, I suspected that if Marco could select his ideal sexual partner, it would be a mirror image of himself.

We stayed silent for a few moments, watching until Beth finally sprang up and somersaulted out of sight.

"Such a pity," Marco said sadly. "She could have a marvellous life, but there's no hope for her with that awful father, guzzling beer from dawn to dusk, and her brother's even worse." He mimed a hypodermic injection. "The pair of them have driven her mother quite mad, so Beth pretty much runs the household, if you can call it that. I'd love to do something to help her, but I don't know what."

"Friendship is the best gift you can give, Marco."

"Yeah, well sometimes it's not enough." He suddenly snapped out of his contemplative mood. "Now look, what time is it? I've got to face Mrs. Twelvetrees at seven, though how I'm supposed to perform with only half an arm left, I don't know. Cancellation due to medical reasons, I think. But I still have to show up to apologise."

"It's nearly half past six. Of course, you don't have a watch any more, do you?"

"No, thanks to your hare-brained scheme of making us climb up that wall like monkeys. Of which Zeki, by the way, resembles one. I could barely award him two out of ten, solely for size. What did you think of him?"

"The thing about Zeki is that he prefers the more mature man. Quite a lot of younger men do, you know."

"Well, the more mature man is welcome to him."

As we gathered up our beach paraphernalia I asked Marco what he told his parents about his arm and the watch.

"Mugged by a local in Beetlebridge. Masses of sympathy, much cursing of the natives, went down like a treat. Course, it means I can't wear the watch now, but I *would* like it back. It was my father's, you know."

"I've got the bits up at Trelawney's, or most of them. I'll tell you what, why don't you take mine for now? I'll get yours repaired for you when I'm back in Spain. Then I can give it to you when I see you again."

He turned to face me. "You don't have to have an excuse, Peter. I'd like to see you again, so I will. It's as simple as that. But when? Are you really going?"

"It looks as if I'd better. Maybe I'll come back next year – but you could even come and see me in Spain."

I could almost hear the wheels of his mind beginning to whirr. "You know…that might just happen. I shall have to give it due consideration. But not now! Let's get a move on, I shall be murdered if I'm late!"

He started bawling Beth's name and she soon appeared from behind the rocks. We bundled everything into the car and I drove back with the accelerator flat to the boards all the way, screeching around the bends and playing havoc with the gearbox. Mahboob had left his cassette of Arab music in the machine, and I played it at full volume as we went, with choruses of 'A Policeman's Lot' thrown in for good measure. Residents of Beetlebridge taking their evening stroll looked on aghast as we lurched past them in a swirl of dust – further proof that the Village up the hill was inhabited by lunatics, as if it were needed.

Marco and Beth dived down onto the floor again as we approached the Village. The sun had set by now, so Marco decided it was safe enough to drive all the way up to the lych-gate.

When the moment came to say goodbye, I leaned over to kiss Beth on both cheeks. She seemed to be fighting back tears. Then without thinking, I reached out to do the same to Marco. He moved instinctively towards me, but then remembered where he was. Instead of offering his cheek, he grabbed my cut hand and locked his fingers in mine, just briefly – did he remember the last time, after all? With the other hand, he removed my watch and pocketed it.

"Give me your address, then," he hissed. I passed him the business card I'd remembered to put in my pocket. "Bye, sweetie. And thanks. For everything."

They clambered out of the car and crept off in the shadows of the church wall where I'd stopped. Just before they rounded the corner, Marco turned and blew the merest hint of a kiss in my direction.

I stayed there for several minutes, my eyes fixed on the point where they'd disappeared from view, wondering when or where I'd next be with Marco. Never in a million years could I have guessed the circumstances that would bring us together again.

Chapter Sixteen

That evening's supper at Trelawney Towers was a muted affair compared to the splendours of Wednesday night's party. Mounting the terrace steps after I'd changed and showered, I felt like a truant schoolboy about to enter the headmaster's office, though I knew I'd complied fully with Trelawney's request not to bring any Blaines or Horrabins anywhere near the house. I paused to draw a deep breath before entering the drawing room where Purvis and Trelawney sat in darkness.

"So, the wanderer returns," Trelawney said.

Purvis picked up a book, moved a paraffin lamp closer to him, and began reading intently.

"Having heard nothing, and given the state you were in last night, we were a little worried. Then you were reported driving a vehicle somewhat erratically down the hill with your two young companions, so at least we knew you were alive."

"That's right, Trelawney, I had a very nice afternoon down on the beach. I was glad to get out of the Village for a while. All of this trouble that's brewing is starting to make me feel like a criminal fleeing justice."

"Which, I am sad to say, is exactly what all of us now are." There was a solemnity in his voice I'd never heard before. "Greta has had the good grace to remind me of a fact that both we and the authorities have conveniently chosen to overlook for these many years past. Namely, that *all* acts of intimacy between persons of the same sex are against the law of this country, and always have been."

"Punishable by several years behind bars," Purvis chimed in tonelessly, without looking up from his book.

"Well, for the record, nothing of that sort has happened between Marco Blaine and myself. Not that it's any of your business – either of you."

I glanced across at Purvis, but he paid me as little attention as I received from Colonel Twelvetrees in the café earlier that day.

"But you chose to spend this afternoon with members of the two families who are responsible for stirring up the trouble."

"Trelawney, an innocent afternoon on the beach with a couple of European kids is far less likely to cause trouble than the procession of goatherds and butchers and desiccated old queens that we've had up here in the last few days. Let alone the last ten years."

I was astonished that I dared to be so forthright with him. He rose from his chair and started pacing up and down the room.

"For your information, Peter, Greta did me the honour of coming in person this afternoon to warn me that she is powerless to stop Commander Blaine's crusade against the immoral minority. He has the ear of too many influential people in the capital. Now I find that tradespeople with whom I've had the friendliest of relations for years suddenly don't want to know me."

Small bubbles of saliva were emerging from the corners of his mouth as his agitation grew.

"I tried to get old Ramzi up here from Beetlebridge to fix the lights when they blew this afternoon. He was almost in tears when he told me he couldn't come. That's why we're sitting here in candlelight. Blaine's obviously launched a vendetta and I am unable to guarantee my guests they can pursue their private lives undisturbed. The same applies to me. And, the ultimate indignity: this house is now being watched by a *policeman*! He has been stationed outside the front door since you left on your excursion."

A rollicking refrain by Gilbert and Sullivan floated through my mind. Serious though the situation was, I found it very hard to stifle a giggle. I looked over at Purvis again, but he remained impassive. His silence was really needling me now, so I decided to tackle him directly.

"And what do you think about it all, Purvis?"

He carefully inserted a piece of paper in the book before closing it and placing it on the coffee table. He drained his glass – a very stiff brandy sour, by the looks of it – and turned towards us at last.

"Deplorable. The whole business. Horrabin can be discounted – he's just a hopeless drunk, and they never do any real damage except to the ones closest to them. But the man Blaine is a fanatic. I've done a bit of business with him, as you know, Trel."

I noted this detail with some surprise. Presumably, then, Blaine was willing to engage the services of a despicable pervert if his financial interests were served.

"Unhinged. But intelligent, rich and powerful – not an uncommon combination, but a highly dangerous one. He'd be delighted to hear you two bickering – it would just prove his view that poofters have as much backbone as a yardful of cackling chickens. People like Blaine only leave you with two alternatives. Nuke'em, or stay well out of the way. It seems Blaine can't be nuked. Not yet. So, the only thing to do is to steer well clear of him. Easy for you and me, Pete. All we need is a ticket out of here. Tough for Trelawney. This is his home. Time to rally round." He peered into his empty glass. "Any chance of a refill, Trel?"

Purvis was quite unruffled as he delivered his analysis of the situation, and he was perfectly right. Trelawney and I had begun to sound like a pair of hysterical schoolgirls.

"Tamir's in the back somewhere getting our dinner," Trelawney replied, "not that I feel much like eating. Perhaps you could ask him to bring one for all of us."

Purvis ambled off towards the kitchen, glass in hand.

"Peter, I'm sorry, again. Purvis is wrong there – actually I know this is no easier for you than for me. Frankly, I was hoping that you and our German friend would, er..."

"Get off together," I supplied.

"Well, yes. That would have been, let us say, a less troublesome choice for all concerned. But it seems that both you and he have chosen otherwise. I don't know what kind of relationship you are developing with Marco, and I doubt whether you can know either, after only a couple of days. If both of you are happy with it, then it must have my blessing. But if his father is going to carry on breathing fire and brimstone like this, it puts all of us – especially you – in an impossible position."

"So...I'd better go."

"I never thought the day would dawn when I'd have to ask you to leave this house, my dear friend, but that day has arrived. For your own safety, I beg of you: get out of this country as quickly as you can."

I was quite unperturbed by the prospect of leaving the Village after less than a week of the month-long stay that I'd planned – normally the highlight of my year. Never having been the victim of an overpowering obsession before, I didn't recognise the true reason for my indifference – there was no point in staying if Marco wasn't there.

"What about you? Are you still going to move Tamir and his wife in here?"

"Yes, I think that's quite a brainwave of Sir Brian's. Even he's worried about the repercussions this could have for them down in town, but he's invited me to stay in their house whenever I like, for as long as I like. They wouldn't dare touch him, he's the most distinguished foreign resident they've got. So, with one thing and another, I have decided..."

Trelawney's lip trembled. I would never have thought it possible, but this ludicrous situation had brought him to the brink of tears.

"I have decided to close the Towers this winter – for the first time in twenty years." He paused to regain his composure. "It's high time I travelled around a bit, and that will leave time for the storm to die down. I may even take up your invitation to come to Spain."

"You'd be a most honoured guest," I said automatically, but with misgivings as I thought how austere he would find Casa Morena compared to his own sumptuous home.

Purvis returned from the kitchen, followed by Tamir bearing the drinks on a tray. "Yes, Trel, it would do you good to be a guest for once. You're always playing host, always in charge, always on parade. Put yourself in the other fellow's shoes for a change. And you know, old boy, you might not be the best chappie to deal with this balls-up."

He certainly had a point. If Trelawney was thrown into a tailspin by a fracas over a window-frame and a hosepipe, he was hardly the ideal person to deal with a matter of this gravity.

"Give it a few months," he went on, "let things take care of themselves for a while, and you'll probably come back to find the problem's gone away. Might be time for old Purvis to call in a few favours. Cheers, gentlemen. To victory."

The three of us raised our glasses half-heartedly. There was nothing more to say. I stared at the floor and Purvis opened his book again.

I'd quite forgotten that Tamir was still in the room but now, his firm, clear voice broke the dismal silence. "Why everyone so sad? No need! In my country, family always look after family. You go, Mr. T, enjoy the winter, see your friends. I stay here, I take care everything. When you come back, problems all gone. You trust me."

Tears began to roll down Trelawney's cheeks now. Even Purvis was visibly touched by the poignancy of the moment as the flickering candlelight played over Tamir's fine features. Trelawney spread his arms wide, and they hugged.

Something approaching the normal relaxed atmosphere of the house slowly began to return as Tamir bustled off to the kitchen. We started to talk of other matters over dinner; as the food and wine went down, we even took bets on who would be the first to seduce the policeman posted outside to spy on us. This prompted me to tell the story of my first sexual encounter for the third time that day. Soon, our conversation was running along the same lines as thousands of others that were doubtless going on all over the world at that very minute, as gently ageing homosexuals — members of that worldwide family as close-knit as any bonded by ties of blood — gathered round candlelit tables to relive and embroider the glories of their countless conquests.

Chapter Seventeen

The three of us met again over a very early breakfast. Florian joined us but he seemed uncharacteristically downhearted and edgy.

I'd offered to drive him and Purvis to town in the hired Citroën. With his usual dexterity, Purvis had secured himself a seat on the noon plane to London. Florian was going on by bus to the see south of the country, and I'd decided to take the long ferry trip back to the Straits and Algeciras, from where I could easily hire a car and drive home in less than a day.

Conversation at the breakfast table was stilted – none of us wanted to speculate on when we would meet again or how the situation would turn out. We kept to mundane matters and feeble jokes in a vain attempt to pretend that nothing much was wrong.

"I take it that our friend from the constabulary made sure none of us were violated in our beds last night," Trelawney said.

Nobody replied. Florian was hardly eating anything for breakfast, though Purvis was tucking into a mound of scrambled eggs that Tamir had produced.

All of a sudden, a manful rhythm punched out on the door knocker startled us all. Tamir went to answer it, and seconds later June came huffing and puffing up the terrace steps. For once, there was not a trace of make-up on her face, and the ravages of the years were all too painfully visible. But even at this hour, she was clearly bursting with the energy that the rest of us were so severely lacking.

"I woke PC Plod up and told him I was coming in to give you lot a round of blow-jobs," she said breezily. "Don't think he got the point.

Anyway, I couldn't let you go without saying goodbye, and what's more, I'm not letting any of you leave unless you make me a promise," she continued while helping herself to coffee and lighting up a cigarette. Jabbing her finger into Florian's chest, she added: "And that includes you, Comrade!" Tamir, who was replenishing the breakfast supplies, suppressed a chortle.

"I'm afraid we can't take you with us, June, if that's what you want," Purvis replied. "Much though we'd like to. But we'd have to strap you to the roof, seeing as Mr. Carter's luggage is taking up most of the space in the car."

"No, no, dearie, the Village is my last address, everybody knows that. Here I am, and here I stay. But one day, sooner or later, when all this crap has been shovelled out of the way, I want the lot of you back here, and we'll have the biggest knees-up this place has ever seen. Nobody's excused, you'll all get your arses back here whatever state you're in. I'll even ring the church bell myself if nobody else will, whether I'm allowed to or not. We'll show the buggers what we're made of!"

Saying goodbye to us, of course, was only half of her purpose. She knew how dejected Trelawney would be after our departure, and she wanted to be there to help him get through. I realised how genuinely fond of her I'd become.

"Time to head out, gentlemen," Trelawney said. We started shuffling down the steps in that hesitant, over-careful way that often precedes a separation. In between making and serving breakfast, Tamir had managed to stow everything into the car, leaving just enough space for one person on the back seat.

In turn, the three of us who were leaving embraced the three who were staying behind. Florian and Tamir were surprisingly distant, barely pecking one another's cheeks. In contrast, Trelawney and Purvis stayed with their arms wrapped around each other for almost a minute.

Luckily, the policeman was not on hand to witness this latest evidence of perversion.

As I hugged June, and thanked her at last for reviving me on Wednesday night, I felt her slip a small package into my jacket pocket. "Shoved under the door last night with a note telling me to give it to you, dear. Now, you will be careful, won't you?"

With a pang of delight, I realised it was the tiny crab that Marco had stunned and wrapped up on the beach for me yesterday. Now it was my turn to bid farewell to Trelawney. Our eyes were moist as we embraced.

"All too short a stay this time, my friend, but one that you will never forget."

"You can say that again," I choked out.

"Go well, Peter. I love you dearly, and I'll see you soon."

Despite the battering he'd taken in the last couple of days, I could sense the old strength charging from his body into mine. The onrush of conflicting emotions was beginning to overpower me, and I was glad to take my position behind the wheel as the others squeezed themselves in. We poked our hands through the car windows as we jolted down the lane, waving our last farewell to the trio on the steps of the Towers. Silhouetted against the growing golden light of the autumn sun, you would have taken them for any ordinary family group saying goodbye to their house-guests: the upright, silver-haired father and his portly but still shapely wife, standing proudly on either side of their strapping son. But in this Village, as I had learned very well, nothing was ever what it seemed to be at first sight. And in that lay its endless fascination.

"Give it time, Pete," Purvis said in an attempt to assuage me, "Trel's far too worked up about this business. I've met Blaine's type before – give them enough rope, and they hang themselves, that's what you usually find." He attempted to turn around in his seat but could only manage half a rotation in the confined space. "All right in the back there, Florian?"

"So, so," Florian snuffled. His cold really sounded quite bad now.

"Sad to be leaving Tamir, Florian?" I tried to put as much kindness into the question as I could.

"Him, yes of course, but all of you, Trelawney, June, and – and – all the other people in the Village. They only allow very special people in that place, I think. I'm sorry, I..." He faltered and his voice gave out with having to shout above the engine noise. "I'm not with me today." Whether it was correct English or not, that was a pretty good description of how we all felt.

Eventually we reached the bus station and Florian quickly extracted his rucksack from the back of the car. I shook his hand firmly; Purvis actually got out of the car and gave him what just about qualified as a hug. Only then did it occur to me that Florian was obliged to travel in the company of both the prospective candidates for his experimental research into sex with the older generation, each of whom had roundly turned him down.

"I hope we meet again, Florian, maybe even in the Village."

"I've a strong feeling I will be back there, Peter. I take June's invitation very seriously. We shall see us!"

With that, he was off into the milling crowds waiting to travel to all corners of the country.

"Right, Pete," Purvis said, turning towards me once we were on our way, "Me and you have never really hit it off, have we? You with your university degrees and books, me with no education except the school of hard knocks. But there's one thing we've got in common."

My stomach lurched. This was certainly not the moment for a discussion of our shared interests in the bedroom.

"We both know what it's like to have a father who's nearer to being your worst enemy than your best friend."

"How the hell do you know that?"

"So I'm right. It takes one to know one. I saw the signs the first time I met you. No need to go into details. Point is, your Marco –"

"He's NOT my Marco! How dare you –"

"Mark my words, Pete, he's not going to let go of you, no matter what. C'mon, I'm not stupid, you're head-over-heels with him and he knows that. You're his ticket out. I've watched him grow up. You'd be surprised how well I know him. He's a great kid, bit of a show-off, far too big for his boots – he'll grow out of that soon enough. But I've also watched Blaine senior change into a monster over the years – I've been in the Village longer than you, remember, and I don't miss much." He paused. "We've not got much time, so I'll put it plain and simple. For God's sake, Pete, get Marco out of the Village, and out of Blaine's clutches. People think old Purvis is a bit short when it comes to principles, but after what I went through as a kid, I swore I'd never stand by and let a youngster be maltreated, and that's what's been happening to Marco."

I was speechless. Either he was demented, or he really knew far more about the Blaines than anyone I'd talked to. And if he'd been helping the Commander with his finances, well, maybe he'd had more of an insight into that household that anyone else. I thought it best to humour him – I'd never seen him in such a rage in all the years of our acquaintance.

"I'll remember what you've said, Purvis. But really, I've no idea if I'll ever see Marco again – we're just..."

"Would do you good to have him around as well, Pete. What was that posh word you came out with last night? Desecrated old queens?" I stopped myself from telling him the word I'd actually used. "Looked in the mirror lately, have you? You're not exactly a bundle of laughs yourself, you know. Not much going on in your life, it strikes me. You're a good bloke deep down, I reckon, but Marco's just what you need to liven you up. Put a bit of spice into your life and get you thinking about somebody else for a change."

I was starting to seethe with anger. The truth usually hurts, of course. I'd heard more than enough, but he hadn't finished yet.

"Anyway, Pete, just remember this: if you don't get him out of there, I *will* – one way or another. Geddit?" He slapped the Citroën's tiny dashboard with the flat of his hand.

Now I really was starting to think I'd got a maniac beside me. Purvis's face had turned from pink to puce. I mumbled my thanks for what he'd said and desperately thought how I could distract him, because his fury was starting to terrify me.

I handed him my mobile phone and asked him to dial the number Mahboob had given me to arrange for the car to be collected. It would be easier for him to make the call in Arabic, I said, hoping his voice wouldn't be recognised.

He jabbered away for a minute or so, and then told me that someone would meet me at the entrance to the ferry port in an hour.

When we arrived at the airport, Purvis made no fuss about leaving – a quick, sweaty handshake and he was off into the departure lounge, wheeling along the two suitcases mentioned so precisely in his contract for the hire of this vehicle a few days before. I turned the car around swiftly and headed straight for the waterfront.

Chapter Eighteen

I'd taken the ferry back to Spain after previous holidays in the Village, so I knew roughly what to expect at the port. You had to cross acres of scorching, cracked concrete before you got anywhere near the boats. Whole families from all over North Africa were camped here, the men decked out in gaudy tribal robes, the womenfolk swathed from head to foot in black, with crates and boxes piled up against their decrepit cars and vans to afford some shade from the merciless sun.

The Village already seemed a million miles away. So did Spain, for that matter. The more I looked, the more I wanted to be across the sea as soon as possible.

By some inexplicable oriental process, Mahboob himself had materialised outside the door to the customs hall. He was conducting an animated discussion with several other paunchy entrepreneurs, all of them fingering their rosary beads as they gabbled away. He spotted me and detached himself from the group.

"So, Mr. Carter, a sudden departure it is. Very wise. Thank you for your custom. I hope we may be allowed to serve you again."

I handed him the keys and said goodbye. An elderly but eager porter started loading my bags onto his trolley, and I followed him to the passport barrier.

I pushed my passport through the opening at the bottom of the grimy guichet window and haggled over the price of my guide's brief services until we agreed on a figure that was almost as much as the ferry fare I'd just paid. It was only when I was left alone with my cases that I realised things were not running quite as smoothly as they should have been.

"*Monsieur Peter Carter, oui, c'est ça?*" the moustachioed official behind the window asked me, his eyes moving in a triangle between my face, his computer screen, and my passport on his side of the glass. I nodded.

"Certain enquiries have to be made before we can authorise your departure. If you'd be so kind as to step through the door to your left."

My stomach began to grind. I was totally unprepared for this kind of trouble, but had no doubt as to what the problem was.

"The officers will help you with your baggage." The icy elegance of formal French did nothing to soothe my nerves. I was ushered into a small whitewashed room with no windows and a couple of wooden benches on either side of a table studded with cigarette burns.

The passport officer poked his head through the door on the far side of the room. "*Le commandant va venir.*"

I sat down wretchedly on one of the benches, remembering what Trelawney had said about criminal acts. I hadn't committed one with Marco, but I certainly had with Zeki. How on earth would I survive in prison conditions here when five minutes in the ferry port had sent me rushing for the boat home?

A week ago, I was a solitary middle-aged bachelor with a reasonable job, free to travel wherever I pleased, without a care in the world. In these few brief days, a tornado had swept through my tranquil existence, propelling me helplessly to this awful moment when my liberty was about to be taken from me.

And whose fault was all of this? The Blaines, the two of them, Marco and the Commander...the Commander...the *commandant*... surely not? Was my punishment about to be administered by Marco's father in person?

My head was in a total spin. I had to get help. Thank God I still had my luggage with me. I retrieved my mobile phone and keyed in Trelawney's house number. He answered on the first ring.

"Peter, I've been expecting your call. Purvis is in the same trouble at the airport. He's got his friend from the Ministry of State on the job, and I've alerted Sir Brian. Stay calm. Say nothing. Help is on its way. This is war, you realise. Can't say any more now. You'll be all right."

Trelawney's words brought me some hope, but they also roused me to fuming rage against the authors of that prejudiced clap-trap in the Telegraph. How dare they set themselves up in judgement on us? How dare they poke their noses into our private lives, forcing my best friend to abandon his home? And there they sat, penning their poisonous letters, too stupid and blind to see they were harbouring the so-called enemy in their own homes. How I would love to see the day when Marco, gallant and strong, stood there without shame and told his father the truth about himself! If I ever got out of here, I would...

At this point, the door swung open and the *commandant* stepped in. A figure more at odds with my mental picture of Marco's father would be hard to imagine. He was a slim, immaculately groomed and deeply tanned man of thirty or so in a starched white officer's uniform. A gleaming black badge identified him as Commandant Ahmad Shams ad-Din. Under different circumstances, I'd have been glad to spend more than a few minutes with him in a windowless room.

His English – or rather, American – was perfect. "I'm sorry you've been detained in this manner, sir, but my officer was only doing his job correctly. You stated your address as a certain house in the Village when you arrived in our country, and our boys had some difficulties up there recently. I'm assured that you're in no way involved, sir, and it will be my pleasure to accompany you on board your vessel now."

I felt a heady surge of relief, but it occurred to me that this might be a polite way of saying I was being thrown out of the country. As the *commandant* handed me my passport, I didn't dare open it to see whether it had been stamped with the dreaded words "DEPORTED

DUE TO SEXUAL MISCONDUCT," as once happened to Alex after an ill-advised adventure in Singapore.

Another porter appeared to load my cases onto a barrow and we strolled through the customs hall and up to the gangplank. The other passengers parted respectfully to let us through, doubtless imagining that I was a VIP being escorted with all due honour.

"I gather you know Sir Brian Bishop, sir," my rescuer said, his tone markedly respectful.

"I do, indeed. I was with him only a couple of nights ago."

"He is a great friend of our nation. I wish there were more men like him to tell the world what our people are really like."

"He certainly has an unusually intimate knowledge of your countryfolk."

"Please pass on my compliments when you speak to him."

"I shall be delighted to do that. I am sure Sir Brian would love to meet you one of these days, Commandant."

"Oh, he already has, sir. On many occasions."

The infinitesimal upward movement of his lips would not have registered as a smile on any camera that might have been monitoring us, but it was sufficient to communicate to me what had transpired on those many occasions. Commandant Shams ad-Din left me with a polite handshake and a crisp salute at the top of the gangplank.

I found myself a quiet corner by the end of the open deck at the top of the boat, where I could stretch out half in the shade of the funnel, half in the comforting sunlight. I opened my passport and flicked through it: no sign of the shameful stamp. Looking around the deck, I spotted a nameplate which told me that I'd crossed the Channel on this selfsame boat as a schoolboy, in the days when it bore the name of Queen Astrid of Belgium.

As the engines began to drone and we nudged our way out of the harbour, I tried to count and catalogue the cascade of different emotions I'd experienced in one short week. I might as well have tried to count the waves as they dissolved in spume against the ship's rusty prow.

Many hours later, the elderly ferryboat crawled along the Straits of Gibraltar, eventually performing a laborious turn that brought her under the lea of the Rock and back around between the outstretched arms of Algeciras harbour, past the promontory known as Both Worlds. The clanking and crashing that signalled our contact with Spanish soil roused me from slumber, as if I were waking from a long dream that had indeed taken me to a second world. Now that I had awoken, could I safely close the door on that other world and return to the comfortable tedium of the one I knew? Or had the events of the past week swept me into new, uncharted waters from which I could never, ever return?

Interlude

A Battered Jewel Box
2009

I was stretched out on the chesterfield in our lounge, still drowsy after my sleepless night. The late summer sun was well up over the Mediterranean, flooding the room with vibrant warmth.

"I think," said Marco, breaking the companionable silence, "that of all the communications I never expected to receive, this one takes the bucket."

He was opening the morning mail on the desk next to the huge painting of himself.

"Biscuit. Takes the biscuit, not bucket," I pointed out vaguely, focusing more on the newspaper that had been delivered with the post.

"How many times have I told you in the last ten years? I amend the English language as I see fit, just like Humpty Dumpty. It's part of my unique charm, sweetie. Anyway, it's one of the few freedoms left to me these days."

"All right, point taken. It's too early in the day for the pity pot. So, what is it?"

"I'll give you the thrill of reading it for yourself."

He backed his wheelchair away from the desk and motored over. The oversized scarlet envelope he handed me was of a quality and mass rarely seen in the twenty-first century, and the heavily embossed invitation card that I slid out was equally impressive.

"Before you say anything, I insist we go. It'll be a total nightmare and utterly hilarious – I can't wait to see their faces turn green as we roll in! Book the tickets now, sweetie, and I'll start planning what I'm going to wear. We'll need to stop off at Madrid to stock up on accessories, I think."

The copper-plate inscription on the card certainly merited the build-up Marco had given it:

Her Excellency Miss Greta Lindberg, Headman of El-Velaj,
Dame Grand Cross of the Order of St. Olav,
cordially invites you to celebrate her One Hundredth Birthday
on November 15, 2009.
RSVP: The Mansion, El-Velaj.
Dress. Lodging.

Neither of us had been back to the Village for years – we made the excuse that Casa Morena kept us too busy, but for a long time we knew it would simply be too painful to revisit the scene of the events that changed our lives for ever. Beth kept us supplied with the latest gossip and scandal, and June was a regular (if somewhat managerial) guest at our hotel.

I fingered the heavily embossed lettering on the invitation with awe.

"For once, I agree with you. It's time we made our peace with that place."

"Well, that remains to be seen. I still have a few scores to settle, and a wheelchair is a remarkably safe place to settle them from. Even that shower of stumblebums would balk at socking a cripple in the jaw."

"Marco, I'm not coming along if the sole purpose of the expedition is for you to engage in a series of screaming matches with the Village idiots."

As was his wont, Marco had seized control of the venture, his script already written and ready to shoot.

"Don't worry – I shall behave impeccably throughout and of course I'll be swamped with sympathy and promoted to hero status forever.

But there are things that need to be said and done, so I shall choose my moments and do them. Do you think it'll be tails for the dinner? They won't show up very well in this thing" – he pounded the arms of the wheelchair – "and I suppose they'll get caught up in the brakes at the back. Oh well, you'll have to keep an eye on that. Devoted carer and all that crap, you'll love it!"

Beth pitched up, ruddy-faced and panting from her morning run. She always made a detour through the bungalows to check that our guests and property had made it through the night without major incident.

"Vomit on the veranda at number five, but otherwise all clear today," she announced.

Marco curled his upper lip in mock horror. "Really? Projectile or otherwise?"

"Do you have to show your intellectual superiority so early in the morning? It's just a pool of puke. Perfectly ordinary. I didn't stop to analyse it. One of the many joys of running an exclusive resort in a country where Larios gin flows like water. Anyway, you guys seem a bit stunned – what's up?" She spotted the scarlet envelope. "And what on earth has arrived in that?"

I got up to pass it to her, and swivelled Marco around so that he could precede us through the French windows and onto the terrace for breakfast.

"Peter, you will take me to Greta's, won't you – pl-eee-ase, *pl-eee-ase*! Say you will?" Marco pleaded.

I nodded my agreement. He reached up and cupped his hand over mine.

Almost all of our bungalows were occupied today, so we had to wait some time before one of the waiters climbed the steps with our tray of croissants and sugar-dusted *ensaimadas*, pungent coffee and, to my delight, a bowl of freshly picked purple figs with droplets of dew still clinging to their satiny skin. Conversation over breakfast at the long teak table on our veranda naturally revolved around speculation on the upcoming centenary.

"I mean, is Greta still capable of meaningful utterance?"

"More than you, Marco. June says she still holds court at Elevenses, and nothing happens in the Village without her say-so."

"Do you think they'll ring the church bell again?" The last time this happened – by special dispensation of the Head of State – was to usher in the new millennium.

"Well, she still has the ear of the powers that be, so I wouldn't be surprised. And there's no telling who'll come down from the capital – one of the top brass, I would think..."

"It'll be nice to see Trelawney again," I chimed in. "And all three of us could do with a break. We haven't been away together since we opened for business."

The reincarnated Casa Morena had opened its doors eighteen months previously as "a resort reserved for the most discriminating of guests". The huge construction project that preceded the opening had dominated our lives for several years. To my surprise, the hotel was already a going concern – not that we needed it to be, after the settlement following Marco's incapacitation.

As Marco and I sipped our coffee and smoked, Beth prepared herself for the numerous challenges posed by another day of catering to the demands of our discriminating clientele.

"Pest control people at eleven o'clock, and I want to be around when those Eastern Europeans in number seven pay their bill. Credit card looked a bit too flexible for my liking when they checked in."

"Rats and Romanians. I don't know how you put up with it, darling."

"What puzzles me isn't *how* I put up so much as *why*, Marco."

"It's because you love it. And you love us – you know that. You wouldn't want to be anywhere else on earth!"

"You might be right, I suppose. Just this once."

She rolled her eyes heavenwards as if to disavow what she'd just said, but I knew as well as she did that Marco's last comment was no less than the truth. Like each of us, she'd been transformed almost beyond recognition by the events since our respective departures from the Village nearly a decade ago. As I looked at this self-assured and surprisingly buxom young woman, I recalled the timid creature who used to cower over her calligraphy book in a corner of June's café. I pitied anyone who attempted to elude payment of their dues under her gimlet eye.

"Any airport pick-ups today, Beth?" I asked.

"Yep. Two Greeks. Romeo's taking the Rolls over at four."

This was one of the special touches that had helped our hotel establish its reputation. Visitors never failed to be impressed when a fifty-year-old Rolls-Royce Silver Cloud pulled up to collect them at the airport, with our stunningly handsome driver-handyman at the wheel.

"Oh, and remember that Federico's coming up to do a wine-tasting tonight," Beth added.

Our friend Federico ran the most fashionable bar along the entire coast, and the sampling sessions he conducted for us on his days off were always a hit with our guests – perhaps because they tended to degenerate into something resembling a game of strip poker as the evening went on.

"Busy day, then. Beth, don't worry about Marco's swim today. I'll take care of him. Sounds like you've got enough on your plate already."

Swimming was a vital part of Marco's daily routine given his condition. His adaptation to life in a wheelchair had been far from smooth or easy. For well over a year after his discharge from hospital, he simply refused to accept that his legs no longer worked. He would drag himself across floors, or up and down steps, in the forlorn belief that his powers of movement would suddenly be restored. They were not, of course, but the cuts and abrasions he sustained were horrific. Then he would burst into fits of body-wrenching sobbing that would give way to uncontrollable screaming, even more distressing for those around him. He took to the whisky bottle during this phase and I saw no point in depriving him. As the alcohol made him more maudlin, he would leaf through the albums of our past visits to flamenco venues across the length and breadth of Spain, or stare with quivering lips at the life-sized painting of his triumphant performance in Granada. Then would come an interval of comatose silence until he awoke, and the sobbing and screaming resumed.

But after about eighteen months, as the work of converting Casa Morena into a luxury resort got into full swing, there was a change. The screaming stopped, the sobbing became less frequent and we no longer found him crawling around the house or gardens in the middle of the night. He even took some interest in wheelchairs and chose an extremely sophisticated motor-powered model that was duly shipped over from California. There was an even more heart-rending aspect of this phase: he still had hope that something could be done. We undertook wearying trips to specialists in London, Miami and even St. Petersburg, only to be told the same disheartening news. Medical science could do nothing to make Marco walk again. Spiritual healers came to the house and laid on hands, or chanted in exotic tongues; masseurs and chiropractors would pound and pummel him, or drench him in exotic oils.

He'd plumbed new depths of desperation when he asked me to take him to Lourdes. We never actually made the trip. Marco wheeled over to me and stared me straight in the eye.

"There's really no point, is there?"

He spoke very softly, but with a resolve I hadn't seen in him for years. "I might just as well stay here and get on with it."

He sobbed, just once, and let a couple of tears moisten his cheek.

Then, after a few deep breaths, he looked up at me with a hint of the old mischief in his eyes.

"Come on sweetie, I'm famished. I'll race you to the kitchen – loser fixes lunch!"

The change in Marco was already apparent that same afternoon. For months, he'd stared on with unfocused eyes as the procession of architects, builders, carpenters and landscapers tramped through the property. On occasion, he would wearily throw in a word or two of Spanish to help Beth as she struggled to get some technicality across to the workmen. Otherwise, he seemed oblivious to the slow-motion chaos that transformed Casa Morena into something from a canvas by Hieronymus Bosch.

Now, however, I watched with delight as he began to take a lively interest in the work – or, at least, some of its less taxing aspects. He wheeled himself along the broad ashlar pathway linking the ten half-built bungalows, entered one of them and subjected it to critical scrutiny.

"Have any of those nincompoops thought what colours these love-nests are going to be painted? We can't just leave everything in terracotta – every cheapjack resort in Spain is full of that. Soothing pastel tones, I think, but bright and breezy. Yes – butter yellow, Wedgwood blue. And what about lighting? Don't tell me you're thinking for one moment of using those obscene fluorescent tubes!"

There was a pile of them on the floor.

"Parchment lampshades, soaring uprisers and dimmers, dimmers..."

Beth and I exchanged glances of muted horror. But this was far better than the months of indifference that had gone before, and at least there was some hope of support with an undertaking that was beginning to overwhelm us. Beth had originally come to Casa Morena to help with the considerable burden of nursing when Marco was finally discharged from hospital. From the moment the idea was first mooted, she was the most enthusiastic backer of the project to turn Casa Morena into a resort. By then, money was no object. We knew the settlement for his paralysis made almost unimaginable sums available. I was in two minds about the whole idea and at that stage, Marco could only focus on his own suffering. Beth, however, immersed herself in the details of the building work and soon revealed her natural flair for managing people quietly, but very firmly.

I used to come across her late at night, immersed in one of the numerous books she ordered online to develop her skills. By the time Casa Morena opened its doors to the first guests, she'd grown naturally into the role of manager. She also recruited a squad of immaculately groomed young men, decked out in khaki shorts and tennis shoes, who darted about the place under her command.

I went into the kitchen to make a cup of coffee and while I was waiting for the kettle to boil, I noticed a small, battered blue jewel box lying on top of one of the kitchen ranges. I knew exactly what it used to contain, for I borrowed it from Trelawney to bring back the remains of Commander Blaine's diving watch all those years ago. Marco found and seized it one day as he was rooting through the chest of drawers in the bedroom.

"I'll have that! It's part of my inheritance, after all!"

I'd never seen it since, and had no idea he ever looked at it; he must have left it there earlier on his way to the bathroom.

I undid the hasp and lifted the lid. Sure enough, there was the smashed dial, with a few fragments of glass and some tarnished screws. Although the leather strap had started to perish, I could still make out the old bloodstains.

But the jewel-case also contained two fragments of rusty grey metal that I couldn't identify at first. Then, with a shudder, I recalled what they must be. I cradled them in my palm and as I did so, my thoughts travelled back in time again, to the events that linked these decaying objects, and the day – nearly ten years before – when I returned to Casa Morena with the little box in my luggage.

Part Two

The Sky You
Gave to Me
1999

Chapter One

It was a grim homecoming indeed on that late autumn day, not long before the turn of the millennium. By the time I was safely back on Spanish soil, I'd begun to tremble with exhaustion. As I drove past the concrete sprawl of the Costa del Sol in sheeting rain, emotions I'd only read about in books washed over me in bewildering succession. Visions of a rosy future alternated with waves of remorse and shame that I could even contemplate a liaison with someone over twenty years my junior. In the end, all I wanted was to be alone for a very long time – to restore the comfortable dullness I was used to.

When I finally arrived, the house seemed even more arid and soulless than I remembered. The arduous drive had drained me completely. At four in the morning, I woke on the lumpy sofa in the main room where I must have dropped off without unpacking or eating. But those few hours of unconsciousness did nothing to bring me peace.

The next day, I drove the hire car down to Aguacate, the small town nearest to Casa Morena. I dropped it off at the rental agency and trudged up and down the main street, buying the sort of tinned and frozen foods that I wouldn't even have considered eating when I was a student. Weary already, I called in at the post office to open my mailbox. I sifted through the usual accumulation of bills and circulars until at the bottom of the pile, I found a handwritten envelope bearing a pair of pretty edelweiss stamps and a Zurich postmark. I didn't recognise the writing at first; on opening it, I was pleased to find that it was quite a long letter from my friend Alex. Knowing how far his disease had advanced, I didn't expect the contents to make easy reading

– even his handwriting seemed straggly and insipid compared to what I remembered of it before.

The doctor in charge of his treatment had "come clean," as he put it. 'A year at most; probably less'. The cancer was spreading, chemotherapy was having no effect and the time had come to put his affairs in order, say some goodbyes and have whatever fun was left to be had.

"Believe it or not, my friend, that includes spending some time with you before my onward journey, so I'd like to come and visit. It will have to be soon: the remission will not last long. I won't apologise in advance for being difficult company, but it will be easier to come now than later, they tell me. There is a particular reason why I want to see you. Call me when you've decided."

The rest of the letter described a boat trip on the lake that he'd made with friends, an attempt at a night out in the Zurich clubs, and harrowing telephone conversations with his mother and other relatives, none of whom could or would believe the news they were hearing. I decided to call him immediately and do whatever I could to grant his wish. I returned to the post office, phoned from there and was lucky to get him at home. We arranged his visit for the following week.

Now, at least, I had a purpose to pursue. Casa Morena was in no state to receive visitors, and I could hardly offer my guest baked beans in the barren kitchen. I thought about taking the easy way out and booking a suite at a hotel on the coast – but no. I would do what I could to turn the place into something like a home, and … what? Give Alex a suitable send-off?

Over the years I'd lived in Casa Morena, I'd managed to make it clear that I wanted only the most distant relations with Elena and her brother Pepe. Their right to live in an ancient cottage on my land was a condition of my purchase contract for the house. Now, at last, they saw me showing some interest in the place, and they forced their way through my defences with offers of help – it would have been stupid as well as discourteous to refuse them. Elena elbowed me out of the way and set about swabbing the floors and removing the grime from every corner of the house. Pepe came to repaint the bedroom Alex would use; new bed linen was bought, plants were lined up on the terrace, wood was chopped and the stove was fired up as the evenings began to turn chilly. Really getting into the spirit of things, Elena brought up a tray of *tortillas* and a rich game stew in an earthenware casserole the night before Alex was to arrive.

Now and again, my thoughts would turn to Marco, but the events over the water seemed more like something I'd read in a novel – somebody else's life, not mine. I was far too preoccupied with the rushed preparations for Alex's visit to wonder if or when I would hear from Marco or the other characters in the Village.

Chapter Two

Alex walked into the arrivals hall at Almería airport looking far better than I'd dared expect. But when we hugged, I saw that his watery blue eyes were somehow focused on a spot in the distance. All through his visit, he never seemed to be looking at whoever or whatever was in front of him, as if he was already only half-present. His face had become more puffy and flaccid in the few weeks since I'd seen him in Zurich, and he now wore a beanie cap to conceal his hair loss.

We stopped off for *tapas* at a café alongside Almería harbour. Conversation did not flow easily at first. I couldn't bring myself to ask him the simple, usually meaningless question that normally gets asked whenever two friends meet – how are you? I started rambling on about some excavations that had started recently in the castle overlooking the harbour. My only near neighbour at Casa Morena, a retired archaeologist, would bore me rigid with the latest details of this pet project of his if I happened to meet him while I was out for a walk. It was hardly what Alex had travelled all this way to hear about.

"Look, Peter, I'm getting quite experienced at handling conversations in these new circumstances of mine. There are a few who simply can't deal with talking to someone who's dying, but with most people, I've found it's best not to skate around the obvious subject, but not to dwell on it either. So, if you want details of the diagnosis, let's get that out of the way now. And then there are lots of other things I want to talk to you about."

"Tell me."

"It's pretty much as I said in the letter. Barring miracles, less than a year. The cancer is now in my spine, and I've found some lumps in my neck as well." He pulled the collar of his shirt sideways. "There – you can feel if you like."

I made myself do it. After all, we were considerably more intimate than this at one stage, although our one attempt at actual sex was quickly abandoned amid gales of laughter. I could feel several wobbly pea-sized growths in the hollow formed by his collarbone. Running my finger over them, I couldn't help thinking this was one of the places on a man's body that I found most arousing. As he well knew.

"Now then, that's enough! As you can see, it's everywhere. Riddled with it – that's the phrase I think is used. How ironic to spend half a lifetime avoiding AIDS and then cop something that carries the same sentence."

"What about the pain?"

"Strange, actually. There isn't really any pain. Bouts of weariness like I've never known. Breathing is hard at times. Awful headaches, that's the worst, but they should stop now I'm refusing more treatment."

"Refusing?"

"Yes. The chemo is utterly gruesome. You lose your vision for a while after you have it, you know – they don't tell you that, do they? And there's no chance of stopping it, so – no more. The doctors have sworn they can keep me comfortable with drugs until I'm ready to call it a day. It's Zurich, after all."

"A clinic?"

Of course, I knew the city had several establishments where the Swiss administered death with the same cool courtesy and efficiency as they showed when managing bank accounts or rack-and-pinion railways.

"Yes. I'm already registered. Paid in advance, as you'd expect. They even take Amex."

"Alex, is there anything – anything whatsoever – I can do to help you?" I realised how feeble my offer was as I spoke.

"Not a thing. Having me here for these few days is more than enough. Everything's as organised as it could be."

Alex drained his glass of wine, but the tray of *tapas* remained untouched.

"You might say that I've taken my life in my hands. Which brings us to what I wanted to talk to you about, if you've had enough of this subject."

"Alex, you can talk about whatever you want with me, whenever you want, as long as you're here. And you're welcome to stay as long as you need."

"Thanks, but a couple of days will be enough for both of us. And my time is limited, as they say."

I was amazed yet relieved that Alex had taken the initiative in this way. We were similar in many respects, but I always knew his strength of character and sheer determination far surpassed mine. He'd achieved high standing in our shared profession without the advantages of a middle-class background or a university education. In fact, he'd hauled himself up by the boot-straps from a ghastly childhood in one of the most depressed parts of Glasgow to a life of professional eminence and comfort in Zurich that many would envy.

I drove us to Aguacate, where I wanted to stop and pick up my mail.

I'd never liked the phrase "my heart leapt" because my literal mind dismissed it as a physical impossibility. But that's what seemed to happen when I saw what the mailbox contained: two personal letters, one from Trelawney and another envelope, adorned with artistic squiggles, from Marco. I pocketed them to savour later.

Alex stared at me in astonishment when I emerged from the post office. "What on earth happened in there? Did you have a knee-trembler with the counter clerk? Your face is completely transformed!"

"No, no, don't be ridiculous. Just a couple of letters I've been waiting for, and both came at once."

"I see. It's your man, I suppose. I was going to wait until we were at your house …."

"What do you mean? What man?"

"What's his name again – Marcus, isn't it?"

"Marco. No – I mean, there isn't anybody. What are you talking about? How did you know his name?"

A broad smile lit up Alex's face and for a brief moment, I saw again the handsome, rugged features that had turned so many eyes in their time, and had even cast their spell over me for a while.

"So what I've heard is true. The ice around your heart is finally thawing! You're in love. And you don't dare to believe it, so you're all of a dither and you think you're going crazy."

"Heard? Who from? You don't know anybody in the Village." He'd never been there and now, clearly, he would never have the chance to go.

"That doesn't matter. You can work it out for yourself. A shrewd observer, let's say. I'm told that a certain someone has started to unlock all that love that's dammed up inside you. At last! But you're terrified of abandoning your lovely, comfortable, solitary life, aren't you?"

"I'm more concerned about being slung into jail or being bludgeoned to death by his father."

Alex sighed. "Denial is an amazing thing. This is Europe, not Africa. Policemen don't come knocking in the middle of the night to haul us out of bed and lock us up anymore. Unless you're planning to conduct this relationship on top of that blasted mountain in Africa, of course. I gather the father is a bit of a bully, but stand up to them like a man and bullies usually run a mile. Anyway, you won't be including him in your household, will you?"

"Relationship? Household? Aren't we jumping the gun a bit?"

"Ah, yes, maybe I am. The prospect of imminent death concentrates the mind, I'm told. No time to waste."

By this point, I'd clearly lost control over the conversation and I had the distressing feeling I was quickly losing control over my future, if I ever had any. The last thing I'd expected was for the focus to be on me at any time during Alex's stay. But now it seemed that I was under the microscope, and he'd diagnosed my recent state of mind more accurately than I was able to. Alex seemed to be mapping out a future for Marco and me on the basis of what I'd tried to dismiss as lewd and improbable fantasies. Part of me wanted to talk endlessly about it, but I desperately needed a break from the daunting subjects our conversation had covered.

"Alex, you don't know how much you've done for me already. You can't imagine the chaos my mind has been in. Thank you, thank you, so, so much − old pal."

I tried to choke back tears but they dribbled down my cheek anyway. We hugged, and from the grip of this dear, dying man, a vibrant charge of strength pulsed through me, unlike anything I'd ever felt upon touching another human being.

"*That's* why I needed to come. You remember I told you I seem doomed to die without knowing what it is to have a lover. I urged you not to repeat my mistake. Now your chance has come, I'm telling you a thousand times over: take it, seize it, Peter, for God's sake do it − do it for my sake, even."

We broke our embrace and got back into the car, staying silent as we headed out into the open country. All of a sudden, the source of Alex's information came to me. How could I not have worked it out immediately?

"Purvis!" I said loudly, but when I looked over, Alex was sleeping peacefully. The lines of premature age had returned to his face as the wan sunlight played over his features. I didn't need his confirmation, anyway – Purvis was Alex's only possible link with the Village. I recalled they'd been in contact over some translation or other, and made a mental note to ask Alex exactly how that had come about.

Maybe Purvis wasn't such a bad sort after all. Perhaps he knew I wouldn't take advice from him, so he shared his concerns with someone I'd be more likely to listen to. If so, his action had certainly brought me relief. It might even have saved me from losing my mind. However, I had a nagging feeling that all was not as it seemed – as usual in the Village.

I remembered the two letters in my pocket and wondered if I could fish Marco's out and open it while I was driving, but we were swerving around the precarious bends on the narrow track over the hills towards Casa Morena.

As I unpacked the car and escorted Alex into the kitchen, I saw he was dazed and barely aware of where he was.

"Rest and some meds," he muttered. "I'll be okay in an hour or two. Just show me where I sleep."

I settled him down in the spare room I'd prepared and helped him unpack a formidable array of tablets and phials from which he assembled his dose.

"Cocktail of drugs!" he mumbled. "How dare they call it that? Some Bloody Mary, this is!" And in barely a minute, he was out for the count.

Chapter Three

He didn't resurface until much later. I poured a beer and lit a cigarette before carefully opening the envelopes.

Trelawney's letter, posted from London, was rather brief and factual. He'd left the Village and the country a few days after we did; he was staying in Doocie's London flat just off Sloane Square for the foreseeable future. He'd talked to Greta a few times on the telephone – she had no news to impart of developments in the Village, but advised him to stay put for a few months. London was cold, it was expensive; the English had become uncivil. The BBC had been taken over by the Irish and the Australians; there were more burkas on the streets of Belgravia than in the alleyways of Beetlebridge. He was unable to make any plans and saw no point in doing so. There was no mention of Tamir, let alone Marco.

Marco's message, most of it written in huge block letters on a page torn out of an exercise book, was equally brief but its tenor was very different.

Dear Peter,

Actually, I enjoyed meeting you. Largely because I've never met anyone remotely like you. You remind me of the extinct species we had to study in Biology. Some of them are quite quaint. But by all appearances you're still alive, so I've decided to make a project out of you. Purpose: to drag you into the twentieth century, which you may have noticed is about to end. Then you might even make it into the twenty-first. The first step is communication – nobody writes letters anymore. Frankly, I'm exhausted already writing this one. Get yourself an e-mail account. Clue: you'll need a computer. You'll manage because you're quite bright, so send me an e-mail when you've finished and I'll fill you in on the next stage. Which I think will have to be wardrobe. TBD.

Love Marco

(Don't read too much into that, by the way. You seem to spend too much time reading between the lines. Try reading the lines instead. M.)
PS. MARCOTHEMAGNIFICENT@SCOTMAIL.COM

I'd just finished reading this for the third or fourth time when Alex wandered in, rubbing his eyes. I gestured to the wine bottle, he nodded, and I poured him a glass.

"You got the news you wanted by the looks of it."

"Really? That obvious?"

"The cat that ate..."

"The cream. All right, I got it. Want to have a look?"

Alex grinned. "How could I not? The suspense is killing me."

I still wasn't used to these cavalier references to his grave state of health, but they seemed to be part of his toolkit for coping, so I attempted something like a chuckle as I handed him the scrappy piece of paper.

He soon let out a guffaw and was howling with mirth before he reached the end.

"It's not *that* funny, Alex..."

"Well, it is, but it's also just so...*honest*. I mean, he simply comes straight out with things I've been longing to say to you for years. I wouldn't call you a dinosaur..."

"Feel free. Go on."

"But you'd really have a far better life if you – er – got more in tune with the times, let's say. How you cope with carbon paper and Tipp-

Ex is beyond me. I wouldn't dream of working without my computer. What a gift to have someone that cares about you enough to turn you into a –"

"PROJECT!" We both bawled the word out together and dissolved into peals of laughter.

"Peter, you're going to have enormous fun with this – the time of your life, truly. But reading this confirms what I've heard – "

"From Purvis."

"All right, from Purvis. What does it matter? Although he did ask me not to reveal his name. Anyway, if Marco can write a letter like that, he's clearly not what you'd call a typical young man, by any stretch of the imagination. Purvis told me he's brilliant – that comes from his mother, by the way: it seems Purvis has had some dealings with the family."

I frowned. "I'm wondering if there's anybody I know that Purvis *hasn't* had dealings with."

"That's beside the point. It's quite a fascinating little document; in fact, the more I look at it. He completely reverses the roles. You'd expect the older guy to sort out the younger guy's life in a situation like this, not the other way around. It's not the sort of thing you'd expect somebody of his age to write."

"I never wanted to get involved with someone so young, you know."

"Well, yes, he's just coming up to twenty. So, there's an age gap. People will wag their fingers and tell you you're a fool or worse. Maybe some of them will be envious. Perhaps you'd prefer someone just coming up to sixty, or over the hill at ninety. He's tall – maybe you'd prefer someone short. He's dark – perhaps you'd prefer someone as white as the driven snow." Alex was becoming quite heated. "He is what he is, Peter. The world out there is full of men ready to walk into each other's lives. If you don't think he's right for you, get back in the queue and wait for the next one."

I wasn't clever enough to avoid the trap he'd set for me. "But he's the first one that's walked into my life since…"

"Me. I did try to walk into your life, but you slammed the door in my face."

This wasn't how I remembered that phase of our friendship at all, and there was more than a hint of aggression in Alex's tone now. "Perhaps someone had better warn Marco if you're planning to do the same to him."

"Oh no, please, please don't!" I cried out without thinking, then realised how desperate I sounded.

"I wouldn't dream of it." Alex's tone softened and his warm smile returned. "I'm sorry I was a bit harsh. But maybe this time you won't let your fear stop you from following it through."

I felt acutely uncomfortable at being confronted with the truth like this.

"You don't know how many more opportunities will come along. Life doesn't go on for ever."

Alex picked the letter up and read it through again as I sat in silence. "God knows what he's really looking for," he said when he'd finished. "Maybe just some affection, or appreciation. He probably has no idea himself. And of course, it's outrageously rude: most kids would expect to get slapped for talking to an adult like that. But it's clearly how he carries on with everybody. I shudder to think how he treats his parents, or how they treat him, for that matter."

"It's not untypical of my conversations with him," I replied. "I can see your point, but I also find the way he talks — well, refreshing, I suppose."

"You would, because you're obsessed with him."

"Obsessed?"

"Have you thought about anything else since you picked your mail up?"

Casting my mind back over the last few hours, I had to admit that he was right. I went over to take Elena's casserole out of the oven and set it down on the table.

"So, Peter, you're up to your neck in this, emotionally. Which also means you don't know how to look after yourself. The object of your fixation is domineering, self-centred, and totally convinced of his own perfection. Like I say, you'll have the time of your life, but you're climbing aboard a roller-coaster. You'll probably get hurt — and don't even ask me how it will all pan out."

"If I take it any further, that is."

"You can opt out right now, but my guess is you'll be down to the computer store as soon as you've seen me onto the plane home, and I don't blame you. But if you're going to do it – then do it properly, and see it through to the end. Never say die!"

"Actually, I was wondering about taking a look in Carrefour if we go shopping tomorrow …"

He chortled merrily again. "Hook, line and sinker. Even further in than I thought. All right, I'll come with you. Is there any more of that stew? First meal I've enjoyed in weeks."

I ladled some more into his bowl and our conversation moved on to the technicalities of connecting me to the modern world, then to other mutual friends and fellow translators. After half an hour or so, I saw his energy draining, so I asked if he had everything he needed in his bedroom.

"Yes, everything's fine there, thanks, but I do have a request."

"Whatever you want."

"Will you sleep with me tonight, Peter? I do mean, sleep."

I hadn't expected this. As I saw it, our friendship had only been able to develop and strengthen once we'd attempted, and forever excluded, a physical relationship.

"You're sure?"

"I'm sure. Or at least stay until the drugs have knocked me out."

I could hardly refuse, though I felt uncomfortable for more reasons than I could identify. As we got ready for bed, I saw that Alex was putting on a pair of old-fashioned pyjamas. Like me, he always used to sleep naked. He saw me looking at them in astonishment.

"Yes, what a sad purchase *that* was – I had to buy them to go into hospital. End of an era. Anyway, I'm used to them now."

After chatting a while, I thought Alex had dozed off and was snoring gently, but when I looked over, I saw that he was still wide awake.

"Anyone looking through the window," he said softly, "would think that we were one of those ageing married couples, so comfortable with each other there's no need for words." He paused and was clearly gasping for breath. "I did want that life with you, you know. Maybe it would have worked, if we'd tried a little harder. Too late now. Too late for everything."

"I didn't realise it went that deep with you."

"For a while." He fell silent again and I could hear the wheezing and rattling in his chest that I'd mistaken for snoring. "You will remember me sometimes, won't you?"

I could find no more words. I simply nodded, reached over and took Alex in my arms; we clung to one another, tighter and tighter, until my old friend's breathing told me that he had fallen into a profound slumber. I must have dropped off soon afterwards, because a sharp pain in my hand awoke me abruptly in the middle of the night. For a moment – a blissful moment – I thought I was back at Trelawney's house in the Village with Marco beside me. Then I realised it was Alex who was now clutching the same hand as Marco had held when it was freshly scarred from the events of that chaotic night just a few weeks before.

I took my decision there and then: *not this time*. This chance I would pursue with all the dedication and determination I could summon. If the world looked down on me because of my choice, so be it. If my quiet life was to be turned upside-down, maybe that's what I needed. And if I failed, if it all came to nothing, I could never chastise myself for passing up a second chance of happiness.

As the first glimmers of dawn began to permeate the room, I made my pledge: whatever it might cost to be with Marco, I would see it through.

Chapter Four

The rest of Alex's brief stay slipped by in a relaxed, intimate atmosphere. We drove over to Mojácar, drank far too much wine at lunchtime and spent the afternoon sleeping it off on a beach, stretched out on our towels watching the sun sink into the darkening Mediterranean.

On one occasion, back at Casa Morena, I found Alex deep in conversation with Pepe in the herb garden behind the cottage where he and Elena lived. Pepe was carefully plucking leaves from the different plants that grew there, rubbing them between his fingers and letting Alex smell or taste them. I'd never heard Pepe talk so much, and I'd no idea that he was so knowledgeable.

Mercifully, there were no more attempts either to skirt or dwell on the issue of Alex's health or the saga of Marco. The exhausting emotions of the first night gave way to easy enjoyment with little speculation on either of our futures. Only occasionally did I abruptly remember that these were almost certainly the last days I would spend with my friend. I suspected he was using his frequent visits to the bathroom to top up the medicines that would give him relief, although never a cure. But whatever drugs he was taking seemed to put him in such good spirits that it was hard to believe the reality.

The trip to the computer department of the huge Carrefour hypermarket near Almería was an eye-opener. Rack after rack was packed with glistening silver and black apparatus whose function I couldn't even guess at.

The place was largely staffed by youngsters, wearing colourful smiley name-badges. One of them rushed forward to assist. He had some sort of snake tattooed on his neck, and both his temples were pierced.

Knowing glances were immediately exchanged. It turned out that he spoke fluent West Coast American. "Sir, we need to check out your connectivity options first, then we'll get onto your tower."

"Tower?" I gasped. "Do we have to build one onto the house?"

Alex emitted an exasperated groan. "It's the box that'll sit on your desk. Peter, dear, I think it's best if you let me handle this. Why don't you go and have a smoke while young Federico and I get down to business?"

Those name-badges nicely eliminated any need for formal introductions. I was glad to see that Alex could still muster enough energy to flirt.

"Okay, hint taken. Should I give you two about half an hour?"

"Forty minutes and we should be done, eh, Federico? We'll fill you in on the details when you come back."

After I'd browsed the shops in the mall for the agreed time, I sauntered back into the computer department to find Alex and Federico eyeball-to-eyeball in earnest discussion.

"Ah, Peter, we're all sorted. Quite a set-up we've put together for you here. Your life will never be the same again."

Alex was beaming. "But connecting it might get a bit complicated. Tomorrow happens to be Federico's day off – "

"So he's kindly offered to come over and fix everything?"

"It will be my pleasure, sir," Federico chimed in. "I know the Casa Morena – I grew up in Aguacate and when I was a kid, we used to have fun on the beach down behind your house. Alejandro told me to come about twelve tomorrow. Is that okay with you, sir?"

"Whatever *Alejandro* says is fine with me, Federico. Look forward to seeing you. *Hasta mañana.*"

Years of living in Spain had taught me that the correct translation of *mañana* is "any day other than today" but just this once, it really did mean "tomorrow" – as was confirmed by the roar of a motorbike approaching Casa Morena slightly before noon next day.

Alex had already established, as if he needed to, that Federico was more than willing to have some "fun" with him. As soon as I was out of earshot, he'd forthrightly announced both his sexuality and his interest in Alex. Things had certainly changed since I was that age. I was genuinely delighted for my friend, and amazed that he had the stamina and guts even to consider going through with it.

"The doctors actually recommend sex, you know, while you still can. They even allow me to take Viagra occasionally with the rest of these concoctions, but I haven't tried it out yet."

Whatever concoctions he'd taken that morning had left him looking at his best – he was positively radiant.

"He seems a nice enough guy," I said, though he was rather too short and stocky to appeal to me. "You obviously clicked with him, so why not?"

"You really have changed, you know, Peter. In the old days you'd have been grumbling about the risks of theft, damage to your property, your reputation. Astonishing what romance can do."

"Don't start on that again, *Alejandro* dear. Anyway, I need to get on with making lunch."

I'd decided to make an effort at providing a decent meal without help from Elena, so I was still slicing ham and frying bell peppers as Federico dismounted from his motorbike. I opened a bottle of wine and poured them each a glass, then left them to tinker with the computer while I got on with the cooking.

By the time I served the food, they'd connected everything. A sequence of images of Seville and Granada was displayed on the screen and bewitching Spanish guitar music was pouring forth from the speakers.

"Impressed?" Alex asked.

"I certainly am," I replied. "Who chose the music? That's – what d'you call it – *bulerías*, isn't it?"

Marco, of course, would have corrected me brusquely.

"Nearly right. It's a *fandango*," Federico chimed in. "Sort of flamenco stuff. This *is* Andalucía, you know! But your computer can do much more. Alejandro tells me e-mail is your priority – we already set up your mailboxes, but we gotta enter an e-mail address for you."

He started fiddling with some controls on the monitor. The accelerating rhythm of the music, punctuated by the thumping of boot-heels and the clacking of castanets, left no doubt as to the activity that inspired it. Federico finished what he was doing and took a deep breath.

"Can I ask you a question first, before we go any further?"

He seemed suddenly bashful, and I detected a blush.

"Sure, anything you like, go ahead!"

"Are you guys partners? I mean, I don't wanna cause any trouble…"

"No," I reassured him. "We're very good, very old friends. The best of friends."

"Wow! *Gracias*! But sir –"

"Call me Peter, please. Or Pedro, if you prefer."

"You really missed out big time, Pedro. Your best friend is an absolute hunk! And such a gentleman, too. And here you are with this marvellous, crazy old house…I was thinking you guys were the perfect couple!"

Alex was grinning again. A shop assistant who'd flitted into our lives barely five minutes ago had come straight out with the truth. I'd missed out, big time. But not this time. No way.

Alex stayed silent, so it was up to me to reply. "Yes…maybe I did miss out. But sometimes it's better to be friends than lovers." I didn't dare look at Alex as I trotted out this feeble comment.

"Anyway, Federico, just – ah – make yourself at home. But not before you've set up my e-mail, please! So, what's this address I have to choose?"

Alex decided to rejoin the conversation. "Anything you like, Peter. You can have something fancy, like that friend of yours – MARCOTHEMAGNIFICENT."

"Yeah, Pedro should have something special."

"I think I'll have something less dramatic, thank you all the same. What about Peter123, or Peter1956, or something like that?"

"Come on, Peter, you can do better than that," Alex groaned. "You need a name that will impress people. One person in particular, remember."

I thought back to Marco's letter and had a sudden inspiration. "Okay, how about 'PTERODACTYL'?"

"That's more like it. We'll help Peter send his first e-mail, and then…"

"Then you're mine, baby!"

Federico was getting more forward by the minute, but I admired his directness. His English wasn't quite up to coping with PTERODACTYL so I ended up as PETERODACTYL@ESPMAIL.ES – even better. I started playing with my new computer while my guests disappeared for what I hoped would be a thoroughly satisfying siesta.

I was so absorbed in discovering the joys, temptations and perils of cyberspace that I lost all track of time. It was already getting dark when Federico ambled drowsily into the kitchen.

"Everything all right?" I asked.

"Sure. He told me the whole story. What a guy. What a fucking shame." Federico punched the kitchen table in anger. "I couldn't believe it. *Hombre*, he was so hot in the sack! But then he got kinda sick. So sudden, the change."

"I know. He has to take a lot of drugs."

"He showed me. I dunno what to say. This was just supposed to be a bit of fun, easy come, easy go, you know. I spent a year in San Francisco, I know how it works. But now I feel – well, I just don't know what I feel, except bad."

I poured him a cup of coffee. I searched desperately for something useful to say, but trite words of comfort were all that came to mind. "Look, Federico, you know you'll probably never see Alex again. Just be happy that you had this one afternoon with him and you made him happy. Is he okay now?"

"Out. Stone cold. Making that awful noise when he breathes." He stared into his coffee mug and something seemed to snap inside him. "Hey...I'd best split. I can't even talk about this. I just wish I could *do* something...but how...oh, *fuck*! Look, it was great meeting you guys, really." He picked up his jacket and shook my hand firmly. "Call me if you want help with the computer. See you around, Pedro. Thanks for everything. Ciao."

With that, he virtually ran out of the kitchen. Never to be seen again, I supposed.

I returned to playing about with the computer, but couldn't help imagining how Federico must be feeling. And admiring his honesty – a casual sex encounter had brought him face to face with mortal illness. He was out of his depth, admitted it and departed with as much grace as he could muster. He'd certainly earned my respect.

I went out for a walk. Alex was slumped over the kitchen table when I returned. As he raised his head, I saw his complexion had taken on a greenish hue, but he had a broad, dreamy smile and his eyes were sparkling.

"So, that's it." He sighed contentedly. "If that was my last fuck on earth, I'll have no complaints. I certainly saved the best till last!"

"That good?"

"Out of this world. Until I took a turn for the worse – Viagra is not a good idea, I discovered – so the whole story came out. He didn't bat an eyelid. Took it as if we were discussing the weather forecast. We talked about it a bit, then he took me back to bed and gave me the best massage I've ever had. I must have fallen asleep after that."

"Yes, he came through an hour or so ago. Pretty cut up."

"Who wouldn't be? I told you there are plenty of people who just can't cope with talking to me, knowing the facts. Well, Federico could certainly give them lessons."

"I suppose that's the end of it?"

"It wouldn't be fair to go any further. He'll be a perfect husband for some lucky guy one day, but it won't be me. I'll remember him as that lover I never had – just for an afternoon. That's probably all I could manage, anyway. And, Peter? Thank you."

"For what?"

"For going to your crazy Village, falling for your Marco, letting him turn your life upside down, letting him force you to get that bloody computer, dragging me to that bloody shop and letting me meet a guy I shall never forget as long as I..."

He cracked up and began sobbing before he could get the last word out. This time I didn't reach over to hug him. Our relationship had changed subtly in the last twenty-four hours. We no longer needed to try to be anything other than friends.

Best friends.

I just placed my hand gently on top of his and waited for his sobs to subside, as they did in less than a minute. Then I got up to pour out the remains of the wine from our hasty lunch.

"Talking of the computer," Alex said, as his smile gradually returned, "How are you getting on with Project Pterodactyl? Have you managed to write the perfect e-mail yet?"

"Well, I think I have, but I haven't actually sent it. Maybe you'd..."

"Cast a critical eye over it? Sure. Let's have a look."

By now I was feeling quite friendly towards the machine and was amused by its various whirrings and flashings. I proudly retrieved the draft and Alex pulled up a chair beside me. I'd written a good couple of pages and as I recall, it started something like: "Dear Marco, I was delighted to receive your letter and hope..."

Alex stopped reading it after a matter of seconds. "No, no, no. You can't write e-mails like the letters your grandma used to write. Get straight to the point and finish it in two or three sentences. This sounds like Henry James writing to the gas board."

"Straight to the point? 'I'm madly in love with you and I'll do anything you want'?"

Alex pursed his lips and expelled a long breath. "You said it, not me! Best to know where you stand, I suppose. But I think you can save that little remark for pillow talk. Let's see what we can come up with..."

Alex's fingers flew across the keyboard at lightning speed. In a few minutes, we agreed on the text of my first e-mail to Marco:

From: peterodactyl@espmail.es
Sent: Monday, October 4, 1999 22:16
To: marcothemagnificent@scotmail.com
Subject: Project Pterodactyl

Dear Marco,

I got your letter, thanks. Yes, I enjoyed your company too. I got a computer and an e-mail addy as you see. What next?

   I've no news of our Village friends, except Trelawney who is miserable and alone in London.

   I have an old Scottish friend staying with me at my house in Spain for a few days. You should visit sometime. It's a bit primitive, but the countryside is lovely.

By the way, is there anything you'd like from Spain?
Keep in touch X Peter

Alex scanned it one last time.

"Yes, that should hit the spot. E-mail addy – that shows him you've picked up a bit of the jargon. You mention Trelawney and me – just as well to remind him you have friends and you're not some desperate recluse waiting to pounce on anyone who comes along. Offering a gift is a nice touch. He'll ask you for booze or fags, I imagine. Now, do you want me to hold your hand while you push the button?"

"I think I can manage, thanks. And it probably won't lead to anything, anyway."

"Now, now. The power of negative thinking. Believe me: he's not going to drop this, and neither are you. I can hardly wait for the next instalment. Actually, I have a slight confession to make."

"Confession?"

"That's right. I've realised I'm a bit jealous of you. I have many faults, though jealousy isn't usually one of them. But my circumstances have changed."

"Alex – you know all about me and emotions. And you know why I'm not very good at them." I'd shared more about my childhood with Alex than I ever did with Trelawney. "The only one I really know about is fear, I suppose. If I'm honest, I don't really know what jealousy is."

"Then I think you'd better learn, because my guess is that you're going to experience it – sooner rather than later, from what I know about Marco already. And from what I know about you."

We were staring into each other's eyes as we spoke. I realised how much I was going to miss this man. "Somebody once explained it to me quite well. Wanting something more than you've ever wanted anything, and not being able to get it, is bad enough. But watching somebody else take what you want, as easily as a bee sucking pollen – that's the pits."

I thought back with a shudder to the night in the Village when I watched the shadows of Marco and Zeki locked in their embrace. Now I could put a name to the agony I experienced back then.

Alex went on, as if he were reciting a poem learned long ago.

"That's when you feel jealousy, pure and simple – people say it's born of love, but the fact is it kills love, and everything else, if you let it. I love life, and my life is slipping away. I don't want to be jealous of you, or anyone else, just because you have time to realise your dreams. But it's fucking hard. Don't think of me too badly, Peter."

I wondered if I'd ever be able to speak so lucidly and calmly about my emotions as Alex. I had a long way to go, judging by recent experience.

"Really, I'm just a sort of emotional cripple, aren't I?"

"No, you're simply a late developer. Through no fault of your own. And you know what? Perhaps someone who's also beginning to grow is the exactly the right mate for you. Maybe he can teach you to love yourself, or maybe you can teach him. It's the work of a lifetime – and you're the lucky one, because that's exactly how long you've got. So, welcome to the human race, Peter!"

Alex got up from his chair and walked over to check the computer. "Nothing in there yet. It's pretty late, but I wouldn't have been surprised if he replied right away. Talking of the time, I'm shattered. When do we need to leave for the airport tomorrow?"

I'd forgotten that Alex's stay was almost over. "About ten, I think."

He seemed to be utterly drained now; the greenish tinge in his face had become more pronounced. He made his way rather unsteadily towards the bedroom but turned to face me as he reached the door.

"Just one last request."

I flinched slightly, and he saw it. Surely not a repetition of his first night here? I truly could not go through with that again.

"Could I possibly have some clean bed sheets? These ones are a bit – "

"No need for details. Of course you can. Just a minute."

I fetched some sheets from the linen cupboard, handed them to him, and we hugged briefly as we said goodnight.

We both slept late the next day. I had to drive to the airport with my foot flat to the boards, so little was said in the car. Just in time, we reached the drop-off point at the airport – "Kiss and Fly," they were calling it now. Alex made our parting very simple.

"Goodbye, and thanks for everything, Peter," he said, and cupped my hands firmly in his. I mumbled a goodbye and he vanished into the terminal before I could say any more. A traffic policeman waved me on urgently, so I drove smartly out of the airport concourse and turned back onto the motorway towards Casa Morena.

I recalled the alternating waves of anguish and bewilderment that swept through me as I drove along this route on my way back from Africa. This time, I was perfectly calm, but profoundly sad, imagining what might have been, and trying to picture what lay ahead for Alex.

I'd offered to go back to Zurich with him, but he refused. He had a support network there – the hospital had lined up a group of "buddies" who could be with him night and day, if he wanted them. I had to accept I'd just seen my friend for the last time.

I couldn't have known that Alex's involvement in my relations with Marco was far from over. In fact, the curtains had not yet opened on the scene in which he was to play the starring role.

Chapter Five

Idawdled deliberately as I drove back home and invented some errands to run in Aguacate. The longer I stayed out, the more likely it was that Marco's reply would be waiting for me when I returned.

Federico had sent a polite e-mail apologising for his hasty departure and offering to meet up "just as friends, like". There were numerous messages from vendors of dubious products who'd already noticed my arrival in cyberspace. But nothing from Marco.

I needed to get on with some work but couldn't settle, so I wandered down to Elena and Pepe's cottage. Elena couldn't stop talking: when was my friend coming back? Such a *gentilhombre*! Lovely of him to spend so much time with Pepe...they got on so well, did I know that *Don Alejandro* had taken some of Pepe's seedlings back to Switzerland? How nice for me to have a companion of my own age! I kept smiling and nodding in what I hoped were the right places. Pepe stood well behind his sister, maintaining his customary silence, but even he seemed to be distinctly more cheery than usual.

I left them to replay their memories of Alex's visit, returned to the house and made straight for the computer.

Yes! There it was, my very first e-mail from Marco, the sign I was craving that he really was interested, that I wasn't just a silly old fool letting his fantasies run wild.

However, the two words in the subject line of his e-mail puzzled me: URGENT! RACINE.

I sat down squarely in front of the monitor and with a little flourish, pressed the mouse button to open it.

"Peter, you're wonderful. I knew you would do it and you have. Full marks. Talking of marks, the old fart who attempts to teach French here hasn't been appreciating my efforts in French literature recently. In fact, if I don't do better on my next essay, I'll be thrown off the course. Which I couldn't give a fuck about. Except it'll bugger up my uni applications. It has to be in on Friday and I've not even started because I've been so busy (thinking about Project P of course, so it's your fault). Do you think you could run up a thousand or so words for me? I know you're into this sort of stuff. Here's the title:

"Masculine women and feminine men: in Racine's world, sexual boundaries do not exist. Discuss, with specific reference to Andromache and Phaedra."

Sounds like a village we know! Simply write it as you normally would, I'll tone down your overblown style and put some deliberate mistakes in — just e-mail it by Thursday evening.

Love and kisses, Marco.

PS. Scots friend, not Scottish. Maybe I'll meet him one day. Maybe I already have. I get around Glasgow quite a bit when they let me out of this dump."

I didn't give a moment's consideration to the ethical implications of this request. Instead, I set about thinking how I could possibly write anything of relevance to the subject.

I'd waded through Racine's seventeenth-century French tragedies myself at school. At university, I had tutorials from one of the world's greatest experts on this very dramatist. But I couldn't remember a word she'd ever said except for "Pass me the ashtray" as she lit up another Gauloise.

Come to think of it, I still had a couple of her books somewhere or other…I abandoned all thoughts of my own work and sent Marco a brief e-mail to say I would do what I could and then went off to ferret out the books.

Somehow or other, I produced a respectable thousand or so words by Thursday afternoon and e-mailed them to Marco with a warm feeling of satisfaction. This was quickly dispelled by a sharp stabbing pain in my stomach, telling me I hadn't eaten for three days. I'd merely nibbled at a packet of biscuits, drunk countless cups of coffee and smoked far too many cigarettes.

Elena appeared on the terrace and strode into the house, casting a scornful glance at the computer.

"No good, that machine. Too much work. You'll be sick." She started coughing and made a show of fanning the stale cigarette smoke away from her. "House needs cleaning. Why don't you take a walk?"

She stopped short of simply telling me to get out, but there was no point arguing.

It was good to breathe in lungfuls of fresh sea air, but I stubbed my toe badly on a rock as I climbed back up the cliff path. I was more exhausted than ever when I limped back to the house. Elena had put another casserole in the oven with a note to say it had to cook for one more hour. I decided to amuse myself by exploring the internet a little more until my dinner was ready. What could I key into the search box? I tried "Blaine"; pages and pages of hits appeared. "Refine search," the machine told me. So I typed "Commander Duncan Blaine, RN."

Several biographies of Marco's father popped up, and even a few photographs of him in full dress uniform, staring austerely into the middle distance. I learned that he had a brilliant naval career, culminating in distinguished service during the Falklands War. More interestingly:

"Duncan Thomas McNair Blaine is the sole heir to the Glasgow-based Blaine cotton and haberdashery empire, with assets estimated at £500-700 million. M, 1971: Geneviève Belgentier of Paris, France and Antananarivo, Madagascar."

Money to burn, Trelawney had said. Of course, I was familiar with Blaine's cotton reels, knitting needles and suchlike – they were always on display in any shop that sold that sort of thing, and I could see the company's thistle logo in my mind's eye. But it had never occurred to me that a fortune of that staggering size could be built on such mundane products.

Ignoring the ominous bubbling noises coming from the kitchen, I followed the link to the Belgentier family. This confirmed that they did indeed have "some sort of firm" in Madagascar. In fact it seemed to own vast tracts of the country, on which it grew tropical fruit for export. Anyway, unimaginable wealth changed nothing – my feelings for Marco would be the same even if his parents were illiterate paupers.

My hunger finally got the better of me. I downed the overcooked casserole with a couple of glasses of wine, then fell into bed and slept like a log for the next twelve hours.

My effort at literary criticism scored an alpha minus. "But old Prendergast smelled a rat because I quoted so many sources. I told him to get connected to the internet, not that he has any idea what it is. You'll have to be careful about that with this next one. Use of English this time – piece of piss for you, but I've got to pass it."

This time he wanted a well-reasoned composition entitled "Music is thawed architecture. Discuss." Well, that would be quite enjoyable – but then I would put a stop to this outrageous form of ghost-writing. When I protested that it defeated the whole purpose of education, Marco pointed out the whole purpose of education was to get a head start in life (as if he needed one, with the Blaine knitting-needle conglomerate and the mango fields of Madagascar to fall back on); and in any case, most of his classmates at the crammer were paying agencies to write their essays, another service which I discovered was available on the internet. As autumn turned into winter, my assignments became more demanding and absurd: "Should Israel be a member of the European Union?" was a particularly thorny question to tackle, but I felt more at home with the Golden Age poets of Spain and "Would you blow up the Channel Tunnel? Give reasons."

Nor were Marco's demands on me limited to essay-writing. The strain of mock exams was so great that he'd run out of cigarettes; could I send two or three cartons over? He 'needed' to go to a party in London at the half term weekend; he could get himself to Glasgow but 'my miserable parents won't cough up for the train ticket.' He persuaded me it would be easier and cheaper to buy an air ticket online and e-mail it to him.

I was vaguely aware that my life, and an increasing amount of my money, was being hijacked, and I kept steeling myself to refuse these requests. But when it came to the crunch, I caved every time. Perhaps it was because of the compliments Marco lavished on me, or the occasional instances when he let his bravado slip.

"You know, Peter, nobody's ever been so kind to me as you. I don't just mean sending fags and writing stupid essays. I come from quite a privileged background as you doubtless know. Silver spoons galore. But sometimes I feel like I'm just a must-have fashion accessory that my parents use to keep up appearances. Or some sort of substitute. Thank you, Peter."

Marco's essays and certain other distractions offered by my new computer kept me so busy that I hardly noticed autumn turning into winter. I corresponded regularly with Alex, although we said little about the progression of his illness. Federico, too, kept sending chirpy little messages. Elena trudged in from time to time with wintery concoctions she left for me to heat up. By and large, though, I was back to living out of tins. I never did much to celebrate Christmas, and was unconcerned when I realised it was only a few days away.

⸺ ⬩⬥⬩ ⸺

It was on the day before Christmas Eve that I noticed an e-mail from a completely unknown sender, although I was now savvy enough to know that the .ch suffix meant that it had come from Switzerland.

From: nils.dettweiler@zbuddies.ch
Sent: Thursday, December 23, 1999 11:42
To: peterodactyl@espmail.es
Subject: Alex Macallister

Dear Peter,

I'm Nils from the Buddies network in Zurich. I found your email in Alex's emergency contact list.

I'm sorry to have to tell you that the inevitable has happened. Alex passed away late last night. We were ready to support him through his illness here in Zurich, but he wanted to spend Christmas with his mother in Glasgow, and it was there that he died. Peacefully, I believe, in his mother's house. It will take some time to arrange the funeral because of the Christmas and New Year holidays. I will go to Glasgow in the next two or three days. I hope to meet you there if you are coming for the funeral.

Sorry this is such a short message, but I have no more words right now.

Yours,
Nils

187

It felt like a dull, muted blow, not the sharp stab of shock or surge of grief I'd expected. He was gone; I felt empty.

I mooned around the kitchen, made a cup of coffee, didn't drink it, poured a glass of wine and drank that, then another. I really wanted to talk to someone – but who? Marco – well, I couldn't call him because I had no phone number for him. Of course, I would write him an e-mail later on. Elena? She and Pepe would certainly be distraught at the loss of their favourite visitor. I pictured Alex in the herb garden with Pepe and felt the first wave of sadness sweep over me. I decided to try Trelawney's number at Doocie's flat in London. He answered on the first ring.

"Doocie residence. Yes?"

Trelawney's tone was clipped, but his voice softened somewhat once he recognised me. "I am in isolation here, Peter, but it is far from splendid. I haven't felt so depleted for a long time. I have become a foreigner in my own country – an object of curiosity, or even ridicule."

I listened while he vented his spleen about the shortcomings of England in general and Doocie's apartment in particular. He was desperate to return to the Village – "Let them put me in the public pillory and pelt me with rancid fruit, if that's what it takes" – but apparently Greta had been pulling strings and oiling wheels, so there was some hope that he might soon resume his old life. "I dread to think what price she will extract for her favours, but whatever it is, it will be worth it."

I repeated my invitation to visit Casa Morena, knowing that he would find the accommodation even less to his liking than Sloane Square; he declined politely and when he finally ran out of steam, I told him my news. He remained silent for so long I had to ask if he was still on the line.

"Yes, I am. How thoughtless of me to ramble on about my own petty problems when you have had such big news. Of course, he was rather more than a friend to you, wasn't he?"

I told him what Alex had revealed to me during his stay, which he claimed to have worked out for himself a long time ago.

"Being rather older than you, I have reluctantly become used to losing friends in one way or another. I treasure my memories of them, but life is lived forwards, not backwards. You too are moving ahead – what news of young Marco?"

I gave him an edited version of our correspondence, omitting any mention of ghosted essays or extravagant air tickets.

"You should be more generous to Marco, you know. In case you hadn't realised, you two are going through what is known as a courtship ritual, and you are the wooer. Based on my not inconsiderable experience in these matters, I advise you to play that part more actively. Your relationship with Marco is not some kind of substitute for what you might or might not have had with Alex, you know."

Substitute? Where had I read that word recently?

"Now, I presume you'll be attending Alex's funeral, which as I understand it will take place in Glasgow. Scotland. The same country where Marco Blaine is currently residing, I believe. Might that coincidence call for some action on your part? In fact, does it not suggest that the wheels of fate have turned ever so slightly in your favour?"

This connection hadn't occurred to me at all. I hadn't even started to think about if or when I might next meet Marco in person. The novelty of contact via e-mail, now on an almost daily basis, was still fresh enough to keep me satisfied with the progress of the relationship, or courtship, or whatever it was.

As soon as I finished talking with Trelawney, I e-mailed Marco, telling him of Alex's death and announcing I could well be in Glasgow within the week. Within a few hours, the wheels of fate had indeed turned to produce a combination of circumstances I could never have envisaged.

Marco was spending the holiday period in Scotland – "parked with a ghastly maiden aunt in Blairgowrie" – but he was confident that good conduct and a plausible excuse would enable him to escape to Glasgow once Hogmanay was over. Just in time to join me for the funeral, which had to be delayed until the third day of the new millennium. When I eventually spoke to Alex's mother on the phone, she was in tears as she told me how one undertaker after another had been unable to offer an earlier date simply because the crematorium was closed for the duration.

"It's not something you'd normally give much thought to, is it, dear?"

The closure of municipal crematoria to mark humanity's advance into the third millennium of the Christian era – no, it was not an issue that most people would need to consider.

Marco, as usual, made no bones about his requirements and intentions.

"I shall meet you at the venue, or whatever you call it for funerals, and stay with you for two nights in an hotel of superior quality. You may book a double bed but the rules will be the same as in the Village. My dear schoolfriend Sadie may join us at some point. I shall need disco both nights after being bored witless at Blairgowrie, so bring dancing shoes. Actually, I don't suppose you have any suitable disco gear, so we shall buy that after the funeral. All clear? Oh, and sweetie, don't forget duty-frees."

The best I could manage was to pack an ancient black suit and a few other drab items from my limited stock of clothes. It was almost midnight when I remembered the old year was about to end. I wandered down to Elena and Pepe's herb garden and plucked a few sprigs of rosemary to leave near Alex's resting-place.

Yes, indeed, I would remember him sometimes. And I would never, ever forget the words of counsel that he had made almost his last journey on earth to give me.

Chapter Six

The first day of the new millennium found me boarding a near-empty night flight from Madrid to Glasgow. A crescent moon shone brilliantly in the clear skies over England. At the start of our long descent, I saw the spires of Oxford silhouetted in sharp outline and the Thames meandering towards the hazy amber glow of London.

I'd never visited Glasgow or anywhere else in Scotland before; I imagined it to be grim or at best featureless. But as the taxi sped through the city's deserted streets, I was surprised to see a magnificent succession of elegant classical buildings, some honey-coloured, others with a rosy tint. The hotel was equally impressive. It consisted of a row of particularly fine Georgian townhouses, subtly illuminated so the sandstone radiated warmth, even at four in the morning. I was welcomed courteously by an elderly retainer who offered to make me a cup of tea, and was escorted to a warm, sumptuously decorated room where I immediately felt at home. There were two single beds rather than the king-size that I'd reserved, but I didn't want to mention this shortcoming at such an hour.

Next morning, an affable receptionist helped me to access my e-mails on the hotel's computer. Nils from Zurich had written again to say he was here in Glasgow; he gave me a number to call so we could meet up. There was also an e-mail from Marco:

'I know I'm immature, and I put on a show of being insensitive. But I do want to give you the best support I can with this, Peter. You've been very good to me. I haven't lost anybody close yet, so I'm not sure how much

help I can be. You don't know anyone here, and Alex was a dear friend of yours, so it can't exactly be easy for you. But we'll get through it okay!"

I called Alex's mother. The phone was answered gruffly by a man who I assumed was a relative.

"Aye, come on down and join the wake, we're expecting another pal of Alex's here from…" He stopped to yell a question across the room he was speaking from. "Wha's that place Alex was hangin' out in?"

From the sounds of it, there was quite a party going on, and the refreshments were clearly not limited to tea and coffee. He came back to me. "Sweden, aye, thass'it. Come on over now, laddie, we'll make you welcome."

A taxi took me to the address, which turned out to be a fairly dilapidated tenement block in Partick. The raucous noise issuing from the windows on the second floor left me in no doubt as to which flat I was looking for. As I rang the doorbell, I started to tremble. This wasn't just Alex's childhood home – it was also behind this door that his life had come to an end. Marco was right – this was not going to be easy.

Nobody answered the bell. I timidly pushed the door open and was nearly knocked over by the fug of cigarette smoke. At least forty people were crammed into the living room and all of them seemed to be talking at once. Every surface was covered with open whisky bottles, ashtrays, discarded glasses and remnants of food. Fiddle music was playing; some of the guests were attempting to sing along. Several young children were playing on the floor, and there was even a pair of screeching infants in push-chairs.

A gigantic red-bearded man in a tracksuit, bare belly bulging over the waistband, seized my hand and pointed me towards the kitchen.

"Elsie's in there, hen – but she's not in a good way, poor lassie, as you can well understand."

He downed a hefty slug of whatever was in his glass and plonked a meaty hand on my shoulder to propel me through the crowd.

Elsie Macallister – I never even knew her first name until now – was indeed in the kitchen with several other women who were assembling sandwiches. She was one of the tiniest, frailest women I've ever seen.

Someone tapped her on the shoulder to signal my arrival. Just as Alex had done during that last visit, she seemed to be focusing on a spot far beyond the room we were in. Her face was drained of all colour; the high-necked black dress she wore and a smudge of bright orange lipstick only emphasised her terrifying pallor. Another of the women whispered in my ear:

"He died in her arms, you know. She'll never get over it, poor thing."

Mrs. Macallister stared at me as if she couldn't quite identify what species of animal I was. Then a brief flash of understanding lit up her face and I saw how pretty she once must have been, and where Alex's good looks came from.

"Thank the Lord!" she exclaimed. "You'll have brought the ham for Alex's tea, I've been waiting for you so long, dearie. He always likes a slice or two of ham wi' his tea..."

She began to dance around in small circles, hands raised above her head, singing snatches of some unrecognisable song in a surprisingly robust soprano voice.

The woman next to me pressed a cellophane bag containing a few slices of bread into my hand. "Give it to her, hen, she won't know the difference from ham. 'Tis a terrible sight to behold, what it's done to her, but there is no loss like the loss of your own first born."

I took one of Elsie Macallister's hands when she stopped dancing and placed the bag in the other. She raised the polythene to her lips and kissed it several times.

"He'll be here for his tea at three tomorrow, he's never late..."

So, this was what it meant to be *grief-stricken*. I managed to tell her how nice it was to meet her; as I made my way out of the kitchen, I heard her telling the others how polite the butcher's boy was.

Feeling quite overwhelmed, I set about making my exit as gracefully as possible. The giant by the door told me I could come back whenever I wanted. "We'll carry on wi' the wake through the night until, you know, the cars come at three tomorrow..."

I spent the rest of the day wandering around Glasgow on my own, drinking coffee and wine in stylish establishments that would not have been out of place on the boulevards of Paris. I enjoyed a visit to Kelvingrove Art Gallery, delighted to find that it housed one of Salvador Dalí's most famous works. I called Nils Dettweiler but there was no reply, so I dined alone and got a good night's sleep ahead of the funeral.

As I was breakfasting in the hotel dining room next morning, the receptionist summoned me to the phone. It was Nils: he was sorry to have missed me yesterday, but his partner was feeling under the weather.

"I hope he's recovered now?"

"Absolutely. He's well enough to come to the funeral, so we'll see you just before three at the Macallisters. By the way, we wondered what you were doing after? Maybe you'd like to go somewhere with us to relax?"

"Well actually, we – I, that is – there was some idea of going out dancing later on. You see..."

"Oh, great! So, is your partner here as well? I was beginning to think we were the only ones!"

"It's a little complicated..."

For a start, Marco wasn't my 'partner' – and relaxing quietly was unlikely to be his idea of how to spend the evening.

"Oh sure, Peter, we all know how complicated things can get when there are queens around! Don't worry, see how it turns out. But the funeral's likely to be heavy going for all of us, so it would be nice to take it easy in good company afterwards."

I brought the conversation to a swift close without committing myself to anything. Complications were arising even before Marco had made an appearance. Judging from past experience, things were likely to become far more chaotic as soon as he was there in the flesh.

To stop my brain from going into overdrive, I spent the rest of the morning in a glorious second-hand bookshop where I became happily immersed in the academic world where I felt safest.

I lost all track of time, and it was almost a quarter to three when I arrived back at the Macallisters' street. Well over a hundred people were milling about in the street, and their general level of inebriation had clearly increased since yesterday. Two men in sober dark suits were standing together in respectful silence, well away from the crowd – I immediately identified them as Nils Dettweiler and his partner. There was no sign whatsoever of Marco.

The Swiss pair were about my own age. One was a tall, lanky fellow with blonde hair and rimless spectacles; the other was stocky but powerfully built, dark enough to pass for a Spaniard. We'd been exchanging stilted pleasantries for barely a minute when a sudden hush fell over the crowd.

I looked around. The hearse was reversing slowly into the street. Hats were removed, heads were bowed, and the gathering took on a distinct air of solemnity.

At this precise juncture, the silence was shattered by a screech of brakes from the other end of the short street as a garish yellow taxi roared up to the space that the hearse was about to occupy. The red-bearded giant I'd met yesterday vigorously motioned the driver to park elsewhere. As the rear door swung open, Marco's strident voice could be heard clearly by each and every one of the assembled mourners.

"Well keep the fucking change then, and use it to buy yourself a map, you numbskull! Call yourself a taxi driver? You couldn't even drive a milk float into a fucking cowshed!"

I rushed over to the yellow cab. As the taxi driver spat out a series of highly colourful obscenities and revved the engine, Marco took his time to extricate himself from the vehicle along with a considerable collection of luggage. He was wearing a kilt and knee-length white socks.

"Stupid wanker thought I wanted to go to the Partick Thistle football ground, which is nowhere near Partick – as anyone who's been in Glasgow more than five minutes should know. I mean, do I *look* like a soccer hooligan?"

"For God's sake shut up!" I hissed, grabbing his hand to drag him across the street and away from the crowd. I caught a powerful whiff of alcohol on his breath. "This is my best friend's funeral and that's the hearse over there, in case you hadn't noticed. Have you been drinking? And what the hell are you wearing? What on earth will people think?"

"Now, now, calm down, Peter." He patted my forearm, rather as one might comfort a yappy dog. "To answer those questions in order: yes, I have, because it's a Scottish funeral and drinking is what people do at Scottish funerals. I have now turned twenty – not that you chose to mark the occasion with a gift – so I'm perfectly within my rights. I am wearing a kilt made of the tartan that belongs to my father's clan, because that's the correct dress at a Scottish funeral. And people will think nothing, either because they're too pissed or because they've got enough on their minds already. This isn't the Village, thank God."

I looked across at the crowd. He was evidently right on all counts. Several of the men from yesterday were now wearing kilts, though none so magnificent as Marco's. And nobody was in the least perturbed by his ungracious arrival – except possibly the Swiss, although they were clearly nonplussed by the entire occasion.

Now there was another commotion at the entrance to the tenement building. Elsie Macallister, wearing a full black veil, was being escorted towards the first car in the cortege by several other women. She was fiercely resisting their efforts to bundle her into the vehicle – I heard her shriek "I have to be at home for him!" – but they finally manoeuvred her onto the back seat where she was sandwiched firmly between two of them. The rest of us were to travel to the crematorium in various cars and minibuses that were lined up along the street.

Marco took me firmly by the elbow and steered me towards the end of the row of vehicles. "Look, Peter, I don't usually apologise for anything, but I'm sorry about just now. You're obviously overwrought already, and I'm supposed to be helping you get through this. I've lived in Scotland most of my life, so I know what it's like here and you don't. We're all one big happy family. And we aren't stuck up our own arses like the English – watching every move people make and scoring their social graces on a scale from one to ten. So just relax and leave it to me, okay? Now, have you got a fag? I'm *gasping*."

I was certainly overwrought – the presence of the coffin had brought home the stark reality of Alex's death, and I'd been wrong-footed by the strangeness of yesterday's and today's events. I offered him my pack of Marlboros. He took one, lit it, removed it from his mouth and placed it in mine, then lit his own.

I couldn't have felt more comforted if he'd flung his arms around me and smothered me in kisses. That tiny gesture changed my mood in an instant. I no longer cared what people thought of me or Marco – I was here to pay my last respects to my friend, and I would do so in whatever way and in whatever company I saw fit. I fingered the sprigs of rosemary in my jacket pocket and we looked on at Alex's coffin as we smoked in silence.

"Is that really him?" Marco asked after a while, his voice now quite reverent.

"Of course it is. I mean, it must be. Well, I'd never given any thought..."

"And that's how it all ends? A box? In the back of a car? It's just – utterly ridiculous!"

I could see that Marco was trying to suppress an urge to burst out laughing, but in the end he couldn't – it came out not as normal, healthy laughter at all, but a kind of insane giggling. I put my arm around his waist and he hid his face on my shoulder. When he lifted his head again, tears were streaming from his eyes but I could see he'd regained his self-control. I passed him my handkerchief and he dried his face. "I'm sorry, Peter," he sighed, "but – well, maybe this is a bit harder than I thought."

He drew a deep breath and clicked back into normal Marco mode. "My God, I've said 'sorry' twice in the last ten minutes! *You're* the one who's supposed to be changing the habits of a lifetime, Peter, not me. Now let's get this show on the road."

The Swiss couple were just ahead of us in the line to join the funeral procession, and the two of them moved back a few places to join us.

Nils extended his hand to Marco. "I'm Nils, Alex's buddy, and this is my partner, Sebastian."

"Call me Sebi, please, everyone always does, except Nils!" Sebastian had a resonant bass voice that matched his Latin looks. "I hear you guys live in Spain – do you like it there?"

I opened my mouth to answer, but realised that Sebi's question was directed at Marco rather than me.

Without batting an eyelid, Marco replied: "Who wouldn't, after Scotland? Actually, Peter lives there permanently, but I still have to spend half the year here – academic reasons. That'll finish soon and then I'll be there full time. Can't wait!"

This was the first I'd heard of it. Of course, Sebi saw nothing unusual in Marco's answer, and he responded brightly. "I'm half Spanish, actually, and I have some family down in Extremadura – but Nils doesn't like the heat, so we visit them in winter when it's almost as cold as here! Partners can be difficult sometimes, can't they?"

He winked at Marco, but Nils looked on stonily.

There was a degree of tension around or between Sebi and Nils – hardly surprising, since today's proceedings must be even more alien to them than they were to me. Nils mentioned the idea of meeting up later on and Marco scribbled down an address for them on his taxi receipt – "I can guarantee there's nothing in Zurich to match this place!" – and we arranged to meet at a disco in the Merchant City district.

Silence reigned in the minibus that took us to the crematorium. I felt unable to break it, though I was bursting to know what Marco meant by this talk of living in Spain.

A sign reading "Welcome to Glasgow Western Necropolis" told us that we'd reached our destination. I'd never seen such a vast burial ground. Our cortege took a full ten minutes to drive through the serried ranks of elaborate Victorian monuments before we reached the chapel.

We were all given orders of service fronted with a photograph of Alex in his heyday, smiling broadly – it was probably at least a decade old. The service was mercifully brief, given the glacial temperature inside the chapel: a couple of hymns and a barely audible eulogy of Alex from a priest who had clearly never met him.

"Alexander went to seek his fortune in a far distant land…"

I could feel Marco starting to shake with silent laughter again, but this time it was perfectly natural and I was tempted to join in. "Switzerland, for God's sake!" he hissed in my ear. EasyJet could get you there in an hour!"

"In his all too brief life, he never knew the blessings of matrimony, but his many friends and even those who had but the briefest contact with him will never forget his endearing charms…"

Marco whispered again, "What's the name of that famous sauna in Zurich, you know, the one with all the Asian rent-boys?" I dug him in the ribs to shut him up because I knew I couldn't contain my own giggles much longer.

Fortunately, the priest soon ran out of nice things to say. He chanted tunelessly for a short while, and then the assembled mourners joined in a feisty rendition of "The Day Thou Gavest, Lord, Is Ended", largely ignoring a recorded organ accompaniment that varied erratically in speed and pitch. The curtains in front of the coffin closed at a suitably dignified pace, and thus ended the living world's farewell to Alex Macallister.

Chapter Seven

We filed out of the chapel and walked round to the display of floral tributes. There was quite a showing of wreaths, arranged around a simple bouquet of white lilies bearing a card with the one word "Ma". Some kind soul must have organised it for her.

I ground the leaves from the rosemary sprigs between my fingers and scattered them over some of the other flowers. Marco took my hand and raised it to his nostrils. "Rosemary. For remembrance, yes?"

"Oh, you know, do you?"

"Hamlet, act four, scene five. I played Horatio in the school play. A miserable waste of my talents – I would have been far better as Ophelia. But they'll live to regret the error of their ways one day, when I'm a star."

"Yes, Marco, what is all this? You seem to have made quite a lot of plans since I last met you, what with living in Spain and..."

"Never mind. To be discussed later. Or rather, I will inform you later. Don't think you're off the hook yet. There'll be a purvey now."

"A *what?*"

"Purvey." He pronounced it to rhyme with 'curvy'. I'd never heard the word. "It's another boozing and gorging session after the funeral. I suppose the English just bung the box in the incinerator and bugger off to their neat little houses to watch Coronation Street. The purvey can go on all night, but I think we can escape after an hour or so."

He was right. The cars ferried us to what looked just like a country pub, set amid extensive gardens, even though we were still within the confines of the city. The sun continued to shine brightly, and anyone would have thought we were members of some social club enjoying our annual outing.

This was a far more lavish and better organised event than the wake back in Partick. A sumptuous buffet was laid out in the function room and waiters were on hand to serve drinks at the tables. There was even a piano, on which an elegantly coiffed young lady in a black satin ball gown was playing softly as we entered. Elsie Macallister was standing by the door, greeting each of the guests with a peck on the cheek or a handshake. She seemed to have recovered miraculously from the state she was in before the funeral, though she still had that far-away look in her eyes. She obviously had no recollection of my previous incarnation as the butcher's boy.

"You'll be Alex's friends from across the water, so you will. My, what a fine kilt, though I cannae place the tartan. Alex never wears his now, you know, not since his schooldays..."

She'd lost her grip on reality, but I was happy she'd regained some composure. I mentioned Elsie's improvement to one of the women I'd seen in the kitchen yesterday.

"Aye, old Doctor Allardice slipped her something to calm her down before the service. She'll be fine for a few hours more, but 'twill last no longer than that. God knows where it will all end, but bless her, at least she can partake of her own son's purvey. As any mother would wish to do, I suppose."

She stared down at her ample bosom as she considered this appalling prospect and took a swig from her glass, as if to dismiss it from her mind. "Now then, you gentlemen have come a long way – will you be giving us a wee turn?"

I couldn't quite grasp what the question meant, so I looked automatically to Marco for an explanation.

"You'll have to excuse Peter. He's a Sassenach, but a good'un." He answered her with a far more pronounced Scots twang than I'd heard back in the Village. "Some of the party will sing, or play, or even dance as the evening goes on, Peter. Do we want to contribute anything?"

"I think you'll have to excuse us…we're very tired after the long journey."

I thought I might as well cash in on the general impression that Europe was located somewhere to the east of the Gobi Desert. Marco silently formed the word 'Chicken!' with his lips.

I spotted Nils and Sebi, gave them a friendly wave, but deliberately steered us to the last two empty seats at an otherwise full table. As we ate and drank considerable amounts of malt whisky, I began to appreciate the musical offerings – most of them were unfamiliar Scottish melodies, but someone played Dvořák's 'Humoresque' on the violin, superbly accompanied by the pianist, and two children gave a touching rendition of 'Amazing Grace'. For the first time since I stepped into Alex's former home, I began to feel relaxed.

Then Elsie Macallister stepped boldly onto the small stage.

Every head turned towards her. Knives and forks were gently placed on plates; all conversation ceased; you could have heard a pin drop. She let the silence continue for a few moments, drew breath and launched, with no accompaniment, into a haunting, lilting lament.

Her soaring voice could easily have graced any opera house in the world. As she came to the end of the first verse, I gathered that the song was called "The Flowers of the Forest."

Before I knew it, Marco had risen from his chair and was walking up to the stage. As she began the second verse, he joined in, singing in absolute harmony with her, his rich baritone perfectly complementing her entrancing soprano. In this new world where I was the outsider and novice, I'd quickly learned not to trust my first reaction – which, in this case, was "How dare he try to steal the show?" But as I looked around, I saw that everyone in the room was spellbound. Many were weeping openly; even the red-bearded man-mountain was sitting with his mouth agape and a look of wonderment on his face.

When the beguiling melody drew to a close, Elsie took Marco in her arms and hugged him tightly to her breast. The whole house broke out into rapturous applause, with shouts of "Bravo!" and "More!".

Ignoring the audience's demands, Marco escorted her politely back to her seat. They sat together for quite a few moments. Elsie was whispering urgently in his ear – I supposed that her delusions were returning, and he was doing a good job of pretending to take her seriously. They clasped hands; he made his way back to our table as people slapped him on the back and offered their congratulations.

I was speechless. The others at our table joined in the adulation, somebody poured him another hefty whisky, and a toast was drunk to him.

"How on earth...?" I began.

"Remember I was incarcerated at a Scottish boarding school for about half my life. We were forced to grind out "Flowers of the Forest" at Founder's Day every year. I feel as if I've known it since I was in the womb."

"I thought dancing was more your thing."

"Oh, it is – as you'll see later tonight. But if we're going to meet up with Tveedledum and Tveedledee at nine, we'd better be out of here soon. I for one will require a lengthy siesta. I'd no idea funerals were so exhausting – and the strain of keeping you out of trouble is simply monumental. So, ten minutes max, and we're away."

We made our polite farewells, took one of the taxis drawn up at the entrance to the pub and were soon on our way to the hotel.

"What did Alex's mother say to you, by the way?" I asked.

He responded sharply. "None of your business. I can tell you this, though: she may have lost her marbles, but she doesn't miss anything. Maybe I'll tell you one day. When I think you're ready."

Chapter Eight

Back in the hotel, Marco swept into the bedroom ahead of me. He began distributing the contents of his luggage around the room with the skill of a seasoned traveller, shifting my possessions out of the way as he saw fit and gradually removing all his clothing except for a skimpy pair of briefs.

"Sorry, sweetie, this must be a little frustrating for you," he said with a simper as he went into the bathroom virtually naked. "But you'd better get used to it if we're going to be spending time together."

He opened the bathroom door again to sling the briefs onto his bed, then stuck his bare backside through the gap and wiggled it provocatively.

"There you are. Special treat because I'm feeling generous. See you later!"

I climbed into my bed in my boxers. It was beyond my capabilities to extract any sense from all the contradictory signals Marco was giving out, so I stopped thinking altogether and fell asleep almost immediately.

I was awakened by a telephone ringing through my dreams. It took me several moments to realise where I was. Marco, now clad in the shortest of Paisley dressing-gowns, was sitting at the desk in the bay window of our room, talking on the phone in subdued, clipped tones. Various documents and brochures were spread out in front of him. He sipped from a glass of white wine as he spoke; the bottle was in an ice-bucket at his feet, and he motioned me to help myself to a glass. He mouthed the word "parents" and tapped his lips with his finger.

I began to feel queasy at this intrusion into my privacy by Commander and Madame Blaine. Marco was talking to them with as much affection as one might show to a cold-call salesman. He brought the conversation to a speedy close and turned to me.

"Feeling better, sweetie? Ready for the next round?"

"Barely. I don't normally live at this pace, you know."

"Quite. No good dawdling along in life. A glass of wine will perk you up nicely. Chateau Plonko from New Zealand, I'm afraid, but it's the best I could find on their wine list. Now, we have about an hour before we head into town, and there are two items on the agenda."

"Being?"

"One: your appearance. Immediate and drastic action is required. Two: planning and strategy. Ditto. Things have just moved forward considerably. My parents called me from Paris, by the way, in case you're worried about the phone bill. We can multi-task. Start washing your hair and I'll fill you in as we go along."

"Wash my hair?"

"Yes. We start with the hair, then deal with the cosmetics and finally, the real challenge: your clothes. Into the bathroom, please."

There seemed to be no point in arguing, so I started shampooing myself in the sink – which, it quickly dawned on me, left him free to speak without the inconvenience of any interruptions.

"To summarise: *you* are head over heels in love with me. I have decided that I rather like you, but I am not in love with you. Nor, I regret to inform you, do I fancy you. However, you are warm-hearted, kind and generous. That much is clear from the help you've given me up to now, far beyond the call of duty. You're a beautiful person, but you're all locked up and closed down – I don't understand why. Even your friends must see that, and tell you so."

I thought of Trelawney's frequent discourses on this subject, and my last conversations with Alex. Nevertheless, Marco was hardly the person I wanted to hear it from again.

"And you desperately want somebody to look after. I, of course, am the ideal candidate, in your eyes. As luck would have it, I also need someone to look after me, in certain ways. You're not quite the ideal candidate, but you're the best that's on offer. Rinse."

"Rinse?"

"Your hair. With cold water. Too many suds and we won't be able to do a thing with it."

I stuck my head under the cold tap; he turned it on full and began gently massaging my scalp.

"You'll have noticed that relations between my parents and I are hardly cordial. I am, frankly, not up to their standards. Too bad. I might be able to live with that. But what I can't live with is their views – or actually, my father's views – on just about everything. They are the complete opposite of mine. For example: he thinks homosexuals should be exterminated, or at least locked up. I am a homosexual. I intend to live as one. Towel!"

I started drying my hair with the towel he offered, but I was doing it so slowly that he took over, inflicting considerable pain as he did so.

"As if that weren't enough, he has no regard for art in any form. As you saw today and will see tonight, I have considerable artistic talent. I intend to develop it and use it, and make it my life. My parents want to turn me into a haberdasher. Stuck in an office calculating the money to be made from knicker-elastic and bra straps. Over my dead body! I'd prefer to empty the dustbins in Beetlebridge for the rest of my life. With me so far?"

Since most of my face was covered by a wet towel, all I could do was grunt.

"Now for the difficult bit. Shoulders straight, head up. It's not bad hair, actually, considering how old it is."

He switched on the hairdryer and started teasing out the hair from the front to the back of my head with a steel comb, drying the separate strands like a professional hairdresser.

"I'm entitled to a year off before I start university, if I ever get admitted. I just persuaded them on the phone to let me spend it on an educational project in Spain – I told them I'd go and feed yak milk to deprived children in Kathmandu if they didn't."

"Educational project? Spain?"

"*Sí señor.* I imagine something could be fixed up in Almería."

I nearly choked.

"Except that's not where I'll be. But my parents have to think I'm there for a year, doing something they consider respectable. They'll pay the fees and a measly allowance. In return for a promise to do an MBA at university and then spend the rest of my life as a fucking shopkeeper. Eyes closed!"

He started rubbing some kind of ointment into my hair, which created a pleasant tingling sensation; then there was more brisk combing and application of hairspray. I'd never bothered with anything other than a short back-and-sides, but now I started to like the feel of this pampering. As to what I was hearing – it all fitted in alarmingly well with what I'd learned about the Blaines. As Beth and Trelawney had both told me: what the Blaines want, the Blaines usually get.

"I'll be coming over to Spain at Easter," he went on: "so you – I mean, we – can fix things regarding the project. With me so far?"

I had no idea of how we were going to "fix things," and something told me it was unwise to let myself be used as a pawn in Marco's elaborate game. But, as he well knew, I was powerless to resist. I finally managed to get a word in edgewise.

"Now have I got this right? You're going to spend a year in Spain, pretending to your parents that you're actually in Almería, where I live. But you'll actually be somewhere else."

"Indeed."

"Where?"

"I shall be in Granada. Where I shall study at the Academia Andaluz de las Artes del Flamenco. It's the best flamenco school in the world, bar none. It's my *passion*, Peter – it's what I was born to do."

"Flamenco? Granada?"

"Yes. You know it?"

"Of course. I sometimes take a break there – it's quite an easy drive from Almería. I suppose I could visit you from time to time. Or you could come over to my house at weekends."

"Actually, Peter, I was thinking...er...maybe you'd like to stay in Granada with me. We could get a little apartment..."

The penny dropped. The trap had been skilfully baited and now it was about to spring shut. I tried not to sound too enthusiastic.

"Not cheap, Granada. And I don't suppose the Academia is a charitable institution."

"Special rates for deserving cases. And they're keen to have foreigners." He pointed back at the desk in the bedroom with his thumb. "I've got all the information already."

"I'm sure you have. And all you want me to do is sign the papers, pay the bill and help you persuade your parents that you're spending the year on some worthy academic venture in Almería. Right?"

He stopped fiddling about with my hair, placed both hands on my shoulders and stared straight into my eyes in the mirror. "Pl-eee-ase, *pl-eee-ase*! Say you'll help me, Peter!"

I heard Trelawney's voice in my mind – *you should be more generous to him, you know. And Alex was there again – your chance has come, so take it, seize it.* The two best friends I'd ever had. But the whole idea sounded dubious and it would stretch my finances to the limit. The school fees would only be the beginning, of course.

Then again, what was I planning to do with the rest of my life if I didn't go along with Marco's scheme?

I remained silent for what I thought was a suitable period of time – just to let him know I wasn't a complete push-over. About five seconds, I should think. "All right, Marco. I'm game. Let's give it a try."

"I knew you would! Thank you, thank you, Peter. It means everything to me."

He threw his arms around me and planted a kiss right on my lips – no tongue, and only for an instant, but even so I thought I was going to faint. "Now, take a look in the mirror. Quite a success, I would say."

It certainly was. My hair had doubled in volume, he'd added a slight auburn tint to match his own, and the old styleless cut was transformed into an interesting series of waves and peaks.

"There. You never know, if we carry on like this, I might get around to fancying you after all! Now, makeup."

"I really don't need any, Marco. I've never worn it and I honestly don't like it on men."

"Trust me. Just a touch here and there." He started fishing tubes and pots out of one of his several toilet bags and began dabbing my face. "Whitener to hide the bags under your eyes...a tiny *touch* of mascara...and a little eyebrow pencil, I think. Eyes closed again, please."

While he daubed and massaged various parts of my face, I pondered the decision I'd made with such disconcerting ease. For a split second, I considered taking it back and finishing the whole charade there and then. But only for a split second. My doubts vanished into thin air as I recalled the exhilaration I'd been feeling all day – and crazy though the proposed adventure might be, it was already giving my life a purpose that had certainly been lacking until now. I couldn't wait to hear what Alex would say when I told him about the plan – and then I remembered, with a sudden pang of sorrow.

"I can hear you thinking. Tell me your thoughts," Marco said as he applied the pencil to my eyebrows with such force that I thought it would cut the skin open.

"Well, to be honest, I'm surprised at myself. But I'm a bit worried about getting on the wrong side of your parents..."

"They'll never know who you really are. And believe me, they'll thank you for taking me off their hands."

"They *do* know I exist, because they've seen me in the Village."

"In one eye and out the other. They couldn't care less about anyone who doesn't fit into their cocktail party circuit, which you definitely don't. *I* expect to have a rough ride with them, but that's the price I shall have to pay for my freedom."

He paused. "I can tell you're excited, Peter. You're starting to come alive! I mean, I do want to give you something in return – I'm not all take and no give, deep down. You love being with me – just look how happy you've been with me today – at a funeral, for God's sake! And just remember how you loved every minute of our time together in the Village! I can't and I won't give you sex, but I will change your life for the better. I promise you that...and I don't make promises lightly."

"I believe you, Marco." And I truly did.

"Right, we're almost out of time. Clothes. I've been through your suitcase. Its contents are *grotesque*, but I cobbled something together earlier on."

He led me briskly by the hand back into the bedroom, where my black suit was laid out on the bed next to a bright pink T-shirt emblazoned with the words "People Like Us Like People Like Us!" in fluorescent rainbow colours.

"I can't...!" I spluttered.

"Yes you can. Just try it. That shirt is a designer garment, by the way. And there's no time to argue, we've to be at the club in fifteen minutes." I put on the trousers and the T-shirt. "Suit jacket over the shoulders, *not* buttoned up. Mind the sleeves and collar, I used boot polish to get rid of the mildew. Now, turn around..."

I caught sight of my reflection in the mirror on the wardrobe door. For a brief instant, I had the impression that a total stranger had somehow entered the room. And quite a handsome one, at that.

Marco stepped back and nodded his approval. "See what the world's been missing all these years? If we can achieve that in one evening, just imagine what can happen in a whole year. Now, call a taxi while I get ready myself. You'll notice I've sacrificed my own preparations for your sake...but then, the beauty of youth needs no adornment."

"Where are we going?" I asked, as he disappeared into the bathroom.

"De La Rue's. They'll know it. Ask for the cab immediately and forthwith, if not sooner."

Marco emerged in surprisingly sober garb – a plain white shirt, tight-fitting black trousers and stacked-heel black patent leather boots. We grabbed our overcoats and headed out into the bitter chill of a clear January night in Glasgow.

Chapter Nine

De La Rue's was an impressive and luxurious establishment, spread over several stories of another graceful building in the Georgian style. A liveried doorman waved us through to the huge dance floor.

We found the Swiss couple upstairs in a secluded alcove. Nils was sipping from a can of Diet Coke, but Sebi had ordered champagne which was standing in an ice-bucket in front of them. He jumped to his feet and deftly poured us a glass each from a bottle that was already nearly empty.

We sat down side by side on the sofa opposite them and began to trade small talk about architecture, the weather, the Glasgow transport system. Soon in need of a cigarette, I asked Marco if there was anywhere we could light up.

"Right at the top – it's got the most stunning view of Glasgow."

Sebi leapt up. "Can I join you? I don't smoke normally, but it's been a stressful day."

Nils scowled. "I'll wait here."

The three of us trooped up a spiral staircase that led into a glassed-in dome with a stupendous view of the city, the glinting Clyde and its stark, ghostly rows of immobile cranes in the distance.

"I have to apologise about Nils," Sebi said as we smoked and admired the vista. "I love him deeply, but this Buddy thing – it's very difficult for him when they die. He stays depressed for days. I understand it, but – well, I never even met this Alex. Nils seems worse this time, somehow. Now he doesn't like it because I want to forget it, relax, have some fun, and..."

"Yes," Marco chimed in. "Actually, I never met Alex either – he was Peter's friend, so of course I wanted to show him some support at the funeral." He turned to me with a simper. "But now it's over, we won't let it spoil our evening out, will we, sweetie?"

Marco was quickly warming to the role of caring partner, no matter how far from reality it might be; and Sebi was clearly impressed by the performance.

"You two seem to get on very well. And so smart, the pair of you – Peter, you look completely different from this afternoon, I almost didn't recognise you!"

I thought I'd play along, just to see how it felt. "Yes, Marco's amazing with fashion – I haven't a clue myself, but he's so good at it, I always just sit back and let him dress me!"

With what I thought was a suitably suave gesture, I adjusted my jacket to make it sit more closely over my shoulders. My fingers came away from the lapels blackened with boot polish. Marco chortled. I stuffed my hands into my trouser pockets and wondered how soon I could get to a bathroom. The music downstairs suddenly soared to a deafening volume, and the whole building started vibrating to the beat of thundering drums.

"FROZEN!" Marco yelled. I looked at him, mystified. "It's the title of the song, sweetie! Madonna! Our heroine!"

I vaguely remembered the T-shirt Marco was wearing when we first met.

"Come on Sebi, you like to dance, let's get down there!"

They raced off to the dance floor. I thought I'd delay my appearance there by checking up on Nils, who was probably as unwilling to dance as I was. I managed to scrub most of the boot polish off my fingers in a toilet half-way down the stairs, though some unsightly traces remained under my nails. I tried to scrape the gunge out with a coin, and only succeeded in painfully cracking my thumbnail. I let out some choice swear-words.

Nils was still hunched in front of his Coke with the same abject expression on his face.

"Mind if I join you again?" I asked, as cheerily as I could.

He gestured me to sit opposite him, but said nothing.

"I can see it's been an upsetting day for you, Nils. Maybe you'd prefer to go back to your hotel now?"

"It's not only today. I've been…an idiot, really. Do you mind if we speak German? Somehow I feel I can talk to you about it…"

He relaxed a little as he lapsed into his own language. He described the Zurich Buddy network; he was a founder member. They started by supporting AIDS patients but soon extended it to gay men coping alone with diseases that received less media attention.

"We're all just ordinary guys – we had some training, elementary nursing, psychology, that sort of thing. I even went on a bereavement course, knowing that some of the men I was helping were bound to die. And they did. Alex was the fifth, actually. But this time it's different."

"Yes, Sebi said you were having a particularly hard time of it."

"Ha! He only knows half the story. You see, I made the one mistake you should never make. I fell for Alex."

"Oh." He was fighting back tears. I really didn't want to add to his anguish by telling him about my own history with Alex, so I waited for him to find his voice again.

"I mean, I fell deeply, totally in love with him. I couldn't think about anything or anyone else. We're about the same age, Peter, you and I – we're old enough to know the difference between a teenage crush and true love. Sebi knew something was going on – but not who it was. I felt so bad at home, I couldn't even touch my own partner, let alone have sex – what a fucking mess."

I thought my emotional crisis when I returned from Africa was bad enough, but this sounded even more agonising. "Did you tell Alex how you felt?"

"That was the worst of it. I made a firm decision to do my duty as a carer and never say a word about my feelings. How could I put that burden on someone who was so ill?"

I tried to imagine how hard it would be to feel for Marco as I did, to be with him, but never to utter a word about my feelings. Nils clearly had an exceptional degree of self-control.

"I hadn't had a proper night's sleep for weeks. I thought I'd go mad if I didn't relieve the pressure inside my head. So, I decided to tell Alex. If that meant losing Sebi, so be it. I knew what I'd say and no matter how he responded, I'd accept it. I had a key to his flat, so I let myself in as usual..."

He was close to tears again. I offered him the last dribble of warm champagne from the bottle, but he waved it away. "It was very quiet. Alex was usually up by that time, watching television or trying to make breakfast in the kitchen. I feared the worst, so I rushed into his bedroom – and there he was, in bed with his arms around some podgy little Spanish guy, covered in tattoos..."

Federico.

My admiration for the young man from Almería shot up. So, he'd travelled all that way to make my friend happy.

"They laughed. They actually *laughed* – they thought it was hilarious that I'd burst in on their – whatever they were doing. He even introduced me to the kid, some money-grabbing layabout, I suppose. He got out of bed to shake my hand, stark naked for God's sake, and didn't seem the least bit embarrassed. Alex told me the kid was moving in with him until...the end. My services were clearly no longer required."

"And did he stay? I mean – is Federico still in Zurich now?" I asked, rather too eagerly.

There was an icy pause. "How do you know his name?"

"I – er – well, they met through me, actually. While Alex was visiting me in Spain."

I was suddenly aware of the flimsy chain of coincidences that shape our lives. If Marco hadn't forced his way into Trelawney's garden that day, if I hadn't "fallen" for him, if I'd already had a computer like almost everyone else did, if Federico hadn't been working in the shop that particular day...

"I'm sorry, Nils. I didn't mean to...How could I possibly have known?"

"Of course. I can't be angry at you." He clearly was, but he stifled it. "And to answer your question, yes, the kid did stay. He was doing everything for Alex – cooking, washing him, taking him to the hospital, they even went on a little holiday in the mountains. I think he's still in Alex's apartment. I'm sure he could smell money."

I wasn't standing for this. "No, I can tell you for sure that Federico isn't like that. To be honest, I couldn't think of anyone better to stay with Alex in those last weeks. Believe me." In fact, I was overjoyed to discover that the last stage of Alex's life had been so very different from what I'd imagined.

I suggested that we should rejoin Marco and Sebi, but Nils couldn't stop talking now the floodgates had opened.

"I don't know what to believe. It was something Alex said that made me change my mind about telling him. He told me, one day, that he was doomed to die without knowing what it is to have a lover. I could have been that lover."

I inhaled deeply. "So could I, Nils. Many years before. But it didn't happen, for either of us. And in the end, Alex had his lover, even if it was only for a short time. Can't you be happy for him?"

He stared down at his can of Coke without answering.

"Anyway, you still have Sebi – I'm no expert on these matters, but somehow I don't think he's going to walk out on you over this."

"And you have Marco. He's quite a character, isn't he? And so handsome...he could have any guy in this place, just by snapping his fingers."

The same thought struck us both at the same time. Our jaws dropped.

"Okay, let's find them," I said.

We elbowed our way through the gyrating crowds as we scoured the dance floor for them. We checked dark alcoves where bodies were sprawled across one another.

We eventually found two empty seats away from the dance floor and flopped onto them, but I quickly gathered why they were vacant. There was an overpowering stench of drains in this particular spot. Sure enough, we'd stationed ourselves directly in front of the establishment's principal lavatories.

I was just turning around to try and console Nils when Sebi emerged from the gents looking distinctly sheepish – followed closely by Marco, whose face was now the colour of ripe rhubarb.

"Peee-taahh!" he yelled, as he lurched over to us and threw his arms around me. "Are you all right, sweetie? I thought you might have passed out with the stress of it all, I know this isn't exactly your scene! Hi Nils, how you doing? C'mon, guys, time to dance!"

He grabbed my hand and started dragging me towards the dance floor. Sebi cautiously took my place next to Nils and they embarked on a clearly painful conversation which I was glad not to overhear.

"So," I bellowed into Marco's ear as he hustled me along, "did you, er, have a good time?"

"She's a complete slut. Didn't you realise we were in the cubicle when you were trying to give yourself a manicure in the upstairs toilet? I thought I was going to die laughing when I saw you farting about through the crack in the door. She couldn't keep her hands off me. And then she demanded more as soon as we got down here!"

Marco's carefree, shameless exuberance got the better of me, and I burst out laughing. The way he referred to men as "she" – I'd forgotten that British gays like to do that – turned the whole episode into an inconsequential farce.

"And she's completely useless! No technique, teeth feel like they've been sharpened with a file – ugh! – and..." He waggled his little finger to indicate what he clearly rated as Sebi's most serious shortcoming. "Three out of ten. If that. Remind me to bypass Switzerland next time I'm crossing the continent. No wonder they've never managed to multiply much."

As he talked, Marco steered us through the heaving mass of bodies to the glass enclosure where the DJ was working. They conferred briefly and he emerged beaming.

"OK, Peter, here we go. Just relax, enjoy – and be proud, if you like."

The dance music stopped abruptly and was replaced by a blare of trumpets, heralding the song about love and insanity that every radio station in Spain had been playing for the last year.

A cry went up from the crowd: "Ricky! Ricky!" and then "Marco! Marco!"

The crowd parted around Marco and a spotlight flashed on above him. What I supposed to be a random area of the dance-floor was actually a circular platform that ascended slowly until Marco's feet were at shoulder level to the rest of the crowd. As he began to dance, all eyes turned towards him.

And no wonder.

On that tiny stage, he pranced and bounded with the vitality and grace of an impala – then all of a sudden, he was crouching gorilla-style with his arms dangling down to the floor. In another split second, his arms shot upwards, first to flourish an imaginary bullfighter's cape, then to pluck invisible castanets from the air; as he raised them aloft, his whole body arched backwards in a pose of supreme sexual provocation. His face was contorted with a succession of violent emotions: blazing rage and shocked grief gave way to ecstatic delirium – how could someone so young possibly understand, let alone convey, feelings of such depth?

Then, in mid-flow, the music came to a sudden halt – but not the beat, which Marco continued to stamp out with his heels as the crowd fell silent in anticipation of what was to come.

Now I realised the boots he was wearing were no ordinary footwear, but genuine *botas de flamenco*, their soles studded with row upon row of pan-headed nails. Their rhythmic pounding echoed across the immense arena.

As he quickened the pace, the spotlight honed in on his feet, but all you could make out was a blur of frenzied movement. In stark contrast, the rest of his body remained miraculously immobile except for his fingers, which he seductively clenched and uncurled above his head. And just when I expected his performance to a close with an even more spectacular turn of speed, exactly the opposite happened. He reduced the rhythm to walking pace – then slower and slower still, until two or three seconds elapsed between each impact.

For the second time that day, I was surrounded by a huge, silent crowd that was held in thrall by just one person.

The crowd waited, breathless – Marco remained still, his head now sunk on his chest, his black-and-white costume standing out in masterly simplicity against the rainbow colours of the crowd.

He stamped just once more; the lights went back on, the music blasted through the speakers again, everyone began to dance – and for a brief moment, Marco was just another somewhat tipsy, giggling youngster before he somersaulted off the platform to land amid his whooping admirers.

His performance left me in a kind of trance. The place was packed with vast numbers of Marco's friends, and it seemed only fair to give him time to enjoy their company. I found myself a stool at a bar and ordered an "energy drink," which didn't seem to have much effect.

So much had happened in one day that I gave up trying to make sense of it. As for the preposterous scheme that Marco had come up with: how on earth could I find some activity that was credible enough for Marco's parents to accept? I kept myself to myself down in Spain, that was the whole point of living in Casa Morena. I hardly ever talked to anybody except...except when I ran into my archaeologist neighbour and had to endure his monologues on the castle excavations! What was his name now? Don Victorio, yes, that was it...maybe he could be drafted in! But even if I could get him to play along, what if Marco's parents found out that he was actually at a flamenco school in Granada?

"Welcome to the human race, Peter," Alex had said to me not long ago. Now I saw his point. The defensive walls I'd so carefully erected around my life were crumbling by the minute. And far from being terrified, I was bursting with eagerness to finish the job of demolishing them and start living a life that had some meaning to it.

I was almost nodding off at the bar when I was aroused by Marco jamming his fingers into my ribcage.

"Wakey-wakey, party ain't over till the fat lady sings!" he screeched. He was accompanied by quite an entourage, including a bulky young woman sporting a moustache of impressive density.

"I'd like you to meet my dear, dear, former classmate and respected mentor, Sadie. Sadie, this is Peter, a translator. Peter, this is Sadie, a dominatrix."

"Charmed, I'm sure," she said, extending the back of her hand. I took the line of least resistance and brushed it with my lips.

She appeared unimpressed by my courtesy. "Blaine, my glass is empty; fill it, please, while I interrogate your – ah – friend."

She passed her pint mug to Marco without so much as a sideways glance, and extracted a cheroot from a miniature strong-box which she then passed to me.

"Isn't this a non-smoking area?" I asked.

"I'll be the judge of that." She stashed the container away somewhere in the folds of her floor-sweeping black robe. "Well, I've heard a bit about you. Quite well preserved for forty-two – have I got that right?"

"Forty-three, actually. I, er..."

"Drink?"

"I already have one, thanks."

"No. I mean, do you drink? To excess?"

"I wouldn't say so."

"Drugs?"

"Well, I take the odd pain-killer for migraine, and I have quite high blood pressure, so..."

"I mean recreational. Crack. Charlie. Ecstasy is getting quite popular with your generation, I gather."

"Good lord, no! I'm sorry, but – "

"Translator, I hear. Great works of literature, or the European lipstick regulations?"

"I wouldn't call them great, but yes, more on the literary side. Now really –"

"So, a steady source of income. House and grounds in Spain, but no UK real estate?"

I'd had enough of this impudent grilling, especially at this late stage of an already exhausting day. "Look, Sadie, it's very nice to meet you, but I find your questions – well, rather intrusive. I mean, what gives you the right –"

"It's not so much a right as a duty. You'll be well aware that Blaine's parents are totally unforthcoming with any form of support for their son, other than financial – and little enough of that, given the obscene fortune on which their arses are parked."

She pursed and then unpursed her lips, and drew heavily on the cheroot. "Blaine's general demeanour didn't win him much of a following among his contemporaries at school, nor yet among the academic staff, as I suppose we must call them. For the members of his fan club here, he's nothing but a circus sideshow. So somebody has to watch out for him. In the absence of any other candidates, I am that someone."

For the first time in this astounding conversation, a slight smile played across her downy face. "I'm not exactly the Mother Hen type, as may be obvious to you. So, some support in my mission would be welcome. But only from a suitably qualified party. Which you appear to be. Congratulations."

"On what, may I ask?"

She paused and blew a funnel of smoke into the air. "On showing the tolerance, patience and sheer resilience that are required to maintain close relations with Marco Blaine. My view is that you have those qualities."

I wasn't much mollified now she was apparently sweetening me up. "And how do you work that out?"

"The vast majority of men would have turned on their heel at any one of the questions I just asked. Or, now that the age of equality has dawned, slapped me in the face. You put up with my outrageous rudeness, you answered honestly and when you reached your limit, you told me so with courtesy."

"So I've passed the test?"

"If you want to put it like that. Don't we all show concern when people we love are getting involved with somebody new? Isn't that something friends do?"

I thought of the time and trouble Alex had taken to guide and warn me as I dithered over taking the plunge with Marco.

"You're right. But now it's my turn to ask the questions, Sadie. What's in it for you? What do you get from being Marco's self-appointed guardian?" I congratulated myself inwardly on stemming the tide and showing some of the resilience she claimed to see in me.

She was unfazed. "The satisfaction of repaying a huge debt. Being the only declared lesbian in a mixed public school with several hundred pupils cooped up on top of a mountain is no laughing matter, I can tell you. The girls are shit scared of you, and the boys hate you for challenging their so-called virility. The girls I can cope with, but the males of the species very soon resort to physical violence when a female refuses to bow to their expectations."

This wasn't a scenario I'd ever given any thought to.

"Blaine is large and powerful, as you'll have noticed. He's responsible for inflicting more than one black eye on his contemporaries and seniors. The captain of rugby had to be rushed to hospital for a very delicate operation on his testicles after Blaine found out he was threatening to circumcise me. I repeat: circumcise. As in Africa. Blaine came close to being expelled for that attack – you can imagine how *that* would have gone down with his parents. That's just one example. I call it loyalty, and I return it in kind."

Yet again, I was seeing Marco in a new light on this day of endless revelations. Now he arrived in person, grasping Sadie's pint of Guinness.

"I hope Sadie hasn't terrified you out of your wits," he said by way of greeting.

"Enough, Blaine," she said as she grabbed the pint from his hand. "Quite how you've managed it I don't know, but you've become acquainted with a gentleman who is, in every respect, your equal. I wish you both well."

She raised her glass in our direction and drained the contents in one gulp.

"I must away to Cowdenbeath. Mr. Carter, it has truly been a pleasure to meet you. You'll know by now that I don't say anything I don't mean. We shall meet again. Be good to one another, please."

With that, she strode out of the room, head erect, without a backward glance.

Marco prodded me in the forearm. "You're thinking again, Peter. I'm not even going to ask how you got through it. She actually called you *Mister* Carter – that says it all! The rest of us only ever get called by our bare surnames. Unfair of me to spring her on you at the end of the day, I know. But we might as well get everything over and done with at one fell swoop. Now, I have only one word to say, as nobody's around to hear: bed!"

"I can't argue with that," I murmured.

"Don't even try. Out. Now."

He grasped my hand and pulled me through a small door into a dark corridor full of pipes and ventilation equipment. It was obviously a refuge for intimate encounters, but I couldn't have responded even if he'd ripped every shred of clothing from my body and thrown himself on me. I suppose. Anyway, nothing of the sort occurred and we quickly emerged in front of a row of taxis, one of which took us briskly to the hotel. Once back in our room, Marco threw his clothes on the floor, jumped naked into his bed and was snoring loudly within minutes.

Chapter Ten

After a huge breakfast next morning, we wrapped up against the blustery wind and went for a long tramp across the rolling parkland opposite the hotel. The weather held up nicely – a sharp wind sent the high clouds scooting across the sky, with shafts of brilliant sunshine every so often. We hiked to the other end of the park, took a bus, and ended up in a cosy French bistro not far from the Merchant City quarter. Without the slightest hint of pretension, Marco ordered us two glasses of *kir* in fluent French and went on to enquire about the day's specials. I'd more or less forgotten that he was a Belgentier as well as a Blaine.

"Are you actually bilingual? Or did you just learn good French?"

"Definitely bilingual. My mother insisted on that. She would rap me over the knuckles if I ever started using English words in French. She's not such a bad old sort, really – God knows how or why she's put up with my father for so long. It's sucked all the love out of her, I think. But let's not get into that. How's Trelawney? I hear he's still in London."

I told him what I knew, and that I planned to visit my old friend on the way back to Spain.

"That man is a mountain. He's helped so many people in the Village, including me. I can't bear to think of him pining away in London. Can't we do something?"

"Apparently Greta's more optimistic that she can fix things now..."

"And if anyone can, she can. Let's drink to that!" Marco raised his glass, and I clinked mine against it. "You know she was a spy during the war, don't you? Although nobody's saying which side she was on!"

Our conversation flowed easily as we recalled the quaint characters who inhabited the Village: Doocie, the Horrabins, June and even Colonel and Mrs. Twelvetrees. Despite what he had to put up with at home, I could see that he had a deep affection for the Village, and I told him so.

"I suppose you're right – if I have a home, that's where it's been. It's magical – but I'm not sure whether it's good magic or bad magic."

"What do you mean?"

"Well, we immigrants don't really have a right to be there, you know. It's an Arab village, and one day they'll take it back. Sometimes the families who owned the houses before the fire come back to visit – the kids look so sad when they see where they should still be living, instead of some grubby tower block in town. Sometimes it feels like the Village is trying to get its own back on us, for walking in and taking everything..."

I'd never considered the Village's history in this light.

"But nothing will change as long as Greta's around, I'm sure."

"You can count on that," Marco agreed. "But after she goes, anything could happen."

After lunch, we strolled around the city centre, talking effortlessly, drifting from one subject to another. Marco's plan for Beth and Sadie to meet and have a steamy affair (utterly impossible, I thought, from what I knew of the two girls, though Marco insisted it was bound to happen); places we'd visited, music we enjoyed (vastly different for each of us) and books we liked (surprisingly similar).

We walked on past De La Rue's and through some very upmarket shopping malls, ending up on the terrace of a smart café.

I'd been saving my idea about my neighbour and the Almería archaeology project for a suitable moment, and this seemed to be it. Marco was overjoyed.

"Of course they'll swallow it! They adore ruins! That's all they do on holiday – tramping across prehistoric rubbish dumps, squealing with joy if they find a Roman lavatory seat. It's perfect, Peter – and he sounds like just the sort of old bore they'll adore!"

I was interrupted by an electronic rendition of the first bars of *Deutschland über Alles* coming from Marco's backpack on the floor beside us.

"Shit. Oh NO," he said as he rummaged through the bag and extracted a bulky old mobile phone. "This is Aunt Claudia's panic phone. I have to carry it for emergencies. I hope she's just checking up."

He answered it, pasting a contrived smile on his face. "Yes...yes...No, for God's sake, she can't have! She's so stupid!" He gestured at me for a cigarette, which I lit and passed to him. "Can't you call the fire brigade? Well, I'm very busy you know, I've got three or four more hours' work to do in the library, and then I meet my teacher..." By now he was clenching his fist in fury. "Oh, all right then, don't worry, Auntie...yes, as soon as I can. Bye-eee!"

I'd worked out what was going to happen, and my face must have showed my disappointment.

"Look, Peter, I can do without you dissolving into tears as well. You can believe this or not, but her cat has got stuck up a tree. She's hysterical and too ashamed to call the fire brigade, so I have to go and rescue the brainless fucking creature. My God, why is my life full of all these helpless old people?"

I wasn't sure whether I was included in this category.

"Don't worry about me," I mumbled. "I'm still tired from yesterday, I can have a perfectly pleasant evening on my own, and..."

"But I'd planned something really special for tonight – to thank you, for all you've done, and now – this fucking *family*...when will it ever end?"

He was nearly in tears. Unless he was an even better actor than I thought, this was no feigned excuse to dump me as soon as he'd secured my agreement to his plan. We paid up, took a taxi back to the hotel and asked it to wait. He raced around the room, flinging his belongings into his bags, swearing violently and then apologising abjectly to me. There was only time for the most hurried goodbye.

"I'll see you at Easter. We'll make it work. You'll see."

"I'll be there."

He dropped his cases to the floor and threw his arms around me.

"Thanks again, Peter. For everything. You'll never regret it, I swear."

With that, he bounded out of the room and down the stairs. The last I saw of him in Glasgow was a furiously waving hand extended from the rear window of the taxi as it turned out of the drive. If I wasn't mistaken, he was miming the clacking of a castanet.

———————

With Marco gone, there was simply no point staying in Glasgow. I'd pledged to visit Trelawney in London, so I took a train to Euston the next day, booked into the Cumberland Hotel at Marble Arch and arranged to visit him that evening.

I located the impressive building that contained Doocie's apartment in Belgravia. Trelawney flung the door wide open as I reached the top of the stairs. He took one look at me and his jaw dropped.

"Peter! You've lost ten years, I can't believe my eyes. Being in love clearly suits you, my friend. Now come along in and make yourself at home!"

He was clearly restored to full form, shrouded in one of his magnificent kaftans, and his flowing silver locks had obviously just been ironed and waved to perfection. His cheeks were rosy and there was an unmistakeable sparkle in his eye. We embraced and he steered me into the sitting room.

"I was fearing the worst, but I see you've managed to make yourself at home here," I said, as I took in the surroundings. Doocie's furniture wouldn't have been out of place in a dentist's waiting room, and the ceiling was covered in yellowing polystyrene tiles. But fresh flowers, floridly-patterned cushions and a scattering of kilims told me that Trelawney had taken matters into his own hands. It was pleasantly warm, and delicious aromas of cumin and coriander wafted through the room. Before I had time to enquire, the kitchen door opened a crack and a swarthy face peeked out.

"Ten minutes, sir?"

"That will be perfect, Rashid," Trelawney boomed in response. "Take your time, dear boy, my friend and I have plenty to talk about." The occupant of the kitchen pulled the door shut again with a smile and a wink.

"Where did you —?"

"At the Café Damascus, down one of those side streets opposite Paddington Station. You must drop in and try their *baba ghanoush* if you're ever in the area. It sent me into such raptures I demanded to offer my congratulations to the chef in person and…the rest is history. Rashid is just rustling up some *falafel* to accompany our aperitifs."

"You never cease to amaze me – I mean, this is London in the depths of winter, and you've virtually recreated the Village here in Belgravia!"

"But not for long. Dear Rashid is a tremendous blessing, but a temporary one – he will stay with me until I set out for home, and then he will resume his post in Paddington. Richer in pocket and, I trust, richer in experience."

"So – you're going back?"

"Indeed. Crisis over," he beamed. "A storm in a tea-glass, as it were. It was all settled this very afternoon. Hence the exceptionally fine beverage I am about to share with you."

The ice-bucket on the coffee table contained a bottle of Bollinger

La Grande Année champagne. It must have cost several times more than a night at the Cumberland. Rashid came in from the kitchen, proudly bearing a tray of sizzling *falafel* balanced professionally on the upturned palm of his right hand. Trelawney eased the cork from the bottle – it shot up and inflicted a healthy dent in Doocie's polystyrene panelling – and we raised our glasses in a toast "to the Village".

Rashid joined in, glugging from a Coke bottle. It really did feel as if we were back in North Africa already.

"So how did you manage it? Greta, I suppose – or Sir Brian?"

"They both rallied round, but in fact it was Purvis who turned up trumps."

"I seem to be hearing that man's name everywhere. You know that Alex did some translating for him before he..."

Trelawney slowly chewed the piece of *falafel* he had bitten off and washed it down with a gulp of Bollinger. "I have to own up about that, Peter. It was I who gave Alex's number to Purvis – you remember, you left it with me once when you were on your way to see him in Switzerland."

"It seems they stayed in touch. He saw fit to tell Alex that I'd fallen head over heels for Marco, you know."

"No, I didn't know. Perhaps I should have handled it differently. I can only apologise, Peter."

"Please don't think about it anymore. Let's just forget it. But, you know, Purvis puzzles me. I just can't make him out."

"It is not my place to judge. All I know is that he has done me the enormous favour of enabling me to return to my own home. So he remains a welcome guest at Trelawney Towers for as long as he wishes to enjoy our company. And, thanks to his intervention, so do you."

I took another of Rashid's *falafels*. Whatever other talents he might have, he was clearly a genius in the kitchen. I kissed my fingers in the Arab gesture of appreciation, and he smiled modestly back at me.

Trelawney would obviously be drawn no further on the subject of Purvis. "So, all is well?"

"A letter has been sent to Greta, personally signed by the Minister who, it would seem, was in Purvis's debt. His Excellency says that he wishes to eliminate any misunderstandings that have arisen due to erroneous reports in the press. And he states, very clearly and for the record, that nationals of all foreign countries — except Israel, naturally — and of any marital status, are welcome to settle and remain in the Village. By command of the Head of State. I called Greta this afternoon and she read it to me. She was quite tearful, and so was I — we go back a few years, you know, Greta and I."

I got up from my chair and went over to hug him. "Trelawney, I'm thrilled for you. The world just didn't seem right without you at home in the Village."

"It *is* my home."

I knew what was coming next. I smiled as my friend repeated his well-worn maxim.

"Trelawney Towers is my name, and Trelawney Towers is my residence — and forever will be!"

Rashid's English was clearly not up to following the details of our conversation, but he grasped that the outcome was happy — so he decided it was time for another toasting ceremony. Giggling, he lifted his Coke bottle high and we joined in, raising our champagne glasses and slapping each other on the back.

"Well, that's enough about me," Trelawney said as he lowered himself cautiously onto the settee, which looked even less welcoming than the one back at Casa Morena. "Now tell me your happy tale."

I settled back in the only armchair in the room and began my story. I choked with emotion as I described the moment when Marco joined Elsie to sing "The Flowers of the Forest". Both Trelawney and I dissolved into laughter at the boot-polish episode. I explained Marco's plan for us to share a flat in Granada, and how it would all have to be concealed from his parents.

By now, Rashid had moved onto the sofa next to him and was dozing off, his head resting in Trelawney's lap, a blissful expression on his face.

"So, have I understood this correctly?" Trelawney asked rather pointedly, after I'd described Marco's departure to rescue Aunt Claudia's cat. "While you were conveniently gagged, and the object of your affections was daubing your face with mascara and the like, you agreed to a scheme that will have you abandoning your home and embarking on a new life with a talented, but unpredictable, young man in Granada. You will also help to trick his parents into believing that he is studiously excavating the remains of some old pile, in an entirely different location, while this adventure unfolds."

I began to cringe as Trelawney set out the bare facts of the situation.

"Furthermore, you are to fund the entire undertaking by continuing to translate obscure works of German literature, or by exhausting your savings, as the case may be. And all of this is fired by a passion the like of which you have never experienced before, and I daresay may never experience again. Is that a fair summary?"

I hung my head and drew heavily on my cigarette. I'd expected rather more support from Trelawney. I opened my mouth to protest, but he stopped me by standing up and raising his index finger in a distinctly Churchillian gesture.

"Congratulations, my friend! Young Marco deserves a medal – he has achieved in a few days what none of us has been able to do in years. He has set you free – you are flying, I've never seen you like this – it's a joy to behold!" He filled our glasses again. "I wish you both every success and happiness in the world. And I look forward, one day, be it sooner or later, to welcoming *both* of you to Trelawney Towers. Once again."

I'd forgotten Trelawney's immense generosity of spirit, his vast experience of life in general and of romantic attachments in particular.

I reached over to shake him by the hand. "Thank you – and thank you on Marco's behalf too," I said rather hoarsely. "But you know the situation with Marco's parents, so I doubt whether we'll be appearing together in the Village any time soon, even in your house."

Trelawney exhaled deeply. "Never underestimate the Village. It has a magic all of its own. Things have a habit of turning out there in precisely the way one could never have expected."

I remembered Marco saying something along the same lines – about good magic and bad magic.

"You may find it hard to believe, but Marco has a high regard for you. A mountain of a man – that's what he calls you," I told him.

Trelawney chuckled wryly. "Those who enjoy the respect of their juniors must live up to certain responsibilities and standards. And I must confess that I have failed, because there is one more detail of this business I have not disclosed to you."

"Look, Trelawney, please don't feel that I'm trying to judge you. I really don't care what you've fixed up with Purvis – I'm just so glad you can go home. When are you flying back?"

"Ah. You've touched on the very point that I forbore to mention. I'm not flying back. My arrangements with Purvis also include the purchase of a motor car. In which he and I shall commence the homeward journey next month."

"Really, Trelawney – that man is taking you to the cleaners. I suppose this is some piece of recycled Japanese rubbish he's ended up with after one of his shady deals."

Trelawney's face turned redder. "No, it's not of oriental origin, actually. It's a *Rolls-Royce Silver Cloud*, manufactured in this country in the year you were born, I believe."

"I won't ask the price, or anything else about it, but I'd be delighted if both of you – yes, both of you – can visit me in Almería on the way down. I'm sure the Roller will make it over the track to my humble home."

"An invitation I shall be glad to accept. And so will Purvis, I'm sure."

I wasn't thrilled at the prospect of Purvis taking his place at my kitchen table, but I had to concede he'd done a huge favour for all of us. He deserved to be treated with a good grace for that reason alone. And after the countless times I'd enjoyed the hospitality of Trelawney's home, this was the first opportunity I'd ever had to return it in kind.

At midnight, Rashid's quartz watch emitted a series of beeps and I took them as my cue to leave. Trelawney and I hugged as we said our farewells, and I stepped out into the crisp night air.

My mood was buoyant as I strode towards Marble Arch. The months leading up to April would be packed with activity and I was keen to get started. Casa Morena would need far more of a facelift than it received for Alex's visit, with Trelawney and Purvis due before Marco arrived. Don Victorio had to be buttonholed and persuaded to take Marco on as an apprentice archaeologist, and I should also drive over to Granada to look at apartments. For too long, the prospect of returning to Casa Morena after a trip abroad had triggered a sinking feeling in the pit of my stomach. But this time, I couldn't wait to get home and get into action. Things had certainly changed.

Chapter Eleven

Almería is not the most beautiful of Spain's provincial capitals, but it was looking its best as my plane swooped down towards the airport. The sun was blazing in a typically cloudless January sky and the Mediterranean was a sparkling sapphire blue. Golden beaches stretched endlessly on either side of the city, and a cluster of gleaming white Africa-bound ferries were tethered at the wharves. The air was so clear that I could even pick out the battlements on top of the castle walls and the twin belfry towers of the cathedral.

I'd barely been back at Casa Morena for five minutes when Elena sauntered into the kitchen. I greeted her as usual:

"*Hola, Doña Elena, ¿qué tal?*"

She stood in the doorway, staring at me without uttering a word. Eventually, she raised her hand to touch the straggling remains of her own once-blond hair, gazed at me in bafflement and managed to expel one syllable.

"*¿Qué?*"

I'd forgotten the transformation of my appearance since I set out for Alex's funeral. "*Ah sí* – a new barber. Scottish style. Suits me, don't you think?"

An event of extreme rarity now occurred – Doña Elena smiled. "*Sí señor.* You look…handsome! And happy! Good, good, good."

I'd never seen her so animated, but her expression became more vexed as she led me into the bathroom. She showed me where rain had burst through the ceiling while I was away, leaving unsightly stains on two of the walls.

"No problem," I said airily. "It's time we had a new bathroom installed, I think. Maybe you could ask one of your cousins..."

I marched her into the sitting room. "And while we're on the subject – this sofa. It needs to go. I'll pop down to the *Corte Inglés* in Almería to choose a new one next week, along with a few other items."

Elena shot me a look to remind me who, in her view, was the boss in this house.

"Yes, well...maybe you'd better come along too, in case I can't decide on the right colour. Could you ask Pepe to come over to the house later – I want to get the garden tidied up, and we'll probably need some help with that as well."

I sat down with her at the kitchen table and she poured us each a cup of coffee. The more I looked around, the more jobs I found needed doing. I told her about the visitors I was expecting and my planned trip to Granada.

"I'll probably invite Don Victorio over for dinner one evening. Time to be friendly with the neighbours. Perhaps you can cook something special for him?"

By this stage, Elena was clearly having doubts as to my sanity. She knew as well as I did that as a dinner companion, Don Victorio was probably without inferiors in the whole of the province. But she seemed to be taking this sudden burst of activity in good part. Maybe I'd been wrong to think that she was perfectly content all these years, doing the bare minimum that was needed to stop Casa Morena from turning into a ruin. And to be fair, I'd never asked anything more of her.

She stood up to return to her cottage, but I motioned her to wait. I took a parcel wrapped in bright tartan paper from one of my bags and presented it to her. She undid the packaging with great caution and placed the contents on the kitchen table. She looked at it as if it were a cow-pat that I'd come across on my travels, encased in a polythene bag to keep it in pristine condition. I pointed to the inscription on the outer wrapper.

"*Great chieftain o' the pudding-race!*"

She prodded it with her index finger, picked it up and sniffed it. "*Pudín?*"

The Spanish word refers to a sweet and creamy egg custard. Nothing could be as different in taste and appearance from the haggis I'd brought her from Scotland.

"Yes, you could say it's a sort of Scottish *pudín*, Elena. I hope you and Pepe will enjoy it."

She thanked me profusely and plodded off to her cottage with the haggis tucked under her arm. Doubtless she would produce it to Pepe as physical evidence that the master of the house had finally lost his wits.

I wasted no time. By the end of the week, clouds of white dust were issuing from the bathroom, where a couple of workmen were hacking away to repair the walls and install a smart new suite.

Pepe was clearly pleased to see me showing some respect for the land that surrounded my house. He drafted in a gang of muscular lads from Aguacate who toiled away from dawn till dusk, mowing, sawing, slashing and hoeing. They would always down tools at two in the afternoon and sprawl out under the shade of the carob trees behind the house for a lengthy picnic lunch, followed by an even longer collective siesta on the grass.

They were about the same age as most of the crowd I'd been mixing with at De La Rue's only a few weeks earlier. But how different these lads were: relaxed, utterly sure of themselves – and *manly*. As I eyed them from the kitchen window, I realised that my appetite for sex had also returned with a vengeance.

I picked a day for furniture shopping in Almería. Elena arrived on the terrace at nine o' clock sharp, decked out in apparel I never imagined she possessed: an elegant dark green twin-set, a matching pill-box hat and even a pair of patent leather court shoes. Put to shame, I dived back into my bedroom to swap my grubby beachwear for slacks and the faithful sports jacket.

Elena clearly revelled in being the centre of attention when we reached the department store. We were treated with a reverence I never experienced on the odd occasion I went shopping there on my own. Her practical tips were also invaluable: this fabric would stain too easily, that one would fray, and castors were out of the question as they always collapsed at "the moment of truth". I began to suspect she'd led a far more colourful life than I'd previously assumed.

I was out for a stroll next day when I heard Don Victorio's Labradors in the distance. Before long, the whole gang of dogs came bounding over the hillocks, followed at some distance by Victorio himself. He was rather an austere figure with a completely bald pate, gold-rimmed spectacles and a greying, pointed beard of the sort sported by Spanish monarchs in the paintings of Velázquez.

"Good day, my Britannic neighbour! Luckily, it is not the twenty-first of October, so I greet you most warmly!"

I hadn't the least idea what he was talking about, especially it was January.

"The Battle of Trafalgar, my friend! A date that our two nations look back on with…different perspectives!"

I'd perhaps underestimated how trying this conversation was likely to be.

"Of course, we have no evidence that your great Lord Nelson ever visited Almería, or the castle. But only the other day, in a room at the castle that we thought was merely a pig-sty or something of the sort, we came across a pair of British gold sovereigns from the reign of George III."

He paused to light his Meerschaum pipe, and I seized the opportunity to utter words that I avoided above all others in my previous encounters with him.

"Actually, Don Victorio, I'm quite interested in the castle."

An expression of delighted anticipation spread across his face. It put me in mind of a missionary who had seen the first glimmerings of faith in a prospective convert.

"Ah, the castle," he began, directing his gaze to the skies as if to thank the Almighty for its existence. "Or the Alcazaba, as we should more correctly call it, remembering its Moorish origins. There are those who say its true beauty lies in the later Christian additions, but I take issue with them. It is the entire structure, the ensemble, that we must appreciate – must *treasure*, indeed. Its essence, if you like."

There was no stemming the tide. I lit a cigarette and hoped that my face betrayed nothing but the most acute interest as the monologue unfolded. I tuned in and out, emitting the odd "Ooh!" and "Really?" to show that I was paying attention.

"Alfonso VII...the cisterns...the Caliph of Cordoba...the stucco work...the kitchens...the revolutionary plumbing..."

Eventually, Don Victorio paused to stoke up his pipe, which had gone out – unsurprisingly, since he never seemed to draw breath. I seized my opportunity and came out with the lines I'd prepared.

"I have a nephew, a nice young man who's going to study Spanish at university next year, and he's looking for a worthwhile way of using his free year. I wondered if..."

"But this is very welcome news! We're always looking for volunteers, and having a British member of the team would, of course, enhance our international standing. In all modesty, I can tell you that interest has already been expressed in our efforts by the Royal Archaeological Institute of London..."

My attention soon drifted again. Don Victorio hadn't enquired whether my "nephew" was enticed by the prospect of spending endless hours under the baking Andalusian sun, sifting through acres of dried mud in the hopes of finding a few fragments of mediaeval sewage pipe – how could anyone not be? But it sounded like he'd swallowed the bait and I was looking forward to reporting this to Marco. Then I realised from a change in Victorio's posture – he was actually looking at me for once – that he'd just asked me a question, though I'd no idea what it was. I pretended my Spanish wasn't quite up to grasping what he meant.

"A contribution...as you know, we are almost entirely dependent on donations and I'm sure if you – or the young man's parents, perhaps – could see their way...not to put too fine a point on it...a few hundred thousand pesetas...sure to guarantee my committee's approval..." So, he wasn't entirely divorced from the concerns of the modern world.

"Marco comes from quite an affluent branch of the family – unlike myself, you understand – so I'm sure some arrangement could be reached. His parents are both keen patrons of academic pursuits..."

The old digger's eyes lit up. "I think it would be best if the young gentleman telephoned me, as soon as possible – there will be preparations to make. I assume he'll be staying at Casa Morena with you?"

"I think you can assume that, yes." He fished a visiting card out of his wallet which read: "Dr. Victorio de Salazar. Vendor and Exporter of Antiquities. Secure and Anonymous Dispatch Worldwide. Discretion Assured." He saw the puzzled look on my face.

"Ah, a slight error on my part, forgive me." He snatched the card back, stuffed it into his pocket and produced another bearing an impressive catalogue of academic credentials.

"This is the one with the correct details. I'll look forward to the call from your – *young man*." He gave the last two words a distinctly lewd emphasis, but I was unconcerned. He thought he knew what I was really up to and I now had a good idea of what *he* was really up to. I wondered how many of Spain's national treasures he'd discreetly dispatched to obsessive collectors across the world. We parted with much shaking of hands and promises to see more of each other as we went our separate ways.

The winter sun was already about to vanish over the horizon when I reached Casa Morena. Most of the workmen had left, a few were still packing up their tools, and calm was once again descending on the house.

Hoping that the shower was connected today, I strode into the bathroom in my boxers. I was startled to find one of the gardeners sitting on the toilet, his jeans – and underpants – around his ankles. He was smoking and reading a magazine which, judging by the majestic erection it had provoked, was not one of the copies of *Newsweek* I kept in a basket on the floor.

He thoughtfully disposed of his cigarette by dropping it down the gap between his buttocks and the lavatory seat. Then he reached out to grab my boxers, lowered them swiftly and began pleasuring me with astonishing tenderness for such a brawny, virile young man. We careened across the hall and into my room in a sort of *paso doble*. The half-hour that followed was the most exquisite I'd ever spent in that bed.

The need for a shower was even more urgent by the time we'd finished, so I was glad to find it still in working order. After we'd towelled one another dry and were dressing, I offered him a cigarette and lit my own; he snapped the filter off his and inhaled deeply. The entire encounter had taken place without words (but by no means in silence). As we smoked, he took the silver locket that hung from a chain around his neck, flipped it open and showed me the photograph it contained. Beaming up at me, I saw a pretty girl cradling a baby that could only have been a few weeks old.

"They're beautiful!" was all I could manage to say.

"My family," he replied, bursting with pride and love. He brushed the photograph with his lips, closed the cover again and turned the locket over. His name was engraved on the back, entwined with that of his wife: *Ana y Romeo*. If ever a name was well-chosen...He tucked it into his shirt, pulled me to him and gave me a farewell kiss of some depth.

"*Nos vemos*," he said with a wink, after I'd walked him out of the house to his motorbike. That could mean anything: we'll see each other. No promises, no commitments, no complications. Easy come, easy go. Maybe he'd remember our moments together with a chuckle as he lay in his wife's arms tonight. Or maybe not.

I went back to my bedroom and lay down in a pleasant daze, savouring this unexpected treat all over again. In fact, I realised, it was the first time I'd had sex since I met Marco. Did I feel disloyal? *Should* I feel disloyal? Nonsense. Marco had made it perfectly clear that sex between us wasn't one of the "items on the agenda". Well, of course, things might change as the year (or years) went on...

My reverie was interrupted by the telephone ringing in the lounge. I rushed out, stark naked, and grabbed the receiver.

"*Sw-eeee-tie*! Are you *always* so difficult to get hold of? I've been trying your number for *ages*, and I'll have you know I'm standing here freezing my balls off in the one phone box they deign to let us use in this *gulag*. I thought you lived the life of a hermit down there in Casa whatever-it's-called?"

How had he managed to pick this particular moment to make his first ever phone call to me? Come to think of it, I thought I'd heard the phone ringing earlier through the closed bedroom door.

"What a nice surprise, Marco! How are you? Is everything all right?"

"Of course it is. But I have some news, and I wanted you to be the first – well, one of the first – to know."

"Yes, I've got some news, too. But tell me yours first."

"I've been awarded a scholarship at St. Andrews. Not just a place, sweetie – a scholarship. Deferred for a year."

"Marco – that's marvellous! It's one of the best universities in the world! Congratulations!"

"Well, congratulations to the examiners for spotting true genius when they see it. Eggs by the crateload on everyone's faces back at my school, of course. Pupil from hell wins Scotland's top academic award. I'd love to see the headmaster's face as he has to read my result out at Speech Day – but sadly, I shall be in Granada by then."

"Thank you for calling me to tell me the news," I replied. "I'm quite touched, actually. Have you told your parents?"

"No, I wanted you to know before them." His voice became more subdued. "Because, Peter, I couldn't have done it without you. All those ridiculous essays – I know you must have cursed me as you were slogging over them – they paid off in the end. Nobody else would have done it. Nobody else has ever helped me like that. But actually..." He paused, and I could hear him drawing a deep breath.

"Is there something else, Marco?"

"Actually, Peter, I don't think I'll ever take the scholarship up."

"But of course you must! St. Andrews, for heavens' sake – it's up there with Oxford and Cambridge. It's the most wonderful start anyone could have in life!"

I realised I'd said exactly the wrong thing as soon as the words were out of my mouth.

"Well, I'm *not* just anyone and, if you recall, I don't exactly *need* a wonderful start in life. But that's not what I mean."

I should have remembered that Marco rarely saw things as any other member of his generation would.

"You mean, you've shown them what you can do, you've had enough of studying and you can't face another three years of it? I think I felt like that when I left school."

"No, it's not that. I mean, even if I'm the most brilliant student they've ever had in Granada – which of course, I will be – I can see that a university degree would still be worth having. Especially from St. Andrews. But..."

An uncharacteristic hint of fear had crept into Marco's voice.

"But what?" I asked, as gently as I could.

"I just have this hunch. An odd sort of feeling deep down. It's simply not going to happen."

I'd never heard Marco's self-confidence ebb away like this.

"Marco, I know you well enough to say that if you want it to happen, it will happen. And you know that, too. We'll talk about it when you're here. Now, do you want to hear the latest from down here?"

"Of course. I'm nearly out of coins. Shoving them in the slot every thirty seconds is wearing me out as well, so get on with it! Tell me every eensy-weensy little detail. In no more than four sentences."

I gave him a concise summary of my conversation with Don Victorio – no mean feat in itself.

"He sounds better and better. Of course my parents will cough up – I can see it now, the Blaine memorial trowel, with their names etched on a little brass plaque. And you've got some dirt on him as well, so he's putty in our hands. I'm proud of you, Peter!"

Should I tell him the rest? Yes. It was time to give as good as I got. "And then I fucked one of the gardeners here."

Silence. "So, it's really been quite a satisfactory day all round," I said.

Despite what Alex had taught me, was I trying to provoke Marco into feeling jealous? If so, I failed miserably.

"Peter, you old *slut*! Lady Chatterley rides again! The *gardener* - how priceless! I was getting worried about you, you know – it's no good saving yourself for the day that will never dawn. I can't wait to get down there myself. Please don't deflower your entire staff before I come. I shall be like a ravenous warthog after another two months in this place! Especially as there's no earthly reason for me to be here now I've got my place at uni. Are you shagging it again?"

I was about to tell him I'd simply leave that up to Romeo when the line was cut. I put the receiver down and silently considered the conversation we'd just had. The only conclusion I came to was that I'd never had so much fun in all my life.

Chapter Twelve

There was no let-up in the hectic pace of activity at Casa Morena as the first signs of spring appeared. It took nearly three weeks for the brigade of gardeners to cut back the rampant undergrowth. The sparkling new bathroom and the bedroom Pepe had repainted for Alex made the other rooms look shabby. I asked the gardeners to stay on and paint the house all the way through. Romeo winked knowingly as I told the gang there was another few weeks' work for them if they wanted it.

Trelawney called to say that the Rolls was almost ready for the long southward journey; he and Purvis would be arriving at the end of February, so I wanted everything to be shipshape by then. Except in the bedrooms, I'd never bothered to cover the windows. In fact, I'd never bothered with anything. No wonder I had to force myself to return to the house after every trip away. Elena set up her ancient sewing machine in the lounge, I fetched material from Almería, and one by one the windows were curtained in cheerful Mediterranean colours.

Half-way through one of these shopping expeditions, I flopped down exhausted in a café on the Rambla, the palm-colonnaded avenue that slices through the mediaeval centre of Almería. I was sipping a cool beer and waiting for the server to come around with his tray of freshly-grilled *tapas* when I spotted a familiar squat figure beetling past the café's terrace.

"Federico!" I yelled. I felt a pang of guilt because I hadn't even found time to send him an e-mail since I returned to Spain.

He seemed genuinely pleased to see me. "Hey, Pedro, long time no see! How you doin', man?"

His American drawl certainly hadn't changed since we last met. "Come and join me. You're looking well!"

I ordered him a beer and we exchanged a few trivial remarks.

"I guess you heard," he said, "I went up to Switzerland and stayed with Alex almost 'til the end."

"Federico, I think what you did was fantastic. I can't even imagine how hard it must have been..."

He rotated his beer glass on its mat and set it carefully at just the angle he wanted. "It wasn't hard at all. He asked me, I went, and I stayed. Simple as that."

"I'm just very, very glad you did. I offered to go back to Switzerland with Alex when he left here, you know. But there's no way I could have given him what you did."

"I'll tell you the truth, Pedro. We stayed in bed almost all the time, day and night, the whole six weeks or whatever. That's all he wanted and all he needed. And I wanted to be there with him. So that's what we did. Don't get me wrong, it wasn't a fuckfest – he got weaker and weaker towards Christmas."

He was making light of it, but I could see his lip quivering as he remembered. He took a gulp of his beer. "Okay, I had to clean him up and all that. But what the hell – can you think of anything worse than dying alone? At least I could give him that. He didn't want to be alone, and he never was."

"I wondered if I'd see you at the funeral in Glasgow. They gave him a great send-off. His mother sang, you know."

"No, we agreed I'd stay in Zurich. He knew he wouldn't make it back. I knew as well. And he wanted to see his mum. So, we said goodbye, and that was that. Fuckin' nightmare getting him on the plane, Swiss treated him like a piece of excess baggage. But once he'd gone, all I had to do was wait."

A flock of seagulls wheeled around the tops of the graceful palm trees that lined the avenue. We let their forlorn cries fill the silence between us.

"I saw Nils at the funeral. He told me he'd met you..."

Federico grabbed one of my Marlboros. "That weirdo! What a fuckin' screwball! I mean, he could see Alex had decided to be with me, but he kept pitching up at the flat, desperate, tongue hanging out of his mouth...wouldn't take no for an answer. I suppose I should feel sorry for him. I hope he doesn't pull the same trick with all the guys he looks after!"

This possibility hadn't occurred to me. With a shudder, I recalled what Sebi said in Glasgow: "It's very difficult for Nils when they die. This isn't the first time it's happened..."

"Anyway, Alex was too nice to tell him to get the hell out, so I had to do it, for both our sakes. That dickhead never even sent me the e-mail to say Alex had passed. I only heard when Alex's lawyer called me after Christmas."

I signalled the waiter to bring two more beers.

"So I suppose you had to sort out the flat?"

"No, the lawyer did all that. Alex introduced me to him before he went. Like, he wasn't out of his mind – he knew what was happening, and he prepared for it. But there was one difficult thing the lawyer told me when he came around to the apartment."

Federico clammed up. I could see he was reluctant to tell me whatever it was. I let him take his time. "Turns out, Alex left me some money. Quite a bit, actually."

"He did that because he wanted to, Federico. People usually leave money to their loved ones."

He pondered this for a moment. "It's just that – well, Nils came straight out and said I was nothing but a rent-boy. I nearly socked him in the jaw. Fuck's sake – I even paid my own bus fare to Switzerland!"

Bus? I'd stayed fairly calm throughout this conversation, though it brought back poignant memories of my own last days with Alex. But now, as I pictured this determined young man, sitting alone, staring out of the window hour after hour as the bus crawled its way from the southernmost tip of Spain to the mountainous heart of Europe, I had to choke back a tear. And he was embarrassed because Alex had, typically, returned his devotion in the only way he could.

I called for the bill. I needed to go in the same direction as Federico, so we crossed to the broad marbled pavement that ran down the centre of the avenue and started strolling towards the sea.

"I guess you're taking a break now?" I asked him. "You must be exhausted after what you've been through."

"Yeah, I'm kinda bushed. Alex kept it together most of the time, but now and again he'd lose it and bite my head off, over silly little things – I'd bought the wrong kind of soup, or forgotten to put the trash out. And there was a lot of …mess when he was losing control of his body. That's when I knew I loved him, I guess. If you can take that sort of crap and keep smiling, and it just doesn't matter, there's gotta be love in there somewhere. You couldn't do it otherwise, could you?"

I wasn't able to reply to his question. It never occurred to me that I'd have to work out the answer for myself one day before too long.

We carried on walking past neat flowerbeds and splashing fountains.

"Anyways," Federico started up again, "I've decided what to do with the money. Or with what's left after I've given my mom some."

"It's none of my business, but I hope you use it for something you really want to do."

"Sure. I'm gonna open a bar. Nothing fancy – but we don't have a proper gay bar in Almería, and I reckon we should have a place where we can all meet up and relax."

"That's a great idea, Federico! Count me in. I know you'll make a go of it."

He walked me through the winding, cobblestoned alleyways of the old town and showed me where he planned to open his bar: a pretty little one-up one-down house in the Moorish style, painted white with an elaborately carved antique wooden door. He proudly tapped the *reja*, the ornate metal grille in front of the door through which couples would conduct their courtships in days gone by — the boy kneeling on the doorstep and the girl peeking out from behind the door.

"I'm gonna call it 'Bar Alex'. I think he'd be quite amused, don't you?"

I could only agree. In fact, I could almost see my old friend chuckling as he watched from on high when the first round of *piñas coladas* was mixed and served. As we parted, Federico promised to keep in touch, and I undertook to be present at the grand opening of Almería's living memorial to Alexander — or *Alejandro* — Macallister.

The year continued to flash by; although the evenings were drawing out, there never seemed to be enough hours in the day to finish all the tasks I set myself. Don Victorio reported his conversation with Marco in glowing terms when I ran into him during an evening walk.

"Rarely have I heard an Anglo-Saxon speak Spanish — true, Castilian Spanish — with such admirable proficiency! What an exceptionally courteous young man..."

I could just imagine Marco turning on the charm.

"His parents were so inspired by our documentation that they immediately sent a most generous cheque for our cause. *Most* satisfactory. I can assure you that your young friend — er, nephew, I mean — will be our honoured guest for as long as he wishes to stay."

I spotted a good chance to prepare the ground for what was actually going to happen. "Of course," I launched out confidently, "I shall want to take him on a few excursions while he's here. As you've gathered, he has a passion for all things Spanish, so I'll show him more of the country. His work for you will be – how can I say this? It will be the academic basis for his stay in Spain. His parents just need to know that he's not wasting his time, like so many of the young people nowadays. And naturally, I wouldn't want him to become a burden on you, Don Victorio."

I paused before plunging the dagger in. "You must be under a lot of pressure, what with your excavations and your *business* to run as well."

He drew heavily on his pipe. His expression was not unlike that of the bull that suddenly realises it has been cornered. Then he forced himself to give me an obliging smile. "I believe I understand you perfectly, *Señor*. I shall be glad to reassure *los Blaine* that their son is under responsible supervision at all times – wherever he might actually be. And naturally, our committee will be glad to accept any further donations they may care to send us."

Signed and sealed, I thought. Trafalgar Day, indeed! Perhaps Victorio hadn't realised that the British didn't build their empire solely on military might. When it came to negotiating skills, we were second to none in the world.

During this orgy of spending, I'd treated myself to an answering machine; its lamp was flashing insistently when I walked into the lounge. Trelawney had called, leaving a number in France for me to ring back. I pictured him and Purvis sailing down the Autoroute du Soleil in the Silver Cloud with the hood down in the spring sunshine, perhaps making a detour to Cannes or Monte-Carlo.

It turned out that he and Purvis were stuck in a hotel with paper sheets and water-repellent towels on an industrial estate just outside Dunkirk. The Rolls was in a garage, having ground to a halt barely half an hour after they had reached French soil.

"I think perhaps the sea voyage didn't agree with her," he said plaintively. I gathered that Purvis was within earshot. "But she's a stalwart old lady, and I'm sure she'll be back on the road in no time. The boys in the garage are treating her like an empress!"

I refrained from enquiring how the boys in the garage were treating Trelawney, and wished them both a safe journey.

The next call came a week later. They'd managed to navigate the *Périphérique* around Paris and were within striking distance of Poitiers when another breakdown occurred. This time, Purvis was obviously not listening in.

"I could have done the journey faster on the back of a fucking elephant – and in more comfort. It seems the suspension wasn't included in the price. Conversation with our friend is becoming, to say the least, strained."

I tried to calm him down. "Now, now, you know why you bought that blasted car, Trelawney. It's part of the deal that lets you go back home. Just keep your mind focused on getting back to the Village. Then you can find a shed to leave it in, forget all about it and get on with your life." I heard him draw breath for another tirade, but the line was suddenly cut.

I heard nothing for almost two more weeks and started to conjure up all sorts of catastrophes: snowdrifts, the Rolls plunging over a precipice as Trelawney failed to negotiate an unexpected twist in the road...

At last, Purvis called me from Barcelona. "Pete, me old pal. How's tricks?"

I cringed. I couldn't imagine how Trelawney had put up with nearly a month of Purvis and his uninvited, overbearing intimacy. I couldn't retaliate with an equally loathsome abbreviation of his first name because none of us knew what it was.

"Fine, thanks. I was worried sick about you two. How are you? How's the car?"

"She's not so good. Not so bright. Thing is, Trel's not as sharp as he used to be. Coordination's gone to pot. Doesn't always remember to use the clutch. A Roller doesn't respond too well to that."

" I wouldn't know. I've never driven one."

"Anyway, I've sorted things out, and we'll be with you on Friday. Late-ish, I reckon, but we'll be there."

"You'd better call me when you get to Aguacate. It's a bit complicated from there to the house, especially in the dark."

"No need, Pete. We've got a bit of local help. They'll get us there. Don't you worry. See you Friday, then." And with that, he rang off.

Local help? God knows who they'd picked up along the road. Probably a gang of ruffians wanting a lift back to Africa. What had I let myself in for now?

The answer became all too clear on Friday evening after an unusually wet day that did nothing to improve my frame of mind. Purvis had made another curt call from Aguacate, so their arrival must surely be imminent. Elena was bustling around in the kitchen, cooking up a *paella* in a huge copper pan. I was busy setting the dining table with the smart new crockery I'd bought in Almería market.

Suddenly, we were stopped in our tracks by thunderous sounds from outside: the roar of a huge engine and the screeching of wheels that were obviously stuck in the mud.

I should have fetched them from Aguacate. I dashed out onto the terrace. A two-tone siren was blaring somewhere, and I was baffled to see shafts of brilliant red and yellow light strafing the sky and the land. Shading my eyes from the glare with my hand, I stumbled through the puddles towards the gate.

As I approached, I saw that the Rolls had indeed made it to Casa

Morena — but not under its own steam. It was strapped precariously onto the raised tracks of an outsized breakdown truck — easily big enough to have transported a coach. In the harsh light from the revolving beacons on top of the rescue vehicle, I could pick out the faces of Purvis (ashen) and Trelawney (puce) behind the windscreen of the Silver Cloud. The truck driver was frantically revving his engine in a vain attempt to escape from the quagmire. His mate had leapt down from the cab and was watching aghast as the entire rig sank further and further into the mud. Pepe had come up from the cottage to join Elena on the terrace and the pair of them were staring open-mouthed at the chaos.

The driver silenced the siren. In the eerie light from the beacon, the entire tableau resembled the scene from a science-fiction film where the spaceship from Mars has landed and the earthlings are waiting to see what kind of creatures will emerge from it. Trelawney had given up any attempt to conceal his true feelings about the car from Purvis.

"Just get me out of this fucking crate!" he bellowed through the half-open window. Then he recovered some of his customary grace. "Peter, how nice to see you. You must excuse the mode of our arrival. I'm afraid I shall have to beg you to extend some elementary hospitality to our rescuers here."

Purvis, meanwhile, had climbed out of the car and with impressive agility, was manoeuvring himself backwards along one of the tracks on the breakdown truck. He sprang to the ground and waddled over to me, hand extended.

"Evening, Pete. Bit of a rum do, eh? Never can tell with a pre-owned vehicle, can you? She sailed down the motorway to Dover like the Queen Mary, but now look at her, poor old girl!"

More like the Titanic, I thought. Purvis grimaced and shifted his eyes sideways to indicate that no mention must be made of Trelawney's allegedly atrocious handling of the "old girl".

Pepe and Elena went into action to deal with the situation. Elena mothered the two breakdown patrolmen up to the house, where she was soon serving up thick black coffee laced with brandy. Pepe dragged a stepladder out of the barn and I helped him position it at the side of the lorry. We managed to coax Trelawney onto it and, with much spluttering and cursing, he eventually made his descent into the mud. Pepe and I virtually had to carry him up to the house.

My plans for the most sophisticated dinner ever held at Casa Morena were quickly abandoned. The seven of us sat around the kitchen table and ladled healthy portions of Elena's steaming *paella* onto the same old plates I'd been using for years. We mopped up the juices with hunks of crusty bread, and washed the feast down with the coarse red wine I'd bought in for the gardeners; then the *coñac* bottle was passed round.

The patrolmen – who, it emerged, had transported the Rolls all the way from Barcelona – soon became quite merry. One of them had a good singing voice and treated us to some bawdy-sounding Catalan folk songs. Purvis seized the ladle and began to beat out the rhythm out on Elena's *paella* pan. They were both burly fellows, not the sort who would have welcomed an invitation to share any of the beds in the house, so I was glad when Elena asked them to stay overnight in the cottage. Even Pepe seemed to be enjoying himself, raising his glass numerous times to welcome the visitors. "*Bienvenidos a Casa Morena!*"

There was no chance of rescuing the luggage from the Rolls before morning, so I found pyjamas for my friends and made sure they were comfortable in their respective bedrooms. As I gently closed Trelawney's door, surveyed the debris in the kitchen and breathed in the lingering aromas of good food, rough wine and strong coffee, it struck me that my long-neglected house might just be turning into a home at last.

Chapter Thirteen

I rose early the next morning with a fuzzy headache, brewed coffee and took it onto the terrace. I was enjoying the first cigarette of the day when I spotted a stout figure clad in a black track-suit lumbering across my land towards the house. At first I thought it was one of the patrolmen but as the figure galloped nearer, I saw it was Purvis taking his morning exercise. I remembered his nimble descent from the breakdown truck the night before; despite his bulk, he was clearly in excellent physical condition.

"Morning, Pete. Lovely day!"

Indeed it was. The storm had died down overnight, the sun was already bright, and wisps of steam floated dreamily above the grass as the rainwater evaporated. Remembering my resolution to treat him with a good grace, I returned his greeting politely.

"Nice place you've got here, Pete. Lick of paint, spot of landscaping – you could do so much with it! Must be worth a fortune, even in this state, I'd imagine."

"Well, I do what I can. I'm not as well off as some of our circle."

"That's all set to change, though, from what I hear. Seems you took notice of what I said last time I saw you. Quite a catch, Marco, if you don't mind me saying so."

I bit my tongue. Enough was enough. "Actually, Purvis, I do mind you saying that. It's Marco I'm in love with, not his family's money."

I felt myself blushing as soon as I realised what I'd said. Of all people to hear my first open declaration of love for Marco, I'd chosen Purvis, who now gave me a benevolent smile.

"Ah, yes – in love, as I thought – and for the first time, Pete, if I'm not much mistaken. Ha! I remember what it was like. Throwing caution to the wind, nothing else matters but being together, for richer, for poorer – usually poorer, as I recall. But as you get older and you go around the block a few more times, you pay a bit more attention to the realities. Which usually means, the green. As opposed to the red."

It took me a moment to grasp the meaning of this revolting turn of phrase. And as he'd chosen to be so blunt, I decided to respond in kind. "So, you always check out the financials before you fuck, do you?"

Purvis let out a muted chuckle. It sounded quite sinister to me. "You could say that – yes, you could. Guilty as charged! Now look here, Pete. According to old Trel, you're a bit pissed off with me because I told Alex you'd become fond of Marco. Also guilty as charged."

He held his hands out for me to slip imaginary handcuffs over his wrists – a well-practised gesture, perhaps. "Thing is," he went on, "I told him that for a purpose."

I'd always regarded Purvis as devious, to say the least, so I was taken aback when he tackled the source of tension between us head-on.

"And what purpose was that?"

"I told you in the car at the airport, remember? If there's one thing I won't stand for, it's kids being treated badly. I want Marco out of that house."

Again, I saw a sudden, quite terrifying flash of rage in Purvis's face. He punched the air with his fist. Clearly, he would still be a formidable opponent in hand-to-hand combat and for a second, I imagined him flooring Commander Blaine with one well-aimed blow. It was not a displeasing prospect.

"I've watched you for a long time, Pete, and you've not been happy for most of that time. Until you met Marco. Or, let's call a spade a spade, until he pounced on you. I saw the change in you – overnight, you might say. But I also saw you were ready to run a mile. Five thousand miles, if you could. And, in my nosey, interfering way, I decided that would be the worst thing you could do."

I didn't know that my feelings were so transparent to everyone. Or, at least, to Purvis.

"Trouble is, Pete, I'm not an intellectual. As you well know. But you *are*. So you don't really listen to what a simple chap like me has to say."

I was about to protest, but I knew he was right.

"Which is why I told Alex what I'd seen and asked him to encourage you not to run away from your chance of happiness. I knew you'd listen to him. You and him being on the same wavelength. I probably poked my nose it where it wasn't wanted. Sorry. Not the first time, not the last. But by the looks of you today, maybe I did the right thing."

He had a point. If he hadn't told Alex, and if Alex hadn't encouraged me, I'd still be living my solitary life in the desolate lair that Casa Morena used to be. He'd helped Trelawney, and now he'd helped me. Maybe it was time to stop judging him and start trying to like him.

"There's nothing to apologise for. You're quite right. Thank you. What you did has helped me – and Marco too, I hope."

"You're welcome."

"Well," I said, to draw our talk to a comfortable close, "I hope you find some happiness too. One good turn, as they say..."

He chuckled. "Oh, don't worry about me, Pete. I have my interests in the Village, you know. But – how shall I put it? – some of us are more discreet than others, let's say."

A sudden resumption of yesterday's mechanical screeching and clanking made further conversation impossible. We dashed round to the back of the house. The patrolmen had managed to extricate their vehicle from the chasm that threatened to engulf it last night. Pepe had brought some planks to help them, and the Rolls was now being winched onto safe ground. As we watched the operation, Trelawney strode up to us wearing a threadbare dressing-gown of mine and a pair of old Wellington boots.

"Peter! I had no idea! All these years, you've persuaded us that you lived a life of abject squalor on an abandoned cattle ranch in the middle of nowhere – but just look at this!" He extended his arms as if showing off a dream property to a potential buyer. "It's paradise! How clever of you to find it, and how lucky you are, my friend!"

In the gentle spring sunlight, flanked by carob and almond trees, I had to admit that the old house made a pretty picture. I'd just never taken the time to appreciate it.

"And furthermore, you have done a great injustice to the lovely lady who has just served me breakfast. Far from being the hatchet-faced harridan you've grumbled about over the years, she is a charming woman of great dignity and grace. In fact, if you don't mind me saying so, I think she is rather *sweet* on you, Peter. There was a distinct glint in her eye whenever she mentioned your name."

I opened my mouth to dismiss this ridiculous suggestion, but then I remembered our happy day shopping in Almería. My opinions of a lot of people seemed to be changing these days.

Meanwhile, the patrolmen had finished unloading the Silver Cloud. They packed up their tools, thanked me warmly for my hospitality and disappeared down the track towards Aguacate with a final blare of the siren.

Trelawney cast a despairing glance at his purchase. Purvis produced a key from his track-suit pocket and stepped over to the car. All that could be heard when he turned the key in the ignition was a feeble farting noise from somewhere beneath its immense bonnet. Trelawney pursed his lips and rubbed his chin with the back of his index finger.

"There's a plane from Almería that'll get you home most days," I said quietly. "Don't worry about the car. I'll keep it safe for you."

"I can't say how embarrassed I am by this unfortunate turn of events," Trelawney whispered. "I'd gladly have handed Purvis the cash for sorting things out with the Ministry, but he said that would be taking advantage of me. He insisted on me having the car as part of the transaction. He has an odd sense of honour about these things. Now I rather fear the old lady's going to be your guest for some time to come."

The stately Rolls-Royce looked utterly incongruous in front of my decrepit barn, although it lent an undeniable touch of class to Casa Morena.

Purvis was now unloading a rather daunting collection of luggage from the boot. I went over to help him, and we began ferrying cases and boxes into the house.

"Looks like you've done quite well out of this, Pete," Purvis said cheerily. "Not everyone gets a Roller dumped on their front doorstep, free, gratis and for nothing. Would be a pity to sell her off for scrap, though."

"I wouldn't dream of it. The car is Trelawney's and I shall look after it for as long as he wants. It's perfectly safe here – I'll probably move it into the barn when the boys have finished clearing all that rubbish out."

"Well, you never know, Pete, she might come in handy one of these days."

I couldn't see how I would ever find any use for an immobilised and ageing vehicle of that size – but then again, nobody could have foreseen the chain of events that would one day give the "old girl" a new lease of life.

We retreated to the kitchen, where Elena was busily restoring order after the previous night's festivities, whistling tunelessly as she worked. I hastened to assure my guests they were welcome to stay for as long as they liked.

"That's very kind of you, Peter, but I really need to resume the life from which I was so summarily exiled. And Purvis, of course, has business to conduct down in the capital..."

"Too right, Trel. Can't keep the punters waiting. So we won't be troubling you for much longer, Pete."

"In any case," Trelawney added, "Marco must be arriving soon – and the day you welcome him to your gorgeous home must be a day that you and he share alone. When is it he's coming?"

"The fifth of April."

That was a date I was hardly likely to forget but, with a stab of panic, I found I had no idea of the date today.

"Good heavens – that's less than a week away! You'll have all our mess to clear up, and the vehicle to move...of course we must be on our way as soon as possible. It would be thoughtless to impose on you even for another day. Don't you agree, Purvis? I suppose we'll have to go into town to buy air tickets, won't we?"

With some pride, I offered to book their flights online. Even Purvis was impressed when I sent an e-mail to the small company that ran the shuttle service, and shortly afterwards printed out two tickets for the evening flight on the very same day. While I was waiting for the answer, I saw that Marco had e-mailed several times to remind me of his various requirements on arrival, the most essential of these being a hairdryer – "assuming, of course, that electric power has finally reached the badlands of Andalucía."

***

Casa Morena was looking superb, inside and out. I'd prepared Alex's old room for Marco to use – I hoped that we'd continue to share a bed, but I wanted to make it clear he was under no obligation.

However, access to the house was now virtually blocked by an elegant but gigantic automobile which the breakdown men had managed to leave stranded in the middle of the track. The truck had also gouged out huge ruts in the ground, so I asked Pepe to summon the gang from Aguacate to move the Rolls into the barn and repair the damage as soon as possible.

Otherwise, everything was in place for Marco's arrival. The Academia had e-mailed from Granada, accepting his registration for a course in "Arte del Flamenco" beginning in early May. I'd had no chance to drive over there and check out apartments, but that was something we could enjoy together. Federico let me know he would be opening Bar Alex in mid-April – just in time for Easter, which was celebrated in Almería with as much fervour and colour as Holy Week in Seville.

I returned from a walk one evening to find the last of the junk stacked neatly outside the barn. I went in and edged my way around the Rolls – there was just enough clearance to walk all the way around it. As I traced the sleek contours of the bonnet and wings with my fingers, I began to understand why people would be prepared to pay so much for one of these vehicles. Like a child in front of a Christmas tree, I was gently caressing the figurine on top of the radiator grille – the Spirit of Ecstasy, I remembered – when I was startled by a loud snorting sound that could only have originated from inside the car.

I peered through the windscreen.

On the front seat was a higgledy-piggledy pile of garments. On the back seat was Romeo, stretched out invitingly, no longer able to choke back his laughter at my fondling of the bodywork.

He daintily removed his underpants, tossed them nonchalantly into the front of the car and kicked the door open with his foot. He yanked me inside. In seconds, my clothes joined his on the front seat, and we were pounding away on that venerable leather upholstery with even more manic vigour than before. Trelawney was right about the suspension: the Rolls failed to respond to our thrashings in any way and at one particularly exhilarating moment, I thought my back was about to be broken.

As our gyrations became more and more frenzied, I was manhandled into the front of the car; Romeo's ingenious use of both gear lever and steering wheel suggested considerable previous experience of in-vehicle intimacy.

Afterwards, as we stretched out again on the back seat, contentedly sharing a cigarette, I wondered how many scenes such as this the "old girl" had witnessed in her long life. And surely, it occurred to me, performing the act on the back seat of a fifty-year-old Rolls-Royce must qualify me and Romeo for membership of some exclusive international association – even if the vehicle was mothballed in an Andalusian outhouse at the time.

I woke up the next morning, the fifth of April, to the enticing aroma of strong coffee wafting into my bedroom. I ambled through to the kitchen where Elena was cooking up a mixture of scrambled eggs, onions and tomatoes. She'd obviously decided that my agenda for today was momentous enough to merit exceptional support on her part. She'd picked out a different shirt than the one I'd attempted to iron the previous afternoon; all my clothes for the day were laid out neatly on a chair by the bathroom door. I showered, dressed, ate the delicious breakfast she'd prepared, and lit a cigarette with my second cup of coffee.

She sat down opposite me at the table. "I'll have lunch ready when you get back. About two o' clock?"

"That's very nice of you, Elena, but really, Marco's just an ordinary visitor. There's no need to go to a lot of trouble."

She shot me a look of utter derision. "Ordinary visitor. Ha!" She swept her arm around in a gesture that took in the various bowls of flowers, the glistening new paintwork, the fancy curtains, the sumptuously upholstered sofa and the other results of my extravagance. Then she winked at me, wagged her finger and repeated a Spanish proverb that I knew well.

"*¡El mundo es de los audaces!*" It means "Faint heart never won fair maiden," but the Spanish version neatly avoids any reference to gender. I could only nod sheepishly in agreement.

She tapped the dial of her watch. "Time to go. Move!"

She hustled me out onto the terrace, pulled the jacket straight over my shoulders and flicked away a fragment of cigarette ash that had landed on the lapel. Our relationship had changed out of all recognition in these last few weeks. I'd really become rather fond of her and on this day of all days, I was very glad of her support.

I started my car, and she waved goodbye to me as if I were a schoolboy racing off to class. I cast a fond glance at the back of the Rolls as I drove past the barn, and headed down the track towards Aguacate and Almería.

Chapter Fourteen

I reached the airport in plenty of time. With Easter fast approaching, extra planes from various parts of Europe were coming in and the arrivals hall was packed. I elbowed my way through the crowd to secure a position behind the barrier that separated greeters from passengers. How would Marco and I greet one another, I wondered? A warm hug, or an avuncular handshake? Maybe even a kiss, of some sort – it wouldn't be out of place in Spain. I'd let him take the initiative.

I tried to work out the perfect route to take through Almería to show the city off. Perhaps a stop for a drink in a sunlit café on the Paseo Maritimo, but nothing to eat because Elena, bless her...

These pleasant thoughts were rudely interrupted when Marco came storming through the arrivals lane, face scarlet, bathed in sweat. He marched straight up to me.

"Marco, welcome to..."

"Scram. Get out. Now!" He ripped open the zip of his shoulder bag and started rooting frantically for something.

"What in God's name...?"

"Parents. Both. Last minute. Here. Now. Looks like they've smelt a rat. They insist on meeting Victorio. Bribed their way onto the plane – typical. Snap their fucking fingers and they think the world stops turning."

He was almost in tears. I wanted to reach over and hug him but the barrier was in the way.

"Look, Marco, it'll be all right, you'll see..."

"You have no idea what they're capable of. I hope Victorio's got nerves of steel. He sounds like a hardened criminal to me – that's good. You're certain you've got him stitched up?"

"I reckon he'll play along. I could call him..."

"You do understand, don't you? If they think Victorio's a fraud, they'll have me back in Glasgow tomorrow."

Marco finally extracted Aunt Claudia's mobile phone from his bag and handed it to me. "Just stay well away and wait until I call you on this. Keep it with you at *all* times, even if you're fucking the gardener. Which I assume is now a frequent occurrence, since I can never get an answer on your house number."

I couldn't even look him in the eye because he was constantly glancing over his shoulder.

"Where are they now? Why didn't they come through with you?"

"I made sure one of their bags got left in Glasgow. My father is probably tearing some poor Spanish baggage handler to shreds as we speak. But I had to get to you, to warn you..." He was very nearly sobbing. "Peter, I didn't want it to be like this...and I swear to God, this will be the last, the very last and final time they ever screw up my life. Now, please, *go!*"

He did manage to stretch over and grasp my wrist as he said this. I felt like bursting into tears myself.

"OK, don't worry about me. How long are they staying? And where?"

"One night only. The most expensive hotel in town, whatever it is. They choose by numbers."

The airport tannoy system croaked into life with a piercing crackle and a series of chimes. I could barely make out the Spanish announcement, but it was repeated in stilted English.

"Meester Marco Blaine, to the lost luggage counter in Arrivals, imm-eee-diately, please. Meester Marco Blaine!"

"Well, at least that part of it worked. Mummy will just have to cope without a change of knickers. I am actually praying – I, Marco the Magnificent, am reduced to *praying* – that the rest of it goes just as well."

"If not?"

"I shall simply have to tell them the truth once and for all. Then at least I'll never have to speak to them again. Or else I'll shove them into one of Victorio's rat-infested dungeons and leave them to rot. I mean it. Now I *have* to go. You too."

I was rapidly losing the power of speech. Marco slung the bag back over his shoulder and was about to head towards the luggage carousels; then he stopped in his tracks and came back towards me. It flashed across my mind that if things went badly, this might even be the last time I would see him. Doubtless he'd had the same thought, and I tried desperately to think of something memorable to say – and what better than "I love you, Marco"?

But he spoke first, with that imploring look that I already knew so well. "Peter – pl-eee-ase, *pl-eee-ase* could you give me a packet of fags? I'm absolutely *gasping*!"

I passed him my packet of Marlboros, watched him stomp around the corner of the corridor into the arrivals area, and made my way back to the car park. I drove through Almería as quickly as I could and then dawdled along the road towards Casa Morena, at a complete loss as to how I should spend the afternoon. Or, if Marco was dragged back to Scotland and that was the end of the affair, the rest of my life.

My spirits sank even lower when I saw the spread Elena had prepared – a tureen of my favourite almond and garlic soup, fresh artichokes and asparagus, and an array of cured ham and sausages. I couldn't even bring myself to nibble a corner of the crisp loaf of bread she'd baked. But she was neither surprised nor perturbed by Marco's failure to show up.

"He'll come when he comes. *Los jóvenes son así.*" That's what youngsters are like. "The food will be just as good tomorrow, or the next day, or the next..."

I packed the phone and a few morsels of the untouched lunch into my haversack, and set out across the hills.

As I took in the views and admired the pretty yellow buds peeking out of the broom bushes, life began not to seem so bad after all. Marco was nothing if not resourceful. I was pessimistic about the outcome of the meeting between Victorio and the Blaines *en famille*, but if anyone could snatch victory from the jaws of defeat, it was Marco. Even if the whole whirlwind adventure ground to a halt now – well, I would have no regrets. The shell I'd built up around my life had been well and truly shattered and – who could tell? Perhaps another, less turbulent relationship lay in store for me.

I hiked down to the beach far below Casa Morena and plunged into the chilly Mediterranean. A good long swim took my mind off everything – including a bank of grey cloud sweeping in from the west.

By the time I swam back to shore the rain was teeming down. I dashed to a cavern I'd used for shelter on previous visits. These sudden spring showers could last for an hour or more, so I set about making myself comfortable. I remembered to check the mobile phone, but of course there was no signal down here. I replaced it neatly in my back-pack, which I then used as a pillow while I snoozed. The rain had stopped when I woke up but the sun was already setting, so I started scrambling back up the rocky path.

I knew that Don Victorio had mobile reception at his house, so I stopped to check the phone near the boundary of his land. To my horror, I couldn't find it in my backpack. I emptied everything out onto the grass. Nothing. The phone must have dropped out of the haversack in the cavern.

I set off back down the rock path in the gathering dusk. I lost my footing once or twice, and the pretty broom bushes now revealed their true nature as a miniature jungle of vicious spines and thorns.

Sure enough, when I reached the cavern, the torch I always carried in my backpack revealed the phone sitting just next to where I'd rested my head. I let out a whoop of joy and raised it above my head as if it were a nugget of gold.

When I reached Don Victorio's finca again, it was shrouded in ominous darkness – surely his encounter with the Blaines in town couldn't have gone on this long? My heart was pounding, my head spinning, and I realised I was talking out loud, telling myself how stupid I'd been.

As the moonlit outline of Casa Morena came into view, the evening calm was pierced by the blaring tones of *Deutschland über Alles* from the phone. I was gasping after the double climb as I grabbed it from my haversack.

"That's enough heavy breathing, Peter. *Now* where the fuck have you been? Two full hours I've been dialling this number!"

"Well, I was in this cave, you see, and I was so tired that I fell asleep, and then the phone was missing so I went back down the cliff again in the dark, and back up ..."

"Never mind all that. I accept that I am surrounded by insanity wherever I go. Now do you want to know what's happened!"

"Of course I do. Go on!"

"Are you sitting down?"

"No. It doesn't matter, I can take it."

He was clearly enjoying keeping me on tenterhooks. He stayed silent, calculating how long I could bear the tension.

"They fell for it. Hook, line and clinker!"

I opened my mouth to correct the idiom, but managed to stop myself. "Wow! You mean – really –?"

"Really. That man Victorio is one of the most disgusting arse-lickers I've ever met in my short life. So, of course, my parents loved him. And he's a smooth operator – he spotted that my father doesn't know the first thing about archaeology, or anything else academic for that matter. As usual, Papa produced the chequebook to shut him up – anything to avoid being shown up in front of my mother. Result: Blaine Twine and Yarn is now an honorary sponsor of his so-called heritage project. And he'll keep on telling them I'm shovelling rubble in that ghastly ruin all year, even if I'm on the moon. He's scared stiff of being found out."

I couldn't yet bring myself to believe that our improbable scheme had succeeded so brilliantly. "Marco, I still can't take it in. So, you won't have to go back to Scotland tomorrow?"

"No. And not for many a year, believe me. You've obviously lost the plot at the moment, sweetie, but I have to congratulate you on finding Victorio. Or are *all* your neighbours complete and utter crooks?"

"Well, there aren't many others. I thought he was a just a fairly harmless old bore who's making a bit of money on the side..."

"I suppose that's why his jaw hit the floor when I introduced my father as the Commander. It's a police rank in Spain as well, you know."

Well done, Marco. He certainly had the knack of manipulating any situation to his advantage. I hoped I'd never be on the receiving end of this particular talent – but, of course, I'd already fallen victim to it. Hook, line, and clinker. "What's more, he's a pervert of the first order. His so-called volunteers are all teenage girls with small brains and big boobs, and he's obviously screwing them senseless in the catacombs or wherever as soon as they down tools. He's probably got a finger in the white slave trade. Of course, my dear mother couldn't see through it – "Ooh, Marco, you'll probably find a nice little girlfriend for yourself while you're working for dear Don Victorio". It took all my effort not to vomit on the spot."

"But we won. You're free. Congratulations. I just want to say –"

Marco interrupted me with a protracted yawn. "I'm sure there's a lot you want to say, Peter, but save it for tomorrow. I'm shattered. I'll make sure they're safely on the plane tomorrow morning, and then you can buy me an *extremely* boozy lunch to celebrate the start of the Real Life of Marco Blaine. Meet me at two in the airport arrivals café. Don't *dare* go anywhere near departures in case you're spotted. And carry the phone in case of fuck-ups. Byeee!"

He ended the call so quickly he couldn't even have heard me say goodnight. For the sake of it, I murmured, "I love you".

I wondered if I'd ever have the courage to say it to his face.

Chapter Fifteen

Marco breezed into the airport cafeteria next afternoon, all smiles. I stood up to welcome him and he made a great show of kissing me on both cheeks before he sat down.

"Free, free, free at last!" He tilted his face towards the ceiling and let out a prolonged, orgasmic groan that caused heads at the neighbouring tables to turn.

"Peter, I'm only going to say this once because I don't want to overinflate your ego. Mine is big enough for the two of us anyway. But I am..."

He paused to order a vodka tonic from the waitress, who shot him a look of pure lust as she tucked the order slip into her bodice. He looked stunning in a superbly tailored suit of pale blue linen and a plain white shirt with a shocking pink tie that he'd lowered to a jaunty angle, presumably as soon as he was out of his parents' sight. He took and lit one of my cigarettes before continuing.

"I am *soooo* grateful to you I could actually kiss your feet – although I won't be going any further up, of course. For all your peculiar ways – and let's just draw a veil over your inexplicable conduct yesterday – you've succeeded where even the likes of Sadie and Beth have failed. You have liberated me from the tyranny of the most unfit parents ever to have produced offspring. So..."

The vodka tonic arrived, and he raised it to his lips. "I drink to your health, Peter Carter, and to the happy days we are about to enjoy together. *¡Salud!*" He drained most of his drink in one swig. "Now. Lunch. Why don't we eat in Almería? I'm quite impressed – nobody ever talks about it, so I thought it was just a shit-pit, but actually it's rather quaint. As long as we steer well clear of that fucking castle."

I remembered there was a little restaurant in the same street as Federico's bar, and it was there that we lingered over the first of the many long, lazy lunches that were to follow that year. Marco's good humour continued throughout the afternoon. He was an excellent mimic and I was in stitches as he recounted his parents' meeting with Don Victorio.

"He even tried to sell them some old pot he'd probably shoplifted from a hundred-peseta store – "Of inestimable value, Commander – it would look well in your lounge-room, Madame" – and of course, they handed over another wad of cash."

He seemed genuinely taken with Almería. Several times on the way home, he grasped my arm and made me stop the car so he could admire buildings I'd long since ceased to notice. We walked all the way around the bullring, as elegant as any in Spain, with its striking crimson and yellow façade.

"Blood and sand, of course," Marco pointed out; the reason for the choice of those colours had never occurred to me. "You should be glad I didn't decide to become a matador – the drag costs a fortune and the medical bills are enormous. And, at least, flamenco dancers tend not to be gored to death during a performance."

Like Alex a few months before, Marco nodded off during the last part of the journey to Casa Morena.

He woke up blearily as I parked the car in front of the terrace. "Where are we? I thought we were going to your house?"

"This is my house. Welcome to Casa Morena!"

"But Peter – it's *gorgeous*! I thought we'd pulled into some posh country hotel for honeymoon couples – I wouldn't put it past you, I know how your mind works. Actually, this is far nicer than any of my parents' places."

"Thank you."

"We'll be off to Granada soon though, won't we? When are we going?"

"There's no point leaving before *Semana Santa* – everything closes, and everyone in Spain goes crazy for the week. Anyway, I think you'll enjoy the carnival here just as much as there."

I was amazed at how quickly we settled into a pleasant domestic routine. I managed to get back to work during the daytimes, speeding through my translations thanks to the computer. Marco would occasionally float into the section of the lounge that I'd partitioned off as a work area to offer a glass of wine or announce dinner was ready. He was a surprisingly good cook, but Elena naturally disapproved of his invasion of the kitchen and relations between them quickly became icy.

"She doesn't like having a rival around, of course," Marco pointed out barely a day after they'd met. I insisted her supposed infatuation with me was just a joke, but he dismissed my protests.

"She drools over you, anybody can see that! But then, some people enjoy spending their lives longing for the impossible," he added with a wicked simper.

I was expecting Marco to demand constant entertainment and excitement, but he seemed perfectly content to spend the days walking in the hills or down to the beach, sitting with Pepe in the garden of their cottage (he christened it the "Hobbit House") or, even more surprising to me, doing little odd jobs around the place. I'd closed and locked the barn doors after Romeo and I had our last memorable encounter there, so a few days passed before Marco found a way in and saw what it contained. He'd realised I didn't like interruptions while I was working, but this discovery merited an exception to the unspoken rule.

"Being here is changing my view of the human race, Peter. I can now see it's quite normal for a translator who lives in a part of Spain that civilisation has barely reached to have a Rolls-Royce hidden away in his barn. I mean – what the *fuck* is it doing there?"

I told him the whole story of its journey to Casa Morena which, naturally, led on to a session of fond reminiscences about the Village and its motley cast of characters.

"Be that as it may, the car is in a disgraceful condition – nobody bothered to clean the mud off the bodywork before they shoved it into the barn. And furthermore, Peter, there are *unspeakable* stains on *all* the seats. Only one fluid leaves marks of that particular type."

I gave him a slightly edited account of what had transpired inside the vehicle.

"My, my, you have come a long way from shagging the sergeant on the police station switchboard, haven't you?"

"We didn't do it *on* the switchboard, actually – he worked on the switchboard, and we..."

"Enough! I shall tackle the car tomorrow. If not for your sake, then for Trelawney's – I suppose I owe him a small debt of gratitude, as I'd never have met you if it weren't for him."

I thought he being sarcastic, but he wasn't. After he'd said this, he took my head between his hands and moved it close to his, staring into my eyes. He moved his tongue seductively across his lips and for a moment, I thought he was going to give me a real kiss; instead, he licked the tip of his index finger and placed it gently on my mouth.

"That's all I can do for now. I like you a lot, but not in that way."

My heart was thumping just as fast as when I answered his phone call outside Don Victorio's house. Maybe I'd better stop kidding myself I could manage to continue this relationship without sex. To complicate matters, Marco decided without hesitation that he wanted to sleep in my bed.

"It's a new experience for me to sleep with somebody. I've decided I rather like it. Look at it this way, sweetie: a lot of people spend a lot of time in bed with somebody else, without actually fucking them. You might even call it normal behaviour."

He would fall asleep almost as soon as his head hit the pillow while I lay beside him, kept awake by a disquieting combination of contentment and frustration. I alternated between hoping that he would reach over and pull me to him, and relief when he didn't – knowing, deep down, that sex at this stage would inevitably spell the end of the relationship we were building. I eventually trained myself to ignore this nightly tantalisation and concentrate instead on being grateful for an end to the long years of loneliness.

The grand opening of Bar Alex was a quintessentially Spanish occasion. The entire front of the house had been opened up, trestle tables and chairs were set up on the street and it looked like most of the neighbours were joining in. We were greeted by an affable, plump lady of about my age, clad in a bright pink smock and a polka-dot bandanna that reminded me of June's back in the Village. She joked and laughed as she flipped home-made *empanadas* and *croquetas* onto guests' plates from a huge frying-pan. It turned out that she was Federico's mother.

A four-piece gypsy band played everything from tangos and *boleros* to Spanish pop. When they launched into the Ricky Martin song Marco had danced to in Glasgow, I expected him to leap onto a table and dominate the proceedings as he did before. But he just looked at me and shook his head.

"No, Peter, this is their party, not mine. Plenty of time for that in Granada. But that's no reason for you and me not to dance – come on, *everybody* dances in Spain!" Though I knew he could easily have outshone every dancer in the bar, he pinned me into a corner and patiently taught me the few simple dance steps I can still perform today.

Federico, of course, was frantically busy – apart from the crowd of neighbours, there must have been at least a hundred guests, many of them in flamboyant garb. A coachload of outlandish characters from the Benidorm clubs had come down especially for the occasion. On this showing, Almería's first gay venue was all set to become a rip-roaring success. Federico took the time to come up and welcome us.

"Hey, Pedro...This must be Marco the Magnificent!" He clapped one hand on each of our shoulders. "Wow, whenever I see you, you're with an absolute hunk – you certainly have good taste in men!"

Quick as a flash, Marco came back at him. "And so do I!"

Federico jumped in to explain. "It was Pedro who introduced me to my Alex. Look, I put a little photo of him on the wall behind the bar. There wouldn't be a bar if it weren't for him. Go take a look, Marco, and give me a call soon, it'd be great to hang out with you guys when things calm down a bit."

He dashed off to welcome a group of gentlemen dressed as nuns who were just making their stately entrance. We wove our way around the dancers to the elegant zinc-topped bar. The framed photo showed Alex in his prime, grinning mischievously and raising a glass of champagne towards the camera, as if to offer it to a waiting customer. The portrait was hardly larger than a paperback book, but to me it seemed to dominate the entire room. Underneath it, Federico had placed a brass plaque with a simple inscription:

Alexander Macallister
1956-1999
Un Gentilhombre

Marco was also studying the photograph intently. I could understand why – after all, he'd attended Alex's funeral, but he'd no idea of what my friend looked like except for the outdated portrait he'd seen on the order of service.

After a while, he turned to me. "Peter, can I ask you a question?"

His voice was uncharacteristically subdued.

"Of course. You don't usually ask permission."

"Did Alex go to Glasgow very often?"

I didn't really know the answer. "I suppose so – after all, his family was there..."

Marco clamped his hand over his mouth in dismay. "Oh. Fuck. Jesus H. Christ! I think I've met him."

I realised immediately that this would not have been a social encounter over tea and scones.

"You mean – "

"I can't be sure. The light wasn't very good. It was in one of the back rooms upstairs at De La Rue's."

"It really doesn't matter, Marco. But you'd perhaps better keep quiet about it when we see Federico again."

"Does Alex have a really *huge* – I mean, an absolutely *monstrous* –"

I cut him short. "Yes, he does. Did. I knew him for years, you know – we often went swimming, so..."

He squinted at the portrait again. "Peter, I reckon it was him. About two years ago. Come to think of it, he said he didn't live in Scotland, though he was definitely Scots. I asked him for a re-match, you see, but he told me it was his last night in town. Oh my *God*!"

"You didn't ask his name?"

"Peter, you really have a lot to learn. You *never* ask people's names in those circumstances. Not that they'd give you a real one. Anyway, it's rude to speak with your mouth full. Mummy taught me that."

I looked across at Alex's photo again – his smile seemed to have become even more impish. So, did he know exactly who we were talking about as we spent all those hours discussing love, lust and jealousy? Or was the whole thing a complete fantasy in Marco's mind? There seemed to be no limit to the sexual permutations that went on – or were imagined – in the "real" gay world that I'd somehow been dragged into. And did it really make any difference if my might-have-been lover and my would-be lover...

Marco interrupted these pointless thoughts. "No use staring at his picture like that, sweetie. He's the only one that knows the answer, and I don't think he's about to tell us. But I do have another rather important question for you."

I just wanted to get another drink and carry on dancing. I was learning that it was an excellent way to forget about the complications of life – which seemed to be increasing by the minute, as they usually did when Marco was around.

"And what's that?"

"What did Alex die of?"

"Do you really need to know?"

"Yes I *do* really need to know. You might say it's a matter of life and death. Do I have to spell out why?"

I hadn't thought of that. "Lung cancer. Nothing else."

"Thank God." For the first and last time, I saw Marco stub out a half-smoked cigarette. "I mean, poor guy. How awful...but, well...I did make an exception to the rules for him. Under the circumstances. Never again."

His face had drained of all colour. He excused himself and rushed off to the toilet; I thought he was about to throw up.

My own response to the emergence of AIDS had been simple: sheer terror. I stopped having sex of any kind for all of the 1980s and well into the 1990s – not that very much had happened since my now legendary fumblings with the policeman. Whispered rumours and harrowing government advertisements stirred up panic and fear that probably saved my life and many others. It was also a reason – or a good excuse – for the life of increasing isolation I'd chosen to lead. But Marco's generation had grown up with fairly clear facts, open discussions and testimony from a growing number of healthy long-term survivors. I still had my doubts as to whether it really was Alex that Marco had met; but by the looks of Marco's face for those few seconds, he'd learned a lesson he would never forget.

His sombre expression as he returned from the bathroom suggested I was right. Wanting to steer the conversation on to lighter matters, I asked him how he thought Trelawney and Purvis would fit into this exotic gathering. But it seemed we were not done with the subject just yet. The nuns were making their way round the crowd, handing out small parcels from flower-baskets. One of them, sporting a heavy ginger beard, now approached us, squeezed my thigh, tweaked Marco's ear and presented us each with a gift-wrapped package.

"They're the Sisters of Perpetual Indulgence, sweetie. We have them in Glasgow too."

I opened my package to find a couple of condoms and a little leaflet in several languages. The headline on the English version was 'Fancy risking your luck?' above a photograph that left no doubt as to the price to be paid for unsafe practices.

I mumbled something about too many coincidences, but Marco waved it away. "You'll always find the Sisters dropping by in any respectable gay bar. The way I feel right now, I might become one myself. How marvellous to live in an age when sex means either nothing at all, or a death sentence. Aren't you glad we're the only couple in here who definitely *won't* end up fucking tonight?" He drained his glass and passed it to me. "I think I need another drink after all this, *pl-eee-ase*, sweetie."

People were already making their way to work in broad daylight when I bribed a taxi to take us to Casa Morena. Marco passed out as soon as we fell into the back seat; I was just about coherent enough to give directions to the driver. I was glad that Elena wasn't around to see us reeling and staggering up the steps, our arms around each other's waists – a spectacle that would surely have demolished any romantic hopes she may have nurtured.

It took us two full days of lounging around and sipping chicken broth to recover fully from that memorable evening.

And then it was time to head for Granada.

Chapter Sixteen

I know of no city that is more instantly captivating than Granada. Approaching from the south, as we did that day, you climb rapidly from the lush palm groves and sugar-cane plantations on the coast into the bleak, boulder-strewn terrain at the western end of the Sierra Nevada. In spring, you encounter the first dribbles of greying snow on the slopes while the memory of the sunlit coast is still fresh in your mind's eye. On and on the road climbs, the landscape ever more arid, the wind howling through the canyons. You're beginning to wonder whether such a laborious journey is really worthwhile when you breast the last rise – and there before you, in all its exotic majesty, is the Palace of the Alhambra, its massive ramparts reddened by the setting sun.

I'd seen this sight many times, but it never failed to send a shiver of anticipation down my spine. As we dropped down towards the city and wound our way around the snail-shell highway that eventually penetrates to its ancient heart, Marco fell silent except for an occasional gasp of wonder.

"I've seen more places in twenty years than most people see in a lifetime, but this beats the lot! And look at those little white houses, all clustered together on the hill up there...just gorgeous!"

"That's the Albaicín. The Moorish quarter. I thought we might look for an apartment there."

"I just can't wait to explore! Please, Peter, when can we go into the Alhambra? Tonight? Tomorrow morning?"

"Actually, our hotel is almost inside the Alhambra precincts. If they've given us a good room, you'll see into the palace from the balcony."

I'd booked us in at the Washington Irving Hotel, named after the nineteenth-century American writer who once followed the route we'd just taken on horseback. Its reception area was crammed with faded engravings from early editions of his 'Tales of the Alhambra', and the rooms were named after characters from his other works. We were assigned to 'Rip Van Winkle' – although the racket from a small construction site below the balcony made it unlikely any of its occupants would emulate Irving's hero.

The view was superb. To the left, the crenellated towers of the Alhambra clustered around the monolithic square palace of the Emperor Charles V; to the right, the tiered gardens of the Generalife with their soaring cypress trees; and as the backdrop, the snow-capped peaks of the Sierra Nevada.

The next day, we made the first of many visits to the Palace itself. I watched with delight as Marco craned his neck to take in the cascading stucco work on the ceilings of each courtyard, cunningly reflected in the myrtle-lined pools and water channels. We watched some restorers at work, crouched on rickety platforms suspended from a roof. The tools they were using to reconstruct the huge expanses of ancient mosaic looked no larger than pencils. We strolled through the immense Generalife gardens, stopping to admire the meticulously trimmed hedges; they were shaped into birds or animals, and there was even one that portrayed a flamenco dancer.

Marvellous though it was to be living in a historic monument, the noise from the building site prompted us to press ahead with our search for an apartment. I wanted a view as good as the one we had from the hotel, but Marco insisted on ground floor accommodation.

"I assure you that neighbours won't appreciate a flamenco dancer practising on the floor above their heads. It's worse than living next to a trombone player."

In the end, we rented the ground floor of a dilapidated villa built around a patio with a little fountain in the middle – a *carmen*, as they call these old Moorish houses in Granada. The rest of the building was unoccupied apart from the owner, an elderly black-veiled lady who was none too steady on her feet when we met her to look the place over. A series of misunderstandings made it clear that she was virtually stone-deaf. Marco jabbed me in the ribs and hissed: "Take it. She wouldn't even notice if we were rehearsing for the Edinburgh Tattoo down here."

Once Marco started his course at the Academia, I realised the wisdom of his choice. I was driven to distraction by hour after hour of thumping and stamping, often accompanied by recordings of tortured singing. He told me it voiced the rage and defiance of gypsies imprisoned and exhibited in wicker cages by the perpetrators of the Spanish Inquisition. The hand-clapping that accompanies flamenco is also an art in its own right, I learned, and this too requires hours of deafening, monotonous rehearsal. But when he returned from class and proudly placed a pair of castanets on our kitchen table, I decided that enough was enough. The weather had warmed up by then, so I decreed that all future practice would take place in the patio.

Strains of gypsy music often floated through the air from neighbouring houses, counterpointed every hour by the bells of the Albaicín's innumerable churches. There was even a mosque within earshot whose muezzin, I'm sure, had installed extra-powerful loudspeakers to make sure that his calls to prayer were audible above the rest of the cacophony. Evenings here were a far cry from the utter silence that prevailed at Casa Morena, but as I watched Marco's increasingly muscular figure pounding away at his daily exercises, I had no desire to return.

That was not the only realisation that struck me as I stretched out on the ottoman, fascinated by the intricate detail of the movements he was performing. Although he'd never looked more handsome, I sensed that the edge of my physical desire for him was becoming blunted. It felt comfortable rather than tantalising to watch him force every muscle in his body into the service of the art he was determined to master. Of course, if he suddenly changed his "rules" and pounced upon me, I probably wouldn't have resisted. But the imperious urge seemed to be fading. I didn't know whether to be relieved or disappointed, so I just accepted it.

The Academia itself was housed in a much larger version of our *carmen*, in a secluded square at the foot of the Albaicín hill. I got into the habit of walking Marco down to school in the mornings. After we'd said goodbye, I'd take a seat in the Academia's tea-garden. A passion for tea – unusual in coffee-addicted Spain – was another legacy left to Granada by the Moors. I sampled a different blend each day as I read the newspaper or watched the comings and goings of flamenco devotees of all ages. Parents or partners of other students would sometimes come up and chat with me. "How's your son getting on?" would be the usual question, and I didn't correct them. But one day the girlfriend of one of the few other male students came and installed herself at my table.

"You're Marco's partner, aren't you?"

"That's right. I think he's in the same class as your..."

"Fiancé. *Madre mía de mi alma*, that boyfriend of yours is so talented – he just outclasses everyone else without even trying. You know that, don't you?"

"I can't really judge. I'm only just starting to learn about flamenco myself."

"Oh yes. He's *phenomenal*. My Juan can't stop talking about him – even at night! Lucky I'm not the jealous type. You're a very fortunate man, you know – and you're going to be a very rich one as well."

"What do you mean?"

"Your Marco is going to be a star. Not just good – he could conquer the world, believe me. You must be very proud!"

I was glad to hear that Marco was making progress: objective self-assessment was not one of his strong points, so I treated his own opinion with caution. But what struck me most about this brief conversation was the casual way she identified me as Marco's partner. Our relationship was a reality: other people could see it and in this country, they accepted it as nothing out of the ordinary.

Although my nights next to Marco were easier now, I began to sense a sort of pent-up tension at odd moments of the day. I'd find myself staring at a handsome man in a café, or just walking along the street. More than once, my look was returned with some hostility, so I decided I'd better find a suitable outlet. Visits to murky corners of the internet were losing their attraction. I thought of returning to Casa Morena on the pretext of checking on the house, hoping to run into Romeo – but that would somehow dispel the magic of these idyllic days in Granada.

Then I came across an online review of an ancient Moorish bath-house not far from the Alhambra. Especially during the siesta hours, it was said to be a "hotbed of fleshly pleasure," so I decided to give it a try.

The delights on offer fell far short of the description. The domed and colonnaded interior had seen better days but was still impressive – more the sort of place I'd have expected in North Africa rather than Spain. There was plenty of time to admire the flaking tilework because the establishment seemed at first to be completely devoid of clients. I eventually wandered into an almost pitch-dark room which, judging from its odour, was probably the alleged hot-bed. I thought I was alone and was muttering to myself about what a waste of time this was when a rasping Cockney voice interrupted me. "Slim pickings today, eh?"

Through the steam, I could just about make out a bulky figure perched on one of the marble benches that ran around the walls. There was no reason why an ageing East Ender should not be whiling away the afternoon in the tepidarium of a Moorish bath-house in Granada but even so, I was quite taken aback.

"Sorry?"

"Not much meat on the slab, is there, love?"

I had to agree. He was clearly an old hand – I presumed I didn't qualify in his eyes as "meat on the slab," so I saw no harm in talking to him for a while. He'd started his adult life as a rent-boy in London, he told me, in the good old days when politicians and high-ranking churchmen could still indulge their sexual predilections without the constant attention of the gutter press.

"Worst thing they ever did, making it legal, if you ask me. It were all so much easier when everything went on behind closed doors."

I saw what he meant. After all, the cloak-and-dagger routine added to the thrill of encounters in the Village. I let my new acquaintance ramble on – he shocked me by dropping several names that I didn't expect to hear in that particular context.

"Anyway, love, change and decay, change and decay, as they say." He expelled a dispirited sigh. "To think I used to 'ave 'em queuing up on the King's Road, twenty quid a throw – and now look at me, I can't even *give* it away!"

Our conversation was interrupted by a screech from somewhere in the darkness behind us.

Then, a voice that I knew all too well yelled in outrage. "No, *not* there, sweetie! Don't even *think* about it – not that you could do anything with that *jelly-bean* you've got hanging there. Out! Now!"

A door slammed. Seconds later, Marco stormed into the room

where we were seated, swathed in towels, one hand clamped to his forehead. "I *ask* you! What's more, he's still got his *socks* on! Mind you, he may have a point, looking at the state of the floor in this dump. Having a nice afternoon, sweetie?"

Yet again, I was amazed by Marco's total composure and utter lack of embarrassment when he met me hard on the heels of a sexual encounter with someone else. The idea of offering an excuse, let alone an apology, for his presence during what I supposed were class hours clearly never crossed his mind. But that also meant I had no cause to feel guilty or ashamed. My new friend tapped Marco on the chest.

"See, darling, you'd have been better off 'aving a few moments of bliss with your old Uncle Barney. Don't say you wasn't offered!"

Marco turned to him with a kindly smile, and ruffled his straggly grey hair. "You know, honey – I think you're probably right. Tell you what – I'll consider it next time. For a fee, of course. It'll set you back a bit more than twenty quid, I'm afraid."

Uncle Barney made an extremely uncouth noise that involved his tongue protruding from his lips and the expulsion of copious amounts of saliva. Marco prodded my ribs.

"C'mon, sweetie – stiff drink on the way back, and then it's time for castanet practice. I put a nice casserole in the oven on low before I dragged myself up here, so we can have a cosy little evening at home."

Uncle Barney expelled another profound sigh. "Some people have all the luck. You're a fortunate man, my friend."

If one person calls you a donkey, my father used to say, you smile and pass them by. But when the second one calls you a donkey, you'd better start braying. I pondered those words as we dressed. Uncle Barney could be heard whistling in the far reaches of the bath-house. I recognised the tune as "Someday My Prince Will Come." If I hear that song today, it revives all the memories of that golden summer, and it never fails to bring a tear to my eye.

Chapter Seventeen

The Academia was an establishment of some standing. It was a family enterprise set up in the 1950s by the distinguished dancer Diego Escobar, who was still to be seen sauntering around the place in an ice-cream suit and Panama hat.

Nowadays, the institution was presided over by his daughter, Dolores Escobar, known throughout the world of flamenco by her stage name: La Furiosa. This formidable lady of imposing stature – she towered a couple of inches above Marco – would emerge from her midnight-blue Mercedes and stride across the courtyard. In the earlier, cooler days of our stay, she was enveloped in a floor-length sable coat that must have cost more money than I was likely to earn in a decade. The reception area of the Academia was lined with photographs of La Furiosa performing before the King, and in the company of celebrities ranging from Nureyev to Elton John.

She took a close personal interest in the progress of every student. On the morning of Marco's first master class with her, he was more nervous than I'd ever seen him. I stayed in the tea-garden until he came out of class and walked up to my table with a crestfallen air.

"What did she say?" I asked him.

"Satisfactory. Then she gave me a sort of faint smile and said I had potential. Well, I know that, but – fuck, this is going to be a long haul, Peter. But I'll make it, if it's the last thing I do!"

Talking the next day with Elvira, the girl whose fiancé was in Marco's class, I learned that La Furiosa was never known to make any comment, favourable or otherwise, either to her students or about them.

"That's her way – she teaches with her feet, not her mouth. So, I tell you: what she said to Marco is worth more than a hundred diplomas from all the dance academies in Spain. All my poor Juan gets is a nod now and then – but usually just silence. It doesn't matter to me, though – I adore him anyway!"

I became quite friendly with Elvira as the summer progressed. She and Juan occasionally accompanied us on our evening outings to flamenco taverns. Sometimes we went to the tourist traps in the caves below the Abbey of Sacromonte; more often, we visited the genuine *tablaos* where impromptu performances continued into the small hours. As time went on, and Marco was gradually accepted into the flamenco community, the venues included schools, youth clubs and even an old people's home.

Jazz is the only other art form I know that is practised in such a relaxed ambience. The dancing can carry on for three or four hours, but you'll be served drinks, a platter of wafer-thin ham and tangy Manchego cheese, or even a whole dinner as you watch. Drinking and smoking are perfectly acceptable during the show, and conversation carries on except during the most dramatic solo routines. After a morning in the tea-garden, and an afternoon working on my laptop by a shady pool in the Generalife gardens, I'd look forward with great anticipation to these extraordinarily civilised evenings. I was quite happy to munch away at whatever delicacies were served in the flamenco venue while Marco moved around the room discussing the finer points of the performance with fellow *aficionados*.

The food was equally delicious at home. As spring gave way to summer, rich stews simmered in an earthenware pot were replaced by the endless variety of sausages, salamis and hams available from Granada's markets and *bodegas*. Marco grew more slender and sinewy, whereas my midriff was beginning to bulge. The folding door on our shower was very narrow and one day I was having some difficulty in edging myself through it sideways. Marco happened to be in the bathroom at the time, and he spotted my clumsy manoeuvrings.

"Hmmm," he said as I eventually extricated myself, "you were nothing but a bag of skin and bones when I first met you, but you're really quite a chunky little monkey now, aren't you?"

He moved closer to me, put his hand on my belly-button and began rubbing my stomach. I saw the contour of his shorts change in an unambiguous way. I was speechless.

"You've seen me operate often enough, sweetie, so you know I like a good bit of meat on the bone..." Now he was massaging the top of my right thigh with insistent circular movements of his fingers. I was as limp as the pennant of a becalmed yacht; I fumbled desperately to prevent the towel around my waist from falling to the floor. I knew I had to stop him, but as I reached out to push his arm away, the towel dropped.

"Oooh, naughty, naughty! It looks like the moment of truth has arrived at last, sweetie!"

"Marco, please – no. Not now. You know it'll ruin everything. You made the rules, for God's sake – *please* can we stick to them?" I couldn't believe I was saying these words after all those nights of torment,

He brushed the tip of my lifeless penis with his little finger. "Really, sweetie, is that the best you can do? Hmmm...seems it wouldn't work out too well, anyway. Rain check, by the looks of it. You can get tablets for that sort of problem, you know – they sell them under the counter at the tobacco shop down the road, in case you didn't know."

"I don't need – I mean, it's just not the right time – Look, Marco, I think we'd better just forget this ever happened."

"But it *did* happen, Peter. Or rather, it *didn't*. And as you're very well aware, I'm not accustomed to being turned down. Just wait until I tell Sadie about this – ageing translator misses out on shag of the century!"

As usual, he was pumping the situation up into a melodrama, but underneath the act I could read the genuine pain of rejection in his face. I felt wretched. The look he gave me was as black as thunder.

"In fact, the balance of my mind is so disturbed that I'm going to call her right now. Bugger the expense. Kindly make yourself decent."

I'd forgotten I was standing there stark naked as I tried to hold a conversation that was beginning to look like it could herald the end of our relationship. Marco stalked out of the room to find the phone, leaving me in utter turmoil. I attempted to calm myself down by doing simple tasks: cleaning my teeth and applying the various lotions and cosmetics that Marco had taught me to use. But my heart was pounding faster and faster, and blood was rushing in my ears. I heard him get through to Sadie, wherever she might be by now.

"Yes, I think it might be dump-the-frump time, darling...you'll never believe what he's just done...after all these months...no, it didn't budge a *millimeter*...what? Of course I did..."

There was such a long silence I assumed he'd ended the call. I finished dressing and walked through into the main room but he still had the mobile phone clamped to his ear. Even from a distance I could hear Sadie, in that voice which could surely shatter tungsten, administering a tongue-lashing that caused Marco's face to drain of all colour.

"All right...yes, I will...no, never...I'm sure he will..."

Eventually, with a look of utter humiliation on his face, he handed the phone to me. "She insists on speaking to you."

I took the phone and greeted her as cheerily as I could.

"Good evening, Mr. Carter. I'm sorry that we have to speak under these unfortunate, not to say *ridiculous* circumstances. I ask you to remember that Blaine is, in some respects, still a child – I would say adolescent, but that's pushing it. He wants what he wants, right now, without a thought for the price to be paid. And we know where *that* comes from, don't we?"

I emitted a croak of some sort by way of reply, but she boomed on.

"For your information, I have placed a ban on Blaine having sexual relations with you until I deem fit, on pain of his losing my friendship for eternity. Now —"

I bridled at this. I tried to break in with a protest about her outrageous interference, but I couldn't stem the torrent.

"You can interrupt me when I've finished. When we last spoke, I complimented you on your tolerance and patience. I do so again. You, at least, have managed to keep a lid on your own lustful intentions which, whether you like it or not, were plain for all the world to see. Fortunately, as I detected, there was — and is — something more noble beneath them. To put it in a nutshell, *I do not want this relationship fucked up. Literally*. By either of you. And as you'll understand, I have used the most powerful weapon at my disposal to make sure that it doesn't happen. I'm not particularly concerned if you think I'm speaking out of place. I act out of love, and loyalty, as I told you before. I can only hope that you two will do the same."

She was right. The only cloud hanging over our relationship had the distinct outlines of an erect male organ. Sadie's threat to Marco had certainly chased it over the horizon, at least for the time being.

"I'll admit you've grasped the situation quite well from wherever it is you are, Sadie..."

"My business, not yours. But I can tell you, I keep a closer eye on both of you than you might imagine. Now, please put this misfortunate episode behind you and get on ... with enjoying your lives and loving one another. Do I make myself clear?"

"As ever, Sadie."

"Goodnight. Until the next time."

"Good..." The connection was broken before I could even get the word out.

Marco had poured both of us a glass of wine and was staring

abashedly into his. "She's right, Peter. I was a fool to try it on. I'm neither blind nor stupid, so I know what you've been through, and I truly admire you for keeping your paws off me all this time. I can't quite believe that..."

He took a slug of his wine. I waited for him to find the words. "...that just for a split second, just a teeny weeny little bit...I wanted you. I mean, look at you – you're not exactly Tom Cruise."

"But better than poor old Uncle Barney."

"I'll give you that much. The poor old sod!" He blew his cigarette smoke up towards the ceiling. "I don't know what came over me. Funny how things turn around, isn't it?"

"That's life, I guess."

"Well, you may never get another opportunity, and I hope you don't regret it."

He was proved right on both counts. There never was to be another opportunity for us to consummate our relationship in that particular way. And to this day, I've never regretted it.

I knew we had to break the mood and move on from the most awkward moment we'd experienced since we met. I didn't know how to do it, but Marco did. He leapt up and rapped out a deafening sequence of thuds with his feet, then swirled around and grabbed my hand to make me join in. I started to laugh as he used his hands to make my legs follow his. I didn't wince in the slightest at this physical contact, so soon after the event in the bathroom. The tension was dispelled; we sat down, panting, and I refilled our glasses. Marco raised his, and I clinked mine against it.

"Enough," he gasped. "Let's head up to Sacromonte, watch one of those tacky tourist shows and get far drunker than we ought to." Which is exactly what we did.

Chapter Eighteen

The temperatures soared as the summer days sped by and the long holiday to mark the Assumption of the Blessed Virgin Mary on 15th August was not far away. To escape the crowds, we started taking trips at the weekends – to the cool white villages of the Alpujarras or the coast, to swim from the beaches at Motril. We also attended our first – and last – bullfight, in the quaint little town of Sanlúcar de Barrameda on the edge of the eerie marshlands of the Guadalquivir delta.

Marco was quite gung-ho about witnessing a bullfight. He tried to persuade me that it was an art form just like flamenco, so it was almost a duty for him to attend. But his enthusiasm waned almost as soon the first bull trotted into the ring. It was a rather skittish animal, and it kept charging into the barrier between the audience and the arena. When you hear the wood splinter as the bull's horns smash into it, you know you're not watching a film. Marco grabbed my arm in terror and would not let go, edging ever closer to me. The creature met its inevitable, bloody end – it was a messy kill – and the old nags came plodding along to drag the bleeding carcass out of the ring. Marco gathered up his bag and camera, and rose to his feet.

"Out. Now, please, sweetie. I knew what a bullfight looks like, I knew the bull was going to die – but nobody told me about the smell! I think I'm going to puke..."

It was certainly an overpowering mixture: blood, fear, and the acrid odour from the contents of the animal's massive bowels and bladder, which were spattered all too visibly across the sand. The idea of entering a bull-ring was never raised again.

Not long after our visit to Sanlúcar, Marco returned from school one afternoon proudly brandishing an envelope.

"Tickets for the event of the year, sweetie! The flamenco show in the Generalife theatre on 15th August. And guess who the star performer will be?"

"You, of course, my sweet."

"Don't be so ridiculous. Doña Dolores herself is dancing! She came into class to give me the tickets in person, and insisted you come to the show with me."

An appearance by La Furiosa was an event not to be missed. Now in her late fifties, she rarely performed in public. Marco had shown me some clips of her in action and even on the small screen, the charisma she exuded was bewitching. I'd walked through the open-air theatre occasionally during my visits to the Alhambra – it is the only ugly structure in the entire complex. Built in the Franco era, apparently with the aim of striking awe into its occupants rather than offering them comfort, I thought it would have been quite a suitable setting for a Nuremberg rally.

"I see we're in the front row of the stalls," I said as I examined the contents of the envelope.

He snatched the envelope back. "I hadn't noticed that...wow, these tickets must be like gold dust! She did say the show was sold out."

"That means there'll be upwards of three thousand people."

"She could pull in thirty thousand. She's an absolute mistress of her art."

Marco's great respect for La Furiosa was clear from the tone of his voice. This period in Granada was certainly changing his character: I couldn't remember him showing any signs of respect for anyone in the past – certainly not his parents, or his teachers, or the various hangers-on who clustered round him on the Glasgow gay scene. Sadie was perhaps the only exception – but she commanded the kind of respect the bull would be wise to show the matador.

We decided to dress smartly for the occasion. I chose an off-white cotton suit with a black silk shirt and Marco wore a black waistcoat embroidered with silver thread I'd bought him in Seville, with a crisp white shirt, set off by a red-and-white bandanna around his neck. When I caught sight of our reflections in a shop window, I paused for a moment as if I'd glimpsed a pair of Hollywood stars.

"Don't you think we look pretty good?"

"Peter, when I took on Project Pterodactyl, I promised you I'd change your life for the better. In every respect, not least your appearance. Promise kept?"

"Kept." I moved my face close to his and blew him a kiss. "Thank you, Marco. For everything."

"*De nada*, sweetie. And there are more changes to come, just you wait and see."

Like all the seats in the theatre, ours were moulded from an exceptionally unaccommodating plastic compound, but we certainly had the best view in the house.

"Stick with me and you'll always be a VIP, sweetie."

"Nice to have friends in high places," I murmured in reply.

"That much I learned from my parents. It's not what you know, it's who you exploit. Though God knows why they're so keen to cosy up to Victorio – he's a complete nobody."

"He's served your purpose very well and you know it."

I'd called him a few times since we'd been in Granada to check that he was keeping the Blaines happy with glowing accounts of their son's progress. I had to put up with the usual rambling descriptions of progress at the dig before he confirmed he'd kept his side of the bargain.

The house lights dimmed and a spotlight was trained on the steps leading up to the stage. Nothing happened for a long time; people began to groan and ask what had gone wrong. Then, having generated exactly the degree of anticipation she wanted, a figure known to every magazine-reader and television viewer in the country strutted onto the boards. This was none other than the Duchess of Alba, Spain's richest, most outrageous, most scorned but best-loved aristocrat, still sprightly in her seventies. Her chaotic tangle of frizzed hair was dyed fire-engine red for this occasion. I estimated that she was wearing several million pounds' worth of jewellery in each ear.

Marco nudged me and whispered: "She married a defrocked priest, you know. And rumour has it that her toy-boy is twenty years younger than her!"

"Shut up, Marco!" I hissed. "We're so near the stage she can probably hear you."

"She wouldn't give a flying fuck. Anyway, younger partners are all the fashion in Spain – you're in good company, sweetie!"

I wasn't sure I wanted to be likened in any way to the ageing but much-restored Duchess. As her introduction wore on, I began to think even Don Victorio would have tired of the sound of his own voice before she did. At long last, she ran out of words, hitched up her skirt and broke into an erratic but vivacious flamenco routine of her own, leaving the stage in a flurry of thumping and finger-snapping. Rather charitably, the audience gave her a lengthy round of applause.

Finally, the moment came for La Furiosa to appear.

The stage was plunged into total darkness; not a sound could be heard from the auditorium. A faint rosy light began to colour the translucent stage curtain from the bottom up. Gradually, a network of criss-crossing bars was projected onto the curtain and behind it, the silhouetted figure of La Furiosa could just be made out, lying face down on a low bed. Very slowly, as if in excruciating pain, she raised herself from the bed and seemed to be crawling across the floor. She eventually managed to lift herself to her full height and look around her – although we could only see her shadow, every one of her movements conveyed the most acute agony.

Then she broke the silence with a horrendous, drawn-out wail. Just in time, I realised that the latticework behind the curtain was real. Of course – it represented the wicker cages that Marco had told me about. La Furiosa spun around and with one tremendous clout, sent the whole structure crashing down towards the audience. For a split second, I thought it was going to land on top of us. As she demolished the cage, she also tore the entire curtain in two with such violence that shreds of it came floating over our heads. And at that precise second, she burst into the most electric, frenetic flamenco routine that I've ever seen, to the thunderous beat of hidden drums and the soaring and plunging strains of the guitars.

To me, this was a completely different dimension of flamenco than anything I'd seen in Granada or elsewhere. Even the best of the dancers in the taverns seemed like amateurs compared to La Furiosa.

She danced for well over half an hour. The sudden shifts in tempo and mood caught the audience unawares, and we could hear them gasping and yowling in astonishment.

After many rounds of applause, there was a pause before the final item. I saw from the programme that it was to be a *fandango* – as I now knew, the extravagant Moorish dance of courtship and unrequited love.

The lights dimmed again. This time, La Furiosa made a perfectly conventional entrance, walking to the centre of the stage. I thought she was about to address the audience, but instead she pointed an imperious finger straight at us. Still I didn't understand, because this finger-wagging is an intrinsic element of the body language of flamenco. Marco had begun to use it himself whenever he felt that my attention was flagging.

It was only when Marco rose from his seat in response to her beckoning that I realised what was about to happen.

Of course – the *fandango* was always a dance for two or more partners, and there was no mention of a male dancer in tonight's cast. As Marco climbed the same steps that the Duchess of Alba had so recently trodden, I was overcome with pride that La Furiosa should invite him to partner her, but trembling with anxiety in case he loused it up.

I needn't have worried. Of course, he couldn't match her half-century of training and experience, but that didn't matter. He danced from his heart, because he was dancing his own story.

He began with a stunning solo exhibition: only now did I see that the money I'd invested had certainly paid dividends. Suddenly, his head disappeared under the silver-threaded waistcoat, as if he were talking to his own heart. As the pace of the dance accelerated, he deftly slipped the garment over his head and tossed it down to me. She gazed at him, captivated, dancing with increasing flamboyance to try to attract his attention. At first, he didn't notice her, then he did; he rejected her advances, she became more and more desperate, he started teasing her – at one point, their bodies were totally intertwined, but somehow you could hear that their feet were stamping out separate rhythms. No words could have expressed infatuation and rejection more exquisitely. Finally, she tired of him and retired to her corner of the stage, where she could once again enjoy dancing for her own pleasure.

But now of course, his interest was aroused; and soon it turned into passion. He did everything to attract her attention: he pirouetted and spun around like a dervish; at lightning speed, he stamped his way across the entire stage to present her with an imaginary flower; he writhed on the floor before her in abject desperation, but all to no avail.

The music that accompanies the *fandango* simply consists of the same insistent theme played again and again, slightly faster each time.

As if the dancing were not enough on its own, the relentless repetitions of the music cranked the tension up to boiling point. I felt that my head would explode under the strain – and I was not the only one, judging from the expressions of my neighbours in the stalls.

At that moment, the guitars and drums stopped; the two dancers came face to face and stood in silence, gazing into each other's eyes. She extended her hand; he took it gently; they kissed. The silence continued, and then all hell was let loose: the music switched up from minor to major and in the last minutes of the performance; the pair of them capered and cavorted across and around the stage in their shared joy. La Furiosa, somehow, seemed to have shed forty years and was dancing with just as much youthful energy as her partner.

Her partner. *My* partner.

The audience erupted in wave after wave of rapturous applause. They yelled and screamed in adulation, hurling flowers and confetti onto the stage. Marco bowed; La Furiosa curtseyed; the musicians, singers and hand-clappers joined them as the house lights came up. Then, in what was and remains the proudest moment of my life, the *grande dame* of the flamenco world stepped aside and led the audience in a standing ovation that lasted a full five minutes for my lovely, wonderful, phenomenal, divinely talented Marco.

I was in floods of tears – the lady sitting next to me became quite concerned, passed me a handkerchief and patted me on the back. "*Bis! Bis! Bis!*" the audience screamed, and naturally there had to be an encore.

They danced – and sang – to music that was in total contrast to what had gone before: a seductive, swaying *rumba* entitled *Tuyo es mi corazón* – "Yours is my heart". Now that we could all relax, the unspoken conventions of flamenco were broken: whatever else might be allowed during a performance, it is absolutely forbidden to clap, sing along or, worst of all, stamp one's feet. But as the *rumba* gathered momentum, the dancers encouraged the audience to do all three: the theatre was soon vibrating to the sound of three thousand or more people joining in with this captivating old melody. I knew the song well – it had been recorded by countless artistes since it was written in the 1930s, and was still a favourite on Spanish radio. I wondered who had chosen it, and why, as I sang the last lines:

> *Mi vida la embellece una esperanza azul,*
> *Mi vida tiene un cielo que le diste tú.*

> Hope flows through my life, like the blue waters of the sea,
> And high above my life, there is the sky you gave to me.

As the last strains of the song died away, the auditorium began to empty. I knew Marco would have to spend time backstage with the other performers, so I remained in my seat to wait for him. I think I could have stayed there quite comfortably all night, savouring and reliving the magic of the evening, imagining the meteoric career that now, beyond a shadow of a doubt, lay ahead for him. I was so deep in reverie that I didn't even notice when he finally came and sat down in the seat next to me. He tapped my shoulder.

"Well, sweetie, will I do?"

"Marco, what a ridiculous question to ask! You saw what the audience thought of you, and La Furiosa herself..."

"I don't mean will I do for them. Will I do for you?"

He looked at me meekly, and I slowly understood what he was asking. Not a single word would come out of my mouth.

"If the Duchess of Alba can do it, so can we. I had to kiss her, by the way – *atrocious* bad breath. She seems perfectly happy with someone nowhere near her age. No matter what people say about it. So – what about you and me?"

"You want to be my partner."

"You got it. Deal?"

Typical Marco. At his age, of course, he couldn't have any understanding of what a partnership actually meant. These things needed to be discussed calmly and in depth, surely? He was having the time of his life in Granada, that was clear. He wanted it to go on for ever; I was the one who had made it possible, so he naturally wanted to sign me up long-term. I recalled Sadie's words: *He's still a child...he wants what he wants, right now, without a thought for the price to be paid.* His view of life was disarmingly simple. I supposed it would do no harm to go along with it.

"Nothing would give me greater pleasure."

"I might have known you'd come out with some hackneyed old cliché like that, sweetie. A simple "yes" would do."

"Then: yes. Yes. Yes."

The theatre was empty by now. He leaned over to me and we kissed. Long, and deep. I broke the kiss first; Marco pulled me back to him for more. Things seemed to be getting more serious than I thought. When our mouths finally separated, I hesitated to ask the question that had forced itself into my mind.

"Em, what about..."

"What Sadie said?"

"Yes. I mean –"

"Can't we just leave that for now? We've got the rest of our lives, after all...and Peter, I'm absolutely *famished.* It's certainly *not* a night for salami and salad by the telly!"

"We'll go somewhere really nice, then. Wherever you like."

"Granada's been so good for us, right from day one – so why don't we go back to the Washington Irving?"

"Sure. Maybe we can even get the same table."

We did, and they'd folded the terrace doors back now the weather had warmed up, so we ate a leisurely supper with a sweeping vista of Granada's floodlit splendours before our eyes. By the time the waiter brought our bill, we were both in a sort of daze – drained by the day's events, and more than a little tipsy after a couple of bottles of wine and sizeable *coñacs* with the coffee.

Afterwards, we lolloped down the Alhambra hill, arm in arm, across the rushing Darro river in its ravine, and all the way home.

As I lay in bed, waiting for him to join me, I couldn't help wondering if the kiss in the theatre would lead on to something more, despite Sadie's dire warning. In a way, it did. As I lay on my side, Marco wrapped his body around mine, his chin resting in the indentation of my collarbone. I felt profoundly at peace, deeply contented.

"Spooning, this is called, you know," he explained. "I'm the big spoon, and you're the little spoon. Night-night, sweetie."

We still "spoon" in bed to this day but, things being as they are, I have become the big spoon and Marco is the little spoon. It's not always the most comfortable position to sleep in, but we were so utterly exhausted that we spent the whole night interlocked.

Which is why the normally unignorable notes of *Deutschland über Alles* blaring from the mobile phone in the next room went unanswered as they rang out repeatedly through the night.

Chapter Nineteen

I t must have been that funereal refrain which dragged me back to consciousness next morning. I was about to lever myself gently out of Marco's embrace and make for the bathroom when it started up again. I never answered it, because Marco's family were virtually the only people who had the number. I ruffled his hair to wake him up.

"Phone."

"Shit."

"I'll fetch it for you."

I brought it from the dining table and handed it to him, but by then it had stopped its beeping. He stared blearily at the little screen.

"Fuck. Twenty-seven missed calls. My parents. From their number in the Village. What the hell do they want now?"

He rolled over into his stomach and stuck his arm out towards me, twitching his first and second fingers. "Fag, sweetie, *pl-eee-ase*. I think I'm going to need it."

No sooner had I lit one for both of us than the vexatious melody began again. He answered the call, exhaling a long funnel of smoke before he spoke.

"Yes, mummy, I'm fine, how...What? He can't have!" Then came a torrent of French that was too fast and garbled for me to decipher.

His face turned crimson as he listened. He sat bolt upright in bed, flicking his cigarette ash furiously onto the floor. "Yes...Well, Don Victorio gave us a few days off, that's why...Of course I will. Today might be difficult...Yes, yes, as soon as I can."

He ended the call with the most frigid of goodbyes and hurled the phone across the bedroom. "Fuck, fuck, double fuck and fuck the fucking lot of them."

He stomped into the bathroom to relieve himself. I knew I had to wait for him to tell me what was happening, but my stomach was already starting to churn with foreboding. He came and sat next to me on the bed, burying his head in his hands.

"Well?" I said, as softly as I could.

"My father. He's been hit by a car. Stupid fucking idiot insisted on walking all the way up the hill from Beetlebridge. Knocked unconscious. A goatherd found him. Saved his life, probably – not that the poor kid'll get any thanks, being one of the filthy germs and perverts, etcetera."

"How is he?"

"Stable, but poorly. That's the word she used. He's in the main hospital in town. She wants me there. He's asked for me, apparently."

"When?"

"Immediately. I can't see any way out of it. I have to go."

The spell was broken. The serene, mellow mood of the night vanished in an instant. It was as if the wicker scaffold had come crashing down, and the curtain shielding our lives from the outside world was rent from top to bottom.

"Peter – I can't do this alone. I just can't." He started sobbing and hid his face in his hands again. "Please will you come with me? Say you will?"

I placed both my hands firmly on his shoulders and stared him in the face. "Of course I will. You don't even have to ask."

"It'll be tricky in the Village. You can't be seen with me, of course. But I'll feel better just knowing you're near. And I can come and see you at Trelawney's."

He attempted a smile, but failed. We breakfasted in almost total silence on the patio.

"I wonder if we'll ever sit here again," he murmured as he topped up our coffee.

"Of course we will. Your mother's probably exaggerating. He's her husband, after all, so she's bound to be panicking."

"I have my doubts. I knew it was all too good to last."

There was no way I could shake him out of his increasingly despondent mood, so I left him to finish breakfast and fired up the computer to book some tickets. There was no direct flight from Granada, and only one seat left on the evening plane from Madrid that would get Marco home. I managed to book connecting flights for him, and decided I'd drive him to Granada airport, then continue down to Algeciras, leave the car there and embark on the long ferry voyage. It would still be faster than waiting for the next plane. I called Trelawney and gave him the news.

"Of course you must stay with me, dear boy! The house is empty apart from Purvis and myself, so Heliotrope will be waiting for you as ever. This is no time to be alone; never forget you are much loved by many in the Village. We shall, as the poet Browning puts it, greet the unseen with a cheer."

I doubted there would be much to cheer about on this particular visit, but I was heartened by Trelawney's words. I knew that, whatever happened, I could count on his support. And somewhat to my surprise, I was actually looking forward to seeing Purvis again.

The atmosphere in the car on our journey to the airport was as grim as it had been at the breakfast table. I took the turning for the car park, but Marco stopped me.

"No, Peter, I'll just get out and go. It's all too painful after...after..."

I reached over to give him some sort of a kiss as he opened the car door, but I barely managed to brush his cheek.

"I'll see you soon, sweetie. I'll get a message to you at Trelawney's whenever I can."

With that, he dashed into the airport. He didn't even turn around or give me a last wave. It was as if the last few months had never happened.

I turned the car around and headed out of Granada along the same route we took when we drove from Almería to begin the adventure that now seemed like a mere illusion. The mountains looked even more hostile and menacing without their covering of snow. Back in the city, the sunlight was benevolent and nourishing; up here, it was harsh and unnerving.

I climbed towards the pass of Suspiro del Moro, the Moor's Sigh: the point where the last of the Moorish kings sighed in despair as he took a final look back at the city and kingdom he was forced to abandon. I, too, knew in my heart that the dream world we'd created for ourselves in Granada had vanished forever. The whole story of the accident might even be a trick: they could have found out that the Almería project was nothing but a subterfuge, and they were going to confront him with it.

As it turned out, all my speculations were well wide of the mark. What awaited us over the water was far beyond anything I could have imagined as the Rock of Gibraltar loomed into view, and I caught my first glimpse of the mist-shrouded coastline of Africa over the water.

Part Three

A Somewhat Different View of Love
2000

Chapter One

Far fewer people have swum the Straits of Gibraltar than have climbed Mount Everest, and the start of my voyage that day gave me a good idea why. The water began churning and boiling as soon as the steamer edged out of Algeciras harbour and turned her back on the Rock. A bitter wind sliced through the Straits, driving me away from my preferred spot on the open deck. I retreated to one of the enclosed lounges packed with migrant workers, their veiled wives and screaming, vomiting children headed home for the late summer holidays.

The wind dropped, only to be replaced by a clammy fog that persisted throughout the long journey. I was chilled to the bone by the time I set foot on the gangplank. Quaking, I stood in line at the passport counter where barely a year before, I was preparing myself for the horrors of life in a prison far from home.

My mood had sunk so low that I was actually bucked up by the normally uninspiring sight of Mahboob, paunch propped atop the balustrade at the far end of the customs hall.

"Lovely to see you as always, Mr. Carter. The limousine is standing by. I, myself, in person, shall have the honour of driving you to Mr. Trelawney's front door."

I told him how glad I was that the residents of Trelawney Towers were once again allowed to partake of his services.

"Ah yes, sir, what an unfortunate misunderstanding that was."

Mahboob scratched the side of his nose, decided he could do better and then inserted his index finger fully into his left nostril for some serious excavation.

"Water under the bridge, Mr. Carter, water under the bridge. I am at your entire disposal for as long as you care to stay in our country. But sad to say, I have to recover the losses I incurred during the suspension, so my prices..."

"Yes, yes, Mr. Mahboob, whatever you say. Now I'm here to visit a sick friend, so there's no time to waste."

"Message received loud and clear, sir."

He was as good as his word, honking his way through the traffic with total disregard for the few traffic lights that were functioning. The next day was the anniversary of the Revolution of the People, Mahboob informed me, so the beach road was cordoned off for a fireworks display. This forced us to make a detour past the drab grey walls of the hospital. Perhaps Marco was inside at this very moment, gripping his father's hand in a poignant deathbed reconciliation scene. Or perhaps he was too late...

The fog cleared as we drove eastwards, so my first glimpse of the Village above us, with a crimson sun setting behind it, was as breathtaking as ever.

Trelawney was poised to greet me on his front doorstep, arms spread wide.

"Welcome back to Trelawney Towers, dear boy – words I never thought I'd say again, but how little we know of what life has in store!"

"I can't say how much I appreciate this, Trelawney, at such short notice –"

"On the contrary, Peter, I am the one who appreciates the chance to offer you my traditional brand of hospitality. Now give dear Mr. Mahboob his pound of flesh, and come on in."

I counted out no less than sixty pounds into Mahboob's eagerly outstretched palm, but I was past complaining or arguing.

Tamir appeared in the half-light of the vestibule behind Trelawney, looking untypically bashful. Although no longer necessary for tactical reasons, his marriage had taken place shortly after Trelawney's return from Europe.

"I am sorry for the trying circumstances that bring you here, Peter. But we also have great cause for celebration."

"Revolution Day? I know the kids sometimes let off fireworks up here, but I've never known you to throw a party for it."

"No, no, not that. Tamir has done his duty!"

Tamir giggled and playfully clutched Trelawney's arm.

"Really? Finished his military service already?"

Conscription was a bane for most young men in this country, but a few banknotes distributed in the right quarters could reduce it to a couple of months.

"Peter, although your personality has blossomed in recent months, you can still be very obtuse. Tamir is now a father-to-be!"

Trelawney seemed as proud as if he had sired the child himself. My energy was flagging, but I tried to show some enthusiasm.

"That's marvellous! Congratulations, Tamir!" I reached out and shook his hand vigorously.

"Now come on in, Peter. I know you're tired, though you look magnificent. Tamir will deal with your luggage."

"Thanks for the compliment, but I feel like death warmed up. I just need to collapse for a few hours, and then I'll have to find out what's happening with Marco's father."

"You should consult Purvis about that. He seems to know what's going on."

Purvis was reclining on a long chair on the terrace, his face concealed behind a copy of the Telegraph which he lowered slightly when I greeted him.

"Evening, Pete," he murmured. "Nice journey?"

"Not particularly."

"Long way to come for a storm in a teacup, really."

"What do you mean?"

"Well from what I hear, old man Blaine was knocked out for a few minutes, bruised and grazed a bit, but nothing serious."

"Thank God for that!"

Purvis took a sip from his glass of chilled white wine. "Seems he's out of hospital and back home already. So they're all cooped up together in their eagle's nest. Happy families, and all that."

My heart went out to Marco. What must he be feeling? He'd moved heaven and earth to liberate himself from his parents – and now, only a few hours after his hard-earned moment of triumph on stage with La Furiosa, they'd yanked him firmly back under their control.

"Do you know where the accident happened?"

"About half-way up the hill, I gather, by that patch of waste ground. I expect you know it."

I did, and so did every other visitor to Trelawney Towers. It was exactly where I'd collected Marco and Beth for our beach excursion on my last visit. It was also a popular spot for discreet encounters. I couldn't help tittering at the thought of Blaine, flat out, his face submerged in the particular sort of detritus which littered that piece of land.

"Anyway, Pete, *they've* hauled young Marco over here, and now he's dragged *you* over here...a touch risky, for you both, I'd say. I think I'd make it a short visit if I were you."

As I unpacked my bag, I found myself in agreement with Purvis. It was beginning to look as if my journey was totally unnecessary. I stretched out on that familiar bed, so weary that the painted cherubs on its canopy seemed to be flying around in circles.

I was awoken by a gentle tapping at the door of my room next morning. Automatically, I rolled over in bed to nudge Marco. But, of course, he wasn't there. I climbed out of the four-poster and plodded over to the door.

Tamir was there, clad in a freshly-laundered white *djellaba*. He held a brass tray with a cup of steaming coffee and a folded page torn from an exercise book, sealed up with an enormous amount of Christmas sellotape. A huge letter "P" was scrawled on it.

"I come help you wake up, Mr. Peter?"

Although a *djellaba* covers almost all the wearer's body, it can be an extremely revealing garment – and as before, Tamir had evidently dispensed with the luxury of underwear. But I decided to resist temptation and anyway, I couldn't wait to see what Marco had written.

"Now, now, Tamir, you're a married man."

"You too, Mr. Peter, you got husband now! You fixed up, I fixed up. Everybody happy."

I envied him his simple view of life. Maybe I could learn from it.

"That's right, Tamir. Everybody's happy now."

"But can still play? Zeki coming to Village today."

For once, this was unwelcome news. All I wanted was to find Marco and get us both back to Spain as soon as possible. If the Commander's accident was really as trivial as Purvis claimed, we could easily be in Granada for the start of his classes after the August break.

Nevertheless, I feigned enthusiasm. "Ooh, that's nice. When's he coming?"

"Afternoon time. Want see you. Want see your husband also."

Well, of course he would. In the usual Village way, the situation was becoming more complicated before I'd even made it out of the bedroom.

"How did this note come, by the way?"

"Gardener boy from Blaine house bringing it early morning. You want answer, I take back."

"Thanks again, Tamir. I'll come and find you if I need to send an answer."

"You welcome, Mr. Peter. Always happy help you. We all same family!"

I felt a sudden rush of warm affection for everyone in this bizarre household. Whatever happened in my life from now on, I knew I'd always have a home here.

As soon as Tamir had closed the door, I ripped Marco's note open and sat on the bed to read it. There were only a few lines:

Sweetie,

This is the biggest load of bullshit I've seen since we were at Sanlúcar. They threw him out of hospital after the first night. Upsetting the other patients too much, I imagine. He has minuscule bruises and a scratch on his face that looks like it was done by a hamster. I just need to get OUT of here NOW! But I'll have to keep them happy for a bit longer. Victorio's done a superb job, I'm sure they don't suspect a thing. The frustration is killing me. Every part of my body feels like it's about to explode. Including and principally my balls. Fortunately, Zeki's around, as I expect you know. Meet me inside the church gate at 2 to decide strategy. Much love kisses etcetera Marco.

PS. Thank you sweetie.

PPS. For fuck's sake don't smile or even look at me if you see me in the street. You know what the Village is like. XX

I knew exactly what emphasis and intonation he would give to each word. It was almost as if he was there with me – I half-expected him to emerge from the bathroom, complaining that he'd run out of some lotion or other.

I knew I'd be counting the minutes until two, but decided to make the most of my free morning. I'd been fond of Beth from the very start, and was eager to see how she'd changed since we last met.

First, though, I walked across to the drawing room and found Trelawney at breakfast, in his usual place at the head of the refectory table. Purvis was nowhere to be seen.

"Peter," Trelawney began, munching his toast. "I'm mindful that your situation has changed since we last breakfasted at this table, and I have great respect for my guests' partners. Of course, you will want and need to see Marco while you're here, and I appreciate you are not at liberty to visit his parents' house."

He wiped his mouth with his napkin, kept in place by two clips suspended from a delicate silver chain around his neck.

"Yes, it's a bit tricky, really. But –"

"Let me finish. The assault on my – our – freedom mounted by the Blaines and their like has been roundly rebuffed, of course. Thanks to Purvis, but at considerable effort and expense. Including the purchase of that ridiculous vehicle which is now marooned on your premises."

"The Rolls is perfectly safe, Trelawney. Pepe checks it every day when I'm not there."

"Sad that I shall probably never drive it again. There really was no need for Purvis to throw it in as part of the deal. But it has served its purpose: we are here."

I refrained from disclosing the purpose it had served for Romeo and me.

"Anyway, Peter, I have to say that my feelings towards Commander Blaine have not mellowed. I cannot imagine any circumstances under which I would ever speak to him, let alone permit him to enter this house."

"Quite. Marco's assured me there's no risk of that. His parents have no idea that I exist. They think Marco's been having the time of his life with a bunch of Spanish schoolgirls, digging up old pots in Almería Castle."

"I'm pleased to hear it. Marco is extremely – er, inventive, shall we say – so I'm sure he has the situation under control. And as he is now evidently your partner, I shall not object if you choose to entertain him in your room. Just be very discreet about it, and be sure to use the rear entrance."

My conscience was relieved when I heard this. Of course, I knew exactly what Marco was going to ask when I met him later at the church. If Trelawney ever found out that my plan for "entertaining" Marco included letting him share the four-poster with Zeki for an hour – well, I'd find some way round the problem. It was the Village, after all. I set out for the Olive Branch in much brighter spirits than when I arrived.

June threw her arms up in delight as I walked through the archway into the café garden. She was positively blooming: perhaps another in her series of admirers had trekked across the Saharan sands to enjoy her favours.

"Oooooh, now there's a sight for sore eyes. Home is the sailor, home from the sea!"

She waddled out from behind her counter and hugged me so tightly that I was gasping for breath. "I don't need to ask how you are, love, I can see for myself. Marco popped in yesterday, so I know a bit of what's been going on – quite the young gentleman he looks now. You two are doing wonders for each other. Sit yourself down and tell your Auntie June all about it."

I looked around. "Is Beth not here today?"

"Nah, I gave her the day off, she'll want to spend as much time as she can with Marco while he's here. Those Blaines don't approve of her, of course – what a pair of stuck-up arseholes *they* are. That won't put her off, she's made of stronger stuff. She's bound to drop in later if you want to see her."

I spent an agreeable hour bringing her up to date while she went about her tasks. I was searching for words to convey the magnificence of Marco's performance with La Furiosa when she placed her hand on my wrist to stop me.

"You really love him, don't you? I mean, *really*."

I looked her in the eye. "Sometimes I'm sure I do – sometimes I just don't know, June. I've never experienced anything like this before, and..." I stammered.

"Take it from one who *does* know, dearie. I can hear it in every word you say. And anyway, it's not what you say, it's what you do – and just look at how much you've done for him."

"Not really – I've spent a bit of money, yes, but...well, it's just been a lot of fun for both of us, that's all."

"Now come on. You've changed him beyond belief. He actually thinks about other people now. He saw I was run off me feet when he came in yesterday, so he came straight behind the counter to help me serve up. He's losing that awful selfishness they taught him up in the big house."

She cast a scornful glance towards the hill that was crowned by the Blaines' mansion, just visible above the palm trees in her garden.

"Now, I've had my fair share of gentleman friends, as you well know – I certainly shan't die guessing. But lightning only strikes once, they say, and when my turn came, I...I..." Her face changed completely. Her usual jollity evaporated, and I saw the edge of a profound sadness that I never suspected was there. "I let it slip through my hands. I wasn't brave enough to go all out for the one I really wanted. What is it they say? Faint heart never won..."

"Something like that, yes. They say the same thing in Spanish."

"I'm sure they do, dearie. But I'm telling you in plain English: you've found him, now stick with him. You'll never regret it. And for your information, I told Marco the same thing yesterday. Now you can tell me to keep my fat nose out of your business."

"I wouldn't dream of it, June. A few people have said similar things recently, so I'm beginning to..."

The rest of my sentence was drowned out by a loud explosion and a series of smaller ones in the alley outside the café. I leapt up in shock to try and see what was going on through the archway, but June was unperturbed.

"Revolution Day, of course. You can't really complain about the kids letting off fire-crackers. It's their country, after all, not ours. Them as works in the houses up here don't have much fun. Let 'em enjoy their day off!"

I'd already forgotten that today was the big public holiday. That explained why Zeki wasn't working and could come down to the Village. Which reminded me – the morning was speeding by, and it would soon be time to get down to the church. I took my leave of June with another bone-crushing hug.

Chapter Two

Two o'clock was fast approaching. The route to the church was all downhill, so I had just enough time. As I turned into the lane that led down to the lych-gate, I very nearly collided with Greta, striding vigorously up the hill towards her house with two bulky bags of shopping. She stopped, placed the carrier bags on the ground, and offered me her hand.

It was a gesture of truly imperial grandeur. I really felt I should kiss it, but I made do with a rather limp shake.

"Peter! It is wonderful to see you back here, so soon after our recent spell of..." She paused to choose the word carefully: "... *unpleasantness*."

"I'm just as glad as everyone else that it's all over, Greta." I had to stop myself from addressing her as 'My Lady'. "We all agree that it was one of your greatest triumphs."

"The point is that I absolutely refuse to have anyone treated as a second-class citizen in this Village. I fought in a war for six long years to defend that principle. Sadly, it has not yet prevailed in the world at large. But in my little domain, if I may call it that, it is sacrosanct."

I stole a look at my watch; I had only a minute to get down to the church, but I couldn't possibly end the conversation before I was dismissed.

"I believe Sir Brian was very helpful in getting things resolved," I said.

"He was, indeed. In fact, he is dining with me tonight. And by way of thanks, I am doing him the honour of cooking our supper with my own two hands. He has my greatest respect."

"And Mr. Purvis played his part too, I hear."

Her smile faded a little. "That is true, to a degree. I shall thank him in due course, at a more public venue. Perhaps over one of dear June's lunchtime specials, as I believe they are called."

So much for *égalité et fraternité* in her empire.

I nodded politely. "Well, if you'll excuse me, Peter, I'd better get these commodities into my kitchen."

A rivulet of water was trickling out of one of her bags, from what looked suspiciously like a pack of frozen fish fingers. The tiny Village shop was not noted for its stock of gourmet delicacies.

"Of course, Greta. I hope we'll meet again soon!"

"Oh, I'm sure we shall. I owe Trelawney a visit, so I'm bound to see you there."

I picked up her bags as she unlocked her door, and placed them on the gilt-legged console table in the hallway.

"Goodbye, Peter. Enjoy your afternoon!" she said, with a trace of amusement in her voice. I had the impression she knew exactly where I was off to, and why.

It was already well after two when I walked through the lych-gate into the churchyard, but Marco was nowhere to be seen. I propped myself against James Anthony Horrabin's gravestone and smoked a cigarette. Still no Marco; his parents had probably banned him from going out or found some petty chore to keep him occupied.

I went over to the lych-gate and was scanning the lane outside when I felt a gentle tap on my shoulder. I turned around, and there he was. He'd scrambled over the back wall of the graveyard under the cover of the cedar trees. I opened my mouth to greet him but he thrust his finger across my lips. Gone was the brash, self-confident Marco of Granada and Glasgow. His complexion had lost its glow; he seemed shrunken and stooping. He pointed to the porch on the side of the little church.

"In there," he whispered. "I'll go, you follow in a minute. We *must* not be seen."

The porch was built to afford shade from the binding sunlight, and it performed its function well. Marco had huddled himself up at the end of a bench next to the church wall. I went to sit next to him but he pushed me away and made me sit opposite him.

"I can see what a strain this has been," I began.

"Too fucking right. The fuss he's making over nothing is just beyond belief. I truly think he's lost his marbles. He has this weird idea it was a deliberate hit-and-run. And what's more, he's convinced Purvis was the driver of the car that knocked him down!"

This didn't seem totally improbable to me, given the way Purvis reacted to any mention of the Commander's name, but I kept my opinion to myself.

"If he thinks that, why doesn't he go and confront Purvis?"

"Not in a million years. Purvis stays in the house of perverts, remember. Infidel territory."

"I thought the two of them got on well – doesn't Purvis do some of his financial stuff for your father?"

"What you mean is, he helps my father avoid paying tax. Obviously, he knows Purvis is a poofter, but somehow that doesn't matter when money's involved. Typical double fucking standards. Something must have gone wrong, so now Purvis can be thrown on the garbage heap with the rest of the queers. Or framed for something he didn't do."

His voice was becoming louder and louder as he vented his anger.

"Look, Marco, it's only for a couple of days more. Your father's not badly injured, so there's no reason for you to stay."

He hung his head low and heaved an enormous sigh. "I can't take it for a minute longer. And he's being so revoltingly *heterosexual* – 'Now, my boy, with all those lovely señoritas around, I hope you know how to use a contraceptive device'…Yuck!"

"Well, at least that proves he doesn't know…"

"What's really going on? That I'm living with a man over twice my age, and we're having an absolute ball – even if our sex life is a bit – well, *peculiar*, wouldn't you say, sweetie?"

Now I could hear some of Marco's old swagger coming back into his voice.

"You could say that, I suppose."

He came out with an exaggerated parody of my words, just like he always used to. *"You could thay that, I thuppose!"* Really, sweetie, you don't get any better, do you? Now look. What I need is a fag and a shag, and a flight out of here, in that order, immediately and forthwith."

I passed him a Marlboro, took one for myself, and we both inhaled deeply. I saw no point in beating about the bush.

"Okay. So, what about Zeki? When do you want the room?"

"Four, I've booked him for. I'm having to bribe the gardener to deliver all these messages. Do you think Trelawney will mind?"

"He told me it's okay for you and me to meet up in the Heliotrope Room, you know, the one I always use."

"I'm unlikely to forget it. Are you having him before or after me?"

"Never you mind," I said as I handed him the key. "Just try to be discreet. I know it's not in your nature, my dear, but…"

Suddenly he stood up, finger to his lips. "Sssssh! What's that?"

We fell silent. A shiver went down my spine as I heard a sort of scraping noise on the other side of the church door.

"There *can't* be anybody in there," Marco hissed. "It's only ever open for the service once a month, or at Christmas and what not."

But he was wrong. The door slowly creaked open, and the doddery figure of Mrs. Twelvetrees emerged. She did a very poor job of feigning surprise at our presence.

"Oh! My, my. Hello, Marco – and Mr. Carter, isn't it? Ah, well, birds of a feather…" She gave us a sickeningly artificial smile. "Now then, boys, you really shouldn't be smoking here. Consecrated ground, you know."

"Sorry, Mrs. Twelvetrees, promise we won't do it again," Marco said in a sing-song schoolboy voice.

"Well, I must be on my way. Greta just wanted me to check if there was any damage after that rainstorm last week. I'd better be getting along to hand in my report." She placed ominous emphasis on the last word. "Good afternoon, gentlemen."

With barely a nod in our direction, she padded across to the lych-gate and disappeared through it, humming tunelessly as she went.

As soon as she was out of sight, I lit two more cigarettes and passed one to Marco.

He clamped one hand to his forehead in despair and thumped the bench with the other.

"Oh. My. God. Holy *shit*. She heard every fucking word."

"She can't have, Marco. She's probably deaf anyway."

"Peter, she was my *piano* teacher. Piano teachers tend not to be hard of hearing. She was listening to everything, fucking nosey old cow."

I replayed some choice excerpts from our conversation in my mind. *Living with a man over twice my age...a peculiar sex life...Trelawney...the Heliotrope Room...Are you having him before or after me?*

Damning was hardly the word.

Marco stubbed his cigarette out on the porch floor and ground it into the consecrated gravel with his heel.

"To hell with it all. I'm going to shag Zeki senseless – God knows I need it, and I've earned it – then I'll go back to the house. If my parents confront me, I'll admit everything, say goodbye to them for ever and come down to you – we'll go out in a blaze of glory, you and me, sweetie, into the sunset!" He punched the air. "In fact, that's what I'll do even if that old ratbag *hasn't* stirred up a storm. Enough is enough. You'll take me back home to Spain, won't you, sweetie? Please?"

There was no question of my resisting his plea. "Of course I will, Marco. You know that."

"I know, I shouldn't even ask. You're the only one that I trust, Peter. You're the only one that I..."

He couldn't say the word. But I was thrilled to see him regain the vital, electric power that had drawn me to him in the first place. He leapt up from the bench and strode out into the sunlight.

"I'll get a message to you tonight, somehow or other. We'll be out of this viper-ridden shit-pit by tomorrow at the latest, you mark my words! Nothing, and nobody, will ever defeat us!"

I knew he was back to full form because, with head held high and arms flailing, he stamped and crashed his way out of the churchyard and through the lych-gate in a frantic sequence of flamenco steps. Even in that mock display, his genius for the dance shone through.

I wish I'd taken a photograph at that moment. It could have hung on the wall at Casa Morena, next to the other portrait of Marco in the full fury of the dance. And there is no doubt as to the title I'd have given it. It would be called 'The Last Fandango'.

Chapter Three

I stayed in the cool of the church porch for a while and pondered the worst that could happen. Marco certainly had the resilience to survive a showdown with his parents. Since he'd no intention of taking over at the helm of the Blaine business empire, his father was deprived of his main bargaining counter – and anyway, with such a brilliant dancing career ahead of him, Marco would soon have no need of financial assistance.

As I sat there in the comforting shade, I admitted to myself for the first time that I would do anything – absolutely anything – for Marco. Perhaps June was right.

On the other hand, if we were lucky, nothing whatsoever would happen. However acute her hearing might be, Mrs. Twelvetrees seemed somewhat disconnected from events around her. She might well not have understood a word we were saying. I could almost picture her musing to herself as she made her way through the Village: *a fag and a shag*...now is that some kind of new-fangled luncheon dish?

I made my way back to the Olive Branch and to my delight, the first person I saw when I walked in was Beth, busily checking a pile of till receipts. She wore a smart black pinafore and a crisp white blouse. The greasy spikes had gone and her raven hair was swept tautly back under a comb. The silver scorpion was still stranded by her eyebrow, the last reminder of the rebellious teenager who had grown into a young lady with a naturally commanding presence.

A broad smile spread across her face when she looked up and spotted me.

"Peter! I've been dying to see you ever since Marco told me you were here! Just let me finish these bills and I'll join you. What can I get you?"

"Isn't it your day off? I'm famished, but I don't want to put you to any trouble, Beth."

"June did give me the day off, but she gets confused with the accounts, poor dear, so it'll be easier tomorrow if I sort out the money now. She's left a fresh tray of toad-in-the-hole in the oven – or there's some tuna and avocado salad, that might be better for you, you know."

She cast a slightly critical glance at my expanded waistline. I opted for the salad, and went over to a table in the far corner of the garden. The only other customer in the place was Colonel Twelvetrees, mercifully unaccompanied by his wife. He had an outsized book open on the table in front of him, but the effort of reading it had defeated him. His head was slumped on his chest, and he was snoring away merrily.

Beth brought the salad to my table and sat down opposite me. "So how did you do it?"

"Do what?"

"Transform Mr. M.T.D. Blaine into a human being, that's what! I never thought I'd say this, but it's actually a pleasure to spend time with him now."

"I honestly don't think I've had much to do with it. He's studying what he really wants to, and now he isn't under his parents' wing so much..."

"It's only his father, you know. His mother's not so bad, really. It was *so* clever of you to find that guy who keeps pumping them with reports about digging up junk in some castle or other!"

"Victorio. He just happens to be my neighbour. I really didn't have to do very much."

"They lap up every word he writes, and believe it all – just goes to show how stupid they are. I mean, Marco's changed a lot, but nobody who knows him could ever imagine him getting his hands dirty!"

The salad was tasty, but it left me hungry. I lit a cigarette and offered her one. She refused with a gentle shake of her head.

"But you know the most amazing thing, Peter? He can't stop talking about *you*."

"Really? Well, we've been sharing quite a small flat for several months, so I suppose that's quite natural."

"Bullshit! I've lived with my brother for fifteen years – shared the same room and the same bed, for God's sake. The last thing I'd dream of telling people is what he does when he wakes up in the morning, the funny way he brushes his teeth, how he goes into a panic if a moth gets into the room at night – I mean, Marco notices everything you do, Peter!"

I was aware that living alone for so long had given me some slightly eccentric ways, but I was surprised Marco found them interesting enough to discuss with anyone else.

"And you should hear him go on about how talented, how professional you are. I don't really understand what it is you do, exactly, but apparently there's nobody else in the world that can do it!"

"Everyone's good at something or other, Beth. Which reminds me: are you still doing your calligraphy?"

Her face lit up. "Of course I am! I wouldn't give it up for the world. I'm not one for knitting or needlework – but give me a pen and some ink, and I can lose myself for hours. Actually, I've got something to show you. I'll just go and fetch it from my bag."

She paused briefly to check whether Colonel Twelvetrees was still displaying any vital signs, and then disappeared behind the counter.

She returned a little later with a large artist's folder from which she unpacked a piece of artwork that was stunning by anyone's standards. She must have spent hours tracing the intricately entwined letters and flourishes.

"Do you recognise it, Peter?"

I thought it looked familiar, and then I understood: it was the ceiling of a room in the Alhambra.

"Beth, that's incredible! Marco and I go up there – used to go up there – nearly every day!"

"I know. He's told me all about it, and how you introduced him to it, of course. And he sent me some great photos, so I used one as the model for this."

"It's called the Hall of the Sisters, I think. You must come over and see the real thing, you know. I could look at this for ages!"

"Then I'll leave you with it for a couple of minutes, 'cos I've got to check something in the kitchen. I won't be long."

I sat there transfixed by the beauty of what she'd created. I was soothed and calmed by the harmony and balance of her drawing – it still has that effect on me whenever I look at it in Casa Morena today.

I glanced up at the majestic palm trees that lined June's garden and the soaring mountains above, now turned purple by the declining sun. The Village was working its magic on me all over again.

But my moments of tranquil contemplation were brusquely interrupted by another salvo of explosions as more firecrackers were let off somewhere outside.

At least, that's what I assumed they were.

There was a clatter as Colonel Twelvetrees awoke from his slumber with a start, clumsily knocking his book and coffee-cup onto the ground. He was sitting bolt upright in his chair, gesticulating wildly with both hands.

"Good God!" he exclaimed. "That was a Browning Mark One. Best automatic pistol ever made. I'd know that sound anywhere! You should've heard 'em firing into the air when we crossed the Rhine in '45. What the devil's going on?"

Two more reports rang out. Now I knew the Colonel was right. I'd heard enough rifles fired by hunters in the hills around Casa Morena to tell the difference between gunshots and fireworks. A knife-like surge of panic swept through me. The shots were followed by a succession of long, gut-wrenching screams.

Then, clear as a bell in the silence of early evening, came Trelawney's voice, yelling for help. Beth came running over and threw herself into my arms.

"Oh my God, my *God*," she shrieked. "Please don't let it be Marco! Please, please, *please*! C'mon, Peter!"

We hurtled down the deserted lanes. Shutters were being drawn back, heads were starting to poke through windows. Trelawney was standing in the street outside his front door, hand clamped over one eye, blood streaming down his cheek.

"He just barged in here – I should never have opened the door – I tried to stop him, but –"

"Who?" As if I needed to ask.

"Blaine. He punched me – threatened me with a gun if I tried to move – then stormed out into the courtyard – Oh, Peter, thank God, you've come."

"Marco. Where's Marco?" I screamed.

"Marco? No, Peter, Marco's not here. Purvis is the only one at home, out on the terrace – that's who Blaine was after."

I knew he was wrong, of course.

"Don't take the girl through there," Trelawney cautioned me.

"You won't stop me, Mr. Towers," Beth shot back at him. "Actually, *you'd* better stay here."

She grasped both his hands and forced him to sit down on his own front doorstep. He'd suddenly turned into a dithering, confused old man, mouthing words but no longer able use his voice. Beth led me by the hand through the front door. She spotted an ornamental Moorish dagger mounted on the wall, tore it from its hooks and thrust it into my hand.

"Here – take this, Peter. It's all we can get. I'll use brute force if necessary." I had no doubt she could and would.

"They'll be in my room, Beth – across the terrace and on the right."

The door of the Heliotrope Room was wide open. I didn't care if it cost me my life, I had to see Marco, I had to clasp him to me one last time. I signalled Beth to stay behind me and stepped into the room, clutching the dagger.

Standing in front of the harmonium in a triumphant pose was Purvis, clad in his trademark safari jacket and shod in heavy brogues – one of which was clamped firmly across the neck of Commander Blaine, who lay prostrate on the floor before him. In his right hand, Purvis held a sizeable grey pistol, its barrel pointed straight at the back of the Commander's skull.

"Shall we shoot the bastard's brains out, or should we stab him in his miserable guts? He's just committed cold-blooded murder. Your choice, Pete." His voice was chillingly calm.

I was mesmerised by my first real sight of Blaine – this man who had earned the hatred of almost everyone I knew. He raised his head slightly and turned it in my direction. His face was not unattractive: he had Marco's high cheekbones and exceptionally long eyelashes. But the eyes they shielded were terrifying. There was a glowering intensity about them that hinted at insanity.

With his other steel-capped shoe, Purvis inflicted a hefty kick on his prisoner's temple.

I sensed Beth come into the room behind me; I heard her gasp of anguish; she clutched my arm with both her hands.

And then I saw the bed.

Zeki was lying on it, stark naked, face up, with a gaping hole in his throat and another in his groin. His blood had poured onto the bedsheets and was trickling onto the floor. His eyes were wide open, gazing up at the flying cherubs on the bed's canopy, but they clearly saw nothing. Nobody could have survived those wounds.

Next to him lay Marco. He was just as motionless, just as naked. Some weird instinct made me thank God he'd been spared the ultimate indignity, for he was lying face down. But that meant I could see the two bleeding gashes at the base of his spine and another on the back of his head.

I staggered across to the bed and knelt beside him. I felt overwhelming relief when I heard him drawing shallow, irregular breaths. I whispered his name, but he couldn't respond. His eyes were closed and from his mouth came an awful low wailing sound like the whine of a scolded dog. I felt a hand clasping and squeezing mine: it was Beth's. She'd crouched down next to me. I reached out to embrace Marco – but froze when a piercing Scots voice barked out.

"Don't you dare touch my son!"

Somehow, Blaine had levered himself out from under Purvis's foot. I suppose Purvis must have been watching me as I tried vainly to comfort Marco. But in the nick of time, Purvis fired a deafening shot into the floorboards, inches away from Blaine's head. Taking advantage of the shock he'd created, Purvis threw down the gun, grabbed Blaine by his shirt collar, yanked him upright and snarled in his face.

"That's enough from you, you fucking cunt."

It was, and remains, the only time I'd ever heard that word used in this house.

Then with his clenched first, Purvis dealt him an almighty blow straight between the eyes. The Commander toppled back onto the floor, as unconscious as the two naked young men on the bed.

Now Trelawney appeared in the doorway, blood still oozing from the wound on his face. He took in the horrific scene and had to turn away.

"I – just don't – understand...I came back home...only for this to happen?"

Purvis interrupted his mumbling. "Trel, we need some rope, or something to tie this bastard down until we can get the police here. And a doctor. Help us."

The request for practical help seemed to bring Trelawney to his senses, reminding him that he was still master of this house.

"Peter, go into my bedroom. There's a portmanteau by the right-hand side of the bed. You'll find some rope and, er, things in there. Bring anything we can use."

I dashed over to the main house and into Trelawney's bedroom. There were, indeed, quite a few "things" in the portmanteau: several whips, gags, blindfolds, some lengths of what looked like tow-rope, and even a pair of handcuffs. I took these and the rope, stuffed the gag into my pocket and raced back over to the Heliotrope Room.

Purvis was delighted with the handcuffs – all the more so because they had some sort of frilly pink material twisted around them. With his foot, he rolled the unconscious Commander over to face the floor, jammed his hands through the rings behind his back and snapped them shut.

"I've sent Beth over to the German doc's house, see if she can rouse him," he announced. I dreaded to think my beloved Marco's life could be in the trembling hands of Dr. Steingass, but there was no other choice.

It sounded like a crowd was beginning to assemble in the courtyard outside. I caught June's voice, firmly telling people to stay away from the Heliotrope Room. Purvis warned me not to attempt to move Marco. All I wanted to do was remain with him until...until it ended, one way or another.

I stayed there, crouching beside him, oblivious to the others in the room except poor Zeki. In death, his hand had dropped down onto the back of Marco's shoulder as if he were bidding him farewell. I thought it could do no harm to hold Marco's hand, which was dangling limply over the side of the bed. I kept squeezing it gently and repeating his name, but he didn't react in any way.

Suddenly, the hubbub outside subsided. The door swung open and Greta Lindberg strode in, head held erect, her face devoid of any trace of emotion as she surveyed the scene before her in silence. She had a gold chain around her neck from which hung an amulet shaped like the emblem on the national flag.

Behind her came Sir Brian Bishop, spruce as ever in a cream tuxedo and yellow bow tie. Though he must have experienced worse atrocities during his long years of service, his jaw dropped in horror as he took in the spectacle.

"Good evening, gentlemen," Greta said as calmly as if she were addressing a church committee meeting. We all mumbled some sort of greeting in return.

"Mr. Purvis. Did you witness this crime?"

"I most certainly did, Greta. Blaine came tearing through the house like a bloody madman, waving the gun – ran right past me, I don't think he even saw me, he was so out of his mind. I chased him but he'd fired the first shot at the Arab's throat before I got into the room. Then I saw him take another shot at...em..."

"The pubic area," Sir Brian supplied.

"Right. Then he took aim again, but what happened was..."

For the first time ever, I saw Purvis overcome with emotion.

"Take your time, Mr. Purvis," Sir Brian said gently, "everybody here is distressed. There's no need to pretend otherwise."

Purvis drew a deep breath and went on. "Marco threw himself on top of the lad, to protect him, I suppose, but Blaine was too late to stop himself – he pulled the trigger anyway – twice more at least – and that's why..."

"Quite," Greta said curtly. "Now, he seems to be properly restrained –" she cast a derisive glance at the handcuffs with their shocking pink festoon – "so can you wake him up, please, somebody?"

Purvis started slapping Blaine's cheeks while Sir Brian fetched a pitcher of cold water from the bathroom, which he splashed over the Commander's face. Blaine's body started twitching and he began to wake up, unable at first to comprehend the situation he was in. His puzzlement turned to disdain as he looked around at the assembled company – Purvis, Sir Brian, Trelawney, myself and Beth, who had returned from her mission and was now hunkered down beside me at the bedside. Hardly a gathering he would normally have graced with his presence. Then he noticed Greta behind him and addressed her:

"Ah, good evening, Greta. I'm so glad you're here. You can clear up this little misunderstanding, I'm sure."

"Good evening, Commander," she said, with not the least hint of contempt. "I have to ask you to state your full name."

"What? I'm perfectly *compos mentis*, Greta. I've had a bit of a shock, but..."

"Your full name, please, Commander."

"You know who I am, Greta. Come on!"

Greta remained silent and did not move a muscle.

"Oh all right, then. I'm Duncan Thomas McNair Blaine. Would you like the letters after my name as well?"

Blaine was trying to stand up but for good measure, Purvis had bound his ankles together with the rope from Trelawney's toy-box. All he could do was writhe around on the floor like a fish thrown ashore in a squall.

"Can you sit him up on that chair, please, Mr. Purvis?"

Purvis manhandled the Commander onto the simple wooden chair that stood in front of the harmonium. Greta took up her stance in front of him, her head towering a good two feet above his. Assuming an expression of the utmost gravity, she intoned:

"In exercise of the authority vested in me by the State, I hereby arrest you, Duncan Thomas McNair Blaine, on suspicion of murder, attempted murder and other charges to be ascertained."

She touched the amulet with the fingers of one hand as she spoke. I half-expected her to ask for the terrifying black skullcap judges used to don when pronouncing sentence of death.

Then the silence was broken by the last sound I expected to hear: Blaine began to cackle with uncontrollable laughter.

"You must be joking, Greta," he said once he'd gained a grip on himself. "It was just an accident."

An expression of utter scorn passed over Greta's face. "Commander, I strongly advise you to say nothing unless you are prepared to have it used against you in court."

Blaine nodded contemptuously at Zeki's inert body. "He was attacking Marco – I was defending my son. You can't be serious, surely? I mean, he's only a dirty Arab queer boy!"

Marco lay there, utterly impassive, unable to respond as every word he'd spoken to me about his father was proved abundantly true.

Greta's patience had clearly come to an end. She stepped closer to him and slapped him hard in the face.

"How dare you?" she snarled.

On withdrawing her hand, she saw that it was flecked with the Commander's blood: the blow inflicted by Purvis had left a crimson wound above his nose.

"A handkerchief and some disinfectant please, Trelawney. You never know what's floating about in a criminal's veins. Now: medical assistance for Marco is paramount. Where's Dr. Steingass?"

Beth began to tell her she was unable to rouse the doctor no matter how hard she hammered on his door, but Sir Brian interrupted her.

"No need for him, Greta. This very capable young lady told me exactly what Marco's symptoms were when we met her on the way into the house. He's in a coma, of course. I used Trelawney's phone to call for an army helicopter. It should be here in minutes. My contact in the military was most obliging."

Sir Brian directed a very faint smile at me as he said this. "My friend will be on board himself," he continued, "and he's bringing a doctor with him."

The babble from outside suddenly increased in volume as the door swung open. In walked June, carrying a tray loaded with teacups, milk and sugar, as well as a bottle of whisky and some glasses. Tamir followed with a huge teapot, which he dropped with a clang as soon as he saw the two bodies sprawled on the bed. June deftly rescued the teapot, set the tray down on the harmonium, and started pouring.

"I don't care what's going on in here, but you lot all need something to calm you down," she said in her most matronly tone. Beth went over to help her hand out drinks to everyone.

Meanwhile, Tamir had rushed over to the bed and was standing beside Zeki. He assumed the posture of Moslem prayer, palms facing upwards, and began quietly reciting in Arabic. He seemed more concerned than shocked. He addressed the company at large.

"Must move him, please. Not correct. Must look to Mecca."

He leant over the body and, with great respect, slowly closed Zeki's eyes and what was left of his mouth. He moved the arms downwards so that they lay by his sides. Tamir's hands became covered in Zeki's blood, but he was unperturbed. Beth fetched a sheet from the wardrobe and the two of them gently laid it over the corpse. My attention was still focused entirely on Marco – he was just managing to breathe – but I was glad that someone was at last showing concern for the other victim of Blaine's attack.

Conversation in the room ground to a halt as we sipped our tea, waiting for help to arrive from the skies. Purvis broke the silence as he bent down to pick up the gun, still lying on the floor where he'd thrown it.

"I'd better put the safety catch on. We don't want any more accidents, do we?"

Greta raised a finger in warning. "Please don't touch it again, Mr. Purvis. The police will want it for evidence."

"But it's the only gun we've got in case chummy here starts his tricks again!"

"Oh no, it's not."

She opened her handbag, reached into it and produced a tiny black revolver, its grip studded with what appeared to be small diamonds. She wielded it with professional ease.

"I've never fired it in peacetime, but I assure you I haven't forgotten how to use it. So, please, leave the murder weapon where it is."

"She's quite right, of course," said Sir Brian, with some authority. "Incidentally, Blaine, where's your wife?"

"She's down at the French consulate, signing some important papers. We have a rather large business to run, you know."

I fingered the gag in my pocket and thought of producing it to spare us any more of his arrogance. Purvis couldn't resist coming back at him.

"It'll be many a year before you're doing any kind of business except slopping out and sewing mailbags, Blaine. If you're lucky — which I hope you're not."

"Now, now," Greta admonished him. "Let us try to be civil, even in these extreme circumstances. We set ourselves certain standards in this Village, and we abide by them, come what may."

As she finished speaking, we heard the throbbing drone of an aircraft engine in the distance. Soon, the thrashing of the helicopter's blades drowned out all other sounds; it must have passed right over the house. Stupidly, I hoped that the tremendous noise would awaken Marco, but he just lay there, immobile except for the slight flaring of his nostrils each time he drew breath.

"They'll have to land in the churchyard, I suppose," Trelawney bellowed above the din, "it's the only flat piece of land we have. Beth, come with me and we'll guide them down to the house."

The noise from the helicopter ceased abruptly and, hardly a minute later, a squad of uniformed soldiers and policemen charged through the door. The doctor, a tall, steely-haired man with a thoroughly business-like air about him, followed close behind them. He wasted no time on greetings and came straight over to me.

"Are you the victim's father?" he asked, unpacking his medical bag.

"No, I'm his…friend. That's his father, over there."

"I see. I must ask you to step aside. His condition is obviously grave, we must get him to hospital immediately – but moving him may cause more damage if it isn't done correctly."

As he spoke, he inserted the tube of a ventilator into Marco's mouth. A soldier began applying dressings to the wounds on Marco's back and skull – the quantity of blood was simply incredible. The doctor produced a collection of syringes already filled with various fluids and proceeded to inject Marco's arms and buttocks. Despite all this, he did not respond.

Moving on swiftly, the doctor signalled the other soldiers to approach the bedside. They wrapped Marco in a blanket and lifted him onto the stretcher that two of them held ready.

While this was happening, the policemen exchanged Commander Blaine's handcuffs for a more robust pair. Sir Brian spoke with them in Arabic while Greta signed the documents they gave her.

"It's easiest if they take him to town in the helicopter too," Sir Brian explained to us. "Quite a luxurious way to go, but I think it's best under the circumstances. He'll be detained in the main prison until charges are brought." Although Blaine was sitting there taking all this in, Sir Brian spoke of him as if he was no longer in the room.

It was a solemn procession that made its way towards the churchyard, up the hill Beth and I had raced down barely a couple of hours earlier. Greta led the way, her bearing as dignified as ever. Sir Brian lagged slightly behind out of respect for her superior standing in the Village. Then came Blaine, frog-marched between two burly policemen and followed closely by two more with rifles cocked. Marco, only the tip of his head now visible under the blanket, was borne on his stretcher with the doctor walking on one side, his eyes fixed constantly on his patient. I walked on the other side, longing just to ruffle Marco's hair but now unable even to touch his hand. Trelawney, Tamir, Purvis, Beth and June brought up the rear, with an assortment of Villagers straggling behind.

The atmosphere at Alex's funeral seemed positively merry compared to the grim aura of this cortege.

We filed through the lych-gate and came face to face with the huge bulk of the helicopter, a jarring intrusion of the modern world into the normally peaceful old churchyard. Standing to attention by its door was a figure I recognised instantly: Commandant Ahmad Shams ad-Din, the memorably handsome officer who eased my passage through passport control on my last departure from the country. Whatever had transpired on the "many occasions" when he'd met Sir Brian was evidently worth a full-scale airborne rescue mission.

He saluted each of us in turn – including Blaine, his fellow officer. Unable to return the salute, Blaine nodded gruffly before his guards shoved him up the boarding ladder and into the aircraft. His son was carefully hoisted in after him, a soldier grasping each corner of his stretcher. I hoped against hope for a sign of recognition from Marco as he vanished from my life for what would surely be the last time, but none came.

Shams ad-Din ordered the rest of his squad on board and paused briefly on the uppermost step to wave us farewell. Greta, Sir Brian, Trelawney, Purvis, June and I stood in line, heads bowed as if we were actually at a funeral. As soon as the engine roared into life, Sir Brian shepherded us all away from the helicopter. Even so, the enormous force of the slipstream flattened us against the churchyard wall.

Dear June put her arm around me, but I brushed her aside. I broke away from the rest of the party, following the path across the churchyard that Marco had capered along that same afternoon when he was still full of life, vigour and defiance.

I reached the porch and threw myself face down onto the bench where he'd sat, hoping somehow to recapture his presence – a whiff of perspiration, perhaps a trace of his usual cologne, but there was nothing except the hard wood and cold stone of the church wall. I lay there alone until the last of the daylight was gone, bawling my heart out. I'd known – oh so briefly – what it is to love another human being. Now, that being had been cruelly snatched from me…and the harmless idyll we'd created for ourselves had been smashed to smithereens by the hand of the one man who surely should have loved his son more than any other.

Eventually I cried myself to sleep – but it was a shallow sleep, invaded by horrific nightmares. I saw Alex standing behind the wicker cage on the great stage of the theatre in Granada, fist raised to the sky, screaming "Never say die!" – and then it was he, not La Furiosa, who demolished the entire structure at a stroke. The scene changed: Marco himself – half-naked, blood gushing from his wounds – was stamping and thrashing his way back along the churchyard path, into the porch where he stood before me. A derisive grin spread across his face, and I even heard his shrill voice: "*Really, sweetie, did you think I'd give up that easily?*"

At that point, I woke up: somehow I knew immediately that my despair had evaporated. Of course Marco was going to survive. He was indestructible. He never yielded. He was Marco the Magnificent. It might take a long time, and it would be the greatest challenge of my life – but I would stay with him night and day, I would nurse him back to health, and he would go on to achieve greater things than either of us could imagine.

Chapter Four

One night at Trelawney's was enough. The day's events had robbed the house of its welcoming warmth, only recently restored after its owner's long absence. The front door was guarded by the same sullen policeman who was posted outside on the last day of my previous visit. The Heliotrope Room was cordoned off; chalk marks all over the house stopped us from walking on any surface that might harbour evidence of Blaine's rampage.

Steingass finally appeared to patch up Trelawney's injuries, leaving one side of his face covered in untidy bandages from which iodine oozed onto his kaftan. A party of robed and bearded Moslem clergy from the Beetlebridge mosque came up to remove Zeki's body. Tamir could be heard in the courtyard, chanting the prescribed lament for the departed in Arabic. He refused to join us in the main room, where Trelawney sat glumly in an armchair, saying very little and shaking his head in disbelief.

I had nothing much to say either. I just wanted the telephone to ring with good news about Marco, but it simply sat there on its little table, obstinately silent. Other than Tamir's incantations, the only sound was the endlessly repeated BBC World Service news on the radio. Purvis made a few half-hearted attempts at conversation.

"I should think he'll get life at least, if not the firing squad – unless they try and wangle diplomatic impunity for him."

"Immunity," I mumbled.

"Yeah, yeah."

The silence resumed. A few minutes later, Purvis got up from his chair and marched out of the house without a word. Soon after that,

I bade Trelawney goodnight and made up the bed in one of the spare guest rooms. Somehow or other, after a lot of tossing and turning, I got off to sleep, comforting myself with the thought that I'd move down to a hotel in town the next day, to be as close to Marco as I could.

The previous evening's gloom still prevailed next morning. Trelawney's face had ballooned during the night; the mess Steingass had made of bandaging his wounds prevented him from eating anything solid. Tamir made him a bowl of porridge which he brought to the table with eyes downcast, barely able to hold back his tears.

I tried to choose the right moment to announce my departure, but there wasn't one. Trelawney greeted my news with a sigh of resignation, his injuries causing him to slur his speech.

"Who wouldn't leave? My beloved house has become a hell-hole. I wish I had some strength to pass on to you, dear boy, but this – this *outrage* – has left me bereft of all resources."

The telephone rang. Tamir answered it and came back to say the call was for me. My hand was trembling wildly as I picked up the receiver.

"Peter, it's Brian Bishop. How are you?"

I thought I was going to collapse on the spot. He was surely calling to tell me the news I least wanted to hear. I didn't even return his greeting.

"Is it Marco? Have you heard from the hospital? I'm on my way now."

"No, there's no news...at least, no change. They called me as a courtesy, but that's all they said. No, I was wondering if you wanted to come down and stay with us for a while. We're only five minutes from the hospital..."

"It's very nice of you, Sir Brian, but..."

"But nothing. And call me Brian, please, this is no time to stand on ceremony. Jean-Louis insists you come. We have a completely separate apartment you can use. If you don't want company, then you shall not have it, but we'll be over in the house if you need us."

The idea began to seem attractive. Sir Brian's imperturbable calm might make him the ideal confidant if the worst happened. I decided to accept.

"I'm so pleased, Peter. I'm sure that's the right decision. Shall I send our driver to fetch you?"

"Thanks anyway – I was going to book in at the Phoenicia, so I've called Mahboob to drive me into town."

"Ha! That old rascal. Well, he knows the way up here, so you shouldn't have any problems. We'll see you later on. Just come whenever you want."

In fact, I could hear the infantile squeaking of the Citroën's horn outside as I brought the conversation to a close. I took my leave of Trelawney and got straight into the car.

"Well, well, Mr. Carter," Mahboob greeted me with a smirk. "We meet yet again in difficult conditions. I can't recall asking any of my respected customers this question before: do you want to go to the hospital, the prison, or both? I'm happy to wait for you at either, of course."

This was what my life had suddenly become. I was leaving the scene of a murder to rush to the bedside of my beloved, who was at death's door, while his father sat in jail, probably awaiting the gallows.

"Neither, Mr. Mahboob," I said wearily. "Take me to Brian Bishop's house, please."

We drove down the hill in silence and turned onto the coast road.

"Bad happenings, Mr. Carter," Mahboob mused as we picked up speed. "You understand why?"

"I don't understand anything anymore."

"Ah – it is not up to us to understand, my friend. El-Velaj has its spirits, you know. They see what happens on the land that is truly theirs, and if they are not happy with it – well, now you see the consequences."

I recalled what Marco had once said – "*Sometimes it feels like the Village is trying to get its own back on us, for walking in and taking everything...*" I suddenly became very glad I was putting distance between myself and the Village, thinking I might never return.

We pulled up outside the monumental gates of Sir Brian's villa. A housekeeper welcomed me in and introduced herself as Marie-Hélène. Her figure was trim and her manner embarrassingly deferential, but her name made me think fondly of Elena – a character from a life that now seemed like a distant dream.

"*Les Messieurs* are in town," she informed me. "They instructed me to ensure you have every comfort you require."

The grounds were enormous, with sweeping views of the city and the sea. The house was not at all what I'd imagined: starkly modern, with vast expanses of plate glass and concrete, and clearly equipped with every amenity one could desire. The apartment was just as bright and stylish. A lunch of French cheeses, pâtés and salad had been laid out, and a note was placed by the telephone:

"Dial 1 and I will come whenever you wish. Dial 0 for anything else. I expect they've impounded your luggage, so there are some clothes in the wardrobe. Bon courage, B."

I showered and changed into a perfectly pressed pair of checked Oxford bags and a white tennis shirt from the wardrobe. Then I braved the early afternoon heat and the brew of noxious gases that filled the streets to make my way to the hospital. The receptionist was business-like and somewhat abrupt at first. But when she located Marco's name and whereabouts on her computer, I caught a sharp intake of breath from behind her veil; her manner changed as she made an effort to convey her concern.

"The Intensive Care Unit is on the top floor, Monsieur. The staff there will tell you how long you can stay with your son."

I thanked her and set out to negotiate the usual maze of corridors and swinging doors. The atmosphere was very different from what I'd experienced on visits to hospitals in Europe. Instead of handkerchief-twisting relatives pacing up and down outside the wards and theatres, whole families of visitors sat cross-legged or knelt silently in carpeted areas reserved for prayer. I found the effect deeply calming, and I'd recovered a degree of composure when I finally located the entrance to the ICU.

The long final illnesses endured gracelessly by my mother and father in turn had made me no stranger to facilities such as these, so I was not taken aback by the routine of scrubbing my hands, donning a surgical gown, face mask and plastic overshoes. A young nurse ushered me into the sterile zone.

"We were expecting you, Monsieur," she said softly. "Madame Blaine mentioned you would be visiting." I didn't give any thought to the implications of this piece of information. "Perhaps you'd like some water before you go in?"

Eager to see Marco now, I declined her kind offer. She led me gently to Marco's bedside, her hand exerting a gentle but welcome pressure on my wrist.

The usual paraphernalia of life support was in place: a polythene tent shrouding the bed, a tangle of tubes plugged into various pulsating and blinking instruments, and a huge oxygen cylinder stationed by the bedside. Had I not known it was Marco lying there, I couldn't possibly have recognised him. Only his closed eyes and the lower part of his forehead were exposed. From the slight rise and fall of his chest, I knew he was breathing. But that was enough.

I stood before him, immobile, speechless.

Automatically, I made my breathing follow his, willing him to inhale with just a little more strength each time, trying to somehow give him the determination to live. Trying to transmit my love through that welter of gadgetry – resisting the urge to rip it all away and throw my arms around him, hold him close to me and tell him how much I loved him.

"You can speak to him, you know, Monsieur. I'm sure you have something you want to say. Who knows whether they can hear us or not? But perhaps it helps."

I'd forgotten that the young nurse was still beside me. She patted the back of my hand.

"I can leave you with him for five minutes, if you like. But no longer, I'm afraid. And I'm sorry, but you mustn't touch him in any way. You understand, I'm sure, Monsieur."

I mumbled a thank-you in her direction, but my eyes were riveted on Marco as she slipped silently out of the cubicle. Alone at last with Marco, I was convulsed by a tidal wave of emotion so powerful I thought I would choke. Frustration, anger, fear, my own inadequacy, my failure to tell him I loved him while he could still hear the words – all of it boiled up, and I erupted into tears.

The nurse was right – there was something I wanted and needed to say to him.

"I love you, Marco," I whispered slowly.

I watched for some sign that he'd heard, that he understood, but nothing came.

I repeated the words, softly, then a little louder, a little faster. "I love you, Marco. Sweetie, I love you."

I thought I detected a faint tremor in his left eyelid.

"Marco, I love you. I always did, and I always will."

He lay there before me, motionless as ever, but there was a bead of sweat on his forehead that wasn't there before...

"I love you, sweetie. Remember, I love you."

I must have carried on like this for a few more minutes when I heard the rustle of a crisply-starched surgical gown behind me. I didn't feel in the least embarrassed; the nurse must have witnessed such scenes many times before, and I felt no need to hide my feelings from her.

The words of the *rumba* from Marco's last performance floated into my mind; I whispered to him once more.

"I love you, Marco Blaine...*Mi vida tiene un cielo que le diste tú.*"

Above my life, there is the sky you gave to me...

I exhaled deeply, and turned around to let the nurse escort me out. But she was not there.

In her place, unmistakeable even in sterile hospital attire, stood Geneviève Blaine. Her remarkable nose held the mask well clear of her mouth, rather defeating its purpose. Her strong, dark brown eyes gazed straight at me, unblinking.

"I'm sorry...I had no idea, I mean..." I stuttered.

I could feel a hot blush spreading across my face and was thankful that most of it was concealed by my own mask.

"There's no need to apologise, Mr. Carter. Although I too am sorry that it has taken *this*" – she raised both her hands, palms upwards, in a quintessentially Gallic gesture – "for you and I to meet at last."

Swathed though she was in an all-enveloping green gown, her poise suggested the kind of power that brooked no resistance.

"I'd better go now. I feel I'm intruding on your precious time with your son, Mrs...em...Madame..."

"Geneviève, please. Yes, I am his mother, and I have every right to be here. But you, Peter Carter, are his lover and, therefore, you too have every right to be here. It is as simple as that."

I was astounded — utterly at a loss for words. What little I'd seen of Commander Blaine matched up exactly to Marco's descriptions of him. But with a few brief words, his mother had completely shattered the image I'd built up of her. And despite the herculean efforts we'd devoted to concealing my existence, she was clearly under no illusion as to the reality of our relationship. Seeing my consternation, she went on.

"You have nothing to fear from me. I am French, as you know. And we French take a somewhat different view of love than you Anglo-Saxons. If there is love, all will be well. If there is no love...well, events like yesterday's will come to pass. I have suspected for some time that my son has your love, and now I know that to be true. So, all will be well. *Voilà.*"

"If he lives," I said, morosely.

"He will. A mother knows these things. He loves; he is loved. He will survive. Believe me."

She reached out, clasped my polythene-gloved hand in hers, and repeated: "*Believe* me, Peter Carter. It is not an easy path you have chosen. Neither is mine. But I see that you, like me, have the strength to follow it through to the end."

She paused, still gripping my hand with considerable force, and said with a smile I couldn't see: "I am delighted to meet you."

She neatly turned her gesture into a formal handshake and stepped back just as the nurse entered the cubicle. It was obviously time for me to leave.

"We shall meet again soon, Peter. I shall be here quite regularly, and so I'm sure will you. There will be much to discuss as Marco's recovery proceeds."

I attempted to take my leave of her in French, which clearly pleased her.

"By the way," she said, with a coquettish glint in her eyes, "I should congratulate you on that pantomime you organised for our benefit in Almería. What was that old fool's name? Vicente?"

"Victorio," I replied without thinking.

"Quite. My husband, of course, was completely taken in. I decided to play along with it. The right decision, *n'est-ce pas?* Whatever happens, I shall always be grateful that you gave my son that one summer of romantic bliss. We all deserve that, I think. Goodbye, Peter. *À bientôt.*"

I stumbled out of the room to make my way down the staircases and past the crowds of crouched, silent visitors into the open air. I drifted back up to Sir Brian's house in a daze and let myself in through the security gate. With a sigh of relief to be safe in that haven of tranquillity again, I threw myself on the bed, too weary even to wonder what the next twist in this never-ending tale would be.

Chapter Five

Any set of circumstances, no matter how harrowing, will sooner or later become commonplace. Within a couple of days, my trips to the hospital had settled into a regular routine. I made three visits a day – morning, mid-afternoon and early evening. I kept hoping for evidence Marco was improving; the only sign of change was the gradual disappearance of some of the machinery that was keeping him alive in his coma. On the third or fourth day, a rather obese, ill-shaven man in a less-than-white coat was scrutinising a monitor by Marco's bed when I walked into the cubicle. From his appearance, I assumed he was some sort of technician servicing the equipment, but he turned out to be the duty doctor.

I asked him how Marco was doing.

"Monsieur Blaine est dans une situation difficile."

A difficult situation – a very French way of putting it. The doctor refused to elaborate, except to say that Marco would be moved into a room on a normal ward very shortly: an *appartement*, he called it. I took my leave of the doctor with as much courtesy as I could muster, and headed out into town to set about filling in the vast expanses of time between those precious ten-minute sessions at the bedside.

The *appartement* was quite pleasant – it even had a small balcony, but there was no indication that Marco would ever be able to sit on it. The oxygen tent was removed and except for the tubes inserted into his nostrils, he looked as if he was just sleeping normally. I was allowed to hold his hand and even mop his forehead with a damp flannel – he seemed to sweat a lot, he would snore and sometimes cough, but that was all.

One day, I entered the room to find a huge bouquet of roses and irises sitting on a table – a colourful card announced that they were from La Furiosa and all the staff and students of the Academia in Granada. "To our much-loved *maestro*," it read – and there were forty or so signatures, little messages and drawings from Marco's teachers and classmates. I couldn't hold back tears as I read through them all. I longed to feel Marco prodding my back and snatching the card – "*I'll* read that first, if you don't mind, sweetie" – but no, not even the flicker of an eyelid.

Beth and June came down from the Village one afternoon to visit Marco with me. June focused more of her attention on me than on Marco.

"You know, he's going to need you more than ever before when he comes out of this. I can see you're not eating properly, dearie – I may have to move down to town to keep an eye on you."

Beth, practical and thoughtful as ever, noticed that Marco's fingernails needed cutting and asked the nurse if she could do the job herself. On receiving permission, she produced a pair of nail scissors from her shoulder-bag and, with immense tenderness and care, gave him a full manicure. As she worked, she talked quietly to him about trivial gossip from the Village: the summer's record temperatures, her brother's latest attempts to woo the girl who worked in the grocery shop. Her presence created a relaxed ambience that was markedly absent from the room on my visits, and I resolved to learn from her example.

Trelawney phoned a few times – he seemed to be slowly hauling himself back into something like his old form. Nevertheless, the shadow of the awful events we had witnessed hung over all of us. Greta, he told me, was carrying on as if nothing had happened, trying to restore some semblance of normality to the community; the

Twelvetrees had vanished from sight since the day of the shootings. Then, a week or so after I'd left the Village, Trelawney announced he'd be driving into town the next day.

"Purvis has asked me to bring him down. I've hardly seen hide nor hair of him since...you know. But it seems he actually has to visit Blaine in jail, to get some financial papers signed. The bastard's never likely to get out, from what Greta says, so I suppose arrangements have to be made. You know our Purvis – nothing gets in the way of business."

"I'm not very good company at the moment," I warned him, "but I'd love to see you."

"I'll drop Purvis off at the prison gates. I'm in no mood to visit convicts, so I'll come straight over to you. Perhaps we could even eat together, if you're up to it."

As soon as Sir Brian heard of the plan, he insisted we all dine together in his house – so just this once, I decided to forego my evening visit to Marco.

It turned out to be the first vaguely pleasant evening I'd spent since the shootings. The housekeeper prepared a whole poached salmon encased in diaphanous puff-pastry, and champagne was served throughout the meal. Trelawney announced his firm resolve to stay in the Village for the rest of his life, come what may. Sir Brian recounted various stories of people who'd recovered well from injuries even more horrific than Marco's. I wasn't convinced but for the first time, I allowed myself to imagine some sort of future with Marco. However, it was Jean-Louis who really enlivened the evening with his racy tales of French theatre life and hilarious impersonations of singers from Piaf to Aznavour, accompanying himself on the piano. The champagne gave way to some of the finest cognac I'd ever tasted and it was past midnight when I staggered back to the apartment for my first full night of undisturbed sleep since I set foot in the country.

On returning from my morning visit to Marco the next day, I found a note pinned to the door of the granny flat.

"Peter, please call over to the house as soon as you can. There's some news I'd prefer to give you in person. I'm here all afternoon. B."

I knew it couldn't be about Marco – I'd seen him only an hour previously and though he was still comatose, I thought I detected more colour in his face; there even seemed to be the hint of a smile playing about his lips.

I raced across to the house. The expressionless housekeeper directed me to the study where Sir Brian sat behind a massive, completely empty mahogany desk. He motioned me to sit down in a leather-upholstered wingback chair.

"I thought we'd had enough shocking news recently, Peter, but – well, there's no nice way of putting this. Commander Blaine was found dead in his cell this morning."

He waited for my reaction, but I was too stunned to speak.

"The prison governor called me – obviously, there are diplomatic implications. I suppose I should be flattered they call me when something like this happens, rather than the Embassy in the capital."

"How did it happen? Do we know?"

I briefly ran through the various ways a white man could meet his end in that particular jail. Perhaps some sort of justice had been served, after all.

"Not for sure, Peter, but we have a good idea. After the governor called me, he sent his driver over to give me this. For safekeeping, as he put it."

Sir Brian opened a drawer and produced a clear plastic sachet containing an assortment of objects, which he set down on the desk between us. Two blister strips – the tablets they once contained had been pressed out – a small plastic tub, and an empty brown medicine bottle with a faded label: the homely blue logo of Boots the Chemist was still visible on it, as was the inscription below it:

The Mixture

Mr. P. Purvis

2 tbsps 3 times/day while symptoms persist.

Bizarrely, I started wondering what the "P" might stand for – this was the nearest I'd come to having any idea of Purvis's first name.

"It looks like a kaolin and morphine bottle," Sir Brian said as I examined the contents of the sachet through the plastic. "But I rather think it contained a somewhat more lethal substance. Pentobarbitone tends to crop up in these situations, I've found."

"Pento...what?"

"You might have heard of Nembutal. Same thing."

I most certainly *had* heard of it. I recalled the night when AIDS was being discussed in Trelawney's house and Purvis told us that he'd laid in a stock of liquid Nembutal to "finish the job" if the need ever arose.

"The pills would probably have done for Blaine on their own," Sir Brian said with a sigh. "But Purvis obviously wasn't taking any chances. There was enough in that bag to finish off a couple of elephants."

We pondered this new turn of events in silence, punctuated only by the slow ticking of an antique grandfather clock in the corner of the room.

"So...what happens now?"

"Not a lot," Sir Brian answered. He took a silver-plated cigarette case from his waistcoat pocket, opened it, and offered it to me. Sobranie Black Russian, I noted with appreciation as I lit one.

"Given where we are, and in view of the potential for embarrassment on all sides, the minimum of fuss will be made. Well, that's what diplomats are for, I suppose – to see that things are done diplomatically." He suppressed the slightest of titters in response to his own half-hearted attempt at a witticism.

"Where's Purvis?"

"A very good question. I don't know. Of course, there's no evidence to suggest that he's guilty of anything. Presumably he presented Blaine with his little gift − rather as one might offer a box of chocolates, I suppose − and left him to take his own decision."

The room filled with the mellow, bitter-sweet aroma of Russian tobacco. I was becoming mildly irritated by Sir Brian's casual approach to this latest news.

"What was in this bag wasn't exactly confectionery, though," I said, tapping it with my forefinger. "How on earth did he get it into Blaine's cell?"

Sir Brian removed the cigarette case from the desk and replaced it with an ashtray from the drawer.

"Well, security in these parts isn't quite what you'd find in Pentonville or Dartmoor. And anyway, Purvis has some standing in the capital as you know, so I shouldn't think he was even searched as he went into the prison. He certainly hasn't been around much since the − ah − events in the Village; and now he's vanished again. Trelawney tells me his luggage is still in one of the rooms at the Towers, but he hasn't clapped eyes on him since they parted company at the prison gates last night. Curious. Dark horse, our Purvis. Always was."

There was a gentle tap at the door of Sir Brian's study. Marie-Hélène made a deferential entrance and asked if she should serve some lunch. Sir Brian invited me to stay, but I needed some time on my own to absorb what I'd just learned.

"I quite understand, Peter. I've seen a thing or two in my time, but I confess to being stupefied by this series of events. And I'm not even close to any of the parties involved. Which reminds me…" He stood up and prepared to escort me out of the house. "I haven't even been able to contact Marco's mother. The – ah – *widow*. I keep trying their number up at the Village, but there's no reply. Trelawney sent someone up there to take a look, but the house is apparently closed and shuttered. I don't know her at all well, but my heart goes out to her. And to you, Peter. I do know what it's like to hold the hand of someone you love, not knowing if he will make it through the night."

He cast a glance at a framed photograph on the wall, of himself and Jean-Louis in formal attire at some gala dinner. Now was definitely not the time to enquire further.

"But for a mother to be faced with the loss of her own first-born son – you and I cannot imagine that grief. I'm told there is no sorrow that can compare."

I'd heard almost the same words not so long ago. The memory of Alex's mother came into my mind, performing her grotesque dance in the kitchen in Glasgow. Elsie Macallister and Geneviève Blaine: I could hardly imagine two more different women, or two more different responses to similarly tragic circumstances.

But Marco was not dead, and he was not going to die, I reminded myself sternly.

And with equal firmness, I forced myself to take my leave of Sir Brian with the respect that he deserved.

"I'm probably not showing it very much at the moment, Brian, but I'm deeply grateful for everything you've done for me. I wouldn't want to be anywhere else while…while all this is going on."

Before I knew it, he enveloped me in a disconcertingly warm embrace. "We've all got to stick together, Peter. Always. And if the worst happens, remember you're still a very attractive man." He hugged me even tighter. "You need never be alone, you know."

I extracted myself from the grip of his muscular arms and made my exit as speedily as I could. I absolutely refused to consider what the manner of his farewell to me implied, and hastened back to the apartment to prepare for my next visit to the hospital.

Chapter Six

I decided to tell Marco the news that same afternoon. He had a right to know, after all. I'd convinced myself he could hear everything I said to him, even if there was no chance of a response. I usually started my visit by talking about trivial details — what I'd seen on the way to the hospital, or what I'd had for lunch. I tried to be as natural about it as Beth, but it was hard to keep going with no sign that anything was getting through to him. I rambled on for a few minutes in this vein, then clenched his hand tightly in mine and put it as simply as I could.

"Marco, your father died last night. He took his own life in prison."

I kept hold of his hand and lowered my face close to his, hoping against hope for a flutter of his eyelashes – how extraordinarily long and beautiful they were, gently curved like the stamens of some exotic flower – but they remained motionless. I longed for his eyelids to part, so I could see those mysterious hazel irises I knew so well. I was thinking I had come to know and love every inch of his body, every little blemish and scar, when I became aware of a slight chafing noise coming from the other side of the bed where the oxygen supply was connected. I looked across to the ugly metal cylinder, fearing a malfunction of the machinery.

What I saw made my heart bound with joy.

With his left hand, Marco was clawing at the plastic tube that led from his nostrils to the cylinder. In fact, he was tugging at it so forcefully it had almost become detached from its socket, and the other end was hanging half-way out of his nose.

I yelled in panic. "You mustn't, darling, you mustn't – it's keeping you alive!"

I pushed the tube firmly back into its connector and tried to move the ventilator into position above the bow of his lip. He resisted – briefly – and then his hand fell back, motionless, onto the bedsheet.

I wanted to hug him and smother him with kisses, but I knew that wasn't allowed, so I just kept gripping his other hand, and told him how proud I was of him. "It's going to be all right, Marco, you're going to make it – *nothing, and nobody, will ever defeat us*, remember?"

I pushed the button to call a nurse. I felt like running out into the corridor to fling my arms around someone and share what had happened. The nurse who answered the call was clearly a seasoned veteran; she saw how excited I was and immediately told me to calm down, in her patient's best interest.

I explained what I'd seen.

"Of course it's a good sign, Monsieur, a very good sign. It usually begins like this – you can imagine, it's not very comfortable to have those tubes inside your nose. It's quite natural for your son to do what he did – he was conscious for a few seconds, perhaps a minute. Now, excuse me please, while I check the monitors. I'd better call the doctor, too."

I wanted her to give me a guarantee this was the start of Marco's return to normal life, but she made it clear she had nothing more to say. The doctor swept into the room a few minutes later. She was a woman of my own age, with a welcome air of efficiency about her that contrasted markedly with the impression made by her colleague in the ICU.

"He didn't open his eyes, you say? Let's hope that will happen soon."

She inserted an instrument into one of his ears. "Now, Monsieur, I have to warn you that difficult times lie ahead. We won't know how much damage there is until he's fully conscious, but judging from the bullet wounds in his spine, and the traumatic injury to the back of his head, I'm afraid there's likely to be extensive paralysis. You must prepare yourself, and you must be ready to help him accept it."

She looked up from her clipboard and removed her half-moon glasses to make direct eye contact with me.

"Is your son an easy-going, cooperative sort of young man, would you say?"

I could hardly think of a less apt description of the Marco I knew.

"Let's say he has enormous determination and willpower. And he was extremely fit before the..."

"Accident," the doctor supplied.

"Where is his mother?" Now her tone was brusque. "I know you are separated from her, but she must be told of this development." I'd long since given up correcting the natural assumption that I was Marco's father. "Her presence will help Marco as well. I saw her here yesterday with her companion, but I don't believe she's visited today."

It did seem odd I hadn't run into Geneviève Blaine at the hospital since our first, memorable encounter. I'd actually been looking forward to seeing her again. I was glad to hear that she was still visiting her son; the "companion" would be one of her cronies from the French consulate, I supposed. Fortunately, the doctor didn't seem particularly interested in a two-way conversation.

"Please make an effort to contact her, Monsieur. Meanwhile, we'd be grateful if you and your family could spend more time here now Marco is starting to recover. We don't really have the staff to post someone in this room all the time. Nurse here will keep watch today, but please arrange for yourself and his mother to be here for the next few days."

I'd barely had time to absorb the news of Blaine's presumed suicide and now, for the first time, I'd been given real hope that Marco would stage some sort of recovery – but I was also getting an idea of the grim challenges that lay ahead.

I stayed with Marco for a few minutes after the doctor left. On my last few visits, I'd begun reading *Lord of the Rings* to him – one of his favourites – but I didn't have the energy to continue now. As I sat there by his side, I saw that his expression had changed: his lips had arranged themselves into a smile of deep satisfaction. I ran my fingers gently through his hair and left the room brimming over with gratitude and optimism.

I decided that next day, I'd go up to the Village to ask Beth and June for help with keeping vigil over Marco. I might even be able to track Geneviève Blaine down while I was there. Sir Brian welcomed the suggestion when I told him that evening:

"That's an excellent idea, Peter. Now look, don't bother calling that old rogue Mahboob to take you up to the Village. You're welcome to have our driver for the whole day."

I set out for the Village after my lunchtime visit to Marco. It was a relief to escape from the stifling city and its incessant hubbub, especially in a luxurious, air-conditioned Mercedes with a driver at the wheel who maintained a professional silence throughout the journey. I called at the Towers first. Tamir looked much more robust than when I last saw him, but he told me that Trelawney was in bed nursing a cold, not to be disturbed. I said I'd return later, and continued on foot to the Olive Branch. Both June and Beth were perched on their stools behind the counter with no customers to serve. The news of Blaine's demise had already reached them through the Village grapevine.

"What that poor woman must be going through," Beth sighed. "First Marco – now her husband – she must have loved him once, mustn't she?"

June and I exchanged glances, but neither of us answered.

"And Marco – how on earth will he cope with this when he wakes up? We all know what Marco thought of his father...but surely he wouldn't have wished him dead...would he?" There was a look of honest bafflement on her face. She clearly couldn't come to grips with the morass of twisted emotions that had driven the events of the past couple of weeks.

"I wouldn't worry too much about Madam Blaine," June said with a sniff. "That's one lady as can look after herself very nicely, thank you. Cool as a cucumber. It's Marco that needs all the support we can give him – and so do you, Peter. Look at the state of you. You're running yourself ragged with all this!"

She reached over and stroked my cheek with the side of her index finger. Her gesture felt enormously reassuring. I realised how much I was missing the way Marco used to show his affection by touching me throughout the day, in so many different ways – grabbing my hand, prodding me in the ribs, or placing a finger over my lips to shut me up. Apart from Sir Brian's ambiguous embrace and the gentle leading of the ICU nurse, I'd been deprived of physical contact since Granada.

"There is some good news," I said. I told them about Marco's first attempts at movement, and repeated the doctor's request for help with keeping watch over him.

"That settles it, then." June slapped the counter with the palm of her hand. "Beth – I'm giving you leave of absence so you can stay down in town and take it in turns with Peter to be by Marco's bedside. He's going to wake up soon, and the first thing he must see is the face of someone he loves – someone that loves him."

Beth's jaw dropped. "But June – I can't! I mean, you can't – there's the business to keep going!"

"Business? Can you see any customers, dearie? Half of 'em have buggered back off to wherever they came from, and the other half are too scared to come out of their front doors in case another maniac decides to use them for target practice! The place is as dead as a doornail."

Beth thought about the idea for a few seconds.

"Well – all right then. On one condition, June – if things pick up again, you'll let me know and I'll come back to help out."

"Agreed," June replied with a roll of her eyes. "Look, darling – it's not the fucking Ritz I'm running here. If I can't manage a glorified greasy spoon on top of a mountain in the middle of nowhere, I might as well give up completely and book myself into an 'ome. You go and get your bag packed now, my girl!"

"Yes," I chimed in, "I'll give you a lift back to town in Sir Brian's car. We're parked outside Trelawney's. I'm walking back down to see him, so meet me there when you're ready."

She gathered up her possessions and hurried off. June offered me a cigarette, took one for herself, and I lit up for both of us.

"It's the best thing for you as well, Peter. If ever I met anyone with a heart of gold, it's Beth. Admit it – you can't cope on your own, and you're pining away for Marco. Like I said, both of you love him, so both of you need to do this together."

We watched the smoke from our cigarettes rise and dissipate in the limpid air.

Eventually, June continued. "I'll come down to town again as soon as I can – and you call me if the going gets rough, right?" She placed both her hands on my shoulders and stared me in the eyes as she spoke.

My voice was quivering with emotion as I answered her. "I will, June, of course, and I can't say how much..."

"Don't bother, darlin'. And by the way," she went on, rising briskly from her stool to see me on my way, "you won't be able to winkle Trelawney out of his lair: he's another one that's too terrified to poke his nose out of his window. Now – be off with you, and get on with what you have to do."

We parted with a hug, and I set out on the climb to the Blaines' house to see if there was any sign of Marco's mother. Never had I seen the Village so deserted. The silence was broken only by a few dogs who howled at me as I passed the homes they guarded. At the Blaines' villa, the shutters were bolted and the gates padlocked. I rattled the gates, but the only response was the echo of their metallic clanking from the rock face that rose behind the house.

I wanted to escape as soon as I could from the unsettling atmosphere that now pervaded the Village like a chilly fog. I hastened back down to the Towers. Tamir had clearly been instructed to allow no-one across the threshold, and it was obviously painful for him to bar me from entry. He handed my suitcase back to me, and couldn't even look me in the face as he spoke.

"Things very bad, Mr. Peter. Better you come back later. Very, very later. Too many troubles."

Night had fallen by the time we reached town. I left Beth at her schoolfriend's house, ten minutes' drive from the hospital. It was too late to visit Marco that evening, so we arranged to meet after my morning visit to him next day.

"I really hope his mother turns up soon," Beth said as we parted. "She's probably been with him while you were up in the Village. You'd think she'd be there all the time, wouldn't you? I mean – what else could she possibly have to do at a time like this?"

Chapter Seven

The answer to that question became abundantly clear when I reached the open door of Marco's room at the hospital shortly before noon on the following day.

Geneviève Blaine was seated on a chair at the foot of Marco's bed, her back to the door.

But she was not alone.

Sitting next to her, almost on her knee, was a man. The man's arm – encased in the worn sleeve of a beige safari jacket – was draped around her neck in a manner suggestive of something more than casual acquaintance.

Of course, I knew exactly who the jacket belonged to.

I stood still, unable to believe my eyes. Perhaps I was hallucinating; maybe there wasn't anyone there at all.

I hesitated too long. Marco's mother sensed my arrival and turned her head slightly in my direction.

She waved me into the room with her free hand. Her other hand, I saw, was being playfully caressed by her companion's podgy fingers.

"Peter! How nice. Do come and join us, please!" she said airily.

I tottered over to Marco's bedside and faced the pair. As I did so, Purvis had the good grace to remove the heel of his hand from the upper slopes of Geneviève Blaine's right bosom.

He addressed me in his usual chummy manner, without the least trace of embarrassment.

"Yeah, nice to see you, Pete. We thought you'd pitch up here sooner or later. Take a pew, why don't you?"

By now I was clinging onto Marco's oxygen cylinder for support.

The way things were going, I'd soon be needing some of its contents to revive me. Marco's mother, at least, was aware of my perturbed state.

"There doesn't seem to be a spare chair for poor Peter. Why don't you run along and fetch one, Peregrine?"

My shock gave way to a fit of giggling I could barely suppress – especially as she pronounced Purvis's long-concealed Christian name with full French gusto, rolling the two 'r's for all they were worth.

"Of course, my angel," he simpered. His hand lingered over hers for a moment longer before he waddled off into the corridor to find a nurse.

Geneviève Blaine turned to me, utterly unruffled. "*En fin de compte,* Peter, all of our secrets are out in the open now, are they not? The cats have been released from their bags, as I believe you English like to say."

My vocal chords seemed to have seized up. I looked at Marco for the first time since I'd entered the room. There was no doubt about it: the smile I'd already detected on his face had become broader and more firmly defined.

I managed to croak out a few disjointed syllables. "So, you and Purvis…may I ask…how long you've…?"

"Been together? Oh, many, many happy years, Peter." Her face was radiant. "Our *liaison* has been going on under everyone's noses since the moment we met. Strange, isn't it? Concealing a secret that's utterly incredible is far easier than covering up a few sordid little details. But of course, you know all about that, don't you? The constant thrill of subterfuge. The endless scheming, the lies upon lies, the ecstasy of those snatched moments with the man you love – never enough, but you accept it all, because you know you'll never be happy without him."

She clapped her hands, clearly revelling in the memories of so many years of dissimulation. I couldn't deny she was telling my story, too.

"So – you knew about Marco and me, all along?"

"Of course! Even if Peregrine hadn't kept me informed, I would have known. I saw it in my son's eyes. I remember the day I saw the change in his look, his whole *aura* – ha! It took me back to the day I first met Peregrine. Can you remember that delicious moment, Peter, when you first saw the person who you *knew* was going to turn your entire life upside down?"

Indeed I could. I glanced over at Marco again and let my eyes dwell on the tiny mole on his cheek, recalling that day we first met in Trelawney's courtyard, barely a year ago.

"Had I been able to give you my blessing, you would have received it," she continued. "How could I not – when I was in almost the same position myself?"

I still didn't feel capable of contributing much to this conversation. "That's nice to know – er – Geneviève."

She certainly didn't seem to be a woman in mourning, but I felt I had to mouth the customary words of condolence.

"I'm so sorry to hear of your husband's passing."

Like an actress at the moment when the cameras roll, Marco's mother moulded her features into an expression somewhat more befitting of widowhood. I couldn't be sure, but I thought I detected the outline of a bruise on her right temple.

"He is at rest." She paused and inhaled deeply. "Poor Duncan. My poor, poor Duncan. When I met him, of course, he was not the tortured, crazed man that he became. The Duncan Blaine I married could never have done – *this*."

She gestured towards her son, still lying there impassively, that eerie smile on his lips. I let the silence grow between us, and then asked, softly: "What happened?"

"What happened? *War* happened, Peter. A war that need never have taken place. You pig-headed English, sailing your Armada down the Atlantic to the ends of the earth, to defend those ridiculous little islands nobody had ever heard of, with your Queen Boadicea egging them on from her nice Georgian town-house in London...Bah! War changes a man, you know – and that war changed my husband into a monster."

Distinguished service during the Falklands War, I remembered reading in Commander Blaine's biography on the internet. I'd hardly paid any attention to that final, preposterous episode of my country's imperial history at the time – I never imagined it could ever have the slightest bearing on my own life. But now, bizarrely, history had caught up with all three of us in this room – not to mention poor Zeki and the Commander himself. Perhaps the gun that fired the fatal shots had even seen service on those 'ridiculous little islands'.

"So you see, Peter, a perfectly ordinary marriage turned into hell on earth. My husband began to change after he came back from the South Atlantic, gradually at first, and then his character became more and more terrifying. Intolerant, and intolerable. I wanted to get out; but Marco had already been born, there were … financial considerations, and we had some standing in society."

Knowing what I did of their circumstances, I had to admire her capacity for understatement.

"Neither of our families would have accepted a divorce without a huge public *fracas*. I became resigned to my fate. And then, when we bought our house in the Village, my salvation arrived. One day, Peregrine walked straight up to my table in June's café – would you believe? – sat himself down, and we began talking as if we'd known each other all of our lives. The only occasion we ever met there, naturally." She let out a wistful sigh. "We were in each other's arms by nightfall."

And, of course, it was also in June's café that I first set eyes on Marco. I could see him now as he was on that autumn day, oozing indifference while his parents argued over some detail on their map. Dear June certainly had a lot to answer for.

My entire attention was riveted on Geneviève Blaine's account of her life, so I hadn't noticed Purvis standing in the doorway, holding a chair for me.

"I'll take you back there one day soon, my darling," I heard him say with a tenderness I thought him incapable of expressing. "The Village idiots can say what they like. D'you know, I can still remember exactly what you were eating – a silly little mushroom omelette! We'll order the same again."

He turned to me, and Marco. "Or perhaps we should make it a foursome, once the boy's back on his feet!"

He made a fuss of carrying the chair into the room and positioning it as close to Marco's bed as he could. There was something appealing – childlike, almost – about the mischievous smile that spread across his face, crinkling the fleshy folds of skin at his temples. Instead of the irritation he'd provoked in me over the years, I suddenly sensed an affinity with him, a sort of comrades-in-arms feeling. Then I realised why. Both of us were profoundly in love, and the objects of our love – mother and son – were both right here in this room.

Marco's mother rose from her chair. "I think we're all in need of refreshment," she said, stifling a yawn. "I'll see if I can find some coffee. I'd prefer something a little stronger myself, but I doubt whether the catering arrangements here run to that. Perry, *chéri*, perhaps you ought to have a little chat with Peter on your own. Why don't you step out onto the balcony? Considering what we're paying them, I don't see why you shouldn't have a smoke while you're out there. I can see you're both desperate."

Purvis looked as grateful as I was for this suggestion. "You don't miss anything, do you, Jenny?"

"You men are very easy to read. Now, off you go."

She marched out of the room in search of coffee. Purvis slid open the glass door leading onto the balcony, and waved me politely through it in front of him.

Chapter Eight

The balcony gave us an uplifting view across the city to the blue-grey foothills of the mountains beyond. Purvis – I couldn't yet face calling him Perry, let alone Peregrine – offered me a miniature cigar, but I refused and lit one of my own Marlboros.

I didn't know how to begin, and Purvis, just this once, seemed lost for words. After a minute or so, I couldn't stand the silence any longer.

Still staring into the distance, I muttered: "So for all those years I've seen you at Trelawney's, you were putting on an act."

He didn't respond.

"You aren't one of us at all – and you never were, were you? We were nothing but a pretext for you. The best cover you could ever have, I suppose."

He tipped his cigar ash over the balustrade. "Now, now, Pete, my friendship isn't a pretence. I might not be one of you, but I've stayed loyal all these years. None of you would even be allowed up in the Village any more if old Purvis hadn't pulled a few strings, as well you know."

"Come on – that suited you very nicely too. Your little game would have been up if we'd all been thrown out. But nobody could suspect you of carrying on with Blaine's wife while you were staying at Trelawney's. The house of perverts, I believe Blaine called it."

"All right, I admit that. But Trelawney, Brian, even you – you're some of the best pals I've got in the world."

"Some of your best friends are poofters. Is that it?"

Without a trace of cynicism, he replied: "All of them, Pete. All of them."

"Did Trelawney know?"

"Of course. We go back years, me and Trel – we were out in the Gulf together, barely out of short trousers. I got him out of a couple of financial scrapes back then and he always felt he was in my debt. Not that I ever saw it that way. He's a true gentleman, is old Trel. Matter of fact, it was him who came up with the idea of me hanging around with you lot – like you say, the best cover I could possibly have in that blasted Village."

I felt a growing admiration for the brazen cheek and sheer persistence that enabled him to keep up the pretence for so long.

"You knew what you wanted – who you wanted – and you went all out to get her."

"You got it in a nutshell, Pete. Faint heart never fucked fair maiden, as they say."

I'd never thought of that particular translation of Elena's favourite Spanish proverb. Purvis offered me his box of tiny cigars again, and this time I took one.

"Can I ask you a question you might not like?"

"I don't see why not," he answered, as he lit the cigar for me.

"Do you find homosexuals revolting?"

He hooted with laughter at this. "Of course not. I don't find any human being revolting – unless I discover they've harmed someone I love." Now his expression suddenly became stern and forbidding. "And that's when the situation got out of control, Pete. Once Jenny told me Blaine had started beating her, his days were numbered, one way or another."

Then I wasn't mistaken. The thick layers of cosmetics on Geneviève Blaine's face had been applied to conceal her injuries.

"So it *was* you driving the car that knocked Blaine out?"

"It wasn't the car that knocked him out. I followed him up the hill and cornered him on that patch of waste ground. I gave him a taste of what he could expect if he didn't stop beating his wife and treating Marco like a criminal. My right hook isn't quite what it was forty years ago, but I can still floor a man half my age."

"But…you were acting as his financial advisor as well, while all this was going on, weren't you?"

He expelled a long stream of smoke through his pursed lips. "Blaine didn't have much choice. He'd got himself into a bit of bother with the tax people in the States. Not wise, Pete. Don't ever fuck with the eagle. As it happened, a few documents came into my possession that showed exactly what he'd been up to."

"Marco's mother gave them to you."

He gave a shrug of his shoulders. "She might have done. Anyway, they weren't the sort of thing you'd want splashed across the newspapers or produced in court. So, we…came to an arrangement. I got him out of shtook, but I made him pay. Can't say I lost any sleep over it."

"So you were blackmailing him, and screwing his wife."

"You could look at it that way, Pete."

I couldn't really see any other way of looking at it.

Purvis carried on with not the slightest sign of remorse. "He got what he deserved. He was an arsehole of the first order, but I didn't realise he was losing his marbles completely. Believe me, if I'd seen what was coming, I'd have finished him off there and then when I had my little chat with him on the hill. We could all have lived happily ever after, and…"

To my astonishment, he was overcome by a fit of sobbing – he could barely get his next words out. "The…*bastard*…would never have done *that*" – he pointed over his shoulder towards Marco's bed – "…to my… my lovely…Jenny's son…"

Without thinking, I placed my hand gently on his shoulder to calm him down – the first time we'd ever made physical contact. His sobs slowly died down, and he fished out a grubby handkerchief to wipe away the tears.

As I watched him, I noticed something about his face I'd never registered before. There was a tiny bump on the bridge of his nose – in exactly the same place as the one on Marco's nose. My fingers knew that spot quite well.

Was that the real explanation for the depth of Purvis's hatred of Blaine, or just another coincidence?

"In the end," I said as calmly as I could, "I assume you gave him the choice. I take it you didn't force those drugs down his throat when you visited him in his cell?"

"No, I left it up to him. It would have been quick – not painless, but better than he had any right to expect. I suppose you could say he did the decent thing. Spared us all even more grief."

We fell silent again. I looked back through the glass at Marco. He'd been as willing a participant in this web of deceit as any of us, but he was the one – of those still living – who'd paid the highest price. His mother had returned and was sitting on the side of his bed, gently stroking his hair – just like any mother reading a bedtime story or singing a lullaby to her infant.

If there is love, all will be well, she'd said. If love alone could restore him to life, he would surely leap from his bed to stomp and pound his way back into our world. But love was clearly not enough, because he continued to lie there, inert, unable to give us the slightest sign he was aware of our presence.

"There is a bright side to all this, you know, Pete."

"Maybe for you. You've got your – *Jenny* – and Blaine's nicely out of the way, by his own hand. But just look through that window: he might not live, and if he does –"

I hurled the remains of the cigar over the balustrade. For a split second, I considered hurling myself over the parapet as well. He must have sensed what was going through my mind, because he grabbed me by both forearms.

"He *will* live, Pete. Jenny's had all his scans sent over to one of the top bods in Europe, and it's not as bad as it looks. He may not recover fully –"

"Wonderful. May not recover fully. What a comfort."

"But he'll have the best chance in the world. Because there's the money to pay for it."

I turned to go back into Marco's room, but Purvis tightened his grip and prevented me from moving.

"You need to know this, Pete. You might not think it makes any difference, but believe me it does. I got Blaine to sign all the papers before I handed over his bag of goodies. The Marco Blaine Trust is now properly constituted."

"And what does that mean?"

"Blaine himself was finished financially, but I split the companies off from his personal affairs and they're all doing fine. The properties as well. So, the trust has a fair bit of income to manage and allocate. In the best interests of Marco. *And of those who safeguard or further his wellbeing* – to quote from a certain document your mate Alex translated for me a while ago, as you might recall. The trust is based in Zurich, as it happens."

"How nice for it," I spat out. I refused to be swayed from my belief that Marco and I were the big losers in this whole tragedy.

"Money saves lives, and money changes lives, Pete. And big money makes big changes. Believe me."

"All right. How much?"

"There'll be income of about ten to fifteen million pounds a year."

"A *year?*" I found myself saying, despite my resolve not to be consoled by any financial details.

"Yup. I'm the chairman of the trust, you see."

"Naturally."

"There were two other members on the board – the Blaines, of course. So there's a vacancy. Which Jenny and I feel you ought to fill."

"I see. I'll think about it when I've got less on my mind."

"It's for Marco, Pete. When all this is over, you'll be in a very nice position. As I told you a while ago."

"And so will you, I suppose."

"Oh no. Jenny is perfectly comfortable in her own right. We shan't have any need to come begging."

I couldn't fully process the information Purvis had just disclosed. Nevertheless, I was shocked to sense the beginnings of a warm glow within me that could only have been kindled by the unimaginable sum he'd mentioned.

"All I'm interested in is getting the best possible treatment for Marco. Nothing else matters. I'll live on the street for the rest of my life if that's what it takes to get him through this."

"I'm sure you would, Pete. But you won't have to."

"Thanks to old Purvis. You've no need to say it."

I remained silent, trying to piece together all I'd just learned. Words I'd heard Trelawney speak in London floated into my mind: *it is not my place to judge.*

"Well, now you know what the situation is, Pete. All the cats are out of the bag, as Jenny so rightly said. We'd better go back in and she'll tell you what's being planned for Marco's treatment."

I was hoping to spend some time on my own with Marco – after all, it was him I'd come to see – but Geneviève Blaine made it clear she was in charge of events, and she had her own priorities. She rose to her feet and began wagging her finger at us as we went through the balcony door. "Whatever else may be happening, I cannot go on without lunch. I've called the Phoenicia and told them to have our usual table ready in half an hour, Perry. Peter, you'll come with us, and..."

I'd warmed to Marco's mother since our first meeting. But living with her son had taught me to stand up for my own rights, too.

"I'm sorry, but I'm meeting Beth at one o'clock."

"Excellent, we'll pick her up. I know she's Marco's closest friend. My husband couldn't stand the sight of her – but that's another problem that won't be troubling us anymore."

She was bustling us out of the room, but I stayed put. "I'll meet you outside the main door. I just want – need – some time with Marco," I said with calm resolve. Judging by the bemused look on her face, Geneviève Blaine obviously didn't have much experience of being contradicted.

"Oh! Excuse me for not thinking of that – of course, you must."

There was a hint of condescension in her voice, as if she were addressing a child that had asked to use the toilet at an inconvenient juncture.

"Downstairs in ten minutes, then," she went on. "I've paid – bribed – one of the nurses to keep watch until one of us comes back. They're hopelessly short-staffed here. That's one reason he's got to be moved."

I let them go on ahead of me and deliberately overstayed the ten minutes allocated, but there was still no suggestion of movement in Marco's hands or any other part of his body. I gave him a gentle goodbye kiss on the forehead and made a leisurely descent of the hospital's staircases to rejoin his mother and her consort.

Chapter Nine

We were delivered to the Phoenicia Hotel in an even more sumptuous limousine than Sir Brian's Mercedes – it seemed a long time since I'd been jolted around in Mahboob's rust-bucket, and I rather missed it.

The "usual table" turned out to be a private dining room with its own terrace giving onto the sea. Lunch was served by liveried waiters who seemed to have an intimate knowledge of our hosts' habits and preferences; the manager appeared shortly after our arrival to present his compliments. This was obviously where they'd been staying since the "events" in the Village. My appetite had vanished again, but the love-birds ate and drank as if there were no tomorrow. Beth took it all in her stride, although the Purvises – as I was starting to think of them – talked over her head rather than to her. She followed me out when I excused myself to go to the toilet.

"She didn't waste any time, did she?" Beth said as she caught up with me.

"You don't seem as surprised as I was when I walked in on them this morning, though. They were almost eating each other, in front of Marco."

"Well, to tell you the truth, June had her suspicions – she doesn't miss much. And I'd spotted them together in Beetlebridge a couple of times."

"D'you think Marco knew? Knows?"

"Probably not. He'd never admit it, but deep down he had his mum on a pedestal."

"We must stop talking about him in the past tense. He's going to get better."

She hung her head in shame at her lapse, but I'd made the same mistake myself.

"Sorry, I wasn't thinking. I'm not used to being in places like this. I can't stand the way they're so wrapped up in each other. It's like Marco's some inconvenient detail that's stopping them from getting on with their lives."

"None of us are thinking straight after what we've been through. Let's not judge them too harshly. I'll stick by Marco come what may —"

"And so will I," she echoed. She raised her hand and we high-fived each other. A pair of grey-suited businessmen gave us a curious glance as they passed by; gestures of that sort were obviously frowned upon in the Phoenicia.

"Come on, Peter, we'd better get in there and find out what she's planning for Marco's treatment. They're already serving dessert, and all we've talked about so far is money and what's to become of the Blaines' house in the Village."

My voice must have been unusually firm when I asked them what was happening, because Geneviève Blaine looked at me in shock.

"There's no need for you to worry about that, Peter. I've been in touch with Professor Vorvoreanu in Paris, and we've decided where Marco will be going as soon as he regains consciousness. The Professor's seen all the scans and talked to the doctors here, and he'll be flying over himself later this week. But he insists that Marco mustn't be transferred until he starts to speak and move."

"And this Professor — is he good?"

"Absolutely. He's head of the trauma department at the Cochin hospital in Paris — it's probably the best place in the world for spinal injuries."

"I see. So, Marco will be moved to Paris."

I was corrected by Purvis, who was just spooning the last of his crème caramel into his mouth. "No, actually. This Professor chappie runs another clinic down south. Much nearer, so we thought that would be better."

"And where's that?"

Placing her spoon and fork neatly on her plate, Geneviève Blaine announced the name of the unlikely destination that was to become home to Beth, myself, and Marco for the next two years.

"Monaco. It's part of the Princess Grace Hospital. Much easier for all concerned. And we have a spare apartment in Monte-Carlo you're welcome to use."

Always as well to have a spare, I thought.

"Perry and I will keep a suite at one of the hotels for our visits. I'm sure you'll both be in agreement with those arrangements," she said with a serene smile that would have done credit to Princess Grace herself.

Beth and I looked at one another, aghast. We truly didn't know whether to laugh or cry. Instead of doing either, Beth nodded sagely and I mumbled my appreciation of the effort that had been made on Marco's behalf. We used the excuse that Beth hadn't seen Marco for several days to escape shortly afterwards, wondering whether coffee and liqueurs at the "usual table" would be followed by the couple's retreat to the "usual bedroom" at the Phoenicia.

Beth and I soon worked out a rota for "minding" Marco. She quickly won the hospital staff over by speaking to them in their own language and treating them as equals rather than inferiors to be bribed or bullied. A cot was moved into the room so she could stay with him at night. I was to cover the daytime shifts and one or other of the nurses would fill in the gaps.

It turned out that the mother of Beth's schoolfriend was about to give birth, so the house she was staying was bursting at the seams with relatives. I asked Sir Brian if she could move into the other bedroom in the granny flat, and of course he gave his approval.

Little things – her toothbrush in the bathroom, coffee left in the pot for me to heat up – reminded me of what it was like to share life with someone else. Unlike Marco, she was obsessively tidy and remarkably quiet. In less than a week, we were behaving like an old married couple, reminding each other about silly little things – change for the drinks machine at the hospital, putting the laundry out for Marie-Hélène – and checking up that we'd each eaten a proper meal that day. It was then, in fact, that the foundations were laid for the communal life that the three of us have shared ever since. Nothing about the arrangement ever needed to be discussed. Beth quietly carved out her own unique role – sister, mother, agony aunt, comforter, optimist, realist – a little of all of those.

As time went on, I realised how smoothly Geneviève Blaine had offloaded most of the responsibility for Marco's care onto us. Her appearances at the hospital were infrequent and brief; there was no question of her participating in the rota. When she did appear, her attention soon wandered to the mobile phone that always seemed to chirp a few minutes after her arrival. Of Purvis, nothing was seen at all; I suspected that the couple's visits to the suite in Monte-Carlo would be few and far between.

It was Marco himself who set the seal on this adroit display of the art of delegation. Beth and I noticed he'd started to move about in his bed. Sometimes he would flail his arms or bleat wordlessly like a sleeper experiencing a nightmare. He seemed to become more active at night: two or three times, he tried to wrench the oxygen tube out of his nose again. But as I watched his torso twisting and writhing, I began to fear he had no movement at all in the lower part of his body.

This was confirmed by Professor Vorvoreanu, a bronzed giant of a man: swept-back white hair and a solid dark blue silk suit, with a peculiar instrument like a dentist's mirror attached to one corner of his horn-rimmed spectacles. He was ushered into Marco's room by Geneviève Blaine, who was clearly displeased to be ejected along with me while he performed a lengthy examination of his patient. His diagnosis was terse.

"His life is not in danger, I am pleased to say. In my opinion, his brain function is unimpaired; but there is paralysis at least from the pelvis downwards. Maybe more. I anticipate a number of operations; two bullets are still lodged close to the spine. I am optimistic – to a degree."

Marco's mother was already shepherding him out of the room, doubtless en route to a lengthy lunch at the "usual table".

I asked when he thought Marco could be moved to Monaco.

"I have every confidence the senior doctor here will be able to make that decision, Monsieur." He gave a smile of forced modesty. "It so happens he trained under me a few years ago. Marco will start to speak soon – and then we shall not waste any time, because he will become agitated. It is usual in these circumstances. But we have ways of dealing with that."

I pondered the sinister implications of this last remark. There was nothing to suggest that Marco could grasp what lay in store for him when he awoke, but I repeated the facts to him in a gentler tone than Vorvoreanu had adopted for his bald résumé. If Marco's mental powers and voice were indeed intact, I anticipated a stormy relationship between the Professor and his patient.

A couple of days later, I was sitting at the bedside reading to Marco when his mother joined us for one of her cameo appearances. We'd just exchanged pleasantries when her mobile phone began to blare, as usual. She was having difficulty extracting it from her handbag, so I reached over to help her, but was prevented from doing so by a tugging on my left hand that made no sense to me at first. After a split second, I saw with a thrill that Marco had taken hold of my wrist and was pulling me back towards him.

A single word issued from his lips.

His voice was more slurred than I'd ever known it, but I recognised that word immediately. His mother, however, did not. She dropped her phone with a clatter and looked at me in puzzlement.

"What? Sweet tea? But Marco detests tea. It's the last thing he'd ask for!"

"No, Geneviève. He said, 'Sweetie.'"

She frowned, still baffled.

"It's – er – what he usually calls me."

Marco continued to hold my hand in a firm grip, but he said no more.

"I'm sorry," I said, "perhaps it would have been better if he'd addressed his first word to you."

"*Mais non!*" she countered immediately. "Men only cry for their mothers when they are dying. Surely you know that? No, no, it's a good sign, a very good sign. The Professor was right – he will live. And now, well – *il est à toi.*"

Those four little words of French implied far more than anything she could have said in her excellent English. He's yours. He's with you. He belongs to you. He's on your side. And: he's your responsibility.

I suppose I was hoping that Marco would stage a lightning recovery: his electric personality would suddenly be switched back on and the flow of bombast and high drama would resume. But the reality proved to be quite different: that single, barely audible word marked the start of a very long haul.

When he next awoke, he asked Beth and I where he was, but we barely had time to tell him before he lapsed back into unconsciousness. A day later, we had to tell him again. It became clear that he had no recollection of any of the events that had led to his paralysis. We soon resorted to supposedly comforting lies of the sort that were spun to my parents throughout their long illnesses. He began to whisper, then shout, and then scream. We told him that everything was all right, he would soon be well, just some minor surgery. I cringed at every untruth that came out of my mouth.

After a fortnight, the decision was made to transfer him to Monaco.

For the first time since the Phoenicia lunch, the four of us – Beth, Purvis, Geneviève Blaine and myself – came together in the VIP suite at the airport, as a heavily anaesthetised Marco was unloaded from an ambulance and wheeled along to join us. A sleek white Learjet was parked on the apron outside, ready to receive the gurney.

Conversation was, to say the least, laboured. Nobody was prepared to bring up the latest development: two days previously, Blaine's body had been laid to rest in a far corner of the Village churchyard. Greta had eventually consented to the burial of a suicide there on condition that the grave was unmarked. Beth looked on uneasily: she was to accompany the party on board. I would return alone to Algeciras and drive up to Monaco, calling in at Granada and Casa Morena on the way.

I exchanged a French triple cheek-kiss with Marco's mother, shook Purvis's clammy hand and gave Beth a long hug before they each vanished into the plane.

I watched the plane taxi to the runway and take off. Then I gazed over at the main airport buildings and the car park where Trelawney, Tamir and I had shared hot sweet coffee on the bonnet of the Land Rover in what seemed like another existence.

I turned my back on the now empty runway and strode purposefully back into the concourse. Soon, I would embark on the last of the voyages past the Rock of Gibraltar that had punctuated the transformation of my life since Marco entered it.

Chapter Ten

I t took me nearly a week to reach Monaco.

In Granada, old Señor Escobar made a point of offering me his condolences in person when I called in at the Academia to settle the final bills (they were waived, of course). "A tragedy for you, and an incalculable loss for our art. We can only pray..."

When I reached Casa Morena, I was shocked at how welcoming my house had become. Even if Marco never returned here, the vibrant colours and homely furnishings would always remind me of the changes he'd triggered. Elena cooked a simple dinner and Pepe joined us at the kitchen table. She expressed her view of the situation in a few simple words: "He's strong. You too. The pair of you will win through." Pepe looked on, nodding his agreement, giving me an occasional smile of encouragement.

I turned the car northwards next morning and followed the autoroute until it swooped and plunged past Cannes and Nice. The winding road down to Monte-Carlo took me near the spot where Princess Grace's car plummeted over the cliffs a decade before. I recalled with a shudder that she was taken to die in the very hospital where Marco now lay paralysed. Although the magnificent Riviera coastline was bathed in golden sunlight, that thought deepened my gloomy mood as I threaded my way through the Principality's immaculate streets. I found the block where the "spare apartment" was located and Beth appeared behind the glass door to let me in.

"Don't be taken in by the name!" she giggled, pointing up at the plaque on the lintel. It bore the words *Le Buckingham Palace*. "About as ancient as the original, I should think, but not quite so luxurious. We'll be all right here, Peter."

She threw her arms around me, took charge of my suitcase and bustled me into the lift. She'd already made some effort to brighten up the drab, functional apartment that was to be our home for nearly two years. Flowers and fruit had been placed on the tables and she'd hung a couple of Berber shawls on the bare walls. From the minuscule balcony, there was a close-up view of the back of a multi-storey car park that added little to the flat's attractions. In time, though, we turned it into a comfortable refuge from the wearying routine of visits to the hospital that were to come.

Marco's first operation was scheduled for the next morning. He'd clearly been sedated in advance by the time we visited him that evening. He knew who we were and mumbled a few incomprehensible words, but I was distressed to see him paler and more disoriented than ever.

That first operation on his spine set the pattern for the many that followed. We sat with him while he came out of the anaesthetic, hopes rising that he would kick his legs out of bed or even just wiggle his toes – then came bitter disappointment when there was no trace of movement beneath the bedsheets. As the operations proceeded, his face became gaunt and drawn. Ugly blotches appeared on his skin, and mucus dribbled from his nostrils.

And yet, I loved him even more.

Once the novelty of living in one of the world's most famous places had worn off, our hospital visits were the only bright spot of the day. We quickly tired of Monaco's manicured beaches and marble-floored malls; star-spotting in the Carrefour supermarket soon lost its fascination.

Sadie appeared: we never did find out how she'd tracked Marco down, or where she was living these days. Her ironclad façade crumbled when she saw Marco's condition, and I'm sure I saw a tiny tear trickle down her massive jowl.

As expected, we saw very little of the Purvises, who waited a respectable six months before formalising their union at a discreet ceremony in the Phoenicia conducted by Sir Brian and the French consul. Occasionally, I was summoned to the lobby of one of Monte-Carlo's grand hotels to attend a meeting of the trust. This merely involved the three of us signing documents to release frightening sums of money into an account opened in my name at an exotically-named bank behind the Casino.

It began to feel like Beth and I would be spending the rest of our lives in the hermetically sealed compartment that was Monaco. The Vertical Village, they were calling it these days. Then, a few weeks into the second year, Professor Vorvoreanu announced that the next operation would be the last.

"After that – and I give no guarantee of the result – all we can offer is physiotherapy and rehabilitation. And frankly, given his mental state, I think we may have to look at some psychiatric assistance as well."

This came as no surprise to me. I knew Marco was being pumped full of drugs to numb the pain and suppress his agitation when he became lucid. I'd witnessed it all before with my parents. It was horrible to see how his keenness of mind had deteriorated into bewilderment or vapidity.

One day, he asked me to listen silently while he counted off the events that had demolished almost the entire structure of his previous his life: Zeki's death; his own near-fatal injuries; his father's imprisonment and suicide; the revelation of his mother's long clandestine affair with Purvis and now, their marriage.

He paused after his enumeration was complete, drew a deep breath and slowly expelled it again.

"You wouldn't believe it if you read it in a novel, would you? So it must all be true," he murmured.

I expected tears or ranting, but he seemed incapable of any emotional response. He merely asked to be left alone for a while.

Beth and I agreed that our aim was to get him out of the hospital as soon as his physical condition allowed. Until the last surgery was completed, he'd barely left his room except to be wheeled to the operating theatre. Sometimes they would take him down to an open courtyard inside the hospital buildings where he would sit like an old man, swathed in blankets and scarves, but at least breathing some fresh air.

He showed some slight signs of physical improvement once the operations stopped. Vorvoreanu devised a regime of massages, physiotherapy and even sea-water treatments in a luxurious spa complex the Prince had recently opened. His legs were inserted into contraptions that forced them to stretch or go through the motions of walking. We were instructed to take him on short outings, up and down the road that led to the *Jardin Exotique*.

We struck up several nodding acquaintances during these excursions: other wheelchair occupants and their wheelers, walkers of squads of beribboned dogs in multiple harnesses, and old ladies who must have spent hours on their makeup before embarking on the five-minute stroll to the corner shop. Monaco was an apt choice for Marco's recovery in one respect at least: in this town where extreme wealth and equally extreme decrepitude were the norm, we certainly didn't stand out from the crowd.

Brilliant yellow mimosa blossoms heralded the arrival of our second spring in the Principality and at last, we began to see hints the Marco we knew might yet return. After his mother and Purvis had paid one of their fleeting visits, he turned to us with a wry smile instead of his customary scowl.

"It's an upgrade for her, I suppose, but there's still room for improvement, wouldn't you say? And that ridiculous little *moustache*...the mind boggles. How *could* she?"

Beth squeezed my hand and winked at me. If his sharpness of tongue was returning, we knew there was hope.

Soon he was asking, then pleading, to be released from hospital. "Take me home, sweetie. Just take me home." He would even mutter the same words in his sleep.

It was Beth who was bold enough to ask: "Where's home, Marco? Back to the Village?"

"Bugger the Village. Your house, of course, Peter. That's where we belong, isn't it? I knew it the first time I saw it..."

For me, that launched a series of trips back to Casa Morena to prepare for his second coming. Ramps had to be built, doorways needed to be widened for the wheelchair, and our bedroom and bathroom had to be remodelled once more.

I didn't expect him to settle down easily, and I wasn't wrong. At best, he was sullen and silent. All too often, though, he vented his frustration by picking silly quarrels with us.

Right from the start, he insisted we sleep together. His tossing and turning in bed kept me awake and his sleep was interrupted by violent nightmares that were terrifying to behold.

Before long, I was suffering from symptoms of sleep deprivation. My energy and appetite dwindled, and I had less and less tolerance for the string of complaints he churned out during the day.

I don't know how I'd have survived this phase without Beth. She was equally firm with both of us, telling him to shut up when she could see I was at breaking point and making sure I ate properly and rested during the day.

Elena adopted a different and highly successful approach to Marco. She treated him as if there was nothing wrong with him. If he was in the kitchen, she'd expect him to shell prawns or chop onions and garlic and then clear up the mess he'd made doing it. He scowled but obeyed her grudgingly; he had enough sense to see that the consequences of crossing her would be dire.

There was only one person whose company he really seemed to enjoy, and that was Pepe. I used to come across the pair of them sitting side by side in the cottage garden. Once, Pepe had rescued a bird with a broken wing. Marco was clutching it while Pepe gently tried to feed it. Sometimes Marco would sit there with a bundle of rushes in his lap, splitting them and passing them to Pepe who would fashion them into the little boxes and baskets he used around the garden. I could usually tell when Marco had been with Pepe because instead of resignation or mounting anger, there was a calmness beneath his silence. I hoped it was a sign he was coming to terms with his plight.

Vorvoreanu's stupor-inducing drugs were replaced by an ever-increasing intake of whisky and cigarettes. Marco asked for cannabis too, and I saw no reason why he shouldn't have it. I went to one of the cafés in Aguacate where it was readily available.

Amid a boisterous crowd of young men downing their evening beers, I spotted Romeo, looking more handsome than ever. He dashed over and gave me an enthusiastic embrace. Shunning temptation, I told him what I needed and why. He sped off on his motorbike and returned in minutes with a foil-wrapped package. Soon he was making regular deliveries to Casa Morena, followed by equally regular sessions of thrashing about with me at various spots in the outhouses or on the land. Exhausted though I was, I could usually summon up enough energy to turn in an adequate performance.

As I was leaving to escort Romeo out after one of these visits, Marco grabbed my wrist to stop me. "Look, Peter. I know exactly what's going on. It's my legs that are fucked, not my brain. But in case you're worried, I want you to know: I couldn't care less. Truly. It doesn't look like our relationship will ever be consummated in that way, now, does it? So, have him as often as you want. Have twenty of them if you like. As long as you're happy, sweetie."

I was developing a guilty conscience about what I'd assumed were our secret trysts, so I was relieved to hear him say this without the least hint of rancour. But then he took hold of both my hands and pulled my face close to his.

"Just – don't leave me, Peter. Don't ever leave me. Promise me you won't – pl-eee-ase, *pl-eee-ase!*"

This was Marco, defeated. I'd never seen it before and I didn't like it. His eyes were moist, but he held back the tears.

"Of course I won't. I love you, Marco."

I'd said it to his face, at long last. But he didn't answer; we kissed, and stayed hugging each other closely for a minute or more, without exchanging words.

"You'd better run along now, sweetie. Romeo hasn't got all evening – remember he has a wife to get back to, so don't wear him out. And anyway, *I* need you back here to get my dinner. I suppose Beth is also out having her fancy tickled in whatever way turns her on."

He began unwrapping the package that Romeo had delivered. "Thank God for drugs! Enjoy your evening, sweetie. Don't worry about little old me."

The prospect of writhing around with Romeo in a muddy ditch had somehow lost its allure, at least for that evening, so I handed him the banknotes for the goods he'd delivered and bade him goodnight. Our encounters continued until, inevitably, they lost their zing. By then, though, the huge project of converting the house into a luxury resort had begun and Romeo became a fixture around the place. He is still our chief handyman and driver while Ana, his wife, is Beth's indispensable second-in command in the kitchen.

I also renewed my friendship with Federico. Beth and I insisted on taking a weekly day off from ministering to Marco's needs, or at least keeping his mind off his misfortunes. We usually ended up at Bar Alex, now firmly established as one of Almería's most popular night-spots. Our household's alcohol consumption had soared dramatically, so we started buying it from Federico by the crateload.

At first, Marco clearly regarded him as a more serious potential rival than Romeo could ever be, and there was a wall of ice between them. That changed after a long conversation they had one afternoon while Beth and I were out swimming. I never did find out exactly what was said, but Federico let it be known that he'd told Marco a few "home truths" – drawn, no doubt, from his own experience of caring for Alex during the last months of his life. Even today, Federico looks after all our bar supplies, and the tour of Almería we offer our guests always ends up with an evening of considerable debauchery at Bar Alex.

It was Trelawney who put forward the idea of converting Casa Morena into a hotel. He came to spend a week with us and was even more enchanted with the house than on his first visit. He praised us lavishly for our efforts to care for Marco, who was in a particularly fractious mood for most of his stay. Trelawney accepted his behaviour with his usual courtesy, but made no secret of his concern for us once we could talk privately.

"What you have done for Marco, and what I see you do every day, merely confirms the strength of character I have always known both of you to possess." He clapped a hand on each of our shoulders. "But, my friends, your admirable devotion is sapping your life-blood, and your spirits! You are both young people."

I opened my mouth to protest, but he wagged an imperious finger to forestall any contradiction.

"Let me be blunt. Dear Marco is not the easiest of patients. And there is little indication his condition will change very much over the years, or decades. Two lifetimes devoted to caring for him will end in frustration and bitterness, mark my words. A hotel would give you another focus for your attention and your energies. Money, as I understand it, is no object. You could keep the house for yourselves and build on the land around it. I beg of you – at least give it some thought."

We did, and we agreed that Trelawney would raise the idea again the next time we were all together at the dinner table. Marco's response was so cuttingly negative that I felt deeply embarrassed for my old friend.

"Sure, sure. Make it into a hotel, for all I care." He stubbed his cigarette out on his dinner plate. "Demolish the whole place and turn it into Disneyland, why not? Buy a fucking spaceship with my father's blood money, and fly to Mars!"

He slammed his fist down on the table and hurled his wineglass to the floor. "I'm off to bed. Enjoy yourselves."

He wheeled himself out of the dining room at breakneck speed. We stared after him in mortified silence. Trelawney was right: the endless stress, and Marco's constant lack of gratitude, were wearing us down. I began to wonder how much longer I could go on. I made my excuses and left Beth and Trelawney to finish their meal while I went for a long walk in the moonlight.

When I eventually tiptoed into the bedroom, Marco was still awake, lying face-down, his head buried in the pillow. It took me a moment to realise the strange noise he was making was that of uncontrollable sobbing.

"I – just – *hate* – myself," he eventually managed to blurt out. "I hate what all this has turned me into, and I hate what I'm doing to you two."

I reached over to comfort him, but he pushed me away.

"I just don't know how the fuck you put up with it. And poor Trelawney – he introduced us, for God's sake! All I'm doing is ruining your life, and Beth's. What fun do you ever have?"

I said nothing. It was painful to hear — yet somehow, his words gave me a glimmer of hope that better things lay ahead.

"Of course you must do the hotel — for yourselves. Beth will be wonderful — and you'll love it, Peter, you really will. Trust Trelawney to come up with the perfect solution. I shall be a sort of phantom mooning about the place, I suppose, kept out of view in case the guests are put off their dinners."

I decided it was time the kid gloves came off. "You're perfectly welcome to spend the rest of your life wallowing in self-pity, Marco. People tell me it can sometimes be quite enjoyable."

For a moment, I thought I'd gone too far — but no. He raised his head from the pillow and emitted something approaching a titter.

"Hmmm. You've been spending too much time with Beth. Or Elena. If *you're* going to get tough with me as well, I suppose I'll have to get my act together."

He let out a protracted yawn. "Now, please come to bed, sweetie. I can see you're exhausted too. No wonder."

That was the night we resumed the habit of spooning — difficult though it was at first, I manoeuvred us into a comfortable position with my arms crossed over Marco's breast. My mind gradually emptied of all thoughts except one — how lucky I was to be there, my limbs wrapped around his: the man I still loved, no matter how hard he was to love, the only one I'd ever truly loved...the only one I ever would love.

Chapter Eleven

Marco apologised contritely to Trelawney next morning, and it was not long before plans were being commissioned, building permits applied for and contractors engaged.

This was the period when Marco still cherished hopes of a miracle cure. We were often absent from Casa Morena on fruitless trips to orthopaedic specialists and alternative healers near and far, leaving Beth to hold the fort as the construction work got under way.

It was not until the morning we were due to set off on that last, desperate journey to Lourdes that the miracle finally happened, a full five years after the shootings in the Village. That was when the Marco we remembered and loved emerged from his long hibernation to resume his habitual position: centre stage, in the full glare of the spotlights. Once he'd decided to abandon the trip, he suddenly started behaving like the young man he still was – I recall him challenging me with a grin: "I'll race you to the kitchen – loser fixes lunch!". (I lost, of course, and we ended up with a hopelessly unhealthy but delicious mess of English sausages, bacon, fried eggs and baked beans).

After his first cursory inspection of progress to date with the construction work, he demanded to see the plans he'd ignored for months. From then on, there was no doubt as to who was in charge.

"This is going to be fun!" he declared ominously as he tore up our modest designs for countrified bungalows and replaced them with his own, ever more fantastic specifications. Four-poster beds, chandeliers, jacuzzi baths of preposterous dimensions; one bungalow was to be equipped by a contractor from Antwerp who specialised in military insignia and black leather accoutrements of whose precise purpose I preferred to remain ignorant.

"We could call this one the Commander's Suite," he said with a wicked chuckle. I was amazed to hear him refer to his father with something approaching humour. In the end, that bungalow was christened "The Boot Camp", to send out the right signals to guests with a predilection for its particular attractions.

Once he'd snapped out of his long torpor, he set about masterminding the conversion of Casa Morena with a vengeance. Several times, I overheard him berating Malcolm, the interior designer who'd been flown in from London at outrageous expense.

"A tented ceiling," I heard him bellowing on one occasion, "cannot be achieved with drawing pins and a pair of surplus bedsheets, sweetie. The folds have to be *coaxed* out from the ceiling rosette!"

And again: "For fuck's sake! *No wicker furniture is ever to be placed indoors*! Didn't your mummy teach you that?"

The poor designer gave up completely after an encounter I witnessed in the dining room, when they were trying out the table settings.

"Golden rule number one, sweetie, and you've broken it. Candles on the dinner table must always be positioned *below* eye level. Especially if the diners include wheelchair users. Of which one happens to be present, in case you hadn't noticed."

The hapless Malcolm was shipped back to London the very next day.

The work proceeded just as well, if not better, without him. Beth would stride about in dungarees and a hard hat, hounding the builders into meeting their deadlines; Marco supervised the artistic aspects from his wheelchair, which he skilfully exploited to reinforce rather than detract from his authority; and I dealt with the never-ending flood of paperwork, bills and even enquiries from the press.

Meetings of the trust were now conducted by e-mail: the Purvises seemed to be spending most of their time in Africa these days, and both Marco and his mother were content to maintain vestigial contact by telephone. Asking for funds to be released for the latest phase of building work was a mere formality.

When the incessant noise and chaos became too much, we would take off on short holidays – San Sebastián to escape from the midsummer heat, or El Hierro in the Canaries to escape from everything. "Anywhere but Monte-fucking-Carlo," as Marco put it.

Eventually, he asked me to take him back to Granada. We never talked about flamenco, although you couldn't have the television on for long in Spain without hearing the plaintive tones of the *cante jondo* that accompanies it. He didn't want to visit the Academia, but the Escobars – La Furiosa and her father – did us the honour of inviting us to an evening of dance at one of the classier *tablaos* in Sacromonte. Marco and La Furiosa whispered occasional comments to each other about the dancers' footwork.

She was invited on stage to perform for a few minutes. Marco gazed at her in silence, a slightly baffled expression on his face I couldn't decipher. It was almost as if he were seeing it all for the first time. He joined in the enthusiastic applause for her performance, and was at his most courteous as we finished our food and wine and made our farewells.

But once the Escobars had left, he turned to me with words that must have given him more pain that any he'd ever spoken.

"Thanks for bringing me, Peter, but this was the last time. No more flamenco, ever."

He sighed, and looked back at the little stage, empty now except for a blood-red carnation that had fallen from behind La Furiosa's ear as she danced.

"That was then, and this is now. Let's go home tomorrow and get on with our lives."

He spoke quietly, but with great composure and serenity.

The loss of the father he hated, and the loss of the art that he loved

– I often wondered what processes were going on in his mind to enable him to live with that double bereavement.

So it was that the programme of entertainment at the opening gala for the *Casa Morena Resort Grand Luxe* included the gypsy band from Bar Alex, two ancient but hilarious drag queens and a luscious stripper who disappointed us all by vanishing with his girlfriend once his principal attraction had been revealed. But there was no flamenco.

I looked on in wonderment at what my once arid home had become. A couple of hundred people were milling around the now beautifully landscaped gardens. Fountains played and torches flared beside the steps and ramps that led down to the floodlit swimming pool. The pretty old house was suffused with warm amber light from the blazing flambeaus. Its new French windows were flung wide open to welcome our guests, who were flocking inside to help themselves from the sumptuous buffet Federico had laid on for us. Marco was stationed beside the long table, immaculate in a purple velvet tuxedo, holding forth about the various vintage wines on offer; Beth flitted here and there among the crowd, making sure that every glass and plate was full.

Everywhere I looked, there were merry faces and smiling eyes. Shrieks of laughter punctuated the hubbub of animated conversation among friends, almost drowning out the exuberant music from the band. Dancing had already begun on the terrace; down below, some of our more overheated guests had stripped off and plunged into the pool. Like so many of the scenes I'd witnessed since the first time my eyes met Marco's in Trelawney's garden, it felt like something out of a dream from which, no matter how hard I tried, I just couldn't seem to wake up.

Epilogue

The Bell Rang Out
a Hundred Times
2009

"Wake UP! Wake up NOW, sweetie!"

Marco was jabbing my ribs with his forefinger and yelling in my ear in his usual fashion. It took me several moments to realise I'd dozed off as I recalled the long procession of events that had brought us to this day. I must have wandered from the kitchen through to the terrace. The coffee I'd made stood stone cold on the table in front of me.

"Peter, there are several *thousand* jobs to do if we're ever to get to Greta's party, and all you can do is lie sprawled there like a geriatric! Shift – ass – *now*!"

"I'm sorry, darling, I was just thinking –"

"Unwise, in your case. What are *those* doing there, might I ask?"

Marco pointed at the little collection of objects I'd placed on the table: the old jewel box, the remains of the Commander's diving watch, and the rusting fragments of the two bullets that had been removed from his spine.

"I found them on the kitchen range," I said. "I haven't seen that box for years, and I didn't even know you still had the two, er..."

"Bullets that nearly killed me. I've been hunting high and low for them. I've decided to take them back to the Village and leave them there, where they belong. The past is the past."

I couldn't have agreed more. The mere sight of the box and its contents had stirred memories that were excruciating to revisit.

"Cancel all engagements for the day," Marco said, "there are wardrobes to be planned, a gift to be decided on – *total* nightmare, nothing could possibly be appropriate – not to mention the travel arrangements."

"Well, we've got a couple of months, the party's not until November. You said we'll need to fly via Madrid, didn't you?"

"I've had an idea."

I groaned inwardly.

"Why don't we drive there in the Rolls? It would be such fun!"

We'd had it completely refurbished over the course of time, and it even had a new engine. As well as using it as our airport shuttle bus, we sometimes allowed guests to take it on occasional picnic trips to isolated locations where, the evidence suggested, the back seat was put to its accustomed use. Otherwise, though, it was almost never driven. Even if you could find a parking space for it, you'd return to find that souvenir-hunters had removed whatever parts of it they could detach. We were already on our fourth Spirit of Ecstasy.

"I don't see why not, if that's what you'd really like. After all, it's actually Trelawney's, so he could keep it if he wants to, and we'll fly back. I see Greta's offering accommodation, but we'll have to stay at the Towers, of course."

Marco's face clouded over for a moment. "All right, but not in … that room."

I placed my hand over his. "No. Not that room. We can book into a hotel in town if it's too much for you."

The Blaines' house in the Village had long since been sold, and Beth's family had been forced to return to England for health reasons.

"Peter, Trelawney's house is where we first met. Everything started there. Trelawney's stood by us through thick and thin." He waved his hand in the direction of the stunning array of white bungalows, the pool and the cascaded gardens below us. "And remember, he was the one who suggested *this*. Of course we shall stay with him. It'll be like coming full circle."

In total contrast to my journey in the opposite direction a decade before, the drive from Casa Morena down to the Straits in that superb vehicle was an utter joy. Snow was glistening on the peaks of the Sierra Nevada when we passed Motril. Beth took the wheel as we swept down past the Rock, resplendent in the sunlight of a cloudless autumn afternoon.

We spent a couple of lazy days on the windswept beaches near Tarifa before boarding the ferry for Africa. The Rolls secured VIP treatment for us on board; we wined and dined in style in the Captain's quarters, then slept our way through the rest of the long voyage. Sir Brian and Jean-Louis were on hand to escort us through the customs and passport checks as we landed.

In next to no time we were turning off the coast road at Beetlebridge to begin the climb to the Village. The infamous piece of waste land had been levelled and concreted over, ready for the construction of an apartment block; new box-like cottages had sprung up on either side of the approach road to the Village.

"Regrettable, I know," said Trelawney when we commented on these changes after exchanging our usual warm greetings. "The barbarians are at the gates of Rome. But believe me, the inner sanctum of the Village is in very good hands, and will remain so."

"Isn't Greta a bit past it now, though?" Marco asked with his customary tact.

"As you'll see tomorrow," he sniffed, "her vigour remains undimmed by time. But it's true, even she is aware that human life is not infinite." Greta's life expectancy was clearly not a subject he wanted to dwell on. "Now, where's Tamir? He'll show you to your rooms and then we'll have a quiet supper before tomorrow's festivities."

Getting Marco's wheelchair through the house and into the

courtyard was no easy feat, with steps and protruding tiles everywhere. I was looking forward to a rest after the long journey, so I was a little disconcerted when Marco announced that he wanted to go out into the Village.

"Do you have to?" I asked, without thinking.

"Yes, Peter, I do have to. Please, will you take me to the churchyard? There's something I want to do there. We'll need a spade, if you can find one. Ask Beth to come too. She's family."

I realised what he wanted – needed – to do, and immediately felt guilty about putting my own interests before his. I called Beth from her room, and it took both of us to propel the wheelchair up the steep hill to the lych-gate.

I found what we were looking for after a few minutes of scanning the graves: a rectangle of cold grey stone that bore no inscription, beneath the cedar trees by the back wall of the churchyard. Marco released a lengthy sigh. "The ground's a bit hard here, but see if you can dig a hole."

We had to chip away at the sun-baked, stony soil for a half an hour to make an indentation of a couple of feet.

"I'm sorry I can't get down to put them in myself, so if you wouldn't mind..."

He handed the jewel box and the watch to me, and the bullets to Beth. We knelt on either side of the hole we'd made and pushed them as far down into the ground as we could. I wondered what an onlooker would made of this bizarre scene: one figure slumped in a wheelchair, two others kneeling before him, piling handfuls of yellow dirt into a pit by the side of an unmarked grave as the sun set over the churchyard.

I was expecting some sort of utterance from Marco, vituperative or perhaps philosophical. However, he said nothing until we'd finished the job and wheeled him through the lych gate. Then he asked us to stop, drew us both close to him and kissed each of us on the lips.

"There are no words, are there?" he said hoarsely. "But thank you. Just like everything else, I couldn't have done it without you. Both of you. Maybe I don't often show it, but I'm just – so – lucky to have you two."

We looked back at Commander Duncan Blaine's last resting place, now almost entirely hidden from view in the gathering dusk, and embarked on the bumpy journey back to Trelawney Towers. Tamir was waiting outside the front door with an anxious look on his face.

"We worried about you, Mr. Peter. Maybe not comfortable in house, maybe too much bad memory? You all okay?"

"Yes, Tamir, don't you worry," Marco assured him in a strong, clear voice. "We're very, very comfortable, and absolutely everything is all right. Absolutely everything."

"Except," Beth added, "we're famished!" She added a word in Arabic; Tamir's expression changed to one of relief, and he ushered us back into the house I knew so well. He'd prepared a lamb and chicken *tajine* for dinner with lashings of *couscous*.

Trelawney had thoughtfully accommodated us as far away as possible from the Heliotrope Room, but we paused and looked silently at its boarded-up door for a moment as we retired for the night.

"He didn't survive," Marco murmured. "And nor did poor Zeki. But we did."

"Sometimes I can't believe –" I began.

"No more. Take me to bed, sweetie."

Whatever spirits may have been abroad in the Village that night, they did not prevent me from sleeping soundly until almost noon on the day of Greta Lindberg's hundredth birthday.

I awoke in an empty bed, and panicked immediately. Back at home, we'd rigged up hand-grips and banisters so Marco could hoist himself out of bed into the chair or inch his way to the bathroom. But I couldn't imagine how he'd extricated himself from the old-fashioned high bed we'd fallen into the previous night. I flung a towel around myself and rushed over to the main house. Eventually, I tracked Trelawney down in his bedroom, muttering to himself as he fiddled about with a top hat that had definitely seen better days.

"Ah! At last! Good morning, Peter. I should have thought of this before. I haven't worn morning dress since I was last at Ascot, must've been thirty years ago or more. I think the topper will have to be jettisoned − but then, my hair has always been my best feature...How are you?"

"I'm worried stiff! Where's Marco?"

"Oh yes. Tamir's taken him down to Beetlebridge. Apparently it was all arranged last night. You were dead to the world, they said, so they just got on with it. Some last-minute shopping, I imagine. There's bugger all worth buying in the Village shop these days."

Suddenly I understood. I knew that Zeki was buried in the cemetery behind the mosque in Beetlebridge. Having visited Blaine's grave, Marco would feel duty bound to pay his respects to the young man whose life his father had taken. Now I saw what he meant when he talked about "things that needed to be done". He was actually using his time here to set the seal on the long process of reconciliation and acceptance that must have gone on within him since we were last in this house together. It didn't surprise me that he'd undertaken this work silently, on his own. He'd never reached out to any of us, but Marco always had his own way of doing everything, and his manner of grieving was no exception.

Time was speeding by. Given how long it had taken to get Marco into his morning suit on the trial run back at home, I was relieved to hear the Land Rover pull up a few minutes later. I went to the front door to help with manoeuvring Marco out of the vehicle, but Tamir and Beth had already done the job between them.

"Afternoon, Mr. Peter," Tamir greeted me. "Wow! You very fit these days!"

I'd forgotten I was standing there virtually naked.

"Yes, sweetie, it's lovely to have a display of your rippling muscles this early in the day, but may I remind you we've to make our entrance in full formal attire in less than an hour?"

Whatever had taken place down in Beetlebridge seemed to have kindled a new vigour in Marco. He was beaming; his skin had a healthy glow and he clearly couldn't wait to get on with the main business of the day.

"Bedroom – now! Beth, come over to us once you've got into your drag, and I'll help you with your make-up at the same time as I do Peter's."

I knew he wasn't joking, because I'd helped him pack a vast array of cosmetics that took up a whole suitcase. To my relief, most of them were used to put the finishing touches to Beth's appearance. Her hair was piled high and studded with tiny reflective sequins that matched her emerald-green gown. There was no doubt about it: she'd emerged triumphant from our years of tribulation and she stood there as a woman who commanded attention and respect.

Trelawney took a photograph of the three of us, one on either side of Marco, as we left the house to head up the hill. It is my favourite portrait of our little family, and it still stands on my desk at home today. In it, I see the love that binds us together and the strength that comes from that unity: but above all, the profound happiness that our shared life has given us.

The Olive Branch was decked out in style for the occasion. Red, white and blue garlands were strung between the palm trees; lavish flower arrangements spilled out of huge jardinières. There was a long top table; Greta sat in the middle. She was clad from head to foot in black, highlighting the outsized silver medallion on her chest with a prancing lion at its centre: presumably the insignia of the Order of St. Olav. Other than that, the only adornment she wore was the modest chain of office I'd noticed around her neck when she arrested Commander Blaine. She seemed quite unchanged since that night, although her helmet of close-cropped hair was now completely white.

Next to her was the Head of State's personal envoy – her junior by a couple of decades at most, judging from his frail appearance. The ministers and diplomats, including Sir Brian, were clustered around Greta. Unlike me, they seemed perfectly at ease in their formal morning dress. The womenfolk in their jewel-laden kaftans created splashes of colour amid the grey.

The three of us were allocated seats right at the end of the top table, with June next to me. As we waited for the food to be served, I picked out a few familiar faces in the sizeable crowd. Doocie was there, flanked by two of his protégées: they seemed to get younger and more glamorous as he aged. Dr. Steingass, looking ten or even twenty years younger since the night he'd bandaged Trelawney's wound, sat hand in hand with a statuesque lady who, I assumed, was responsible for his rejuvenation.

But most of the gathering was made up of newcomers to the Village since we were last there: family groups – Europeans, Indians and even some Chinese, with children of various ages in tow. Perhaps Greta's vision of the Village as a miniature commonwealth of nations had finally been realised.

Then I spotted another wheelchair parked at one of the smaller tables towards the back of the garden. If it hadn't been for the faded scarlet mess jacket that hung loosely from the shoulders of its occupant, I'd never have recognised Colonel Twelvetrees – age or illness had clearly taken its toll. There was no sign of his wife, as far as I could see. Before Marco could stop me, I got up from my seat and went across to him. If this visit was about laying the past to rest, I would play my part too.

He was already half-asleep, so I tapped him gently on the shoulder to rouse him.

"Ah – yes – young Carter, isn't it? One of Trelawney's crowd, if I recall?"

"That's right. He's my best friend, actually, Colonel. Is Mrs. Twelvetrees not with you today?"

He paused, a distant look in his eyes, as if he had to think quite hard about the answer.

"No, no, I'm afraid not. My dear wife passed away some time ago. Four years, I think it was."

"I'm sorry to hear that."

"My poor Mary...she went into a terrible decline," he snuffled. "Never seemed the same after the night of the – you know, you were there. Kept muttering to herself – all she could say was 'I shouldn't have told him...I shouldn't have told him'...I never did find out what it was all about."

I knew exactly what it was all about, of course, but I saw no need to enlighten him. So, it *was* Mrs. Twelvetrees who had triggered the chain of death and catastrophic injury – her loose tongue had cost her dear. I left the Colonel and returned to the top table, saddened by the knowledge that yet another life had been ruined on that awful night.

The waiters were starting to serve the food. Greta had obviously decided that the menu should honour the customs of her native country. The starter consisted of grey slivers of some hopefully endangered species of fish floating in a sauce of bilious hue. Matters did not improve as the subsequent courses were produced.

"Thank God the Norwegians never got around to making wine," Marco groaned as he poured himself more of the excellent local claret that was flowing freely.

"I could've put on a far better spread than this load of old tack," June added, holding her glass out to him for a refill. "Bangers and mash would've gone down a treat. But Greta always has her own way – always has, always will."

Speeches were delivered by the dignitaries as we prodded and picked at a dessert of something resembling rice pudding.

Finally, Greta rose to her feet, stately as ever. In measured tones, she treated us to a blow-by-blow account of the Village's history, not tempered by humility about her own part in it. The heady wine and leaden rice pudding had made me drowsy, so my attention was dwindling and my eyes began to close. I was vaguely aware of a long pause. Marco elbowed me, and I thought we were supposed to applaud – but then I saw that Greta was still standing, and was in the process of lifting the chain of office from her neck and over her head.

"I now have the honour of performing my last official duty as Headman," she proclaimed. "It lies within my power to choose my successor, and I have done so. Your Excellencies, ladies and gentlemen, friends: it is my great pleasure to transfer my authority to the second Headman in the history of this Village. I call upon Mr. Trelawney Towers to take this chain of office, and I wish him much happiness in the position I have held for almost half a century. Trelawney, please!"

The audience was stunned into silence, broken only by an indignant squawk from Colonel Twelvetrees. "But Greta, he's a bally poo—"

The last word of his utterance was lost in the rising tide of cheering and applause that swelled to a crescendo as Greta passed the chain to Trelawney. After some fumbling, he slipped it over his head and patted the amulet as it came to rest on his chest.

I'm sure the loudest cheers in the whole gathering came from the three of us and June, who was on her feet and punching the air in delight. We raised our glasses in Trelawney's direction, but he was too busy acknowledging the applause to notice. Greta caught our gesture and responded in kind. The nod she gave us spoke volumes.

"She was always on our side, even if she couldn't show it," said Beth as the cacophony died down.

"I'd gladly crawl over there and kiss the hem of her garment," Marco added. "It might almost be worth coming back and living here, with Trelawney on the throne. I wouldn't have missed this for the world!"

"You'll *have* to give him the Rolls back now, Peter," Beth went on. "Can't very well be a monarch without a state carriage."

In fact, we did leave the Silver Cloud in the Village. Trelawney still drives it to meetings in the smart building that now contains the council chamber, a clinic and a school for the local children in the newly developed area on the outskirts of the Village – one of the many projects he has launched since taking over from Greta.

He tapped the microphone to gain the audience's attention. His voice was clearly choked with emotion, but he managed to be as gracious as ever.

"This is Greta's day, so I shall limit my remarks to thanking her, and all of you, for the greatest honour that could ever be granted to me."

He paused to draw breath and mop his brow with an enormous pink handkerchief.

"And now, I invite you all to proceed to the churchyard where, by special dispensation of the Head of State, the church bell will be rung one hundred times to mark this joyful occasion."

Glasses were drained and chairs tucked noisily behind tables as the guests fell into line behind Greta, Trelawney and the envoy from the capital. Dusk was fast approaching and there was an autumnal chill in the air, so we were glad to find that hot punch was being served as we passed through the lych-gate into the churchyard. Some of the new generation of houseboys and gardeners had been pressed into service to ladle it rather sloppily into stoneware mugs. Greta herself was standing by the table to welcome each guest in person. Most of the party received only a few words of formal greeting with their mug of *gløgg*, as the concoction was apparently called in Norway, but Marco was the exception. With impressive agility, Greta dropped to a crouching position so she could look him in the eye.

"Marco Blaine, what a fine man you have become!" she told him, in a voice loud enough for everyone nearby to hear. "Now, I have a question for you. Do you remember when you were a little boy and you broke into my garden to steal my strawberries?"

It was rare to see Marco cowed by anyone, but I saw it now. "I'm s-s-s-sorry, Greta – but I was just a kid, you know."

"Yes you were, but you managed something no-one else has ever done."

Her garden was surrounded by forbidding brick walls. We used to fantasise about her dancing naked by the full moon in there, or growing marijuana plants for her personal consumption.

"Can you remember what I told you when I discovered you in my strawberry bed?"

"I – er, no, I don't think so."

"I said that you were a young man of great determination. And how did you answer?"

"I can't remember that, either." Marco was becoming more and more flustered. The last thing he'd expected was to be upbraided for a childhood misdemeanour, and I thought it was a little unreasonable of Greta to bring it up so many years later.

"You said you didn't know what 'determination' meant. Well, Marco, I think you fully understand the meaning of that word now." She patted the back of his hand. "*Never give up* – remember me by those words, please."

Now Greta turned to Beth and myself with a benevolent smile. "I wish the three of you long and happy lives together. Thank you so much for coming today – I know it was not an easy journey to make. But you will leave our Village with peace in your hearts."

She rose to her full height and pinched Marco affectionately on the cheek as we wheeled him into the churchyard where the guests had arranged themselves into a circle facing the church porch. In front of it stood a tall-backed chair that could easily have accommodated the monarch of a small country. After the last stragglers had joined the circle, Greta strode over to her throne, bowed briefly and sat.

I'd seen the bell once when she showed me over the church many years before – it was cast in bronze and measured a good four feet in diameter. Ringing it a hundred times was going to take a good quarter of an hour. The task was to be performed, I saw, by a young family of northern Europeans: blond-haired, blue-eyed parents with a matching pair of children tricked out in sailor suits. As the father turned briefly in my direction, I thought his features seemed vaguely familiar, so I walked over to the porch to confirm my suspicion.

"Peter!"

"Florian! It's marvellous to see you here! So, you kept your promise to June, eh?"

"I said I'd come back, and I did. And not alone, as you see – this is my lovely wife, Magda, and these are our twins, Mario and Maria. Children, say hello to – ah – Uncle Peter!"

I let this pass without protest as the children greeted me politely – they really were classic beauties in the Teutonic mould.

"So, you reached your conclusion, then, Florian?"

"Yes indeed, as you can see – I reached the right conclusion, for me. A very happy conclusion. Did you know we bought the Blaines' old house?"

I knew it had eventually been bought by someone with a German name – Kleinschmidt, or some such – because I'd seen it mentioned in one of the business reports for Marco's trust.

"I'm glad to think the house will be home to a happy family. I know you're busy, so I'll leave you to it, Florian."

"You can't imagine what an honour this is. I felt so proud when Greta asked us. We really belong here now."

I had an idea I might be looking at the third Headman of the Village, once Trelawney's reign was over. I said my goodbyes to Florian's picture-book family and walked back to take my position beside Marco's chair.

The first chime rang out. Its echo rebounded from the rock face above the Village, reaching us just as the bell was tolled for the second time. The ringers began counting the chimes out loud, and the assembled guests soon joined in. The rhythmic clanging of the bell, the reverberations and the chanting had a hypnotic effect on me. Somehow, this was turning into a much more moving experience than I was expecting, especially after that rather uninspiring afternoon dinner.

Twenty-three, twenty-four, twenty-five...

I looked around the circle of Villagers, their faces lit by lanterns suspended from the trees now night had almost fallen. Gathered here, I could see almost all of the characters who played parts in the drama that had unfolded over the last decade: Trelawney, bursting with pride at his elevation to the rank of first citizen, with Tamir standing just as proudly by his side; behind them were Tamir's wife and the baby, who'd now grown into a pretty little girl. There were Sir Brian and Jean-Louis, relaxed and elegant, easily the most handsome couple present; dear June; the much-diminished Colonel Twelvetrees; Greta herself; even old Mahboob was here, lurking in the shadows ready to offer his services to the unsuspecting; and right beside me, my beloved Beth and Marco...

Forty-three, forty-four, forty-five...

Some, of course, were absent. I thought of Zeki, the most innocent victim of all. I pictured his tanned face, wreathed in smiles, on that long-ago night when I emerged onto the balcony of the Heliotrope

Room brandishing a golf umbrella. Geneviève and Peregrine Purvis had decided not to attend. I could understand why: the mortal remains of Duncan Blaine were uncomfortably close to where we were standing. I imagined that Mary Twelvetrees would have been buried here as well.

Sixty-three, sixty-four...

I felt the usual prod in my ribs and looked down to find Marco holding out what looked like a birthday card – something he'd thoughtfully prepared for Greta, I supposed. He turned the card over, and I was startled to see Alex Macallister's face grinning up at me. It was a copy of the order of service for his funeral.

"Why...what have you brought that here for?" I asked him, quite taken aback.

"There's something inside I'd like you to read."

"Can't it wait?"

"No, I've decided this is the time and place, sweetie."

"But – Alex's funeral? What's that got to do with today?"

"Do you remember when I went over to sit with Alex's mum after we sang the song? You asked me what she said, and I told you to mind your own business. But I wrote down what she told me. Word for word. Please read it to me."

I opened the much-thumbed card, and read:

"That man loves you like no other man ever will, dearie. You love him
too, but you don't know it yet. Learn to accept his love, learn to love him
back, and you'll never regret it for the rest of your life."

My voice cracked up as I read out Elsie Macallister's words, all these years later. Marco took the card from me and drew me close to him.

"She was right. It's taken a while, but I've followed her instructions to the letter."

He drew a deep breath before declaring for the first time, but not the last: "I love you, Peter."

"I love you too, Marco, and..."

He placed his finger over my lips to silence me.

We kissed — heedless of the Villagers gathered around us, and unheeded by all of them – even Beth, whose eyes were riveted on the perspiring bell-ringers in the porch.

Eighty-one, eighty-two...

It was the most beautiful moment of my life, a moment I wanted to savour and prolong. But at that exact point, one of the white-robed waiters came bustling up with a jug of steaming *glögg*.

Marco brought us down to earth.

"Well, how convenient. A toast, don't you think?"

He drained his mug and thrust it out for a refill. But he misjudged the movement, caught the boy off balance, and the scalding hot contents of the jug spilled into his lap. I tried to catch another waiter's attention to get a towel, and girded myself for the torrent of abuse that Marco was bound to spew forth.

But when I turned towards him, I saw an expression of utter shock on his face.

Ninety-eight...ninety-nine...

"Peter — I can't believe it — my knees are burning! I can feel! Oh my God, my God, *I can feel!* I couldn't feel anything before, and now I can feel!"

He'd managed to tell the story of my entire life in one simple sentence. That was the priceless gift that this long, long journey had given me: at last I, too, could feel.

Marco grasped my hand and pulled me close to him. As our eyes locked, I dared to wonder if the dream that had woken me so many times might yet, one day, come true ...

The church bell rang out for the hundredth time. A resounding cheer went up from the crowd, and a dazzling salvo of fireworks soared into the starry sky – the sky, high above our lives, that we had given to each other.

Author's Thanks

A big thank you to all those friends and colleagues who have encouraged me in this work. You all know who you are, but special thanks to Sandie and Joe; to Frances for prompting me to go past Part One; and also Charles and Gareth in Malaysia. Without your help, this would still be a collection of ideas on a few scraps of paper.

About the Author

ROBIN HELLABY was born in Lincolnshire in the 1950s and has since spent time in over 50 countries. The highlights of Robin's worldwide career as a broadcaster, interpreter and translator included witnessing the Iranian revolution first-hand, 'scooping' the death of Rudolf Hess in Spandau prison, and working on the documentation for Noël Coward's estate.

Notable clients have ranged from business executives with their own jets (and banks) to refugees desperate for asylum.

Robin's soulmate eventually appeared in a remote corner of South-East Asia where the couple now lead a quiet life writing, painting, travelling at a slow pace, and growing pineapples.

Robin Hellaby is now working on a second novel that delves into the past of some characters portrayed in this book.